The Descent of the Drowned

ANA LAL DIN

This is a work of fiction. Names, characters, places, and incidents are either the product of the author's imagination or are used fictitiously. Any resemblance to actual people, alive or dead, is purely coincidental.

For more information: www.laldinana.net

Triggers: Physical and emotional abuse, mention of rape and sodomisation, sexual assault, suicide, bigotry, drug abuse, and human trafficking.

Calligraphy: Ana Hernández
Illustration: Marcela Bolívar [www.marcelabolivar.com]
Interior: Damonza

ISBN 978-1-8380465-0-7

First Edition

For the Rohingya People
May your prayers be heard and your tears be repaid

PART I

"Of the Nāgin came the Birth of Sin."

Shamsuddin Codex, Volume II, *Foreword*

PROLOGUE

Roma walked through a sea of slaughtered serpents.

A malevolent wind pulled at her hair and yanked at her skirts. It hissed out consonants and vowels, every sound so coarse, so rancorous that she wanted to shield her ears from their perpetual whiplash. The cold pierced her skin, sinking obstinate claws deep into her bones, and the skies carried a sinister resemblance to a yawning chasm that descended upon the world to swallow it whole.

Treading on bloodstained sloughs, she approached the immense shape of a blackened banyan tree standing upon a hill. Naked boughs strained toward her with a soundless hunger, snatching at the air, sensing her presence. She felt their baleful yearning to drape around her shell. Blood seeped from the banyan's roots, trickling toward her feet, and the taste of the banyan's victims stained her tongue.

CHAPTER 1

Gripping another bough, Roma climbed higher into the banyan from her dream with familiar ease. A crooked web of long-necked trunks encased the core, crawling over each other in a devoted attempt to touch the skies. Drooping strands suspended from the branches and entangled like lovers. Brushing her fingertips over the crevices, she tipped back her head, but she still couldn't see the end of the aged banyan for the intricate canopy above.

There should have been the sound of birds and apes, yet it was silent as if even the spirits roaming the aerial roots drowsed. She shivered despite the dry heat. If not for the tingling sense of a timeless presence withdrawn deep into the heart of the tree, she might have thought it was deceased. The sole indication of life was an ivory-skinned cobra napping in the cradle of a limb. She skimmed her fingers over the cobra's smooth head. Stirring from the slumber, the cobra unfurled its long body with languid grace, the thin membrane clearing over its glossy black eyes.

"We're not so different, are we?" she asked softly. "We're both at home here in the banyan."

It hissed in consent.

She peered past it into the courtyard below.

The stretch of land enclosed by sandstone walls served as a burial ground where those of a higher caste—the higher *zaat*—cremated their people. Thick, black smoke rose from a sacred altar, swirling upward in sensual patterns. The soot clung to her tongue, itching in her throat as the wild fire danced upon the motionless bones below. She chewed on her bottom lip. Death had an awful taste that reminded her of oppressive darkness and inescapable rot.

The High Priest of Biranpur stepped forward. Sādin Saheb was an overweight man with a double chin that slouched over the rigid collar of his royal blue robe. The fabric was unembellished as a silent statement of his dedication to an unmaterialistic existence. Sweat glistened on the black symbols of Lord Biran, God of Creation, drawn on his shaved head, and large beads coursed down his forehead into his caterpillar eyebrows.

"Death shall pass," he chanted. "Life shall remain." Even from the distance, each syllable sounded as clear as if he spoke into Roma's ear. Her skin prickled in unease. She had known him for her entire life and never once had he shown compassion, so it didn't astound her that his eyes remained devoid of sympathy for the dead woman in the bed of fire.

The tales circulating on the demise of Gabrielle Saheba were ominous. People said she had been possessed and driven to the brink of madness. Roma couldn't imagine her so. She had seen Gabrielle Saheba carrying the street orphans and feeding them smoked corncobs from the Grand Market many times. The higher *zaat* woman had appeared sound. And beautiful as well. With skin that shimmered like gold in the sun, hair like polished wood, and almond-shaped eyes the colour of spring leaves. She should have been a Khanum—a queen—in a faraway summer kingdom, not the Second Wife of the Firawn of the West and the East Strip.

"It's the will of the High Lord," Sādin Saheb professed. "And so shall it be."

"So shall it be," the crowd repeated.

Resting her chin on the bough, Roma watched the assembly in their lavish silk and velvet fashions. Humans believed they were artful at deception, but their expressions, voices, and movements exposed their innermost condition—the restless glances toward the skies, the impatient sighs, and the hushed chatter revealed their apathy for the tragedy they pretended to mourn.

It was a play.

Amma said Roma chose to see the abjection of human nature. That she always searched for a lie to bare, an illusion to shatter, and she would never find happiness because lies and illusions were how humans survived. Amma told her that she observed excessive details about the world and lacked a sense of self-preservation, but Roma thought the teacher of their temple lacked perspective, yet she had enough sense of self-preservation not to speak her mind in Amma's presence.

The desiccated breeze caught Roma's veil, but she was all too absorbed in the cremation ritual to care when the sheer fabric slipped from her head. The cobra slithered closer along the branch, tasting the air with a forked tongue, and her fingers trailed over its sleek scales.

"I don't like fires," she whispered.

The First Wife of the Firawn stepped to the altar. People called her Mā Saheb because she oversaw Durra, the northern province of the West Strip, in the Firawn's absence. She was the embodiment of elegance in a fitted, black silk blouse with a plunging neckline and an ankle-length, black silk skirt—the garments named a *choli* and *lehenga* among the lower *zaat*. Gold rings and bracelets adorned her pale limbs. An organza veil descended from the crown of her head down to her hips. The crest of her *zaat* was inked in gold around her bare navel in the regal contour of a hooded cobra. Mā Saheb was stunning in an untouchable and delicate manner. Perhaps it was why she had a slave with an umbrella by her side to shield her fair skin from the sun.

Roma tipped her head to the side. How the higher *zaat* liked to flaunt their wealth even when at a cremation for one of their own.

The fire perished with the bones. Sādin Saheb gathered the ashes in an urn. Roma had seen similar urns inside the temple of Lamiapur. They contained the ashes of her kind. *Lamiadasis.* The slaves of Mother Lamia, one of the Goddess-Wives of Lord Biran and Goddess-Mother to his three hundred and sixty children. Rawiya Mai, their resident storyteller and oldest *lamiadasi*, claimed the souls of the dead would never find rest if their ashes were confined. Roma wasn't certain what she believed, but there were times when she wanted to open the urns and throw the contents to the winds.

Click.

Her eyes were drawn to a young man leaning on a wall much too close to where she lingered. The consistent clicking came from a lighter in his hand. His skin was neither dark nor light, but an earthy meld of both, and the sharp bones of his face held shadows. Black hair was trimmed close to his head on the sides. His expression betrayed no emotion, yet his shoulders were rigid and a vein pounded in his temple.

She inched forward for a better look at him.

"Leviathan Saheb," Sādin Saheb said, beckoning the young man to the altar.

Roma might not have seen him before, but none could mistake his name.

Leviathan Blackburn. The Firawn's only son. The one whom people whispered about and called *bezaat*—without a caste—because of his alleged blood relation to the casteless clans.

When he didn't move, Mā Saheb turned toward him. "Leviathan," she called insistently with her lips downturned.

The Firawn's son looked up then. His hooded eyes were a cold, daunting grey. Roma swallowed forcibly. Sensing her sudden discomfort, the cobra glided over her arm and curled protectively around her neck, hissing toward the courtyard. Her eyes followed the Firawn's son as he sauntered toward the altar. He was tall and broad with the form of a soldier, or perhaps a hunter. His gait had an unpredictable element to it, as if he might slide his hands into his pockets or begin snapping necks.

Her throat tied itself into a knot. He hadn't done anything to stir her fears, yet she was unnerved. Men of his frame and aura caused a prickle of panic down her back. Dipping her chin, she heaved in a deep breath as Mā Saheb passed him a gold ash capsule. The Firawn's son took it without a word or a glance, crouching down and lowering it into a hole in the ground hollowed out for the ceremonial burial.

Biting her bottom lip, Roma pressed her nails into the bark. She wanted to shout at him to spring the ashes and allow the tempestuous winds to snatch them—anything but the impending doom. Mā Saheb touched her fingertips to his shoulder, and the vein in his temple thumped harder. There was a faint smile on her lips. She was aware of his imperceptible reaction, even though he didn't move an inch. He only stared into the hole for the longest moment, and then his eyes lifted, catching Roma's over the bough.

She scrambled down, scraping her bare forearms on the bristly edges of the banyan. Startled by her abrupt drop, the cobra hissed with displeasure around her neck. Slouching behind the trunks, she rubbed a palm over her heart, but it refused to be soothed. The blistering fingers of the wind combed through her hair, making it dance like a black ribbon ensnared by a desert storm.

For how long had he known of her presence? *How* had he known? No one in the courtyard had noticed her. No one but him. Amma would be livid if she found out that not only had Roma intruded on a higher *zaat* burial, but she had been seen as well. They weren't to be noticed unless it was to the sound of drums in an ornamented hall and in the ceremonial costume of a *lamiadasi*.

Drawing the cobra over her head, Roma settled it on one of the lower branches before descending the hill and sprinting across the plains, as if she could erase the moment her face had burned into the memory of the Firawn's son.

She ran along the seam of Kobe Lake. It sparkled beneath the mile-long stone bridge that strained between the enormous black-iron gates of Ferozi, the northern city of the higher *zaat*, and Sefu, the village of the lower *zaat*. The lake was receding because of the drought, which now plagued Durra for long stretches of time. Rare cloudbursts provided some relief, but they never lasted more than a day. Dirt and waste contaminated the lake, so the villagers drew water from the stepwell instead. Even so, the water was boiled before consumption to avoid diseases.

The Wardens patrolled the high stone walls of Ferozi clad in dark blue uniforms with silver clasps and buckles, their weapons glinting on their waists. They were the protectors of the higher *zaat* cities, but oftentimes they roamed the village tavern for drinks and women. They weren't as frightening as the Firawn's other soldiers, the Rangers, in their head-to-toe steel armour and steel masks shaped like horned demons. Roma had seen them as a child when they were called upon for a public execution of two farmers, who had blended pulverised bricks with flour to cheat the tax collectors. It had reminded all the villagers one couldn't deceive the Firawn and what happened if one still attempted it.

When she thought of the Firawn now, the eyes of his son perturbed her, and her throat felt full of cotton. He couldn't have caught more than a glimpse of her face.

With an unreliable sense of calm, Roma reached the village and drew the veil over her face. Sefu rested in the heart of the steppe. It was a serpentine labyrinth of sloping stairs, crisscrossing alleys, and cockeyed clusters of sandstone houses with colourful latticework windows. The rooftops revealed a netting of washing lines with bright garments drying in the late evening heat. Some houses had red ribbons placed by the tenants. Those belonged to the Women of the Flags. Women whom no one would hire for labour, disreputable for servicing men in trade for food, medicine, and coin. They were considered lesser than the clans, but the village men still knocked on their doors in the cover of night.

The Horn of the Gods sounded once over Sefu, announcing the arrival of dusk as the last trace of light dwindled from the skies. Roma ascended the fractured steps into an alley and stepped around the open sewers that gaped in the ground. The sour smell of waste permeated the air. Cats and hounds with flea-infested pelts pawed through the garbage for scraps of food beside sleeping orphans. Shouts spilled out from the windows, families arguing and children wailing.

Darkness blanketed the village when Roma climbed the sandstone wall that encompassed Lamiapur. The gate was locked at sundown. She couldn't hear the drums or the lutes. Her sisters must have ended dance practice to attend prayers in the temple. She hesitated. Amma would have noticed her absence by now. Roma wasn't her favourite *lamiadasi*, but she was her most skilled performer when it came to the sacred dance of their goddess. It wouldn't shelter her from Amma's punishments, though.

Leaping down into the courtyard, Roma shook the dust from the folds of her *lehenga*. She might still be able to sneak inside the temple and—

"Roma?"

Roma winced. Pressing her lips together, she turned as Sunbel stepped under the spectral light of the moon. She was in their practice attire; a yellow backless *choli* with green patch-border work and an ankle-length *lehenga*. It was custom for the slaves of the gods—*dēvadasis*—to be inked with their *zaat*. Small, mythological patterns and symbols decorated the corners of Sunbel's blue eyes, her chin, and the length of her throat, mirroring the symbols that adorned Roma. Sunbel's fair skin and golden hair made her a favoured *lamiadasi* among the patrons. Ever since her auction seven years in the past, Sunbel had served a multitude of patrons, but recently, she was pardoned from her service because she was with child again.

"You weren't at practice and prayers," Sunbel said, caressing her growing bump. She hadn't told her patron about her pregnancy. It wouldn't matter. The patrons never claimed their children. If she birthed a boy, he would become a *birandasi*, a slave of Lord Biran, and serve in Biranpur like her three other sons. If she birthed a girl, she would become a *lamiadasi*, and serve Mother Lamia in Lamiapur like the rest of them.

Sunbel glanced down at Roma's slippers. Mud stained the synthetic fabric and encrusted the flat, stiff bottoms. "You were with Khiraa and Sara again, weren't you?" Her eyebrows drew together. "You shouldn't visit the camp so often. Amma hasn't said anything yet, but if you miss prayers—"

"Khiraa's brother is gone," Roma interrupted.

Sunbel blinked. "Did the Wardens take him?" she asked out of courtesy more than interest.

"There was no raid. He left on his own."

"Why would he do that?"

Roma didn't answer. The condemnatory tone in Sunbel's voice made her feel like she was the one to abandon her family.

"What're you two whispering about?"

Glancing over Sunbel's shoulder, Roma met Yoshi's eyes. She was swinging her long braid with an ill-boding smile. The light of the moon illuminated the freckles on her angular face. She placed a hand on her voluptuous hip at their silence. "Amma sent me to see if you'd returned. I've never seen her so furious. But then, no one ever missed practice and prayers before. I can't decide if you're brave or stupid, Roma."

"Yoshi," Sunbel chided.

Her eyes widened. "What did I say now?" she asked, touching her collarbone. "I was only worried about her like you." She looked at Roma. "At least tell me you skipped duties over something important, like a higher *zaat* patron?"

Ignoring her comment, Roma slipped past her, but Yoshi's derisive laughter pursued her across the courtyard. There were four sandstone sheds in Lamiapur shared by all eleven *lamiadasis*. Each consisted of handwoven sleeping mats and mirrors in single chambers. Roma shared hers with Sunbel, Nilo, and Yoshi, but Nilo lived with her current patron. They hadn't heard from her for over a moon now.

The previous time Caliana was the one sent to live with her patron. His jealous wife had forcefully poured the Witch's Shade potion down her throat so she would never bear children. Caliana was taken to the Kāhinah, their village soothsayer, whom people believed possessed hidden knowledge. She told Caliana to perform a ritual under the full moon in the Sacred Month of Uzzā, but it didn't heal Caliana. Amma was furious. She said it was the sacred obligation of a *lamiadasi* to birth children. Caliana had failed her service and it mattered not that she was abused.

Lamiadasis were forever to take the blame. If there was a drought, the *lamiadasis* must have failed to appease the gods. If a village woman was barren, the *lamiadasi* who blessed her must have had a spoiled fortune.

Fearing Amma wouldn't be in a benevolent mood now that Roma had failed as well, she stalled outside Amma's shed, bracing herself for the punishment.

CHAPTER 2

Burning oil lamps bathed Amma in a warm glow that didn't harmonise with the stern shimmer in her kohl-rimmed, green eyes. Roma stepped over to where she reclined on a *charpai*—a low, wooden bedstead with a middle portion of rope netting—dressed in a turmeric-coloured *choli* and *lehenga*. A traditional *nath* clasped Amma's left nostril, and lac-filled bracelets clutched her thick wrists.

"*Yē*," Amma beckoned in Khansāri, her hard voice cracking like a whip across Roma's back. She motioned a heavily ringed hand to the handwoven mat spread over the ground in front of her. "*Basa*." Lowering herself on the mat, Roma looked at Amma's painted toenails. The rings on her toes had beaded chains linking to her anklets; the skin of her feet was calloused from decades of dancing upon soil and stone. Amma curled a hand around the mouthpiece of a hookah, her cheeks sucking in as she inhaled, and the water in the base of the hookah bubbled. "You didn't attend practice and prayers."

"I apologise."

"Your apology lacks sincerity." Gripping her chin, Amma turned Roma's face upward. Her nails pressed into Roma's skin. She suppressed a wince and returned Amma's stare. "What to do with you? Hm? You've been useless to me for three years because of that ruined face."

The scars weren't the reason Roma hadn't served. Amma had hesitated ever since she found Roma in the bathing chamber with a dull, bloodstained knife in her hand and cuts on her face when she was fourteen. She had used the knife on herself with the knowledge that it would taint more than her skin. It would taint her as a *dēvadasi*. Despoiled *dēvadasis* weren't offered to patrons. The Kāhinah had told Amma that Roma would have to repent for the self-harm she had caused. She would have to be reauctioned once she was rinsed of her sin.

Every *dēvadasi* was auctioned when she received her blood, but if she didn't receive it before the age of thirteen—as it had been with Roma—the local Kāhinah performed an astrological forecast to determine the most auspicious time for the auction. It was always a threatening fact to Roma that she couldn't be pardoned from service forever. She sensed an unnerving change in Amma now and feared that shrewd shine in her eyes.

"I've consulted with the Kāhinah," Amma said. The signature pendant of a *lamiadasi* glinted from between the bulging folds of her bosom. The triple-headed cobra with a pointed tail was the sacred symbol of Mother Lamia, Goddess of Virtuosity. "You'll be auctioned on the sixteenth auspicious night of the Festival of the High Lord."

Roma's chest compressed until she could hardly breathe. Clutching the bracelet on her wrist, she struggled not to panic. Amma released her chin with a none-too-gentle shove. "*Jā*. Practise till dawn," she dismissed. "And, Roma?" She waited for Roma to turn on the threshold. "Don't even think about harming yourself because it won't work this time. The Kāhinah is prepared for any future incidents. We're *dēvadasis*. We're chosen by the gods to serve. The sooner you accept it, the easier it'll be. I've been patient, *ladoba*. You won't disgrace me in front of Sādin Saheb and the village again, or I'll slit your throat myself, *samajalē?*"

Roma found her voice. "*Hō*, Amma," she answered.

The carved basins beside the temple stairs held a bucket of water. She pressed a palm to the wall and dragged in several breaths. Her pulse thrashed in her ears. She couldn't silence Amma's voice as it writhed inside her head. She was to be auctioned again. Three years she had lived in fear of it, unaware of the Kāhinah's prediction, and now the wait was over. Her fingers itched to touch the scars marring her skin. She cupped her hands in the bucket and splashed the cold water on her face. Droplets dripped from the *nath* in her nose.

When she was four years old, she had been dedicated to Mother Lamia. Girls were delivered to the temples if they were birthed under a full moon in a sacred month, or if they were abandoned as babes on the temple steps like Roma. Others, such as Yoshi and Sunbel, were born into it because their birth-mothers were *lamiadasis*. If families underwent misfortune, they dedicated their daughters to appease the gods and to receive salvation. People didn't devote their daughters to Mother Lamia as often as they did to Mother Uzzā, Goddess of Fertility and Battle, and Mother Manāt, Goddess of Fortune and Trade, as they preferred seeking the favours of the goddesses of fertility and wealth rather than virtuosity.

Customarily, the dedication ceremony was a communal celebration, and the villagers participated in the sacred rites. It was said *dēvadasis* were immune to widowhood. They were wedded to their god or goddess in body and soul, and they could never wed anyone else. The worst crime *dēvadasis* could commit was to abandon their service or refuse patrons. Roma was raised with this truth. She had been told she too was chosen. When one was placed at the feet of the Mother Goddess herself, one became her vessel for life. Sacred to the touch. Wasn't it the reason men entered patronships with them? They all wanted to lie with a goddess.

Goddess.

They called *lamiadasis* goddesses at times of convenience, but otherwise, they treated them as less than human. Roma had seen her sisters abused. And she too was—

She dissolved the thought before it could form in full.

Pressing the back of her hand against her wet lips, she straightened herself. She wouldn't crumble. Perhaps her fortune had spared her for the past three years, but she would have to learn to breathe in the same world as her sisters.

If she had survived it before, she could survive it again.

Ascending the sandstone stairs to the terrace, Roma peered up at the temple. It stretched up high, supported by pillars with decorative murals and cornices. One of the murals depicted Mother Lamia as a lover in a human's embrace. Her *lamiadasi*-sisters loved the tales of their goddess. They loved *her*. Roma was once filled with a similar reverent devotion for her, but she discovered early on that none of what she felt was real. It was fabricated. Amma said to fear Mother Lamia, and so she feared her. Amma said to love Mother Lamia, and so she loved her. She could no longer tell what her emotions were or what was planted within her.

The deep fracture within her faith tormented her. She wasn't supposed to question what her sisters loved and respected—what was divine—and there were nights when she was furious with herself for not feeling as they did, for not accepting as they had. For having a mind that questioned relentlessly. Wouldn't it be easier if she ceased to speculate altogether? If she simply lived as her sisters lived? Without question, without thought.

Sunbel's soft footfalls sounded on the temple stairs. "Are you all right?" she asked in a cautious tone. "What did Amma say?"

It occurred to Roma that Sunbel must have known about her auction. They must all have known. She was a fool. She hadn't noticed how careful her sisters were when they spoke of the festival around her. They were afraid to reveal Amma's plans for her. Perhaps they considered her frail. Perhaps they thought she might become hysterical, grip a knife, and slash her own face again.

"Roma—"

"Have you ever thought of leaving Lamiapur?"

The stricken expression on Sunbel's face should have made her regret the question, but she looked into Sunbel's startled eyes and waited for her answer.

"Why would you ask that?" Sunbel whispered. "You can't—You—" Drawing in a breath, she reached for her hand. Roma withdrew. She didn't like to be touched and Sunbel knew that very well. "It's never been easy for you to enter patronships. I know, Roma, I understand. What happened was—it was unfortunate."

"Unfortunate?"

"What I mean is—I can help you through your auction if you let me," she amended. "This is your home. We're your sisters. And you can't abandon your service *na*? We're *lamiadasis*—"

"We're human," Roma interrupted. "Doesn't that count for anything?"

"We've been given a greater purpose—"

She stepped away. "I have to practise," she said, slipping inside the antechamber where the bronze statue of Mother Lamia stood upon a dais, naked but for a crown of sprouting cobra heads. Their gods and goddesses all possessed half-human and half-animal traits, signifying the duality in their nature. The left side of Mother Lamia's face belonged to her counterpart Aranyada—Dark Goddess of Chaos, Violence, and Vengeance—carved in the shape of a cobra's face. When Roma passed the dais, she didn't touch her feet in respect. If Mother Lamia wanted to smite her for insolence, she was welcome to it.

Perhaps it would spare her the auction.

Pushing aside the gossamer drapes, she glided into the practice hall where they danced for hours to the sound of drums every day. She struck a match and ignited the oil lamps. The painted murals on the stained-glass screens came to life in the lamplight. Gods and goddesses with their *dēvadasis.* Her eyes dwelled on the *lamiadasis* in graceful poses as they denoted the love, passion, and beauty of Mother Lamia. Roma didn't know much of their history. She wished she did. It might have helped her understand why she was chosen as a sacred slave. How had it come to be this way? They couldn't always have been *dēvadasis.* Why couldn't they abandon this path and choose another?

Sliding down against the screen, she wrapped her arms around her legs. Whenever she thought of her future, she felt a painful pressure in her throat. Whenever she thought of her existence, she felt a scream build within her head. Ghanima Mai, an elder clan woman from the camp, told a tale once. The clans believed in a god, the Creator or *Rabb*, as they called him, and in the tale, the Creator created the first soul. He commanded it to enter a vacant human body. The soul barely dipped inside before it returned to him. The Creator demanded to know why it had disobeyed him, and the soul answered it was too dark, too enclosed within the vessel. The Creator commanded it twice more until it stayed put.

The suffocation the soul must have experienced—Roma understood it. She felt it. She was trapped in this skin and all she wanted was out.

"Tai?"

Lifting her head, Roma looked up at Chirag. He blinked sleepily as he walked into the hall. His brown hair stuck out to all sides. He never combed it unless Roma sat him down to brush it herself. She shifted her legs. Chirag curled up on the tiles with his head in her lap, entwining his small fingers with hers, and she didn't pull away, even as she instinctively wanted to. His was the only touch she allowed, the only touch she endured. Perhaps it was because she had raised him while his birthmother—Amma—ignored his existence, or perhaps it was because they shared a similar wound.

Chirag should have already been dedicated to Lord Biran. She didn't know the reason for Amma's decision to spare him, except Amma never acted out of pure compassion. Chirag would never be safe because Amma could choose to deliver him to Biranpur at any moment. The constant threat of it was enough that Roma attempted to keep him out of her hair, so as not to provoke her into such an action.

“Did you have another nightmare?” she asked. He nodded. “What was it this time?”

“Fire.” His free hand played with the sonorous bells on one of her anklets. The lamplight danced in his troubled, green eyes. “Lots of fire.”

“Tell me more.”

“The gods were angry.”

The gods were always angry. That was why people lived in constant fear of them. It was as if one couldn’t worship them out of love or want. Anger, punishment, and revenge were the traits by which they were defined. Ghanima Mai was different in her perception of the clan god. She placed emphasis on forgiveness and mercy. She had a perpetual sense of peace about her that Roma sought out again and again because it soothed her like cool balm on a burn.

“What did they do?” she asked.

“They made the stars weep.”

“Is it what scared you?” He shook his head. She caressed his hair. “Then what?”

“We were all burning,” he whispered. “We were all burning—except you.”

CHAPTER 3

Rage was a greedy bastard.

Rolling his shoulders, Leviathan relaxed his arms, fists up and elbows down. He reeked of death, of loss. He had yet to wash the stench of smoke from his skin. When he shut his eyes, he saw flames eating away at his mother's flesh. They were all he could see, all he could think about, and he knew they'd burn in his sleep for years to come. He'd wanted to bury her with honour, respect, but she'd been tossed into the fire.

She'd suffered in death as she'd suffered in life.

Sucking in a deep breath, he calibrated his stance, focusing on the balanced weight of his build and his steadily pumping heart—trying not to think or feel. The chamber was quiet as a tomb. His head rang like in the aftermath of an explosion. Ghosts of demons he couldn't put to rest. The satisfying snap of his knuckles on hard leather cleared some of the noise, so he picked up speed and attacked, rapidly transmitting the energy from his body's momentum to his passive opponent, using his fists, elbows, and knees to strike. It was all about that raw power. The faster you accelerated your mass, the more force you produced behind every crushing blow.

It wasn't enough to distract him, not enough to make him forget.

He should've been with her. Should've known something wasn't right.

He was her son.

Was.

Stabbing faster and harder, he let the redundant whip fill his head. It didn't calm the boiling rage rising inside him. The Firawn had kept him in the dark about her condition. He hadn't told Leviathan it was serious, hadn't mentioned it when she died, and he sure as hell hadn't bothered showing up for her cremation. None of it surprised Leviathan. Enraged him? Yeah. He was imagining the Firawn's conceited face on the receiving end of his punches right about now.

She was never anything more than an opportunity to the Firawn. He knew that. Even she'd known that. He'd seen it in her tears too many times to count. She was always an armour, standing between him and the man who called himself his father, sacrificing her self-respect to protect him when she wanted to return home to the south. She'd wanted to leave, but she'd stayed for him. And he hadn't even been there as she took her last breath.

He clenched his teeth.

There was somebody else who'd known about his mother's condition. Somebody else who'd kept it from him until it was too late, making sure that he could do nothing. His hate for Cecilia Blackburn was like a living beast, dark and foul, distinctive in its ugliness. He cared none for what she claimed. An organ failure? It might've ended his mother's life, but it wasn't what killed her. Cecilia had a hand in it. That sick woman was capable of anything. He needed proof. Just one excuse to destroy her, and he would.

Smack.

He needed peace.

Smack.

He wanted blood.

Catching the sack between his fists, he pressed his brow to it. He hated this place, but his whole life he had one purpose: Getting through the Guild's training and returning to his mother, so he'd be free of what the Firawn made him. With her, he was just Levi. Not a soldier, not a killer. Maybe he could've found his way back to that untainted version of himself through her, but it hadn't only been her body burning in those flames. His identity had burned with her.

The tightness in his chest increased.

He hadn't gone to the camp. He'd thought of going a hundred times, but the clans wouldn't want to see him, and he didn't want to hurt them any more than he already had. He was sure that they'd heard the rumours, heard of his deeds in the southeast. How was he supposed to look them in the eyes? It was better that he stayed away. Better for all of them. The camp used to be his escape from the palace as a kid—a second home—and he'd been worthy of it.

Not anymore.

His muscles tensed at a subtle movement in his peripheral vision. Turning his head, he looked down at a two-foot scrawny girl with a thumb stuck in her mouth. She tilted her head back, peering up at him in return. Chewing back a curse, he neutralised his features, locking his emotions behind a steel mask.

"You again, huh?" he said roughly.

He crossed to a backless divan under a stained-glass window of a camel. He was staying in a separate precinct of al-Abyad Mahal, so he wouldn't have to run into Cecilia. Not much had changed in the quarters since his last leave. It was the same handcrafted ornate dressers and closets; the same blue and white tiles with their gold calligraphy on the walls. He hadn't missed it, any of it. His mother was his home, not this place.

The girl still hadn't blinked. He held her curious stare as he unwrapped the tape from his hands and flexed them. She was good. Not even a flutter of those thick, curved lashes. Leaning forward on his elbows, he signalled for her to come closer, and she practically danced over on her toes. He studied her face. Pale skin, button nose, and huge, brown eyes. Beauty tended to draw attention. That was a given. Beauty among slaves? That was a curse.

"Your name?"

"Yaya," she babbled.

He cocked his eyebrows. "Yaya?" he repeated sceptically.

She shook her head.

"*Yaya.*"

"It's what I said."

"*Nā.*"

"Why don't you teach me, then?"

"Yaya."

His mouth quirked.

A woman appeared in the corridor outside his door. She was of average height, full-bodied. Dark eyes set in a wide face with a stubborn chin. The features combined with her light skin tone marked her Darian descent. She was a slave like every other Darian and Suran who was brought to the Strips after the Khanate collapsed.

Avoiding Leviathan's stare, the woman held out a hand. "Haya," she called, all nerves. "*Yē*, Haya, *lavakara.*" Her Khansāri dialect was soft and rounded, or maybe he'd just been in the south too long.

Looking back at the kid, Leviathan nodded toward her mother.

"Go," he said.

Haya bounced on her toes and bumped her brow against his before she ran over to her mother's side. He blinked, surprised. As he stood, the woman pulled Haya close. There was protectiveness in the move, a lioness in her eyes. Maybe he wouldn't have to worry about the kid after all.

"I apologise for my daughter, Saheb."

"Why did she do that?"

The woman bowed her head. "Haya can't express her affection in words, Saheb," she explained, retreating into the archway as he reached the door. She was a cagey woman. Posture stiff, chin jutting out. He didn't blame her for being guarded. He was the Firawn's son, and he didn't look kind. "I'll make sure she doesn't disturb you again."

"She doesn't bother me," he responded and, on impulse, brushed a finger under Haya's chin. The kid beamed up at him as if he'd dropped candy in her hands.

"Time for bed, Haya," the woman prompted, tugging Haya out of his reach, then hesitantly added, "Welcome home, Saheb."

Burned and buried it.

Tossing the tape on the bed, he rubbed his hands over his face. He wouldn't get any sleep tonight, so he might as well head down to the stables, clean all the travelling sweat and grime off of Cinder's coat. She'd like that. Hell, he'd like that. It'd provide some much-needed distraction.

As he walked through the archway to the stairs, Malev fell in step with him. His companion hadn't changed out of his travelling clothes either, his *kurta* and trousers covered in dust. "Junho got in touch with our contact," Malev said in his quiet way. "He can meet us tomorrow at midnight."

"Sounds good."

"What if he has something?"

"I'll deal with it."

"And what of the Firawn, brother? You know there'll be consequences."

"I'm counting on it."

Malev frowned. "Is it really worth it?"

Leviathan stopped and turned. The look in his eyes was cold, but he knew Malev saw past it to the anguish behind the ice, and Leviathan could tell that he regretted the question. "If that bitch had anything to do with her death," he said, his voice calm, "I'll ruin her. Then I'll take the consequences."

The ground level was all arched windows, gold sconces, and silk curtains. More decorative tiles, pillars, and cut-diamond chandeliers. It was nothing compared to the palace itself, which was one of the largest structures in the Strips and a polished symbol of the Firawn's grand prosperity. You could always tell a ruler's character by the size of his residence, but a large, gilded chair never made a king.

Kicking aside one of the white gold chairs in his way, Leviathan moved toward the panelled doors. Cecilia chose that moment to waltz in, closely followed by her personal slave, Marduk—a skinny rat with a thick bottom lip, habitual twitch, and a half-bald head covered by a fez. He stuck to her like a parasite, living under her protection. He'd need it when the coinlenders finally came for him.

"Leviathan."

He hated her voice. The sickly sweet way she said his name. It made him want to smash something. He didn't pause, didn't slow down. She stepped in front of him, forcing him to stop. Her skin-tight gown rippled like water. "The festival begins tomorrow night. It's tradition for the leading higher *zaat* families to attend the celebrations," she said. "Now that you're home, your presence will be expected."

Leviathan's mouth curved in cold amusement. She'd never believed in the gods of the lower *zaat*. It was a political game to show the people that their customs were revered, their rituals honoured, so they'd feel important, and it was an excuse for the higher *zaat* to indulge in wine and fashion.

"My mother's soul has barely left her body and you want to celebrate?" he said. "Those are your customs, not mine."

Cecilia reached up to brush his hair. He moved his head, avoiding her touch, and swallowed his irritation at the triumphant gleam in her eyes. "You're a Blackburn, no?" She trailed her fingers over the collar of his sleeveless undershirt. "Then you must make an appearance. The lower *zaat* look to your father as a god. He would've attended as well, but he has an important meeting—"

"Planning another massacre? Some god."

Her smirk vanished. "I won't have you shame our name, Leviathan," she bit out.

He exhaled through his teeth, whistling lowly. "Don't you think words like *shame* lose their value coming from somebody like you?"

She slapped him.

The rage in her eyes was worth it. Her face shook, lips curling back in a primal snarl. There she was, the demoness. He chuckled under his breath. Enough of her stepmother act. This right here was the Cecilia Blackburn that he sought to unmask.

"I think *shame* is a word only you'd be familiar with, Leviathan," she snarled, "or did you forget it was a tribal whore that birthed you?"

He slipped his hands into his pockets to keep them from wrapping around her throat. "Pretty hard to forget something you repeat every day like a god-damn echo."

"Address me with respect."

"You haven't earned it."

She trembled for another second before her smile twitched back in place. "Your father wouldn't appreciate your rude demeanour. Should I remind you of what happened when you were last a disappointment to him?" Tilting her head, she stepped closer. "He banished you for fifteen years. I wonder what punishment he'd come up with if you ever disappointed him again."

Leviathan's eyes drilled into hers. Steady, stony. Leaning into her, he turned his mouth to her ear. "I'm not a six-year-old kid anymore. You can't whip me, can't lock me up. You sure as hell can't put me in Verdite for another fifteen years, but do try, *Mā* Saheb. Tell him what a big disappointment I am. This time, I'll make sure you go to hell with me."

Cecilia narrowed her eyes. "The Guild of Guardianship has done a poor task of straightening out your character," she snapped.

"I prefer it crooked," he said, and moved around her.

She laughed abruptly, breezing to a settee. "It's strange seeing you stand so tall and brave now. I'm amused. Marduk, do you remember when he was a boy? He would cling to Gabrielle's skirt and follow her around. She could hardly catch a moment without him."

Leviathan froze.

A crude smile climbed her mouth, eyes fixed on him. "Do you remember how terrified he always was?" Her fingers traced circles on the back of the settee. "Darkness, crowds, and sounds. Oh, he startled so easily."

Marduk howled on cue, Cecilia's laughter rang in the hall, and Malev clenched his hands.

"A fainthearted boy," Marduk brayed.

"It was necessary to inform his father of his sensitivities."

Marduk rubbed his earlobe. "Very necessary, Mā Saheb," he echoed.

"Blackburns can't be weak."

"True, true, Mā Saheb."

"It was rather fortunate I brought it to his attention, or Leviathan wouldn't have become such a daring young man today," Cecilia continued. "Being separated from Gabrielle has done wonders."

"Mā Saheb," Marduk snickered. She raised her eyebrows in question. "Remember how he slept in her lap? He would never leave her bed."

Malev looked to Leviathan. His companion wasn't of a temperamental nature, but those blue eyes seethed with quiet rage now. He waited for a sign, any sign. Leviathan gave him none. Regardless of their friendship, Malev's family were bottom-feeders in the hierarchy of the higher *zaat,* and an insult from him would give Cecilia a reason to damage him however she could. And she would, knowing it'd hurt Leviathan.

It was one price he wasn't willing to pay.

"Oh, I remember," she crooned.

Marduk's shoulders vibrated with laughter. "And when Firawn Sai punished him—" he went on. "She sobbed like a—"

Leviathan pulled Malev's gun from his waistband, pressing the barrel to Marduk's brow, and the slave's slick voice died in his throat. Gaze flinty, face cold, Leviathan calculated. He calculated the advantages and disadvantages of blowing Marduk's brains out. He let it show in his eyes and watched it dawn in Marduk's.

The slave shook again, but not with laughter. Sweat leaked from his pores, rolling down his ashen skin. "Mā—Mā—Mā Saheb—" he spluttered, spittle on his bottom lip.

Cecilia rose. "What is this, Leviathan?" she demanded. "Have you lost your mind?"

"I don't know." He cocked the gun. "Maybe we should find out."

Marduk shrieked, half-sobbing, half-pleading. Leviathan let him sweat it. Cecilia was paler than usual. A rare treat. She stepped toward him. "Leviathan," she said again, grating on his nerves. "Put it down *now.*"

"Do you know why people don't build houses near a volcano?" he asked, eyes on Marduk, his hand disturbingly steady. "Because it makes no sound before it erupts."

"Leviathan—"

Click.

Cecilia covered her ears with a jolt. Marduk screamed, his eyes squeezing shut, his voice hitting a note that had the diamonds in the chandelier shivering before it dropped to a strangled wheeze. Realising his head was still intact, the slave lurched on his feet.

Leviathan pushed the mouth of the gun against his brow. "Next time, I'll plant the bullet in your brain," he warned softly. "*Samajalē?*"

Marduk made a wretched noise in his throat. Using the gun as leverage, Leviathan shoved him out of the way.

"You'll hear from your father," Cecilia screeched after him. "I'll make certain—"

He slammed the doors on her threats.

CHAPTER 4

"THE CLANS BELIEVE hell is an incarnate creature," Rawiya Mai said, sitting under the awning of a crippled willow with Meriel and Goldie in Lamiapur's courtyard.

Carrying clay pails on her head and hip, Roma crossed to the basins and poured all the water from the pails into a large bucket before turning toward the old *lamiadasi*. Thick, white hair cascaded down Rawiya Mai's hunched back in glossy waves, and there was furrowed skin where her eyes should have been.

When she was a young woman, a patron had thrown acid in them because he abhorred their colour. He had called them 'eyes of the Subyan,' a demoness from a breed of magical creatures called the Ghaib. Villagers wore brass or iron amulets for protection against them and warned their children not to soil trees and lakes as they were home to the Ghaib. If one became possessed, one was taken to the Kāhinah. Amma would often take Nilo because she murmured to herself and seemed as if she weren't in the same world as them.

A covert smile lingered on Rawiya Mai's shrivelled lips. "They believe hell will rear up his head from the core of the earth, open his bottomless eyes and toothless maw, and devour the sinners in one mouthful." She made a sudden snatching motion with a clawed hand. Goldie gasped. The cadence of Rawiya Mai's voice crackled like fire licking across wood. "He will complain that he is so full, but he will never stop eating."

"Imagine being eaten alive," Goldie said with a shiver. Her corkscrew tresses were wrestled into a braid that rested like a golden serpent down her back. With her fair skin and blue eyes, she resembled her older sister in blood, Sunbel, more than their birthmother, Hani.

Meriel snorted. "They're stupid to believe such tales," she stated, patting her sleeping daughter, Aimi, in her lap.

"We'll be reborn, won't we?" Goldie asked. "Amma says we will."

Roma didn't want to be reborn into this world. Humans were savages who considered themselves civilised. They didn't hunt for survival, no, but for sport. She witnessed how they persecuted the clans, saying they weren't a part of their people, because the clans had a separate culture, language, and faith, and because they looked different, but there was inexpressible beauty in what was different. If people ever shed their prejudices and cared to know the clans, they wouldn't be bound to their own senseless hatred.

"We're privileged," Meriel said with a proud lift of her chin. "Mother Lamia chose us."

The conviction in her voice needled Roma. She glanced at Aimi's tiny hand wrapped around her birthmother's finger. Aimi didn't know that in a few years she would be dedicated to Mother Lamia, and the hand she clutched so desperately in her sleep would become the hand that shackled her. Roma knew Meriel wasn't to blame. She was raised by her birthmother, Binti, with the same belief as them, but Roma still wondered how a parent could wish a fate such as her own upon her child. She wondered how Amma had bound her daughter, Yoshi, to that fate; how Binti had bound her two sons and Meriel; how Hani had bound Sunbel and would soon bind Goldie.

Perhaps it wasn't so difficult to deliver one's child. After all, Roma's birthmother never cared to place her in Amma's lap but abandoned her on the steps of Lamiapur like an orphan.

Perhaps the human heart was a cold creature.

Rawiya Mai sighed. "We are loved and we are hated. We are fortunate and unfortunate, pure and impure, auspicious and inauspicious. Indeed, how privileged we are."

"Do you believe in a hell, Mai?" Goldie asked.

"Hell is a conviction among the clans. Just as we have shaped our lives to gain the favours of our gods, they have shaped theirs to please their god."

"Why do they believe in a god who'll put them in hell?"

"Why do we believe in a goddess who would have us worship men?"

Rawiya Mai tipped her face toward the sun. "Conviction is a powerful being, *ladoba*. It builds and destroys in equal measure."

"We don't worship men. We worship the gods," Meriel corrected. "Patrons are vessels of Lord Biran just like we're vessels of Mother Lamia. And we should be grateful for our sacred *zaat* because we're safe. If we didn't worship—"

"Safety is an illusion," Roma interrupted. Meriel and Goldie turned their heads toward her. "And the nature of an illusion is to deceive."

Rawiya Mai stretched her spindly legs with another secretive smile, popping her bones, and Roma didn't know if she were laughing at her. Lifting the bucket of water, Roma moved toward the temple stairs as Hani descended with a platter of blessed fruits from the ceremonial chamber. She was dressed in customary red; the colour of Mother Lamia. All colours were sacred but black and white. Denoting vengeance and death, they were forbidden to *dēvadasis*.

"What's going on here?" Hani demanded. "Didn't Amma send you down to sanctify our anklets for tonight, Meriel? Everyone's busy preparing for the festival, and here you're resting in the shade."

Meriel blushed. "Aimi was hungry, Tai. She fell asleep after I—"

"Give her to Goldie."

"*Hō,* Tai."

Hani plucked the bucket from Roma's hands. "Run to the marketplace and fetch two pails of milk. Amma has already paid Jirani Bhau. Take Yoshi with you. And, Mai—it's festival season. You know it's ill-fated to fill the girls' heads with tales of other gods during such an auspicious month," she said in a reproaching tone.

"Lamia *re*," Rawiya Mai groaned. "Go prepare for the festival, Hani. Do not chew my brain."

Drawing her braid to the front, Roma lifted the sheer veil over her head. Her cobra pendant hung from the tie at the end of the braid, brushing her thigh as she walked toward the gate. Since a woman's hair was considered a part of her womanhood, it was a dishonour—a humiliation parallel to publicly stripping her naked—for women to cut their hair, and so Roma and her sisters braided it to keep it in order.

Yoshi was outside. The bells on her anklet chinked in rhythm as she tapped her foot and hummed a love ballad to herself. "You took your sweet time," she said in her obliquely spiteful manner. "Mai must've been spinning another riveting tale."

Roma drew the veil over her face without a word and started down the decline to the street below. It wasn't yet noon, but Sefu was already thronged with people from villages all over Durra, and the paths were peppered with camel, mule, and cow dung. Some had pilgrimaged from the southern provinces of Intisar and Urooj to visit Lord Biran's temple in celebration of the Sacred Month of Biran. The village men dressed in full-sleeved, knee-length *kurtas* with hip-high slits in the sides and layered turbans on their heads, while the village women wore *cholis* and *lehengas*. Single-chained *mathapattis* adorned their hairlines. Large *naths* attached to chains dangled from their noses beneath the veils drawn over their faces.

The houses and doors were painted red and blue. Garlands decorated the balconies, paper lanterns drooped from lines between rooftops. A nomadic lower *zaat* of songsters occupied the street corners, singing ballads about love and magic, playing sitars and drums as the women spun in dizzying circles. Serpent charmers danced around cobras before a cheering horde, as if evading their venomous bites, but no one noticed that the cobras' maws were sewn closed. When they perished from starvation, the charmers would sell their sloughs to the Kāhinah, who would make amulets for protection.

Roma paused with a pang in her belly at the sight of the cobras.

"Perhaps you should worry about your own skin," Yoshi suggested. "It's soon to be sold after all. Doesn't it bother you that we all knew about your auction?" Tipping toward Roma's ear, she lowered her voice to a stage-whisper. "Are you afraid? Your last time was a mean experience, but you can never predict what sort of patron you'll receive. There's always the chance you'll end up with an even nastier one—"

Grabbing the top of her braid, Roma yanked back Yoshi's head. She squealed in pain, squinting against the glaring sun. "Keep on spreading your poison, Yoshi," Roma said, hauling Yoshi along by her pleated hair. "And I'll pull that bitter tongue from your throat."

When Roma released her, Yoshi stumbled. "*Vēshya*," she hissed after Roma.

Boys dallied in the alleys, pursuing girls with leers and whistles. Roma didn't look at them as she hurried through. If she listened to their crude propositions, she would feel soiled before she was out in the street again. She almost collided with one of them when he stepped in her path. Saber was the son of a seamster—and the boy who had once cornered Chirag.

Rubbing his hands, he sneered at her. "Watch your step, sister, or you'll fall at my feet," he teased. He continued to block her path as she moved to sidestep him. "How's pretty little Chirag? We haven't seen him around for a while. Tell him to come by soon. We'll show him what it means to be a *hijra* in case he didn't catch on the last time."

"Get out of the way," Yoshi snapped.

"Get out of the way," he mimicked. His chums snickered. "Girls say one thing and mean another." Noticing the blatant hatred in Roma's stare, he smirked. "You going to hit me? Go ahead." Leaning forward, he turned his cheek, tapping his jaw. "I don't mind your hands on me."

Yoshi reached for her arm. Shaking her off, Roma held his leering stare. He was a tormentor only to those who submitted to him out of fear. She didn't fear him. "If you ever come near Chirag again, I won't hit you, Saber, I'll sever your pathetic little manhood. And then what will you have left to parade around the village?"

Saber's cheeks reddened as his hooting mates fell against the alley walls in boisterous laughter.

"Come on, Roma," Yoshi insisted. "Don't waste time on alley hounds."

Gliding around Saber, Roma followed her. "Go on and run, *vēshya,*" Saber shouted. "Tell Chirag I'll see him again soon."

Sellers lounged in the confined stalls of the Grand Market and bellowed their prices. There were abundant shelves of bright-coloured fabrics; cabinets filled with headpieces, nosepieces, earpieces, and bangles; sacks holding vibrant spices and dried fruits; walls covered with handwoven purses and slippers. Suncatchers swung from the ceiling of a stall bursting with dyed lanterns and potteries painted with floral patterns were mounded on top of one another. Meat and vegetable stalls vied for space. Dyers stirred cauldrons. Men sold incense oils and other sacred offerings for the gods.

People jostled each other to barter in loud, insistent voices while their children wailed in the heat. Smoke climbed the air from enormous iron pans in which *dhaba* owners fried kebabs made of minced meat and bone marrow, or cooked chicken and lamb stews. The sight and scents lured Roma's senses as she weaved through the thick crowd.

Jirani's stall was near the end of the marketplace by a stretch that overlooked the stepwell and the shrines of Tanuf, Goddess of the Sun, and Sahar, Goddess of the Dawn. He was a thickset man in a dirt-stained *kurta* below which he wore the traditional *dhoti* of the lower *zaat*—a long length of fabric that was wrapped around the legs, folded, and knotted around the waist.

Craning his neck from behind one of his cows, he smiled with warmth when he saw Roma. "Good morning to you, *bitiya*."

"And to you, Bhau," Roma greeted back. "Hani Tai sent us for milk."

"Ah, yes." Wiping his hands in a scarf on his shoulder, he removed the lid of a steel container and lifted it to pour fresh milk into two steel pails. The thick, black thread around his throat was tied to a pendant etched with the shape of a cow's head; the *zaat* symbol of a milkman. "How is Jainaba Begum?"

"Amma is well."

"Goldie and Aimi?"

"Cheerful."

He laughed and nodded. Yoshi hummed absentmindedly again.

Roma kneeled to rub the head of a lamb through the wooden bars of the fence. "You're still selling Jingle to the butcher?" she asked.

"*Hō*. With the recent rise of taxes, I've no choice, *bitiya*," he answered, scratching his black beard. It was unkempt like the wild curls under the twirled layers of his orange turban. "We must all feed our families *na*. Here's your delivery." The small, brass cuffs on his ear glinted as he stepped into the sunlight to hand her the milk. "You needn't hurry with bringing back the pails."

Roma caressed Jingle one last time before she rose to her feet to take the pails, but a shriek made her spin toward a girl sprinting barefoot through the horde in a blue, tarnished kaftan. Telltale curlicue patterns were painted above her eyebrows and down the bridge of her nose, and clan cuffs engraved with tribal symbols clasped her wrists.

The clans weren't welcome in the village. They were considered casteless and unclean, so Sara's appearance provoked cries of disdain. People shouted vile names and recoiled from her, evading even her shadow in fear of pollution, demanding she return to her *dirty camp*, but she didn't seem to hear them.

"*Kāy jhāle*?" Roma asked the second Sara reached her. Dread churned in her belly at the tears in Sara's brown eyes. "What's wrong?"

"Wardens," Sara panted. "Wardens took Khiraa."

CHAPTER 5

THE SKIES SPLIT with a rumble. Men, women, and children burst out in euphoric cheers when Ruda, Goddess of Rain, unleashed her power upon Sefu. Profuse sheets of rain poured from the darkened clouds, lashing the streets and alleys. It sounded like a thousand drums pounding a battle beat. Sellers shoved their carts inside their stalls and lowered metal sliders as a shield against the pitiless shower. Garments were ripped from washing lines on the rooftops. People fell on their knees, praising Ruda and her brother Quzah, God of Thunder, for the eviction of the dearth, their eyes swarming with tears of relief.

Roma threaded through the dancing horde, skipping over drains filled with rainwater and running down slick stairs out of the village. Her *choli* stuck to her skin, her *lehenga* tangled around her legs, and her slippers splashed in the mud. Tearing across the steppe, she reached the fringe of an expansive stretch where the camp sat in a sodden bundle. The smell of human waste prickled in her nose as she passed the latrine pits dug out in the ground.

An assembly of phantoms had gathered outside Ghanima Mai's slumping tarp. Clan men and women stood in their soaked garments, the painted patterns on their skin smeared by the downpour, the colour streaming down their faces like ink, and their eyes hollow with muted pain. She had known them ever since she first met Khiraa and Sara in the steppe when she was a child. She had watched them grow harder over time as their loved ones perished from diseases, as their hope for a kinder future diminished like the flame of a melting candle. They were now wintry forms that assembled to grieve out of habit, but they possessed no more tears to shed.

Turning toward Ghanima Mai's tarp, she glanced at Khiraa's younger brother, Seth, who perched on a lump of wood with his arms around his legs and his hands clasped between his knees. Rainwater dripped from the tips of his brown hair. He didn't look up at her. Roma ducked inside the tarp to the stuttering beat of her own pulse, anticipating the worst.

Khiraa lay on a soiled mat with her swollen eyes closed. There was blood everywhere. It was in her damp hair and on her pallid skin. It stained her threadbare kaftan and her exposed calves. Bruises discoloured her skin, blooming on her face and forearms, darkening around her thin wrists. Her chest barely lifted when she breathed. Roma recoiled inwardly at her shattered state as it elicited emotions Roma had entombed in the farthest nook of her mind.

Her fingers trembled.

Ghanima Mai sat beside Khiraa. The black, cotton shawl on her head covered her silver hair, and her hands dipped a ragged cloth in a tin bowl with rainwater. Thick veins swelled beneath her dark, creased skin as she twirled the cloth, squeezing out the moisture, and cleaned the blood from Khiraa's arms. Tribal earpieces dragged down Ghanima Mai's large earlobes and her tribal *nath* glinted in her nose in the light from a cracked lantern Roma had once salvaged after Hani threw it out. The deepened lines of Ghanima Mai's face told tales of pain, but her back was straight as she nursed another injured daughter of the clans.

Removing her wet slippers, Roma kneeled beside the old clan woman. "Mazin assaulted a Warden and stole his weapon before he ran," Ghanima Mai explained, a tranquillity in her voice which clashed with the concern in her sunken eyes. "We didn't know until the Wardens raided our camp at dawn. They took Khiraa and raped her."

Roma swallowed a tart lump in her throat, but the sourness on her tongue only thickened. Khiraa's older brother knew the law. He knew the Wardens would raid the camp and punish his family for his actions. It was one thing to run. She understood how he couldn't live in the dirt with diseases all around him, his people perishing in the heat of the day and the chill of the night. What she didn't understand was how he could abandon his siblings to the malice of the Firawn's soldiers.

Why did he attack a Warden and doom Khiraa?

The drum of the rain and Khiraa's shallow breaths were the only sounds until Sara arrived and retreated to a corner.

"What do we do, Mai?" she whispered helplessly.

"We care for her. May our Rabb ease her pain."

No god could help her now. A parasite had invaded Khiraa's body and attached itself to her soul. Once she roused from the merciful darkness, she would bleed in places Ghanima Mai's cloth couldn't reach. She would feel their hands on her again and again. She would scream within her head, and no one would hear her. She would never be the same because the Khiraa they knew had been destroyed.

Kanoni ducked inside the tarp with more cloths in her arms. She wore a black *choli* that covered her belly—unlike the *cholis* of village women—and a black *lehenga*, with her long ebony hair braided under a shawl. Curlicue tribal patterns were drawn in dark henna between her thick eyebrows and on the back of her hands. Her tribal bracelets clanged when she kneeled to lift the hem of Khiraa's kaftan.

"Has she stopped bleeding?" Ghanima Mai asked.

"*Nā*. Roma, help me with the cloths. Sara, cover us with a blanket."

Rushing to her feet, Sara held up the blanket to shield Khiraa from view. Roma doused a cloth in the rainwater, handing it to Kanoni and holding up Khiraa's kaftan so Kanoni could clean her lower parts. "*Harami saale*," Kanoni cursed. "They should've just killed her. It would've been mercy. If I ever see Mazin again, I'll wring his damned neck, *māshapath*."

"Don't swear on your mother," Ghanima Mai scolded. "It's disrespectful."

"How much more brutality must we endure?"

"Kanoni, not now, please."

"It'll never stop," Seth snapped. Roma couldn't see him for the blanket, but the anger and pain in his voice caused a physical ache within her heart. "We have to do it. We have to stop it ourselves."

"Seth," Ghanima Mai said in a gentle voice.

"They hurt my sister. They should pay."

Ghanima Mai drew a startled breath when Seth ran back outside. Kanoni looked to Roma, so she hurried after him. The rain battered her as she pursued him across the muddied stretch in bare feet. She didn't want to imagine what the Wardens would do to him if he attacked them. The butcher's son was sodomised after his sister eloped with a higher *zaat* man. Many others were tortured for lesser crimes. They had flogged Kanoni for looking in their eyes, pushing her down on her knees and lashing her back until she was unable to stand. They never needed much of a reason to torment the villagers, but they needed none at all to harass the clans.

Catching Seth's sleeve before he could reach the outskirt of the camp, Roma spun him around to face her. "Seth, stop. You can't go near the Wardens—"

"I don't care," he shouted, pulling free with force. She discovered an awful fracture in his eyes. They churned with an emotion she knew too well. Despair. "Mai always says to be patient. She says the Creator will ease our pain. But we're alone, Tai." His dripping hair flopped from side to side as he shook his head. "Nobody cares about us. If Mazin Bhau hadn't left—the Wardens wouldn't have—none of it would've happened, *yani*." His breath hitched in his throat and tears flooded his eyes. He looked so much younger than his twelve years. "Abba said—he said to protect our sister—" His voice cracked.

"Seth," Roma said softly, forcing herself to close her arms around him. He clenched his hands in her drenched veil where it slumped against her back, and she held him until his body stopped trembling from his soundless sobs.

Until he could breathe again.

CHAPTER 6

IT WAS LONG past dawn when Leviathan stepped into the shower. Hot water pounded his flesh, washed the smoke, sweat, and grime from his skin. Bracing his hands on the wall, he bent his head, shutting his eyes as the tension slowly bled from his muscles. Slaves had scattered in the stables on his arrival. Palace guards had watched him with unease. It wasn't just his reputation that made people nervous, he knew, it was the iron in his build and the skill in his movements. He didn't care to bridle it. There was no point in hiding his nature, no point in pretending he was anything but a Cutthroat, a soldier of darkness, one of thirteen who'd graduated from the notorious Guild of al-Mawt in northern Suradun.

The advanced training was established by the Firawn to build an elite group of soldiers known as the Assassins of al-Mawt. Few had the psychological and physical stamina to survive it. To make it into the Firawn's exclusive Black Guard. Most graduated as Wardens and Rangers from the Guild of Guardianship in Verdite, depending on how well they fared in the Tribunals—the painstaking trials Junior and Senior Recruits had to pass in order to rise in rank—but the Firawn hadn't given Leviathan a choice but to take on the advanced training once he'd passed the Tribunals.

And he'd endured.

He had countless scars and a tattoo along his spine as a testament that he'd lived through things worse than death. It rippled under the roasting stream, the Firawn's mark, a hooded cobra, and he felt it stretch, heard it hiss. Poised to strike, maw wide open. It moved like it had a life of its own. The black ink was fused with a drop of magic and poison from the deadliest serpent in the Strips. His body was immune to it. He recalled the look of pride on the Firawn's face when he'd outlasted the ceremony without the need for healers to extract the poison.

He pressed his brow to the damp wall. Fifteen years in the military city for one mistake. He'd pondered more than once, in all that time, what would've happened if he'd done what the Firawn had demanded of him that day. What would his life have been like if he'd been by his mother's side? Would she be alive, or would he still have failed to protect her? He shook his head on a humourless chuckle. She'd never needed his protection. He'd needed hers.

And didn't he still?

If she'd heard of his deeds in the southeast, it would've broken her heart.

"I'm a long way from the man you wanted me to be, Amma," he whispered.

The door to his chamber banged open.

"Bhau," Junho shouted.

Wrapping a towel around his hips, Leviathan stepped into the chamber. Malev leaned on the wall, his brawny arms crossed over his chest. He was two hundred and fifty pounds of clean muscle compared to Junho's one hundred and thirty, and still he moved with more grace than him. And less bloody noise.

Junho shoved a hand through his hair. "Bhau," he sputtered again.

"*Kāy*?" Leviathan asked with patience, yanking on a plain black *kurta* and trousers. "Need special permission to run your mouth today? Spit it out."

"Wardens raided the camp at dawn, Bhau."

His hands froze on the laces of his boot.

"Mazin assaulted a Warden," Malev elaborated. "They took his sister. Khiraa."

Little Khiraa. He remembered her from when he'd gone down to the camp on his last leave. A sweet, wide-eyed kid. She'd be no older than fourteen now. Junho was still talking. They beat her, he said. They raped her. The words burrowed into Leviathan's brain, drawing visuals, making him sick to his stomach. The control he'd barely regained in the stables slipped his hold, and rage was on him in a red haze.

"Where is she now?"

"Back in the camp, Bhau," Junho answered. "Her kid brother found her in a shed."

Seth.

"How many of them?"

"Three, Bhau."

Shutting his eyes, Leviathan fought for composure. Emotion was a liability. If you could be cold, it wouldn't overpower you. Wasn't it the lesson that the Firawn had drilled into his head in twisted, innovative ways until he'd mastered it to his satisfaction? For a dangerous minute, he fumbled for a grip on that cold rationality. He needed to keep his head clear, or he'd lose it.

Junho punched the leather sack hanging in the corner, cursing in every Khansāri dialect he knew. "I say we line them up and slit their throats," he growled. "Let me do it, Bhau."

"They didn't break the law," Malev pointed out, face grim. "They upheld it."

Junho frowned. "Wait. What law?" Being an orphaned kid assigned to Leviathan as his personal slave, Junho had never been exposed to the system like the lower *zaat* and street orphans were. He was still innocent in some ways, and maybe Leviathan was too protective of him. He had to be. The kid rarely used his head.

"Honour rape," Malev answered.

"What the hell does that mean?"

"Specific penalties are issued if someone of a higher *zaat* is assaulted and honour rape is the most common punishment in Durra. It's given to the closest relative in the felon's absence."

"What the hell?" Junho exploded. "Don't they have to go through the Panchayat?"

"The Panchayat is for the lower *zaat*, Junho, not the clans."

Even then, it didn't serve the people. Every village had a Panchayat, a council of the wealthiest elders, entrusted to settle matters between the higher and lower *zaat*. Instead, they bargained with the higher *zaat*. They were granted riches like land and coin in exchange for loyalty, all while the lower *zaat* placed their blind faith in a justice system that didn't exist. As for the clans, Panchayats weren't needed. They were already excluded from society, a stateless ethnicity forced to live in camps without legal claim to any piece of land, without livestock or clean water—their people humiliated, exploited, starving to death on the borders of society. There were no laws protecting them, no decrees securing their basic human rights.

They'd have to be considered humans for that.

Inhaling deeply, Leviathan managed to put a leash on his anger and let the cold, rational part of his brain take the lead. He shoved to his feet and reached for his knives.

"Junho."

"*Hō*, Bhau?"

"Summon the Wardens to the camp." If they refused to come, he'd find them, cut them open, and bring their entrails.

Dead or alive, he'd have them at Khiraa's feet.

Something dark and ugly had awakened inside of him. Something he'd felt too often and crushed. Something he no longer cared to tame. The bastards had walked into his people's camp and taken a sister of his. They'd put their filthy hands on her, condemned her to a lifetime of torment. Their deeds were as primal and twisted as their laws, so he'd meet them on their turf.

He'd be primal, he'd be twisted.

If it was a jungle rule they sought—it was a jungle rule they'd get.

CHAPTER 7

STRANGERS CAME TO the camp.

Roma hovered behind Seth, staring toward the two tall men slicing through the stalwart sheets of rain with long strides. The clans stirred in sudden unease, their steeped bodies clustering closer together. Murmurs spread among them. Their anxiousness was palpable in the dissonant cadences of their voices and the furrows of concern between their eyebrows.

Lifting the veil over her head, Roma shielded her face from the cloudburst and the strangers. The dark-skinned one in a deep blue *kurta* and black trousers appeared like a giant with shockingly broad shoulders and thick arms. It loaned his body violence that failed to harmonise with his serene gait. A copper bracelet engraved with a blazing sun clasped his wrist and marked him as higher *zaat*.

The second stranger's black *kurta* plastered to his body. A leather string dangled from his neck and rounded on a pendant shaped like a curved sword. Rain dripped from his face. When he lifted his head, his eyes latched onto Roma's. Her pulse stumbled at the sharp awareness in his stare. It was as if he didn't even need to search for her. Not then, in the banyan, and not now.

"Bhau," Seth said in a reverent voice. "It's Levi Bhau."

Rushing to Ghanima Mai's tarp, Seth disappeared inside. The Firawn's son strode to the semicircle formed by the clans and Roma held on to her veil in fear that he would recognise her. His expression was barren and his eyes raked over the assembly. None of them greeted him. They only stared in condemnatory silence. She didn't know what business the Firawn's son might have in the camp, but she thought him brash for meeting their stares without a flicker of shame. His ancestors were tyrants. His father was one. Centuries in the past, the invaders had come in their ships, causing an irreversible rift between the Khansan people and forcing the clans to live like hunted animals, and now the blood of the Firawn stood in their camp without humility.

Ghanima Mai ducked out of the tarp with her shawl drawn over her head. When she saw the men, her eyes rounded and glowed, and her lips upturned in a smile. Roma's eyebrows stitched together. Why wasn't Ghanima Mai unsettled by their presence?

The dark-skinned stranger moved toward her first. Leaning down, he touched her feet, brushing his fingertips between his eyebrows and to his lips in the gesture of respect given to the elders. It was peculiar seeing someone of a higher *zaat* practise the Khansan custom.

Ghanima Mai caressed his head before he rose to his full height. "Malev," she said. "How you've grown."

"With your blessings, Mai," he said in Khansāri with a rough southern burr. His voice was a chest-deep rumble. "You're more beautiful than I recall."

Her laughter spilled into space. "Rascal," she said tenderly. Her eyes dashed to the Firawn's son, her mirth collapsing while her smile remained. He lingered a few paces behind Malev, watching her with unreadable eyes. She nodded imperceptibly. It was as if he waited for that sign. Moving toward her without hesitation now, he leaned down to touch her feet like Malev, and Roma noticed a change in his impassive expression when Ghanima Mai placed her hand on his shoulder. It was as subtle as a breeze rustling the desert sages. His eyes closed for a heartbeat—and then he pressed his fingertips between his eyebrows and against his lips.

"It's been four years, Levi." Ghanima Mai's eyes glistened with tears. "Is this how you greet your Mai upon your return?" Stepping closer to her, he slid his arms around her, cupping the back of her head. She pressed her face against his chest with shoulders that trembled from her silent sobs. "I knew you'd come. My heart knew."

A vein in his throat thumped. "I'm too late," he said in a quiet voice.

"I tried to stop them," Seth said beside Ghanima Mai. "But I couldn't—" He lowered his eyes to his stained feet and his hands clenched at his sides. "I couldn't protect her."

The Firawn's son clasped Seth's shoulder. "Look at me, Seth." He waited until Seth lifted his eyes. "You took care of her. That's what a brother would do."

"Bhau!"

The shout came from another stranger. He was younger than the Firawn's son and the one called Malev. Dripping black hair fell over his forehead in an uneven mess as he walked toward them with an aggressiveness to his gait. His feline eyes glared dark in a triangular face. Two nosepieces sat in his nostril—a pin and a ring—and cuffs adorned his left ear, yet the ornaments weren't etched with the symbols of any known *zaat*. Neither was the threaded bracelet with a crescent pendant around his right wrist.

"Pay your respects," the Firawn's son told him.

Ghanima Mai laughed when he reached down awkwardly to touch her feet. "You must be Junho. Levi told me so much about you."

His eyes widened a fraction, but when he looked at the Firawn's son, he received no attention. "Bhau?" he inquired with an unexpected grin that diminished the fire in him and turned him into a child.

"Did you find them?"

"*Hō*, Bhau. They're coming."

Ghanima Mai glanced between them. "Levi," she said in an alarmed voice. "What's happening?"

"Justice for Khiraa, Mai." There was a vindictive shine in Junho's eyes. "Bhau's justice."

"Dauid, send the children inside," she called to one of the clan men. "You, too, Seth. Go inside."

"I don't want to."

"Seth—"

The thunder of hooves sounded over the rain. People inched back when three Wardens rode into the camp on large, black mounts. They wore their blue uniforms and the steel on their forearms dripped water. Roma had seen them in the village many times. The twins—Taras and Timur—were of identical height with shorn red hair. The third Warden, Nen, was the son of a potter who had joined the Firawn's military so his father could be exempted from taxation.

The Wardens dismounted. Their steel-tipped boots splashed fountains of mud when they bounded to the ground. Ghanima Mai failed to persuade Seth to return inside the tarp. His fists had whitened. She rested her hand on his shoulder, squeezing it to keep him in place as the Wardens strolled forward with arrogance in their strides and guns at their waists.

With a nervous swallow, Roma licked her lips. She didn't have much knowledge of the Firawn's soldiers with the exception that the Wardens held less power than the Rangers who terrorised the east. She had heard of the brutal massacres from Ghanima Mai. The clan woman had escaped across the eastern border to seek refuge in the West Strip when the Rangers attacked her camp.

Taras dipped his head in the mockery of a bow. "You summoned us. We're here," he said, waiting a telltale moment before he added, "Saheb."

Junho cracked his knuckles, stepping forward, but Malev's strong arm blocked him. Tipping back his head, the Firawn's son closed his eyes against the rain. When he opened them again, Roma saw that a darkness had taken root, and it drove a terrible shiver down her back. The Firawn's son moved toward the Wardens and his companions followed him.

Taras glanced around at the clans with a sneer, oblivious to the approaching danger. "If I may speak out of term, Saheb," he drawled. "It doesn't seem suitable to meet out here in the slums when…" His words faded as Malev and Junho circled them.

Everyone watched the Firawn's son, drawn to the power which seeped from his presence. Roma couldn't tear her eyes from him. She sensed it as well—that power—and it felt familiar, even though she couldn't place it. The clans might despise him, but they looked to him now with a taste for it.

And so did she.

"Get down on your knees," he said.

Taras lifted an eyebrow. Looking at Malev to his right, Nen gulped, kneeling without reluctance. It astonished Roma that the other two Wardens disobeyed a direct order from the Firawn's son. They measured him with one word apparent in their eyes: *Bezaat.*

"You must be joking, Saheb," Timur remarked.

"*Ay, harami,*" Junho snarled. "You see Bhau laughing?"

"Who're you calling a bastard? Lowlife son of a bitch."

Junho started toward him, but the Firawn's son inclined his head, and he stopped. Taras stroked a hand along his clean-shaven jaw in a casual, uninterested motion. "Look, Saheb," he reasoned in a scornful voice. The Firawn's son didn't react to the derogatory tone like his glowering companion. "We're Wardens. We kneel only to the Firawn."

"You'll kneel to me."

Before Taras could process the statement, Junho had kicked Timur behind his knees and his bones snapped, eliciting a guttural moan from his throat as he dropped in the mud. Taras stared down at his groaning brother in a moment of utter shock which quickly spun into fury. His face contorted and his fingers twitched near his gun, but he didn't pull it on the Firawn's son.

It would have been treason.

Glaring at the Firawn's son, Taras kneeled. "You can't treat us like—"

Seth closed the distance and struck him hard across the face. A collective roar rose from the clans, resonating over the camp and drowning out the assailing rain. The fervour in the sound reverberated in the passionate beats of Roma's heart. Her breath spilled out in a deep, satisfied sigh. Taras looked stunned, and then he raised his fist with a vicious growl.

"Seth," Ghanima Mai shouted.

Roma took a startled step toward Seth, but stilled as the Firawn's son caught Taras' wrist in a blur of movement. Twisting his arm around at a painful angle, the Firawn's son pushed him downward, forcing a groan from his throat. Short-tempered breaths rushed in and out of his flaring nostrils as he pressed his lips into a bloodless line.

"Go ahead," the Firawn's son said. "Give me a reason to detach the other."

Taras' face turned a darker shade of red. He didn't move when Seth struck him a second time and a third. It was impossible to determine whose blood was on his fist as Seth continued to attack until he had no more strength left in his emaciated frame. Spitting in the Warden's face, he walked back to Ghanima Mai, the hatred sweltering in his red-rimmed eyes. She wrapped her arms around him, and he trembled in her embrace, as afraid as he was furious.

Taras straightened himself. Blood poured from his broken nose and lips. He was smeared in rain, mud, and blood, and stripped of his pride. The malice in his stare promised Seth torment before he turned his eyes to the Firawn's son.

"I won't forget this humiliation. *Bezaat* bastard."

The world seemed to hush.

Surging forward, Junho caught Taras by the collar and pressed a gun against his forehead. "What did you say? Piece of shit," he shouted. Roma's lips moved behind her soaked veil in a silent chant that urged Junho to shoot him. He should scream. He should bleed more than Khiraa. "Say it again, *harami saala*—"

"Junho."

"Say it one more time—"

Moving with shocking speed, the Firawn's son shoved Junho back a full step. There was a tolerant expression on his face, but his eyes were dark. "Sit your ass down," he said in a levelled voice. When Junho continued to stare past him at the Warden with murderous eyes, he shoved him once more and harder this time. "*Now.*"

Junho's upper lip twitched in disgust, but he ripped his stare from Taras.

"That's right. Put a leash on your rabid hound," Taras derided, cupping his dislocated shoulder. "You get it now, don't you? You're not above the law. And we" —he raised his chin— "are the law."

The Firawn's son turned and crouched down. "Laws are made by men," he said with unnerving calm. "I'm a man. Which means I can make my own laws." Junho pitched his gun and the Firawn's son caught it out of the air. His hand moved smoothly over the steel, drawing a *click*, which drained the blood from the Warden's face.

"You can't—"

"Didn't we just establish the rules of legislation?"

"You won't get away with it. We're higher *zaat*." Dragging his collar away from his neck, Taras revealed a pendant with an encircled silver flame around his throat. "Silvers."

"Aren't you curious about your penalty? Because I am. Junho?"

"*Hō*, Bhau?"

"What's the penalty for rape?"

Junho showed his teeth. "Death, Bhau," he answered.

"Death," said the Firawn's son.

CHAPTER 8

"Son of a bitch," Timur bellowed and drew his gun.

Roma jolted as the blast sounded through the camp, inciting another fervent roar from the clans, and they started to chant a battle verse in Ancient Khansāri. The ominous tone behind the dark lyrics of punishment caused the hair on Roma's forearms to stand on end. It was a language so old, so forgotten, that she shouldn't have understood it, but the melodic rolls and aspirated sounds appealed to her like a memory hovering at the edges of her mind, only to skitter away when she reached for it. She shivered from a deep unease within her.

Timur had fallen. Blood oozed through his trousers from a wound between his legs, merging with the rain, and agonised moans ripped from his throat while he writhed on the ground. Wheeling onto his stomach, he coughed, pressing his forehead into the mud. Nen stared down at him in silence with enlarged pupils and a face as white as bone. She tasted his fear like a delicate vibration against her tongue.

"You shot my brother," Taras hissed, spitting furiously. "You bastard. There'll be consequences. When the Firawn hears about this—"

"He'll be pissed." Ignoring Timur's aggrieved sobs, the Firawn's son dropped his hand on Taras' injured shoulder and the Warden winced. "But you see, you're a Warden. Me? I'm one of his biggest investments. Since financial losses matter more to him than human losses" —his gaze glided over the camp before it returned to Taras— "he'll give me a warning and move on, while you're buried six feet in the ground, burning up in hell. Those are consequences I can live with."

Malev chuckled.

Rising to his feet, the Firawn's son shoved his gun under the Warden's jaw and forced his head up. The protruding veins in Taras' throat strained. "It was a woman who birthed you," he said, driving Taras' head further back until it was painfully horizontal. "And when you put your filthy hands on Khiraa, you assaulted your own mother."

Taras let out a hoarse laugh. "Oh, I see how it is. You're a sympathiser because your birthmother was a tribal bitch. The Firawn's personal whore."

The Firawn's son stilled. An unsettling emotion shivered in the misty swirls of his eyes and Roma sensed a fire in him. It compelled her to seek cover lest she be burned. She thought that he would kill the Warden now, but he lowered his gun and stepped back from him.

Junho pushed an impatient hand through his hair. "Bhau?"

"Not much of a man, are you?" Taras sneered. "You make me sick."

"Let me kill him, Bhau."

"Everyone knows you came out of a tribal whore. You'll always be *bezaat*, and we'll always be the superior *zaat*. It's been that way for centuries, mate."

"*Bhau*."

"And these vermin?" Taras glanced around at the hollow faces of the clans. "They should suffer. We should cleanse the entire state of their dirty blood before they breed more vermin like you."

"Give me the gun, Bhau."

"That little bitch you're talking about? She deserved what she got. If she doesn't kill herself after what we did to her, we'll just pay her another visit—"

The violent blast jarred Roma's senses, reverberating within her head, while Taras collapsed with a hole through his. A second blast silenced Timur's groans. The Firawn's son had killed them. Peering at their still bodies, Roma tasted a metallic tang in the rain. A terrible knot uncoiled within her chest as the inebriating rush of gratification coursed through her shell. Their deaths calmed a storm that she hadn't known existed inside of her until she felt it dispel at the sight of their lifeblood. It pooled beneath them in the mud where such perpetrators belonged.

This wouldn't mend Khiraa's soul, but vengeance wasn't meant to heal.

It was meant to cause pain.

Nen trembled. His eyes snagged on the Firawn's son. "I didn't do anything," he stuttered out. "I didn't—I never touched her, I swear it. I only watched. Please—Bhau Saheb, I only—"

"Watched," the Firawn's son said. Drawing a knife, he tossed it to Malev. "Take his eyes. Make sure he never watches again."

"Bhau Saheb!" Nen screamed, struggling helplessly against Malev's hold as he dragged him out of the camp. "Bhau, please!"

The Firawn's son returned the gun to Junho. "Take the bodies to the shed, burn it to the ground." Junho nodded and picked up Timur's body, throwing it over his shoulder with surprising strength and striding toward the mounts. The Firawn's son crossed to Ghanima Mai and touched her feet. "*Jāto*, Mai."

Then he turned to leave.

"Just what're you trying to prove?" Kanoni demanded. He stopped. She stepped forward from the semicircle of witnesses. "That you came to avenge Khiraa? When it was men of your *zaat* who raped her?"

"It's not a matter of *zaat*, but of protection." There was no fire nor frost in his voice. His tone was respectful. Subservient. He esteemed her. "Today, they took Khiraa. Tomorrow, they might've taken somebody else. Silence has a price."

"You're saying we didn't fight for our own," Kanoni rebuked. "That we allowed this to happen."

Junho lobbed Taras' body over one of the mounts' back. "Tai," he objected. "That's not what Bhau—" He fell silent when the Firawn's son angled his head and, huffing out a breath, guided the mounts out of the camp.

Kanoni's upper lip lifted in resentment. "What do you know of our circumstances? You're one of *them*. You come here" —she jabbed a finger toward the ground— "with your privileged *zaat* all but stamped on your forehead like a badge of honour, and you lecture us about silence. Do you know what it's like to sing your children to the sleep of death? To watch them starve while you whisper empty promises in their ears?"

Roma pressed her lips together with a heaviness in her belly as she remembered how Kanoni had fallen apart when her twins perished from hunger, how she had clutched their tiny bodies in her arms and screamed from anger and grief, and Roma hadn't known what to do except stand and watch with tears in her throat as Ghanima Mai and the other clan women attempted to take the babes from Kanoni.

"Have you ever feared the Firawn's soldiers would raid your home and kill your husband because he chooses to defend it?" Kanoni's eyes shimmered with furious tears that refused to fall. Her voice trembled. "Don't you come here and pass judgement. Your people invaded our lands. Thieves *saale*." She spat at his feet. He didn't move, but his eyes lowered. "Generations of our children have been born in camps. We have no clean water, no food. Your healers won't treat us because your father issued a ban promising execution to anyone who helps us. We're forced to watch our loved ones die. Do you know what that's like, *Saheb*?"

The Firawn's son flinched at the title.

"Kanoni," Ghanima Mai chided. "*Thāmb re*."

"*Nā*, Mai. All we do is stay calm while his people rob us, *yani*." Looking at Ghanima Mai, Kanoni pointed toward the Firawn's son. "This boy comes around once in a decade and acts like he's one of us." She whipped around to face him again. "Killing the Wardens doesn't redeem you."

Ghanima Mai frowned. "Be reasonable, Kanoni. Levi didn't do it for himself. He did it for Khiraa. Don't you see the risk he's taken for her?"

"What risk? The Firawn will never harm his precious son. And there's no punishment worse than the one we suffer, Mai. It doesn't matter to him, or his people, because it's not affecting any of them."

His eyes lifted to hers. "*You* are my people," he told her.

She raised a hand to stop him. "We're not the same. Badriya birthed you, but your father raised you. It's his values in you, his teachings. The whispers of your deeds have reached far into the north, *ya* Blade of the Firawn."

He tensed at Kanoni's words. Ghanima Mai squeezed her eyes closed in wordless pain. She didn't defend him now. Roma glanced between her and the Firawn's son through the rain. What did Kanoni mean by *Blade of the Firawn*? What deeds?

Dauid, one of the clan men, touched Kanoni's arm. "*Khallas*, Kanoni," he said. "Enough. There's no point in digging up corpses."

The shawl slipped from Kanoni's head when she pushed Dauid's hand aside and glowered at the Firawn's son. "Do you know what happened to Salehe? You don't. You never cared to know. When the Wardens took my sister, he fought for her, and they cut him down." A tear spilled over her cheek and the Firawn's son swallowed. "Even as my husband was dead, they didn't allow him an ounce of respect. They soiled his corpse. They pissed on him." Her abrupt laughter was an anguished sound, like shattering glass, and it ended on a breathless sob. "And you call *us* barbaric. You tell us that *we* are inhumane. You can torment us all you want, but should we defend ourselves, then we're a threat to your system." She swivelled on her heels to leave. "Hypocrisy."

"Tai."

Kanoni stilled.

Roma didn't know if it was because the Firawn's son had used the honorific for a sister or because of the unveiled regret in his voice. He took a step toward Kanoni, but she shook her head. "We don't need your pity or sympathy," she told him, swiping at the raindrops along her jaw with the back of her hand in a harsh motion. "Give us food. Give us weapons. Can you give us anything at all, Leviathan Silvius Blackburn?"

He made a subtle movement with his head as if her words had physically struck him. Closing the distance, she reached for the collar of his *kurta*, yanking the silk for emphasis. "What can we expect from someone who wears the label of our oppressor?" There was no anger in her voice anymore, only emptiness. "Don't come here again." She ducked inside the tarp, leaving him standing in the rain, and soon the clans dispersed as well.

Ghanima Mai's bottom lip trembled. "*Ladoba*," she called to him.

The Firawn's son looked at her with darkened eyes. Grabbing the collar of his *kurta*, he dragged it over his head and, crumbling it between his hands, threw it down on the ground before he walked away from the camp.

CHAPTER 9

Roma pressed a cool cloth to Khiraa's forehead. Khiraa's agonised cries carried through the camp, sounding louder as the rain slowed to a sprinkle. Air rushed in and out of her chest in shallow gasps. Kanoni cleaned her injuries again in an attempt to ward against infection with the rainwater Seth collected in the tin bowls. It was impossible to persuade Khiraa to drink despite her parched state, so Kanoni forced her by pinching her nose.

With her eyes averted from Khiraa's bruises, Roma touched another cloth to her inner wrist where her pulse jittered. The sight of her in this condition nauseated Roma. She swallowed the acidic knot in her throat, but it didn't dissolve the queasiness. There was a time when she was the one with similar injuries on her shell. She sat back on her haunches with restless feet that wanted to bolt.

Ducking under the tarp, Ghanima Mai brushed her shawl back from her head, sprinkling rain on Roma. The drops sent a shiver through her. Ghanima Mai had a vial in her hand and Kanoni rose to take it. "What's this, Mai?" she asked, sounding as if she already knew because her tone was accusatory.

"It's medicine."

"It's magic."

Tipping her head to the side, Roma scrutinised the lucent, crystalline vial. She had heard of herbal medicine bonded with magic, available only to the higher *zaat* through their healers. The vial looked ordinary. She expected magic to shimmer much like the blue lights from the torches on the city walls, or at least provide some indication of its preternatural properties, but it was as clear and still as water.

Rawiya Mai said magic had once saturated Khansadun's soil. There was so much colour, she claimed, so much life. Acres of wheat like polished gold. Gardens of exotic blossoms in bright orange, red, blue, and violet that could heal or poison. Trees abloom with mangoes and persimmons, sweet-and-sour pomegranates, saline olives and sweet dates. Magic still endured in some places, such as the Sleeping Forest, and Roma often heard folk ballads about it from the nomadic songsters in the village.

Imagining a prosperous land was hard when all she knew was a bleached and barren world. Magic had either withdrawn like the banyan's spirit or been drained from the earth by the Firawn and those before him. It was used to light their torches and heal their people. There were even rumours that the Firawn consumed magic to sustain his youth, while others believed he was touched by the gods.

Ghanima Mai snatched the vial out of Kanoni's hand. "Yes, but it's *ruhani* magic," she argued. "The Creator has permitted all Light Magic to humankind."

"Where did you get it?"

"Does it matter? It'll heal Khiraa's injuries."

"You got it from him."

"What do you want, Kanoni? You have a problem if Levi helps, and you have a problem if he doesn't help. I won't see Khiraa in pain just because you're too proud to accept the potion."

Roma glanced between them for a tense moment.

Kanoni sighed. "Fine." She held out her hand for the vial and Ghanima Mai placed it in her palm. Kneeling beside Khiraa, Kanoni pinched her nose again, pouring the liquid past her lips. Roma stared in wonder as Khiraa healed, the cuts sewing together by invisible needles and the swollenness sinking away into her skin. Her cries eased into silence and her breaths slowed, deepened, to the beat of sleep.

How many illnesses could be cured in the camp with such mere vials of magic? The skin diseases, infections, and fevers could all end with one swallow. It was inhumane to keep the potions from the clans and the lower *zaat*. Why shouldn't they have a right to the same medicine as the higher *zaat*?

Leaning back on her heels, Kanoni concealed a yawn behind her hand. "I must tend to Maryam's newborn," she said in a drained voice.

"Go see to her," Ghanima Mai said. "I'll look after Khiraa."

Roma waited for Kanoni to leave before she looked at the old clan woman.

"Mai?"

"Yes, *ladoba*?"

"You care for the Firawn's son."

"Yes."

"Why?"

Ghanima Mai was silent for so long that Roma didn't think she would answer, so she watched the folds of the clan woman's skin, the silver sheen of her thinning hair, the deep furrows around her lips, and imagined her as a young woman. There was always a profound sadness about her as if she had seen too much darkness, experienced too much loss, and now wished to close her eyes against it all, yet she continued to live and care for people with a maternal touch. Roma liked the smallest detail about her—from how she smelled to how she walked with a poise that was nothing like the artificial gait of a *lamiadasi*.

"I knew his birthmother," Ghanima Mai said at last and Roma met her eyes. The shade of brown reminded her of the dark honey that Amma kept on a shelf in her shed. "Badriya. That was her name. She was taken in by a higher *zaat* sympathiser whose daughter, Gabrielle, was her age, and they were raised as sisters. When Gabrielle was married to the Firawn, Badriya chose to follow as her *bandi*, so she'd be allowed to stay by her side."

Draping her arms around her legs, Roma rested her chin on her knees. *Bandis* were female slaves provided as a part of a wealthy woman's dowry. She didn't understand why anyone would choose to become a *bandi*. Perhaps it was because their livelihood was secured if they served in a higher *zaat* household. They wouldn't need for food or a roof over their heads.

"The Firawn didn't know she was from the clans?"

"Badriya looked more Suran than tribal."

"Did he ever find out?"

"Eventually. By then Badriya was pregnant with his child. The Firawn has a weakness for beauty. It's why he married Gabrielle. It's why he forced himself on Badriya when she denied him." Lowering herself beside Khiraa, Ghanima Mai drew a ragged blanket over them both. "I first met Badriya when she brought food to our camp. She'd sleep on an empty belly herself but always delivered what food she could from the palace kitchens. She watched the healers around Gabrielle, learned how to nurse, and gave similar aid to us. She debated politics with the men and often left them frustrated." Ghanima Mai burst into laughter, her thin shoulders bopping, then she vanished deeper into the past. "Gabrielle was just fifteen when she was married. Her father didn't wish it, but one doesn't refuse the Firawn. She became pregnant, miscarried, and fell ill."

"Gabrielle Saheba lost her child?"

"Children. Twice in her third month, once in her fifth month. That third time Gabrielle was forced to give birth as the child was dead in her womb. Badriya said Gabrielle would awaken in the middle of the night, convinced she heard her child crying somewhere."

Roma twirled a loose thread from her damp *lehenga* around her finger. Losing children happened often in her village. Sometimes because a husband couldn't feed another mouth, so the midwife came to remove the child from his wife's womb. Other times because a mother-in-law believed that the child her daughter-in-law carried was female.

What would Roma have done if she had become pregnant after her first auction? She twisted the thread until it snapped. "Was it an illness that killed Gabrielle Saheba?" she asked after a moment of silence.

A gust of wind almost extinguished the light from the lantern. Ghanima Mai reached out and cupped a hand over the crack to shield the flame inside it. "I don't know, *ladoba*. Gabrielle didn't speak of her illness when she visited our camp with Levi. She brought him here because she wanted him to know where he came from, to know his people," she explained. "She thought if he shared a bond with his birthmother's people, it might strengthen him, protect him, but she had to be careful. The Firawn had forbidden any contact between us."

"If he's the child of a clan woman, why did the Firawn claim him?"

"Perhaps because he had no other heirs, or perhaps because there were rumours he was impotent and Gabrielle was never pregnant. The Creator knows." Ghanima Mai folded her arm under her head like a cushion. "You asked why I care for Levi. Well, I've witnessed his birthmother's resilience and compassion, and though he has never known her, I see her heart beating inside of him. I have faith in him yet."

How could Ghanima Mai have faith in someone who she hadn't known for years? Kanoni didn't trust him. She despised him. What did she call him? Blade of the Firawn. She said they had heard of his deeds. What could he possibly have done to earn the abhorrence of his birthmother's people?

The Horn of the Gods sounded across the steppe, proclaiming the fall of night and calling people to prayers. Roma hurried to her feet. She had forgotten about Yoshi, the milk, and the Festival of the High Lord. Turning toward Ghanima Mai, she parted her lips to speak, but the clan woman had fallen asleep within seconds.

Sprinting out of the camp, Roma returned to Sefu's streets which swarmed with villagers dressed in their best garments, lighting paper lanterns, setting up *dhabas* of broiling snacks and stalls of bright kites. Children had their faces painted with vibrant powder, their masks resembling the demons that Lord Biran slaughtered in the divine stories. Colourful paper was pinned to their shoulders and arms like faery wings.

Southern higher *zaat* families arrived on ornamented camels from Intisar and Urooj. Roma could always tell them apart from the northern higher *zaat* by their fashion. The men wrapped their heads in silk turbans adorned with bejewelled pins. They favoured tailored silk trousers—*churidar*—which gathered at the ankles in creases, and long velvet coats—*sherwani*—embroidered with the threadwork of mythological battles, elephants, and peacocks.

Their women fancied *sarees* stitched from lavish silk blends, embellished with similar threadwork and pearls. The southern *cholis* came in all shapes. Backless, shoulderless, or buttoned to the throat; full sleeves, short sleeves, or sleeveless. Copper and silver symbols of their *zaat* shimmered on their gold-dusted skin whenever their bodies moved to the indolent rocking of the camels. Their choice of hair ornament was the *maangtikka* shaped as a beaded chain with a gold-plated pendant and encrusted gemstone attached to the end. It rested on the centre hairline so the decoration piece lingered on the forehead.

Slipping through Lamiapur's gate, Roma slid inside the bathing chamber to bathe before someone caught her overdue return. She changed into a ceremonial backless *choli* which had the cobra motifs of Mother Lamia woven on the half sleeves, and a matching *lehenga* with patch-border work stitched among the heavy folds.

Sunbel stepped into their shed with a cheerful smile as Roma pinned the veil on her shoulder, pulling it across her chest, over her bare belly, and hooking the end behind her back. "I love festival season," her sister gushed, fastening a *jadai* to the length of Roma's braid. The traditional hair ornament for *lamiadasis* had bells pinioned to each triple-headed cobra brooch. "I love the music and colours and mood. Everyone's so spirited, and there's free food."

Drawing a brass *kamarbandh*—another ceremonial ornament—around her waist, Roma hooked it and moved on to the double-chained *mathapatti.* She didn't look in the mirror, avoiding her own reflection, even as she applied thick lines of kohl to her eyes and painted her lips with a practiced hand.

"The lanterns look so beautiful. Oh, and the puppeteers! My favourite play is the one where Lord Biran sees Mother Lamia for the first time," Sunbel continued. "It's so romantic how he pursues her. How he catches her wrist and refuses to let go. She struggles at first, but then accepts his love."

Yes. How romantic that he forced his love on her.

"But the best part is the dancing, isn't it?"

Roma couldn't deny that. She didn't dance as a devotion to the gods. She danced because she was inexplicably drawn to rhythm and movement, unable to resist the call of the pounding drums, trilling flutes, and strumming sitars.

"Sun?"

"Yes?"

"Don't you wonder why we must take patrons? Why we can't just dance?" she asked, slipping on the bangles and bracelets.

Sunbel blinked. "We take patrons because it's the will of the High Lord and the Mother Goddess, Roma. It's as simple as that." Crinkling her nose, she nudged Roma's forehead with a fingertip. "The things that go on inside that head of yours." With a laugh, she sashayed out into the courtyard to join their sisters.

Running her fingers over one of the enamelled bracelets, Roma stared down at Nilo's untouched sleeping mat. Would they see her tonight? Roma doubted it. Nilo's patron wouldn't even allow her a short visit to Lamiapur or have them visit her. It was a relief to Amma. She wanted to keep Nilo out of Lamiapur, as if she were an embarrassment to her, like Chirag, or worse.

A curse.

"Tai, look," Chirag called, running into the shed. Spinning around in front of Roma, he laughed, the bright pink fabric of Goldie's *lehenga* sweeping the air. "Isn't it pretty?"

Her heart leaped into her throat. Rushing past him, she pulled the curtain, hiding him from sight. "Where are your trousers?" she demanded.

The corners of his lips lowered at her chastising tone. "I'm wearing them under my *lehenga*," he answered.

"You know what'll happen if Amma sees you in a *lehenga*." She unravelled the strings with quick hands and the *lehenga* collapsed around his feet. "Step out." His shoulders slumped and tears glistened in his eyes as he obeyed. Standing slowly, she cupped his face, brushing her thumbs over his damp cheekbones. "I shouldn't have scolded you. I'm sorry." She touched her ear-lobes in a playful sign of regret. "Forgive me?" He wrapped his arms around her waist. "You remember what happened last time?"

He nodded.

It wasn't just that Amma had beaten him when he had put on Goldie's bangles and tinted his lips red, but she had threatened to deliver him to the hijra quarters in their village. Hijras were considered an abomination because they were born neither complete male nor female. Fathers killed their sons out of shame or delivered them to the Guru in the nearest hijra quarters where they were raised as prostitutes. It was how they survived. Rejected by their own families and villages, they were abused, pursued, and denied access to temples and shrines, yet simultaneously people tolerated their existence because it was believed they could curse or bless a person.

Whenever Chirag returned to Lamiapur in tears because the village boys had chased and beaten him, Binti said it was because he was only half human. She advised Amma to hand Chirag over to the hijra quarters, but Amma ignored her advice. Roma didn't trust her reason for allowing him to remain in Lamiapur, and she didn't want to fear for his future, so she would protect him however she could. If it meant that she had to subdue his love for *lehengas* and lip tints.

Nudging him back, she looked down at him. "Do you want to wear kohl?"

The dejection dissipated from his eyes. "Yes," he said, bobbing his head. Taking the small, brass vial from the shelf, she shook it and took out the stick, framing his eyes with the black powder. Men wore kohl because it warded against the evil eye, and so no one would care if Chirag wore it, too.

"When we leave Lamiapur," she said, "I want you to stay close to Amma."

"Because of Saber Bhau?"

"Don't call him Bhau. He's no brother to you. Come, or we'll be late."

Torches illuminated the temple of Mother Lamia with a passionate red glow against the walls and pillared archways. The *lamiadasis* gathered near the temple stairs dressed in similar emerald, scarlet, and yellow *cholis* and *lehengas* with sheer veils that shimmered in the torchlight. Rawiya Mai perched beneath the willow, chewing on a betel leaf and patting Aimi to sleep in her lap, while Hani herded everyone into a line with stern orders and irritable nudges.

For as long as Roma had known the older *lamiadasi*, Hani had been the severest worshipper of Mother Lamia. When she wasn't engaged with chores, she sat at Mother Lamia's dais with rosaries in her hands, met Sādin Saheb for spiritual sessions, or shared tales about punishment with Roma and her sisters as if they needed to fear the gods more than they already did.

Roma joined the line in front of the temple stairs, and Yoshi stepped to her side. "You abandoned me with the milk," she whispered.

"Why didn't you tell on me?"

"I still might. Is your friend all right?"

Glancing at Yoshi, Roma folded her arms. Her sister could be vindictive, but at times she surprised her. "Khiraa is alive," she answered.

"Hush," Hani ordered. "Sādin Saheb has arrived."

Sādin Saheb entered the courtyard with four *birandasis* clad in their traditional blue kaftans. The scorpion symbol of the God of Creation was threaded onto their sleeves. Amma plastered on a humble expression for Sādin Saheb, appearing a queen in her ornaments, even as she lowered her head. "It's an honour, Sādin Saheb," she greeted him. "Roma, *yē*."

Roma stepped forward and Sādin Saheb's stare slid to her. The calculative look in his eyes under those caterpillar eyebrows was jarringly identical to the one in Amma's. Taking the platter from Hani, Roma placed it on the ground and raised a pitcher of milk, pouring it over his feet before wiping them down with a cloth.

The *birandasis* ascended the temple stairs to the antechamber behind Sādin Saheb and carried out the statue of Mother Lamia as Sādin Saheb chanted praises of Lord Biran in Middle Khansāri, leading them all across the courtyard, through Lamiapur's gate, and to the street below. Blossoms rained down on them from the waiting villagers the moment their procession turned the corner. Amma lifted her chin with a proud smile, her lavishly adorned hand swinging the cobra pendant, while Goldie and Chirag danced to the drums, and Caliana, Ara, and Sunbel laughed, pointing at the paper lanterns that carried wishes to the gods.

Despite being among the festivities with her sisters, Roma's haunted mind lingered on Khiraa. A part of her wanted to dance, to become one with the beats, but Khiraa's bruised skin had brought back memories of her own past.

A past that she knew would soon become her present.

CHAPTER 10

The white-haired owner of the stall handed Leviathan black tea in a tulip-shaped glass. He looked ancient, all hunched shoulders and crinkled skin, moving as if his brittle bones might break. Mute as he was, he patted Leviathan's cheek in a show of affection, his toothless smile kinder than Leviathan deserved. He pondered about the old man's family, whether he had any, and how many decades he'd spent out here on this jam-packed street offering tea for the rags on his body.

"Why didn't you say anything?" Malev asked.

"What about?"

"Kanoni accused you, brother. You didn't counter her arguments."

Leviathan leaned forward on his elbows, boots propped up on the bench. Taking a slow swig of his drink, he watched people haggle prices and scold their kids. They'd decorated the streets, slapped paint on the surfaces of their houses. To celebrate what? Some mythical story of their worthless gods. Forfeiting livestock for empty statues, following ancient customs, and making prostitutes out of their daughters. It was easier to rule a people once you put the fear of gods in them, once you convinced them poverty was a divine punishment, not the consequence of men's greed.

Even the pretentious higher *zaat* came down from their thrones to indulge in the local festivities. Those with copper symbols—the Coppers—were of native Khansan bloodlines like Malev's family. Rich, educated bloodlines. After the Khanate's invasion, these families were invited into the exclusive circle of the colonialists—the Silvers—due to their inherited wealth, and promised permanent fortune and exemption from the alms that the wealthiest people were taxed with under the Khanate. So they joined the higher *zaat*.

"Kanoni's right," Leviathan responded at length. "I wasn't around."

"It wasn't your choice."

"Wasn't it?"

"The Firawn sentenced you, brother. I'm not saying you did right by them. Just saying you had your reasons." Malev gave him a sidelong glance. "Maybe you should've shared those reasons with her."

Looking into the dark bottom of his glass, Leviathan swirled it, as if it held answers to questions he hadn't yet asked. He would've been lying if he said Kanoni's words hadn't cut to the quick, hadn't made him want to somehow prove that he wasn't the Firawn's hound, but he was in the Black Guard. That was as good as any hound.

When he'd walked into the camp, he hadn't expected a warm welcome. Part of him was terrified to face the clans. Mai had looked at him, right at him, and he'd frozen. She had that same smile, the one she'd had when he visited the camp as a kid, when he climbed onto her back each time she went down in prayer, but he wasn't that kid anymore. He saw the hate and fear in their eyes, saw how they watched him like he came to slaughter them all, and a sadistic side of him embraced it.

"Kanoni's pissed at me," he said. "She has a right to be."

"Means she still cares, right?"

Leviathan shook his head. "The clans are living in camps, starving to death, fearing raid and rape. They've got nothing."

"You're not responsible for that."

"Maybe being human makes us all responsible," he murmured, recalling Kanoni's words. *'Can you give us anything at all?'* His jaw set. "They need food and weapons."

"What do you have in mind?"

His mouth quirked without humour. It didn't surprise him anymore how easily Malev read him. They'd known each other from the early days of boyhood, been bound as friends before brothers, and if anybody could decode his silence it was Malev. With somebody else, it would've unsettled him, made him cautious, but he trusted Malev with his life. Trusting somebody and depending on them were two different things, though. If Leviathan had learned a lesson at the Guild he valued now more than ever after his mother's death, it was to never rely on anybody but himself. You could lose everything and unless you were self-reliant, it'd destroy you.

"Water can be drawn from the stepwell at night," Leviathan finally said, observing a father getting his son a frozen dessert at a *kulfi* stall before lifting him up to sit on his shoulders. "Talk to a few of the boys from the camp. We'll need their help."

"Ilyas and Adam?"

"And Mahir. He's got muscle."

Malev leaned against the table. "What about food and weapons?" he asked, rubbing his chin.

Seizing caravans of weapons was too dangerous. Not just because he didn't have the manpower to do it but suppliers would place the clans under suspicion, and the Commanders of the Wings would send out Rangers to raid the camps. Even if they didn't find traces of the weapons, they'd make sure the clans paid the price. They already thought of the camps as breeding grounds for rebels, and they'd grab any opportunity to assault them. He'd seen it happen. He'd walked on soil soaked in his people's blood, had spilled some of that blood himself.

He swallowed hard.

Don't open that door.

Setting another lock on it, he refocused. "I've got spare knives. Give them to the men and women. They'll need to hide them in case of raids, but it's something. Food is stocked up in the city storage, logged and tallied on taxation day, and the storage is guarded front and back. There's a third access on the roof."

"You want to climb the building? Junho's going to love that," Malev said with a half-smile. "What if we can't get past the sentries?"

No attempts had been made on inner-city structures for decades. The city walls were impassable, making the Wardens guarding the cities less alert, less observant, and with Wardens like Burian and Denis stationed outside Ferozi's food storage, it'd be easy to scale the structure, break in through the access on the roof, and swipe what they needed. The two sentries left their posts to meet up around the corner for smokes and backbiting whenever they could get away with it.

"If we can't get past the sentries, I'll have to get the floor plans of the storage and locate its weak point," Leviathan said. Some stall owner was boiling meat. His stomach clenched. He hated that smell.

"Too time-consuming?" Malev asked, amused.

"Beyond a doubt."

He preferred the result over the effort. Quick, efficient means that led him straight to his objective in less time and groundwork. The approach he'd calibrate according to the equipment and manpower obtainable to him. Which, in this case, were limited. "We do it tomorrow night during Burian's and Denis' watch." They'd need the right gear. A crossbow, a grappling hook, and a few leather bags for the haul—

A loud procession emerged around the corner. Men hammered away on large drums. Women and kids danced. There was something distinctly savage about it all, about the pounding beats and chiming bells, the shrieking colours and entrancing mood. It almost made a man want to forget the world was drowning in its own blood. His heart thumped as it did before a hunt. His eyes cut to a band of women in clothes and charms complimenting every dip and curve of their bodies. One of them had dark skin and darker hair. The end of it reached past her hips. She had an hourglass waist and a serious mouth. Pretty eyes, sultry, bold and black, like volcanic ash.

And interestingly familiar.

She was the girl from the banyan. The one who'd watched him. She'd been in the camp, trying to blend in with the clans, but he'd sensed her before he'd seen her—just like at his mother's cremation. Something about her held his attention. Something more than female, more than sensual. Something quick, sharp, and temperamental, like a threatened serpent.

The nerves along his spine pulled tight. He drained his glass and set it down. Dropping a silver coin as payment for the tea—more than necessary, not enough to embarrass the old Babu—he leaped off the table and moved along the side of the packed street, winding slowly through the spectating masses and keeping pace with the procession.

With her.

His gaze skimmed down to her squared shoulders, the straight spine. He recognised unbreakable strength when he saw it. That brazen stare of hers never wavered. She watched the world with cynicism. There was heat in her. There was power. He doubted she had any clue about it, or she wouldn't have settled for the herd. She'd have led armies and burned down cities.

If he wanted to test his theory for a second, it was because seeing such potential pulled at him like a battlefield before the bloody call of war, the empty stretch that'd soon sing with the sound of steel against steel.

The procession turned near the bridge.

Toward Biranpur.

"*Dēvadasis,*" Malev said from behind him. "Slaves of the gods."

"Sacred prostitutes," he said, eyes still on her. *Dēvadasis* were considered a sub-*zaat.* Neither human nor goddess. He'd seen the likes of them in the south. Centuries ago, they were temple dancers, but when the Khanate ended, the system of *dēvadasis* took on a socio-economical form. The High Priests were taxed in exchange for keeping their temples and positions. Girls were auctioned in the name of whatever goddess they served, sold out by the High Priests, forced into a sacred service of what was essentially prostitution. Their income was divided between the state and the High Priests. Now, parents dedicated their daughters with promises of becoming goddesses in the temples.

All for coin.

Maybe if the *dēvadasis* learned about their history, they'd know the truth, but they were illiterate. Education was a privilege of the higher *zaat,* not the common people, and another way to control the lower *zaat.*

"Bhau." Junho pushed his way through the crowd to Leviathan's side. "Our contact is meeting us at Nox." He followed Leviathan's and Malev's line of sight. "What're we looking at?"

"Your future wife," Leviathan said.

Junho rubbed the back of his head. "*Ay,* Bhau," he said with an embarrassed grin.

"Did you tell Zuberi to keep an eye on the camp?"

"*Hō,* Bhau. But—what about the Firawn?"

"What about him?"

"You think he's heard about the Wardens yet?"

The Firawn knew, and he'd send for Leviathan. After he made him wait for however long it suited him. Despite what the Firawn might think, it wouldn't keep Leviathan up at night. If he'd feared the consequences, he wouldn't have killed the Wardens. He made it his business to know what he could lose and whatever he risked, he was *willing* to lose.

"I'll know when he does," was all he said. "Let's move."

CHAPTER 11

"BIRAN, BIRAN, BIRAN," the villagers chanted.

Biranpur's alabaster temple rose on sumptuously carved pillars decorated with hundreds of lights. Fountains shaped as gods and goddesses in graceful postures were embraced by large, shallow ponds covered with rootless white blossoms. Roma glanced toward the separate terraces raised on platforms where the higher *zaat* lounged on velvet cushions. Gilded tables on short legs overflowed with platters full of pomegranates, mangoes, apples, cantaloupes, and guavas—the fruits so rich in colour from magic they appeared artificial.

The northern higher *zaat* men were swathed in cowl-style silk *kurtas* and *dhotis*, and velvet vests in metallic shades with gold chains and buttons. Embroidered shawls draped over their shoulders and pulled around the back to recline over their arms. The women dressed in embellished silk gowns with threadwork and beads, and enamelled gold belts clutching their waists. Gemstones shimmered on their silk and velvet slippers. While the southern women wore *maangtikkas*, the northern women also wore *jhoomars*—a multiple-chained, beaded ornament with jewels pinned on the side of the head.

Favouring an ethnic fusion designed by a tailor from Prince Jasadan's royal court in the East Strip, the higher *zaat* paraded their wealth in front of each other as if it were a competition. Perhaps if Roma had been raised in gold and glimmer, she too would have desired the spectacle of the material world and feared to ever part with it, but to live with such a fear seemed burdensome.

"They look like they've descended from the stars," Ara shouted over the noise. Her brown eyes shone bright with want. "Khalfani is a masterful tailor."

Caliana nodded. "I can't wait to see what Mā Saheb wears," she shouted back.

The villagers pressed in from all sides as the chanting reached a crescendo. Looking around at the faces of the men, Roma's belly churned with unease, knowing some among them would bid on her during her auction on the sixteenth night. She buried that thought in the barred recesses of her mind along with the others she refused to revisit, turning instead to watch the *birandasis* as they lifted Mother Lamia onto a dais in the centre of the courtyard beside the polished carnelian statue of Lord Biran. Gold cuffs with scorpion carvings clasped his wrists. His hands held a sword that pointed downward because the God of Creation was also a warrior god.

"Move, rats," someone bellowed. "Move."

The crowd parted.

Eunuchs in brown *kurtas* and *dhotis* carried a stunning palanquin fashioned in brilliant white gold to the temple stairs where it was lowered. Six *bandis* assembled by the golden silk curtain. They wore black *cholis*, *lehenga*s, and sheer black veils. Silver *naths* with chains adorned their noses, revealing their higher rank among *bandis*.

The shouting slave was the same one Roma had seen with Mā Saheb at the cremation. Adjusting his fez, he pushed aside the palanquin's curtains. Mā Saheb's unadorned hand appeared from within the palanquin, touching the slave's wrist for balance as she slid out. It was as if she were enveloped in mists and stars. Her silver pashmina gown with its sparkling *zari* embroidery spilled from her slim shoulders to her narrow slippers. The plunging neckline exposed skin so pale Roma saw blue veins running like rivers beneath it. Her ice blond hair was looped into a knot and her fair eyebrows were almost invisible over pale blue eyes.

Everyone bowed low in reverence.

Amma sashayed toward Mā Saheb with a platter holding a bowl of honey, blessed water, neem leaves, and a beaded bracelet with a copper coin. Dipping her head, Amma looked at Mā Saheb from under her eyelashes. "It's an honour to have you grace our festival again, Mā Saheb. Would you allow me to bless you?"

Mā Saheb's dark red lips upturned in a cool smile. "How could I refuse the slaves of the Mother Goddess? After all, you're the reason the gods remain content with us, aren't you?"

"I'm humbled, Mā Saheb, *meharbani.*" Amma touched her fingers to her forehead in the sign of gratitude. Dousing the neem leaves in the blessed water, she sprinkled it twice on Mā Saheb and tied the beaded bracelet around her wrist. When Mā Saheb accepted the spoonful of honey, Amma's smile broadened. "May Mother Lamia keep her hand over your family. So shall it be."

"So shall it be," the crowd resounded.

Mā Saheb ascended the temple stairs to the terrace reserved for her, the Firawn, and their closest relatives who were yet to arrive for the festival. Her *bandis* hurried after her, sweeping out the folds of her gown on one of the divans and pouring wine into a crystal glass for her. The slave rubbed his earlobe. Stepping back to stand against the temple wall with his shoulders hunched, he folded his hands over his bulging belly, staring down his nose at the villagers. Roma supposed that he considered himself superior to them because of his status as Mā Saheb's personal slave.

Higher *zaat* men and women approached Mā Saheb to greet her, hoping she would invite them to sit with her. She didn't. Roma wouldn't want to be in her presence. She appeared composed, dignified, but her eyes held a precarious shine, as if she might shift from collected to unhinged within a second. The villagers continued to gawp at her. The reverence in their stares was as much fear as it was awe for the Firawn's First Wife, and Roma noticed a pleased curve to the corners of her lips. How must it feel to have such power that one couldn't be touched? How must it be to never have to fear persecution and enslavement? The privileged slept like kings and queens on the ashes of the slaves.

Roma looked at Sādin Saheb with his *birandasis* behind him, their hands folded, their expressions bland, and she despised how he sat like a master in his chair and feasted without a care in the world. Sādin Saheb didn't have to reside under tarps, starve, or lie with men. He wasn't born female nor into a lesser *zaat.* Priesthood was the highest caste among the lower *zaat.* Roma wanted to know who had created this structure. Who had decided that people should be divided into *zaat* and that some castes should be superior to others?

It was an injustice.

The Kāhinah emerged in a black kaftan from the horde and Roma turned away from Sādin Saheb. Rosaries rested around the Kāhinah's neck. The soothsayer was an old woman, but her hair was black as starless night skies. The phases of the moon were inked on her forehead in a long line that ended between her shaved eyebrows. It was the symbol of Dhu'l-Samawi, God of Stars and Constellations, whom the Kāhins and Kāhinahs worshipped.

Untying her coarse tresses, the Kāhinah spread her arms and released a scream that shredded the silence. Drumbeaters struck a rumbling beat. She swung her hair in aggressive loops, stomping her naked feet on the tiles. Dropping on her knees, she raised the Conch of Dhu'l-Samawi to her lips. The deep note was always an ominous sound—like the call of death.

The Festival of the High Lord had begun.

Roma and her sisters settled in a wide circle around the statues on the dais. The warm glow from braziers, lanterns, and oil lamps dyed them in hues of red and orange. The musicians sat down behind the songsters with their instruments, and the drumbeaters rubbed their hands in dust. Amma cavorted to the centre, her adornments glittering in the lamplight, and the higher *zaat* lowered their wine glasses to watch her. The generous amount of kohl lining her eyes resembled war paint as she whipped on the heels of her synthetic satin slippers.

"It's the Festival of the High Lord in the Sacred Month of Biran," she announced. "In this blessed month, Lord Biran himself descends upon the earth to walk among his devotees, accompanied by his beloved Goddess-Wife. Tonight, the Daughters of Mother Lamia will praise our High Lord. We shall celebrate and be coloured in his divine hue. So shall it be."

"So shall it be," the people cheered.

Roma bowed in obeisance with her sisters, sanctifying herself for the performance. The sound of drumbeats rippled through the air and vibrated against her skin. It beckoned her blood. The *lamiadasis* spun around the statues, leaping through the air on invisible wings, swinging in and out between one another, and spiralling back into formation, their skirts unfolding to reveal the sacred patterns stitched onto the folds. The beat quickened to Amma's tapping fingers as she pulsed away on a hookah beside Sādin Saheb.

The instruments fell silent and the *lamiadasis* stilled as one.

Then they withdrew with the exception of Roma.

The strumming sitar met the drums and Roma matched the beats. Her hands painted illustrations, her expressions denoted emotions in a depiction of devotion, and she flowed like water to form regal poses as she told the famous tale of how Lord Biran fell in love with Mother Lamia, how he pursued her, and how she resisted his courtship. The bells on her anklets tailed the cadences and syllables that the songsters enounced. She was the oceanic eyes of a lover, the storm of a sweet scent, and the touch of two hearts. She was Mother Lamia's seductive gait, her sultry gaze as Lord Biran blocked her path, and then she was her surrender.

She bowed for benediction to loud cheers.

Swanning toward Roma, Amma smacked her lips. "Flawless," she exclaimed over the wild noise. "Mother Lamia has blessed you, *ladoba*." There was a time when Roma had wanted her praise and sacrificed for it, but her acclaim tonight fell through the abyss in Roma's chest, and the hollowness smothered her.

"Will you teach me this dance, Roma Tai?" Goldie begged, bouncing on her feet.

"Not tonight, Goldie," Sunbel laughed. "Look, there's seafood."

It was a festival custom for the higher *zaat* to provide food. Flatbread and sour bread sat stacked in piles on platters. Puffed rice merged with dark, roasted soybeans, and split red lentils were mounted in bowls. Smoke curled in the air from the fried fish and prawns. There were desserts as well. Sliced sweet potatoes soaked in lemon juice and spices. Persimmons, bananas, and honey cakes. Shots of rice beer were passed around along with bright red sherbet.

Meanwhile, the higher *zaat* were served with bowls of soup made from diced meat and rice beer. Marinated chicken, lamb, and buffalo stews simmered in tagines alongside stews of string beans, chickpeas, and caramelised onions. Dumplings stuffed with minced meat were poured atop steamed rice. Smaller plates held dried mushrooms, diced ginger, and fresh yoghurt next to apricot chutney and mint chutney. There were apples dipped in caramel, nuts, and betel leaves swollen with a sweet paste and tobacco. Betel leaves were a delicacy among the lower *zaat*, but the higher *zaat* had taken to the habit.

The scents mingled and drenched the air, but the aromas didn't coax Roma's appetite. She peered at the food with a belly that revolted. A feast much like this one would be served on her auction night. She released an unstable breath. Distressing her heart with thoughts of it wouldn't alter her fate. The provoked desire for even a false sense of power compelled her to reach for a platter. She would sneak all she could to the camp. Seth and the other clan children would love the fish with flatbread. Khiraa and Sara had a sweet tooth—

"Roma?" Hani called.

Roma repressed a sigh. "Yes, Tai," she said in an impatient voice.

"Watch your tone. Have you seen Yoshi?"

"Not since our performance."

"Find her now. Amma has a patron for her. He wants to meet her."

Deserting the food with reluctance, Roma searched the courtyard for Yoshi, passing a swarm of people captivated by two sword dancers leaping in sharp circles with their curved swords. They were clad in white *kurtas* with leather around their waists and wrists. Their loose trousers slimmed toward the end and vanished inside battered boots. Their faces were concealed behind shemaghs that twirled around their heads, like flat turbans, and left only the eyes visible. It was spellbinding how their blades arched and severed, glided and slashed, in graceful motions that made her pulse quicken. She almost felt the presence of twin hilts in her own hands. It felt as familiar to her as the rug beater when she pounded the sleeping mats in Lamiapur.

Forcing herself to move on from the sword dancers, she hurried past the puppeteers, acrobats, and serpent charmers. Perhaps Yoshi had returned to Lamiapur for some reason. Roma stepped out on the plains and pulled in a deep breath. The air was barren despite the earlier cloudburst. It seemed Ruda had withdrawn again. People said the East Strip was arid ever since the Great Drought trundled across it. They believed it was a punishment from the gods and feared a similar fate awaited Durra.

Gliding across the plains, Roma reached the bottom of the hill, stealing a moment to herself. The banyan stretched up high toward the skies with its crown contoured in the light of the crescent moon. She had dreamed of it as far back as she could remember. She had dreamed of roots and blood. Perhaps it should have disturbed her, but she felt a profound kinship to the ancient tree.

She climbed the hill. Touching one of the pillars, she sensed the banyan's spirit. If she closed her eyes, if she concentrated, it was as if a heart pulsed against her palm. A sign of life in the desolate plains. The heartbeat resonated within her like she had known it forever.

Before even the world's existence.

The wind rustled the banyan's strands. She heard soft laughter. It was a gentle vibration in the air. Frowning in wonder, she slipped in between the roots, circling a larger trunk to discover Yoshi in the arms of a stranger on the other side. Yoshi's head whipped around and her eyes widened. She pushed away from him as if that might decriminalise the situation. The man's copper bracelet branded him as higher *zaat*. Tearing her eyes from it, Roma swivelled on her heels and descended the hill.

"Roma, wait." Yoshi rushed after her and reached for her arm. "Just *wait*."

Roma shoved at her hand. "Never touch me," she warned.

"Aren't you going to ask me why I was with him?"

"No."

"We're in love."

"Don't tell me."

"Why?"

"Because the less I know, the less I have to tell Amma."

The colour drained from Yoshi's face. "You can't tell her. You can't, Roma," she insisted, looking like she might snatch Roma's arm again. With her nails this time.

"Consorting with someone of a higher *zaat* is forbidden unless he's your patron, Yoshi."

"I don't care. It's a stupid law." When Roma shook her head, Yoshi spoke in a softer voice. "*Aikā*, Roma, listen. We may not be sisters in blood, but we're still sisters in service, aren't we? I'm asking you to keep silent. It won't be for long."

"What does that mean?" Roma demanded. Yoshi pressed her lips together. "Yoshi. What do you mean?"

"You know how it is with our *zaat*. We can't abandon our service. We can't even be bought free. But I have a chance at freedom if I leave with Danyal."

Staring at Yoshi, Roma took a step toward her. "Have you forgotten what happened to Idris when his sister ran with a higher *zaat* man?"

"I remember it just fine."

"And still you'd run?"

"Should I sacrifice myself instead?" Yoshi spat. "Should I continue to serve patrons until I'm old like Mai and some *harami* throws acid on me? Or perhaps until I lose my mind and mutilate my own face like you?"

Roma jerked back. She didn't want to dwell on the volatile emotions rising within her at Yoshi's harsh words. They were too painful and vicious. She met Yoshi's heated stare. "Chirag is your brother in blood," she said in a quiet voice, "and he'll be punished if you run."

"Oh, come down from your high horse, Roma. Like you never thought of running? The difference is you can't do it. Does it anger you that I don't have the same moral dilemma as you? You haven't even seen half of what we have. You had one bad experience and it broke you, but the rest of us have had many more. *I've* had many more. I won't live the rest of my life as the worthless object of some patron's carnal desire."

Yoshi's eyes seared with an anguish Roma was too familiar with. She always thought she was the only one haunted, the only one who couldn't breathe in Lamiapur, but now she realised she wasn't, and she didn't know what to say. Yoshi wouldn't run. She might break a rule or two behind Amma's back, but she would never abandon her service.

None of them would.

Shaking her head, Yoshi crossed her arms. "I won't be ruled like I don't have a soul of my own," she said bitterly. "They remove your dignity as a human. They destroy who you are, Roma. That's how they control you."

"Yoshi—"

"You don't know what it's like to be treated as a person. You don't know what it's like to love because you've never loved anyone. Are you even capable of it or did he take that away from you as well?"

A deep fracture split within Roma at her sister's brutal words. Yoshi drew another breath to continue her tirade, but her tongue faltered when she looked into Roma's eyes.

Roma swallowed past the burn in her throat.

"Don't ever see him again."

CHAPTER 12

REMOVING THE DUST-COATED shemagh from his face, Leviathan led Cinder toward the hitching rail. Wisam was a ghost district a few miles southeast of Ferozi closest to Ashura Desert's border. The heat of the steppes eased with the night's chill, but the dry taste of the desert still hung like a reminder of its capricious power. Beaten-down sandstone houses lay empty, except for the mice and scorpions hiding in the craters. The area was notorious for its pulsating nightspot where the restless youth came for nocturnal splurges. They'd named it Nox. It was three stories of corroded stone, stripped down to the bones of its former splendour.

Leviathan loosened Cinder's reins and brushed a hand along her smooth flank. She stood at sixteen hands. Like the rare Suran breeds, she was larger, stronger, faster than any desert-bred mare, her coat the colour of scorched coal, and her eyes dark and intelligent. He'd bought her from an abusive mount trader when he was hardly more than a boy himself. There were enough well-trained mounts to choose from at the Guild, but when he saw Cinder, beaten, broken, he wasn't able to walk away. He got her out, helped her heal, earned her trust. She hadn't made it easy on him. She'd given him a few scars of his own. He liked that she'd tested him, demanded before she'd given. He never tied her up, letting her know she had a choice—and she never left, letting him know they were equals now.

Approaching the guard at the entrance, Leviathan gave him a clipped nod. "Yeol. New cut?" His straight-faced jab was returned with a lopsided grin from Yeol as the guy rubbed a big hand over his bald head. Leviathan knew him since his trainee days at a blacksmith's in Nuru, before Yeol decided that forging steel wasn't his strongest skill. He'd always been bald.

"Grow some hair, man," Junho teased, clasping Yeol's forearm. "That mug's not going to charm any ladies on its own."

"Yeah, 'cause they're all throwing themselves at your princess locks, *saale*," Yeol chuckled, and held the door open for them.

The hard bass hit Leviathan first, pumping into the overloaded space from an unseen source, and the smell of ripe sweat and strong alcohol stuck in his throat. The squadrons were awash in neon light from a cobalt dome above. Leviathan's eyes roved over the dancing crowd. Magic fuelled this place, charging the air, getting under his skin, and his muscles bunched up in response. Annoyed at the patent buzz, he rubbed the back of his corded neck. He hated that tug in his gut, that pull. It'd pass in a minute, but it'd be a long, grating minute. Nobody else around him felt it.

Just him.

The owner of Nox, Sparrow, was a reclusive drug trader from the harem of drug trades in Hunoon. That was how he got his hands on the most desired resource in the Strips: Magic. He provided drugs like the Blue Lotus, and the more prevalent Night Queen, to traders in exchange for bottled magic. A levelled trade. Considering drugs were how the lower *zaat* survived in the east. The Night Queen was a hallucinogen in larger doses, cheaper than food, and the lower *zaat* consumed it, fed it to their kids, to kill their hunger. Drug addiction was another consequence of the invasion.

Apart from his permanent base in Hunoon, Nox was Sparrow's second goldmine. A neutral zone, easy to blend into. You'd see people of every *zaat* in here. As far as Leviathan knew about Sparrow's consignments, they took place underground in black markets to avoid exposure. Tapping the Khansan soil for magic outside the Firawn's jurisdiction and delivering it to anybody but the Firawn resulted in a death sentence.

People still risked their lives for survival—and some for greed.

Leviathan shouldered his way through the throbbing horde caught in their trance. Bodies drenched in sweat, eyes glassy, pupils dilated. The Ghameq danced to life, spreading like a black mist over the mob, inhaling their gritty emotions. Their nature was to drink and arouse. Anger, fear, lust, violence—the Ghameq feasted on it. At times, they clung to humans like parasites to feed. This particular Ghaib tribe could get inside your head and twist what you saw. While most of the Ghaib were created from elemental energies like fire or water, others were of the essence of darkness like the Ghameq. Some tribes could solidify, turn from energy to matter, but they were essentially creatures of energies, which meant they were invisible to humans.

Except to Leviathan.

There was a reason, he knew, but his compulsive search for an answer hadn't brought him any closer to it.

Tendrils of darkness swirled around him now, licking across his skin, rasping in his ear, the words uttered in Ancient Khansāri—a language he'd never studied and shouldn't have known.

'*Taste, drink, devour.*'

A girl stumbled into him with a drunken smile and tilted her head back in invitation. "Kiss," she slurred.

He pulled her arms from his waist. "Sure," he said, passing her on to Junho.

"But—Bhau—" Junho sputtered, catching her helplessly. Malev slapped his shoulder with a quick grin, following Leviathan to the staircase. The first floor was a rectangular space with divans, tables, and chairs. It was less crowded, less loud. Leviathan didn't drop the hood of his cloak as he assessed the couples scattered around the space. His eyes came to rest on a scrawny guy by a corner table. He was five-ten with unwashed hair scraped back into a bun. His wide brow glistened with sweat, his nose crooked from one too many fights.

Cutting across the space to him, Leviathan pulled out a chair and straddled it. "Been a while, Kai. You avoiding me?" he asked, easy on the tone. Malev leaned on the railing, eyes trained on the crowd downstairs, ears trained on them.

"You can never be too careful," Kai answered, leg jittering under the table, fingers tapping the side of his beer bottle. His nails were gnawed to the flesh. "Especially when working for you."

"You hurt my feelings."

Kai snorted. "No offence, Bhau, but you commission me for shit that could get me in some serious fucking trouble if I ever got caught."

"Don't get caught."

"Easier said than done. You know I don't do well with tiny cells and torture."

Everything people did in this world was for profit. It didn't matter if it was spiritual, intellectual, or financial. That was how Leviathan met Kai. He wanted information and Kai wanted coin. It was a mutual business relationship. Kai had an uncanny ability to dig up anything between heaven and hell, and he sold it to the highest bidder. He was in the bottom-feeder fraternity of a people who made their living off of the dirt in society. People who lived in the shadows, non-existent, until somebody needed information.

Having detached himself from the drunken company downstairs, Junho emerged at the top of the stairs and joined their meeting. Leviathan cocked his head at Kai. "You seem to be doing just fine to me. Rumour has it you've been hanging out with human traders in Makhmoor. Making new friends, Kai?" he asked in a cold voice.

Kai choked on his beer. "It was a commission," he defended, regaining his breath. "I get paid for information; I deliver. For the record, they weren't traders. They were handlers. And I wasn't hanging *with* them, I was hanging *around* them. Big difference."

"Right. Handlers work for traders, genius," Junho remarked.

"No shit. I'm not a fucking idiot."

"Could've fooled me."

Malev inclined his head. "What kind of commission?" he asked curiously.

"Do I get paid for the answer?"

"How about I kick your skinny ass?" Junho suggested. "That payment enough for you?"

Shooting Junho a dirty look, Kai turned to Malev. "Remember those kids who went missing from a few villages some weeks ago? Word is it's a gang operation linked to the human trade."

"Why's your client interested in missing children?"

"Like I said, I get paid for the information. If I started asking questions, I'd be out of work."

Jaw set, Leviathan leaned forward. He didn't have time for small talk. "What do you have for me, Kai?"

"What about my coin?"

"Did Bhau ever cheat you out of your coin before?" Junho snarled. "You know the drill. Give the information, take your payment."

"It was a risky charge," Kai insisted.

"*Ay*, Ponyface," Junho spat. "I'm three seconds from hanging you upside down by your balls—" A warning glance from Leviathan cut him off. He crossed his arms and glared at Kai in dark silence.

Taking out a leather pouch, Leviathan tossed it to Kai. "Talk."

Juggling the pouch between his gnarled hands, Kai cleared his throat at the dangerous gleam in Leviathan's stare. "I looked into it like you asked," he said, shifting in his chair. Leviathan narrowed his eyes and Kai licked his lips. "I did. I don't make half-assed work, Bhau. You know that."

Leviathan's voice was lethally soft. "Where's my information, Kai?"

Kai gulped. "I got nothing."

"Wrong answer."

"*Aikā*—Bhau—Just listen for a second. There was no information to dig up. No medical reports, no leads, nothing, I swear. I even pulled on some dicey contacts—"

Leviathan stared at him, cold-faced, and Kai chewed back his words.

"He's lying," Junho growled.

"I'm not. I swear I'm not. Why the hell would I lie? I'm not fucking suicidal. The healer never documented anything."

"Healers document everything," Malev interjected. "It's the law."

"He didn't document *this*. I swear on my mother's life, Bhau."

"You don't have a mother, *saale*," Junho said, grabbing a fistful of his shirt, dragging him halfway out of his chair. "Let me rearrange your ugly face. Maybe then you'll talk."

Kai paled under the blue cast on his face from the dome above.

"Let him go."

"But, Bhau—"

Leviathan's eyes sliced to Junho. He dropped their contact back in the chair with a reluctant huff, and Kai's bones all but rattled from the impact.

There was ice in Leviathan's voice. "The healer?" he asked quietly.

"I didn't find a lead on him either," Kai answered, straightening his shirt. "It's like he's vanished from the face of the earth."

Of course he has.

Rage simmered in Leviathan's gut. He'd been unable to stamp it out for days. Now it smouldered. Waiting for a lit match. He'd counted on getting the information on his mother's illness from the time she got sick to the time of her death, counted on getting proof she was killed and *how* she was killed. Kai was a crafty kid, but he wasn't lying. Leviathan would've smelled it on him. The fact was no record existed on his mother's organ failure, her body was ashes, and her healer was likely worm food by now.

Clenching his teeth, he pushed down the frustration, the grief, and held on tight to the rage like a lifeline. His struggle enticed the Ghameq. Lithe, ink-like vines churned in the air around him, circling him, feasting on his emotions, and their raw whispers goaded him to unleash the beast he'd locked up inside.

'*Blood,*' they demanded. '*Ruin.*'

Junho shot him a wary glance. "Bhau, don't worry. We'll figure it out. I'll talk to one of our contacts in Nuru—I'll find out." Leviathan didn't move, didn't speak. He sat still as a marble statue. Malev looked at him, eyes worried, and Junho turned on Kai. "You know what, Ponyface? Payment's cancelled. No information, no coin. Give it back."

"Hey," Kai protested, glancing between them, his hands clutching the pouch. "I did my part. Not my fault it was an empty search. Bhau, come on." He looked beseechingly at Leviathan as Junho tried to pry the pouch from his grip. "Wait a damn second. I—"

"Let him have his coin," Leviathan said, and stood.

Moving to the stairs, he descended into the pulsing sea below and shoved through the crowd, *out*. His blood pounded in his ears. His fists ached. Knowing his emotions governed him—and that they shouldn't—didn't make it easier to shut them down. He wanted to confront his mother's killer. He couldn't. Not without proof. Cecilia was under the Firawn's protection. If he went after her without solid evidence of her crime, it'd push the Firawn too far. He was willing to risk his life, but not his freedom, because he needed it to help the clans. It was a promise he'd made his mother when he buried her ashes. The Firawn valued cold, hard logic. Reason. So Leviathan had wanted the medical records and the healer in order to use both against Cecilia.

A reasonable incentive to punish her.

It wasn't in his nature to forfeit. He couldn't accept that it ended here. Wouldn't. His hands might be temporarily tied, but he'd find some evidence of Cecilia's crime, and when he did, he'd make her pay for it. Give her a slow, painful death. Watch the light fade from her eyes.

Would it bring him peace? Maybe not. But he thought he'd enjoy it.

Cinder snorted with a jerk of her head and bumped her muzzle against his shoulder for attention. Lifting her head, he murmured soft words in Khansāri, stroking her long neck as she uncoiled, knot by knot, to his touch. There was one place he hadn't yet visited; one path he hadn't yet tried. He'd been avoiding it. Too many memories were linked to his mother's private quarters. All too much pain.

Malev's footfalls sounded behind him.

"You all right, brother?"

Swinging into the saddle, Leviathan turned Cinder around. His head throbbed. He couldn't think straight, couldn't breathe right. He needed speed, the hills ahead, and solitude. "Return to the city," he told Malev.

"This thing Kai mentioned about the missing children—"

"We're done here."

Malev's eyebrows pulled low. "What happened to 'being human makes us all responsible'?" he asked without spite, without accusation.

"Guess I'm not human after all."

"She's gone, brother."

Leviathan's hands clenched the reins as the sole indication he wasn't made of stone. His teeth set. *Taken*. Not once, but twice. His mother was taken from him as a kid, then again as an adult, and she'd suffered the most for it. She'd been alone in the palace, at Cecilia's mercy, and he'd never—he swallowed hard—he'd never protected her. Never shielded her from that bitch's hatred. The Firawn had closed his fist around him and he'd accepted the sentence, allowed the Firawn's will to shape him.

What kind of son was he if not weak?

Ever since the moment he'd received the news of her death, he was coming undone. Years of feeling nothing and now he felt too much. Too fucking much. Like always, the chaos inside him and the rage made him dangerously quiet.

Malev watched him. "You can't help her anymore," he added.

"Don't you think I know that?"

"I do."

"Then what's your point?"

"You know she cared about children. It wasn't charity, but love. You think she'd want you to turn your back on them?"

Leviathan's eyes snapped to his. "Low blow, Malev."

"Necessary. Tell me you don't give a damn. Tell me you can walk away right now, and it won't eat you up inside the minute you do, and I'll let it go."

He said nothing.

"It doesn't end with her, brother. Who you are doesn't end with her."

Wrong.

It'd always started and ended with her.

CHAPTER 13

The sun burned against Roma's bare back as she squatted in front of the basins and tipped a bucket of water over the *lehengas*. Scrubbing a bar of lavender-scented soap into the folds, she swiped at the sweat on her cheek with a shoulder before picking up the beater and pounding the lathered materials. Her chores were to dust off their sleeping mats, wash their garments, and carry pails of water from the stepwell to Lamiapur. The latter had strengthened her. It was now a meditative routine she preferred over cleaning the temple. She never minded the charring heat while she worked because it served as a soothing cocoon, but today it failed to abolish the chill within her bones.

Khiraa hadn't eaten for days. Ghanima Mai's attempts at persuasion proved futile. The despair in Khiraa's tears made it harder to be around her. Even though Roma didn't allow herself to think of her auction, she was reminded of it whenever she saw Khiraa curled up on the mat—and the overwhelming panic that followed clogged Roma's throat.

"Mai, tell me another tale," Goldie whined.

Rawiya Mai laughed. Her calloused feet arched and swayed like sunflowers adoring the sun. She turned a silver ring with a black stone on her finger that seemed to glow red when it caught the light. "You want another tale, do you? Which one should it be this time?" she pondered out loud, tapping her chin. "Ah, let me tell you the one about the most ancient and powerful clan in Khansadun."

"I want to hear a tale about magic," Goldie sulked.

"This *is* a tale about magic."

"But—"

"Bring me the jar."

Goldie's eyes widened. "The jar? Really?" she squealed.

Springing to her feet, she dashed into Rawiya Mai's shed and returned seconds later with a brass jar engraved with curlicue patterns. Roma moved to the washing lines that strained between the sheds, shaking out their garments and hanging them to dry, the fabrics spattering cool drops on her skin, but her attention was on Rawiya Mai. Meriel stopped mashing rice for Aimi as the old *lamiadasi* reached into the tarnished jar.

Even the birds hushed in the willow to watch her.

When Rawiya Mai pulled out her cupped hand, it was full of sand the scarlet colour of ripe apples that shimmered in the sunlight. "Listen, now." She swung her arm in a wide arch and the magic grains spilled through the air but didn't fall to the ground. Whirling with unpredictable force, they amassed in front of a gasping Goldie. "There was once a realm forged by magic dwelling in the earth. A realm concealed from the eyes of other dimensions."

With mesmerising haste, the sand weaved into tall mountains and trees, turbulent seas and desert dunes before Rawiya Mai had uttered the words. "There were the mysterious chants of the Whispering Mountains, the ever-changing paths of the Sleeping Forest, the treacherous depths of the Bitter Sea, and the volatile nature of the Raging Desert."

Goldie's eyes never left the sand. "Amma says we used to live with the clans," she whispered as if afraid her voice would disrupt the imagery.

Folding a betel leaf bursting with sweet paste and tobacco, Rawiya Mai shoved it into her mouth, the orange juice from the paste staining her lips. "It is true that we once lived as one nation. We had our separate cultures and customs, but we did not condemn each other. In the olden times, Khansadun was governed by the Khan. A ruler chosen from the most competent clan. This clan was called Banu Yardan. That is, the children of Yardan."

The iridescent sand rippled and divided into two bands of men with large bodies. The ones on the right wrestled while the ones on the left wrote on scrolls. "There were two bloodlines of Yardan. The Qabilids derived from his firstborn son, Qabil, and trained in warfare. The Habilids derived from his second-born son, Habil, and were scholars above all else. When the Khan at the time, a Habilid named Taib, departed without appointing his successor, it caused a vicious feud between the tribes."

Pulling their swords, the men attacked one another. Roma forgot about the *cholis* that still awaited their turn in the basins as Rawiya Mai went on. "Who was the worthiest ruler? The Qabilids persisted that Jehangir bin Aurangzeb should be Khan, for they wanted a descendant of Qabil on the seat. The Habilids demanded that Sultan bin Taib should rule, for he was the son of the former Khan. To avoid bloodshed, their council—the Shura—decided there would be a test."

Rawiya Mai wiped a line of juice from her chin. "For decades the people had been tormented by a tribe of the Ghaib named the Nar who abused their powers to mislead humans." The men had already transformed into tall creatures with hair whipping around their heads and flames shivering in their palms. "Their progenitor, Iblīs, considered humankind to be an inferior race. His hatred drove him to enslave humans by darkening their souls. His followers taught the men forbidden magic—*sihr*—and possessed the women." Sand creatures descended on the unmistakable forms of sand women. Roma thought she heard the echo of cries and the hair on her forearms stood on end. "The women thrashed in terror, screaming and struggling, but they could not see their perpetrators."

A faceless figure rose from their midst and sauntered forward. His long hair was tied back on the crown of his head and his lean frame held power. Roma should have been disturbed at the assault of the women, but his tall shape and arrogant stride consumed her, and she was unable to look elsewhere. Her mind painted his eyes—crimson like smokeless flames—in a faultless, raw-boned face with lips that curved into a superior smile. The touch of fear made her step back from him. When he tipped his head to the side, she heard a whisper within her head.

"*Nirbaya.*"

The name reverberated like a phantom call in her ears. Familiar, but foreign. Found, but lost. The sand twirled into one mass, taking his form with it, and Roma caught her breath. Licking her lips, she looked at the others. Goldie was pale and quiet. Meriel jolted when Aimi wailed.

"The women birthed the children of the Nar and abandoned the babes in the deserts and the woods to die," Rawiya Mai revealed. "Those who lived were called the Shunned and it is said the colour of their eyes is like liquid gold. The essence of what the clans believe the Nar were created from."

"The Seven Fires of Hell," Meriel murmured.

Goldie shuddered. "Are all of the Ghaib evil?" she asked in a small voice.

"*Nā, ladoba*. Some are cruel or kind. Some are dangerous or harmless. They are complex creatures of free will just like humankind."

"What happened next with the Qabilids and Habilids?"

"The Shura declared that the one who could save their people from the Nar would become Khan. Sultan set out for battle with a great legion while Jehangir returned to his chamber. He was not a rich man, nor did he possess a legion. He had nothing but his faith."

"What did he do then?" Goldie asked.

The sand answered her question as it twirled into the shape of a man bowed down in prayer. "Jehangir did not believe a human force could subdue the Nar because they were creatures of magic. So, he prayed for the power to shield his people. The Habilids laughed at him and the Qabilids were ashamed of him. Then, one night, a hoopoe bird came to his window. Jehangir believed it to be a sign and followed it to a lone tree. It looked awful. The branches were rotted and black, and serpent heads grew on them like hellish fruit."

Stepping closer to his sand form, Roma watched Jehangir while he inspected the tree. It stirred at his touch and shook its branches, and her heart pounded faster. Her mind wanted to paint his face like it had painted the other, but she struggled to draw his features as if an impenetrable wall stood between them and made it impossible for her to see him. Glancing at Rawiya Mai, she realised the old *lamiadasi's* head was tipped toward her with a smile.

"The tree revealed its name to Jehangir. It was called Zaqqum. If Jehangir could solve a riddle, it said, it would give him the power to save his people."

"I love riddles." Goldie clapped her hands. "What did it ask him?"

"What is the nearest thing to man and what is the farthest thing from man?"

"What's the answer, Mai?"

"Guess," Rawiya Mai cackled.

"Death." The answer slipped out of Roma before she had thought it. She couldn't remember where she had heard the riddle, but it felt as familiar to her as her own thoughts. "The other is time."

"Time?" Meriel asked.

"Because it passes and doesn't return."

An increasing disturbance rose in Roma's chest like nausea and shepherded her back to the basins. She didn't want to dwell on the sense of recognition bonded with the riddle. Lifting one of the empty pails to her head and another to her hip, she rushed out of Lamiapur, distancing herself from the magic sand, Rawiya Mai, and the tale. She took the fastest path through the village square where people had gathered for a public punishment. It was a custom for widows to be inherited by their sons upon the death of their husbands. Oftentimes their sons would take them as wives. If a woman refused to accept her son as a husband, she was placed under house arrest for a year, and the villagers amassed to throw cow dung at her upon her release.

Thinking it the reason for the crowd, Roma was about to pass through when a scream compelled her to stop. The repetitive, hoarse sound was all too distinguishable. With a quickening pulse, Roma lowered the pails on the ground and pushed past people to the heart of the circle. A girl sat in the dirt. Her head was shaved so close to the scalp that it bled while her oval face was smeared with coal.

"Nilo," Roma whispered. Nilo raised her arms over her head for protection as the villagers threw stones at her. "Stop! Stop!" Running to her sister, Roma shielded Nilo with her own shell, jolting and gasping when the pebbles struck against the exposed skin on her back.

"Stop this madness," Jirani shouted, shoving through the crowd. "Have you no conscience?"

"Conscience, Jirani Bhau?" The wife of Nilo's patron strutted forward with a lifted chin. She was a large woman with a generous chest that wobbled whenever she moved. "This girl is a serpent. She deserves to be punished."

"What has she done, Zenobia?" Jirani asked.

"The little whore tried to seduce my son. When he refused her, she attacked him."

"That's a lie," Roma snapped, staring at Zenobia. "You know it's a lie." Saber must have sought Nilo out, and Nilo must have fought his advances. If she had let him touch her, Zenobia never would have cared, but Nilo had caused a scene, and Zenobia was a proud woman.

"Stay out of this matter, Roma," Zenobia hissed.

Jirani crossed his arms. "Have you any witnesses?" he inquired with patience.

"Saber said—"

"Have you any witnesses beside your son?" When Zenobia's mouth opened and closed without a sound, Jirani shook his head. "You can't convict her without witnesses."

"Jirani Bhau," Hani called from among the horde, rushing toward them. Someone must have run to Lamiapur for aid. Roma's shoulders eased the slightest bit, but the tangle of resentment remained. Nilo started snapping her fingers, and Roma slowly kneeled beside her.

"It's all right." Battling her own discomfort, Roma reached out to touch Nilo's shoulder, but Nilo jolted, and Roma withdrew her hand. "It's just me, Nilo." She didn't know how to calm her down out here where the glares from the crowd distressed Nilo to the point that she was about to have a nervous episode.

"*Meharbani*, Jirani Bhau. We can handle it from here," Hani said. Jirani hesitated. Then he nodded and abandoned the circle. Hani turned to Zenobia. "Let's take the matter to Lamiapur, Zenobia Tai."

"*Nā*, Hani. We'll decide right here in front of the village."

"What has Nilo done to upset you?"

Heat spread through Roma at Hani's question. They had shaved Nilo's head, smeared her face with coal, and stoned her, but Hani was concerned *Zenobia* was upset? She bit down on her tongue to keep silent before she said something impudent to Hani.

"What hasn't she done?" Zenobia quipped. Her loud, scornful voice vexed Roma. "She bewitched my husband, but that wasn't enough. She had to beguile my poor son, too. You dancing girls need to remember your place, Hani."

Roma gripped her *lehenga*. This woman couldn't keep her husband and creep of a son in line, so she turned her bitterness toward them.

"*Lamiadasis*." Spinning her cobra pendant, Amma came through the crowd, strutting over to stand in front of Zenobia. "We're *lamiadasis*. And a word of caution, Zeno. It's dangerous to question the character of Mother Lamia's sacred daughters." She tipped forward with a smirk. "Unless you care to birth cripples in the future."

"Jainaba Begum," Zenobia warned.

Amma pursed her lips and flicked a hand. "Such pride. Where do you acquire it, Zeno? You were born, raised, and married into a *zaat* of seamsters. Your brother paid one hundred *fals* for my Meriel and now his obnoxious wife is blessed with a son, isn't she?"

"We know your importance, Jainaba Begum," another woman reproved.

"It doesn't mean we let you into our homes with pleasure. If it weren't for the Mother Goddess—"

"Your men would still crawl to my gate and ask for the sacred touch of a *lamiadasi*. What can I say? We have a pull," Amma smiled. "You may call it a divine connection, and one that has brought you lot a great deal of fortune."

"If you're sacred to the gods, why hasn't your service brought us lasting rain?" Zenobia scoffed. "Perhaps it's time to dedicate that abomination you call a boy to the High Lord. Perhaps the gods will stop punishing our village then."

Roma stiffened in response to Zenobia's threat.

Catching the cobra pendant in her hand on a spin, Amma tipped her head to the side. "Tread with care, Zeno. The supplication of a *lamiadasi* is no less than a curse."

"Hm," Zenobia replied with a jerk of her head. "I showed your girl mercy today, Jainaba Begum, but if she comes near my son again, I'll parade her naked through the village as the shameless *vēshya* she is."

Rising on her feet with ire, Roma stepped between them. "Saber is no paragon of sainthood. None of your sons are," she remarked, looking around at the villagers. The fire now blistering in her voice was powered by their derisive stares. "They loiter in the alleys like lustful hounds harassing any girl that passes through, so instead of shaming us, teach your boys to lower their eyes and keep their hands to themselves."

Shouts of anger and contempt erupted among the people.

"How dare you?" Zenobia snapped. "I'll teach you respect."

Roma caught Zenobia's hand before it connected with her cheek. Holding on while the seamstress pulled and twisted her wrist, Roma met her furious stare. "I know how to raise my hand as well, Tai, but I'll forgive you for this one."

Amma laughed.

Zenobia's cheeks burned as Roma released her wrist. "It's a sacred season, girl. Consider yourself fortunate I don't summon the Panchayat over this little skirmish," she hissed and turned to Amma. "I suggest you discipline your whores, Jainaba Begum. They should know their place." Swivelling on her heels, she marched out of the square, and the villagers shook their heads and scattered in the wake of her departure.

"*Vēshya.* Who does she think she is?" Amma spat. "We're the daughters of the Mother Goddess. Without our service, they'd all die from starvation. They'd bear no children. They should weep at our feet in gratitude."

"Forget them, Amma," Hani soothed. "What do we do with Nilo?"

"What's there to do? I'll have to find a patron who'll take her. *Satyanāsh*."

CHAPTER 14

"Mā Saheb's relatives have arrived for the festival at last," Sunbel said as Roma stepped into the shed with a cup of water for Nilo, but Nilo was fast asleep on the sleeping mat in the corner. Sunbel dusted her fair cheekbones with pink powder. "Her parents can read the stars. Did you know, Roma?"

"No."

Suppressing her irritation at Sunbel's delighted mood, Roma kneeled beside Nilo, placing the cup on the ground and spreading a blanket over her. Aggravated bruises marred the skin on her arms. She had been beaten under Zenobia's roof. The sudden desire to throw the cup against the wall rose within Roma. Serrated memories crawled out of a nook in her mind and threatened to tear her resolve apart, so she curled her hands until her nails sliced into her palms.

"People say that Firawn Sai paid a handsome dowry for Mā Saheb's hand."

"Because she can read the stars?" Taking the kohl from the shelf, Yoshi pushed Sunbel to the left and positioned herself in front of the mirror, painting wings at the corners of her eyes. "And here I thought it was because her hymen was made of gold."

"Do you always have to speak in such crude terms?"

"*Hō*. You know what else people say about the Firawn?" Yoshi asked. "That he uses Dark Magic. It's why he doesn't age like a normal person."

"Hush, Yoshi. We shouldn't gossip about him."

"It's not as if he can hear me."

"The gods can hear you."

"The gods have better things to do than listen to gossip."

Pulling in a deep breath, Roma uncurled her hands and changed into her ceremonial attire for the night while her sisters quarrelled on. The *lehenga* was heavier than her other costumes because Binti had stitched three layers together with an elaborate pattern of pink blossoms on the inner indigo layer, and indigo paisley designs on the outer pink layer to enchant the audience throughout her spins.

It was all in honour of her performance tonight.

She searched the large chest for the bracelets which matched her bangles, tossing aside garments, slippers, and adornments, battling an overwhelming frustration that throttled her patience. The earpieces burned her earlobes, the pendant smothered her neck, and the chain of the *nath* scratched against her cheekbone. All she wanted in that moment was to tear it all off.

"Looking for these?" Yoshi jangled four lac-filled bracelets bejewelled with triple-headed cobras in front of Roma's face. She snatched them from Yoshi's hand. "You seem tense, Roma. Is it because of your auction?"

"Yoshi," Sunbel warned.

"It's painful when you don't know who your patron might be or what he might do, isn't it?"

Throwing the bracelets aside, Roma spun toward Yoshi, but Sunbel stepped between them. "Stop it, Yoshi," she scolded. "You're being cruel."

"Am I being crueller than all of you who kept her auction a secret from her?" Yoshi asked with a bite in her voice. She looked past Sunbel at Roma. "At least, I'm honest."

Hani appeared on the threshold. "Roma," she called. "Thana's son is ill. We have some spare rice. Take it to her and don't linger. It'll be nightfall soon. Here." She held out a cotton pouch and Roma ripped her stare from Yoshi's to take it. Relieved to have an excuse to leave, even for a short while, Roma drew the veil over her head and slid out of Lamiapur.

People, carts, and mounts crowded the entwining streets, but it wasn't long before she climbed the fragmented steps to Thana's sandstone house. The sharp resonance of laughter sounded from the hijra quarters further down the street. She touched the padlock dangling from Thana's door handle, knocking it twice against the orange-painted surface before stepping into the dark chamber. Stairs led to the rooftop where Thana sent her children when she served men. It was a rectangular space with buckets outside an alcove that held a latrine pit. The red ribbon billowed on the front wall and marked Thana as one of the Flags.

Sitting on a *charpai* beside her sleeping son, Thana nursed her daughter and patted her bottom in a recurrent motion. Roma saw the bruises on her face when she looked up with a tired smile. "Roma, come and sit," she said. "How's Jainaba Begum and the others?"

"They're well. What about you, Tai?"

"Apart from Juma's fever? Well enough." Thana pulled her breast from Tisha's mouth. "I suppose it was bound to happen. He was playing in the drains yesterday."

"Bhau isn't home?"

Her lips twisted at the mention of her husband. "No. Hopefully, his drunken ass has fallen in Kobe Lake this time. *Harami* stole the coins I'd saved for emergencies." She shook her head. "Men. Cook and clean for them, birth and raise their children. Still, they treat you like waste. They'll tell a woman she's less, so they can believe they're more." Her mood lightened the slightest bit when Roma passed her the cotton pouch. "Thank Jainaba Begum for me."

"I will." Roma unknotted a corner of her veil and spilled sixteen *fals* into her palm. "This should be enough for a small dose of medicine."

Thana's shoulders stiffened. "You know I don't accept coin for charity," she said in an even voice.

"It's not for you, but for Juma."

"*Nā*."

"I don't want them. They were given to me by the village men for my performance."

Lifting her chin with pinched lips, Thana held on to her pride for another moment, then released it with a sigh and took the coins. "*Meharbani, jaan*."

"Have you eaten?" Roma asked.

"I've no appetite."

"Tai—"

"I'm just tired. I need sleep, is all, and I'll be as good as new. I'll lie down with Tisha for an hour or so. *Jā*. I'm all right."

Roma understood her wish for solitude. The need for sanctioning the fall of all walls, all pretences of strength, to just be with one's enervations. She understood because she too craved the same. It was a moment in which she recognised herself in Thana. Hani would have claimed the life of a *lamiadasi* carried no resemblance to the life of a prostitute. *Lamiadasis* were sanctified vessels of Mother Lamia, but Roma remembered Rawiya Mai's remark about how they were 'pure and impure,' and it felt like the bitter truth.

Her auction loomed like a black tempest on the horizon. With each dawn, she felt more and more anxious. Amma was right. Struggling against the confines of their *zaat* only caused pain. She should accept what was her world and what was her worth like her sisters had. Mother Lamia had determined her fate.

She would forever remain a *lamiadasi.*

Stepping out into the street again, Roma had no heart for Lamiapur. There were still a few hours until the celebrations, so she glided toward the steppe. It might be hard to see Khiraa, yet it was harder to be surrounded by chinking anklets. She couldn't remove her own, but at least she could escape everyone else's, and keep her thoughts from wandering to where darkness dwelled. Kanoni and the clan women would be happier for it when they received the henna she had taken from the ceremonial chamber. She enjoyed watching them draw tribal symbols on their skin.

The crush of the crowd eased as she reached the outer border, but her footfalls slowed. A deceitful silence rested like a shroud of bereavement over the steppe. She tasted sorrow. Bunching up the *lehenga* in her hands, she ran to the camp, stopping when she saw the clans gathered outside Ghanima Mai's tarp. Her eyes sought Seth or Sara but found Kanoni standing with her arms folded over her chest and her face drained of emotion. Roma stared at the detached clan woman, hoping the abysmal churning within her belly was misplaced. Dauid ducked out of the tarp then, and in his arms, he cradled a shape swathed in a white sheet.

Her breath snagged in her throat.

The limp form looked like so many others carried out of the camp, draped in white, but she peered at it as if she had never seen the colour of death. The harshness of the silence screeched in her ears, louder than a keening wail, until she wanted to press her hands against them.

Ghanima Mai emerged with a pale Seth. The pain in his eyes burned into Roma's heart. Leading the people, Dauid carried Khiraa's body to the trench beyond the camp where they buried their dead. Roma didn't follow. Maryam sobbed and cradled her babe as if she feared her child might be snatched from her next. Perhaps it was wise. It seemed death was a thief that came and went with such stealth none heard his footfalls.

Sara ran toward Roma and clutched her hands. "Roma," she sobbed. "Khiraa is gone. She's gone." She didn't seem to notice when Roma pulled out of her grip. "Seth thought she was asleep. We needed more wood, so he left and—Mai was with Maryam Tai." Leaning forward, Sara held her arms against her belly as tears streamed down her cheeks. "Khiraa broke Mai's lantern—there was so much blood. Her wrists and—so much blood. We couldn't save her."

Khiraa had killed herself. She had done it to herself.

With the shards of the lantern Roma had brought for Ghanima Mai.

Roma walked to the edge of the trench in a stupor. The Firawn's son and his companions had arrived. They helped Dauid and the other clan men lower Khiraa into her grave. People cupped their hands in prayer, and Roma clutched her elbows. She was ill with some emotion she couldn't grasp. There was a terrible ache within her chest. Pressing a hand over her breastbone, she curled her fingers as if to dig out her heart. She knew the death of the soul because she had experienced the irrevocable destruction of her own. She had seen that same destruction in Khiraa. It was ironic. She had avoided mirrors for three years, but suddenly Khiraa became her reflection—and she had run from her when she should have supported her.

"*Inna lillaahi wa innaa ilayhi raaji'oon*," Ghanima Mai said. The recitation reminded them that they belonged to the Creator to whom they would return and the potency behind those words hardened the men and women gathered around the grave.

"I can't believe she's gone," Sara whispered, stepping to Roma's side. "She was the strong one. I'm scared now. If she could break—" Her voice cracked. She drew an audible breath. "Mai says it's a difficult time for our people, a time when holding on to faith is like holding on to burning coal, but we must believe."

"Believe in what?"

"That things will change. That good will prevail in the end."

"What's the point, if it's the end?"

"I don't know," Sara wept. "All I know is I have to believe."

Roma couldn't provide Sara with the comfort she sought. She couldn't speak the words of strength she needed. Perhaps because Roma found herself frighteningly close to believing in nothing at all.

Sara looked at her. "Khiraa loved you." A coldness spread within Roma. She wanted to tell her to shut her mouth because she didn't want to hear what she couldn't feel. "She always said you made her want to be strong like a warrior."

A hollow laugh caught in Roma's throat. She wasn't strong. If she had been a warrior, she would have fought for the possession of her own shell. She would have never let someone touch her. Never let someone ruin her.

No.

She would have spilled blood.

CHAPTER 15

"It shouldn't have happened," Kanoni said, resting an elbow on her knee and leaning her forehead against her palm. "Khiraa shouldn't have done it."

Roma stared down at the stains of blood that tarnished Khiraa's folded kaftan where it lay on the sleeping mat Ghanima Mai shared with her. It was all that was left of her now. Ghanima Mai would clean it and pass it on to Sara or someone else in the camp. Even the smallest piece of fabric held too much value to the clans because it could cover one more person and shield them from the cold clutch of the night.

Brushing her timeworn hands over her face, Ghanima Mai completed her prayer. She must have found peace whenever she touched her forehead to the ground in submission to her god since she remained in that position longer than the others. "Khiraa was in pain," she said in a soft tone and stretched out her legs with a wince. "We shouldn't blame her."

Had Khiraa been frightened as her breath waned from her chest? Had she been relieved it would soon be over? A desperate part of Roma craved to know how Khiraa found the courage to slice where it mattered. Where it would end her life.

Perhaps it wasn't about courage at all. Perhaps it was about conviction.

"It'll happen again," Kanoni said.

"We must bear our hardships with patience. It's a test," Ghanima Mai insisted. "As with all tests, we must endure."

Kanoni dropped her hand. "So the Creator makes us all suffer to test our patience, our endurance?" Sarcasm and bitterness marred her voice. "Well, that makes it all right, then."

"The Creator hasn't caused our situation, but he has given us free will," Ghanima Mai answered, lowering herself on the sleeping mat. "The test is what we choose to do in the condition we're in. It's people who harm people, Kanoni, not our Rabb."

"And what of our desolation?"

"If not in this life, He'll compensate us in the Hereafter."

"Your existential yammer would hold a lot more weight if Khiraa was alive, Mai. Patience wasn't enough to sustain her, nor was the Creator."

Ghanima Mai sighed. "Khiraa's soul hasn't yet found rest and you've started. We must keep our silence in the wake of death, Kanoni. We must do our best with what we have."

"We have nothing."

"We have our faith."

"And when has our faith ever saved lives? You can't just cup your hands in prayer and expect the Creator to drop a solution into them. We must fight. We need—Mai. Are you even listening to me?"

"I am. But for now, we must grieve."

Roma scratched the paint from one of her bangles with her nail in a repetitive motion. Gods were cruel. Mother Lamia had to know how much Roma wanted to escape her auction, but she never aided her in the past nor intervened now.

Was it a test? What was the point of it?

"Dauid and Baha agree with me," Kanoni persisted. She tipped forward, folding her hands in her lap and looking intently at Ghanima Mai. Golden light from the declining candle sharpened the bones of Kanoni's face. "Dauid says there's a new opposition rising in the east known as the White Wolves. They raid caravans and deliver the loot to the eastern camps. He says they have people in the villages. We could contact one of them—"

"They can't be trusted."

"We have to try."

"It's been centuries, Kanoni, and none of the oppositions that have risen and fallen over time ever aided our people. They used us as a shield for their own purposes. We can't trust rebels."

"We can't change anything if we don't take a risk, *yani*."

The frustration in Kanoni's voice pervaded the silence that followed. Kanoni wanted a rebellion. She would chance her life to alter her own circumstances. Roma looked at her in quiet admiration. Kanoni stared outside with a testiness etched into the hard lines around her mouth. The caged intensity in her eyes unnerved Roma. She recognised it from herself. Kanoni felt trapped, as if her hands were shackled, her feet chained, and she wanted to break the bonds, but feared how it would impact those she cared for.

Ghanima Mai softened. "*Ladoba*," she murmured.

"I have to do something. This wait for change is pointless, Mai. It won't happen unless we *make* it happen." Kanoni whipped her head to the side to look at Ghanima Mai again. Her hands twitched in restless verve. "Give the White Wolves a chance. They could be the opposition we've been waiting for."

"Kanoni—"

"Why don't you want to fight?"

Glancing at Ghanima Mai, Roma discerned a vigilant shiver in her eyes. "I do. But this war can't be won as long as our people are divided. We need a strong leader, a righteous leader, to unite us and show us how to battle the forces of the Firawn."

Kanoni arched her eyebrows. "And you believe this leader will be Leviathan," she said in a sarcastic tone. Ghanima Mai remained silent. She stretched her gaunt arms, popping her bones, and the fire that had just bled from Kanoni's eyes reignited. "Have you had another precognitive dream?"

"Perhaps."

"It's bullshit."

"You just refuse to believe because you're angry with Levi."

"I'm not angry with him. I hate him."

"You two are more alike than you'd ever admit."

"Don't compare us, Mai. It's insulting. I'm not like him. For one thing, I've never killed innocent people."

A chill slithered down Roma's back. "Innocent people?" she repeated. Ghanima Mai and Kanoni looked at her then as if only now remembering her presence. "Has he killed innocent people?"

"We heard the rumours about him and his deeds," Kanoni said, "and for a long time, we couldn't believe that Badriya's son had become one of the monsters we feared."

"We don't know what happened."

"We know enough, Mai. They don't call him 'Blade of the Firawn' for nothing. He executed our people. After all, it's in his blood." Her lips twisted in disgust. "Children of demons become demons."

Ghanima Mai's eyebrows knitted together. "His father might be a demon, but his mothers weren't. You'd do well to remember that."

Kanoni scoffed. "He was raised by the Firawn, not Badriya and Gabrielle. There's no honour in him, no remorse. He's manipulative like his father. That's why he summoned the Wardens and killed them in front of us. He wanted us to think it was for Khiraa when in truth—"

"Don't twist his intentions," Ghanima Mai reprimanded, pushing herself up to sit with an elbow on her knee. "Levi could've shot that Warden when he degraded him, when he degraded Badriya, but he stepped back, and he didn't kill him until he threatened Khiraa. What does that tell you? He didn't seek revenge for himself, but justice for her. Look at me."

Ghanima Mai waited until Kanoni met her stare and then placed a hand over her heart. "I've seen it in him, Kanoni. I've seen his need for us. We're his family. We're his one link to humanity in a place where he's surrounded by the likes of the Firawn's military and that repulsive serpent, Cecilia, and you want to sever that link? You want to send him straight into the Firawn's void?"

The tears in Kanoni's eyes could have been pain, temper, or bitterness. "Even if that were so," Ghanima Mai continued with dignified calm, "Levi would never become his father. The boy lived fifteen years in that demon's cave and didn't become him—No, stop shaking your head and listen to me. You have to understand that when a child is isolated and cultivated by a beast, he'll make mistakes."

Kanoni narrowed her eyes. "Don't make excuses for him, Mai. A traumatic childhood doesn't justify his actions. It doesn't make him a victim now. Thousands of children are abused in this world but don't become monsters like him. It's a choice, not fate."

Choice, not fate.

The words stuck within Roma's head. What was choice and what was fate? She realised she didn't know.

"I'm not excusing his actions, Kanoni. All the years in the military have changed him and not for the better. I don't deny it. But there's good in him as well. Badriya and Gabrielle are both within him. Look at him properly next time. Look into him—"

"He murdered our people," Kanoni said in a quivering voice. "He was our hope and he murdered his *own* people." Blinking back the tears, she steadied herself with a deep breath. "He chose a different path. We can't trust a traitor."

"The truth is, Kanoni, you wanted him to be our weapon," Ghanima Mai said gently. "And instead he became the Firawn's."

"That's not fair. You know I never saw him as a weapon."

"Perhaps not in your heart."

Kanoni was silent for a long moment. Roma could tell from her frown that Ghanima Mai's words troubled her. Pushing her shawl down, Kanoni untied her dark curls, massaging the back of her neck. There was a scar on the side of her throat where a Warden had slashed her when she fought to protect her husband. It was strange how they were all survivors somehow. Kinfolk related by their internal and external scars, as if they could look at each other and read every personal tale from how deep a cut went, or how hollow someone's eyes were. It seemed to be their identity now, an identity whose weight they had paid in blood, or with their very souls.

"It's not the oppression at the hand of the Firawn that burns," Kanoni started in a calmer tone. "It's not about Levi or even the invaders. The Khanate couldn't have been destroyed without aid from the inside, without the Blood Traitor who sold his soul and killed his own brother-in-law for the throne. It's about our people's betrayal, too. The massacres in the east didn't begin with Rangers, Mai, but with villagers. We're all of Khansadun's soil, but they participated in butchering our people, driving us out of our homes, sacrificing our skins to protect their own. We starve on their thresholds, and they ignore it."

"There are those who care," Ghanima Mai said with a soft smile, reaching over to squeeze Roma's knee. "Roma always brought us food and cared for our children. Jirani, too, provides us with what he can despite the decree that prohibits any aid."

"Roma and Jirani are different. The village ignores us. And that *harami* descendant of the Blood Traitor who sits in the palace in Badru and watches his people die? Treachery's in his blood. May the Creator grant him and his lineage the lowest depths of Hell."

"The time of the tyrants will end."

"When, Mai? When all of Khansadun's soil dampens with our blood?"

"The lash of the Creator's whip makes no sound, Kanoni."

"Perhaps we're supposed to be the whip. Have you ever thought of that?"

The Horn of the Gods reverberated in the distance. Roma closed her eyes. She didn't want to join the festival tonight. She didn't want to dance when Khiraa had just been lowered into her grave.

Ghanima Mai brushed a hand over Roma's head and Roma jolted at the touch. "Are you all right, *ladoba*? You've gone pale."

"I should—the festival," Roma stuttered out.

"*Rabbrakha,* Roma," Kanoni said.

"*Rabbrakha.*"

Sefu was still crowded when Roma returned. She shirked the crammed streets and instead chanced the alleys, but the slender paths were all deserted. Following the curving limb of an alley, she climbed the steps to the vacated street below Lamiapur.

Then she stopped.

"Jingle?"

The lamb sniffed a pile of dung outside a house and the bell around her neck rang when she shook her head. Roma squatted down beside her. "Did you slip out again?" she said, cupping Jingle's furred head in her hands. The lamb brayed. "The fence needs to be mended, or Jirani Bhau might lose you before the butcher can have you. That wouldn't be so bad, would it? Perhaps I should let you wander to your freedom." Yet she couldn't do that to Jirani. He needed the coin for his family. Rubbing Jingle's ear, she sighed and lifted the lamb into her arms.

The Grand Market seemed larger when abandoned. The stalls were sealed with metal sliders and padlocked to safeguard the inventory. Roma slid past them to Jirani's stall. The sound of her chinking anklets breached the silence otherwise interrupted by the crickets' song. Darkness shrouded the patch encased by a wooden fence. Two of the bars were unhinged. Jingle had discovered a few pushes made them drop away which left enough space for her to slip through.

She was too clever for a lamb.

Herding Jingle back inside, Roma climbed the fence, dropping down on the other side. She found a rope near the sleeping cows. The roof creaked. She stilled. The wood was old, she reminded herself, but her heart took a moment to calm down. Twisting the rope around the bars, she tied them together, ensuring they wouldn't come loose again.

There was a vibration in the air. She swivelled on her heels and peered into the shadows, her heart in her throat, but she was alone. Her eyes roamed the stall and lingered on one of the steel containers Jirani filled with milk. The askew lid exposed the inside of the container. Lizards and insects tended to fall into uncovered pails and containers, so people kept them sealed to avoid contamination. Perhaps Jirani had been in a rush and forgotten to cover this one.

Stepping toward the container, she touched the cool lid, her hand pale under the light of the moon, and caught the glint of an object within it. When she reached inside it, her fingers brushed cold metal. She pulled it out and stared at it.

A knife.

The container was full of knives. Long knives, short knives. Narrow and broad. She tossed it back into the container and the metal clanged. Retreating until her back collided with one of the cows, she jumped as it mooed in complaint, rushing to the fence and climbing out of the stall only to stop when two figures appeared in her path as if they were waiting for her. She recognised their white garments and covered faces.

The sword dancers.

Spinning around, she ran in the opposite direction, but a shadow leaped from the roof and blocked her escape. Her heart knocked against her ribs. She breathed in shallow gasps, taking an involuntary step back. He was tall, lean, and clad in black. His black hair reached past his shoulders. It was braided close to his head in side rows with small, silver cuffs. A scarf concealed the lower part of his face and one of his eyebrows had a crosswise scar through it. Golden eyes studied her. Golden eyes like molten amber just as in Rawiya Mai's tale of the children of the Nar.

Roma forced her throat to swallow.

"Take the weapons," he ordered. His voice was deep and dark, but with an amused note to it, and his accent was eastern. The two men disappeared inside Jirani's stall. The clinks of metal sounded in the night as they emptied the containers.

She wanted to run. But she knew she wouldn't reach far before he caught her.

Because he wasn't human.

She didn't like how he watched her, taking in her face as if pledging it to his memory, all while his eyes danced with the mirth she had heard in his voice, but she refused to lower her stare, even as he must have noticed the careering pulse in her throat. The other men returned with large sacks and hurried past her without sparing her a glance. She would have been relieved if only their leader had followed them.

He lingered.

She curled her hands at her sides as he sauntered toward her. His eyes were a spell. His scent was a thrill. Neither deceived her senses. She wasn't touched by his inhuman charms. Only disturbed. She wanted to recoil like a cornered mouse before a lion, but she remained where she was as he closed the distance.

To her surprise and relief, he moved around her.

Her breath tumbled out only to tighten again when he stalled beside her. Holding her defiant stare, he leaned down to level their eyes.

"*Wallahi*," he whispered. "*Ainaky todamerani rajolan*."

Then he was gone.

CHAPTER 16

THE DESERT WAS soaked in blood.

Mutilated bodies lay in pools of red, severed heads were piled on each other. Death poisoned the air. Thick and metallic. Leviathan's stomach turned hard as stone, heavy as lead, as he looked down at the clan men kneeling before him. Yet his heart was cold, his mind was a black hole. He didn't shoot. Guns were useless in the desert because magic still writhed beneath the ancient sand. It sensed his purpose. The cruel intention in his muscles. He pulled his sword from the scabbard on his back and felt the magic roil under him.

"In the name of the Firawn, Lord of the West and the East," he said, his voice like death's whisper. "You're sentenced for treason." The men stared up at him. Some in terror, some in tears. Their faces blurred, sharpened, blurred. The blade glinted when he raised it and cut them down one at a time, the steel slicing through flesh and bone, the heads dropping and rolling in the sand.

Slashing his way through the rank, he reached the last man.

He was old, silver-haired.

Leviathan hesitated.

The man smiled. "Go on, boy," he said with calm. "Slay me with your sword, so I may return to my one and only lord."

"You're not afraid."

"I fear none but my Rabb. You'll know fear, too, *ya* Blade of the Firawn. You'll know the price of the blood on your soul."

Leviathan breathed the cold in his chest. "I've no soul." Lifting his sword, he detached the man's head, but it wasn't silver hair drowning in a red puddle.

It was black as the night. Dark skin, full lips. A woman. He'd never seen her before, but he knew who she was the moment he met her eyes.

Grey like thunder. Grey like his own.

His eyes flashed open.

Tilting his head forward, he rubbed his face, the stubble scratching against his calloused palms. His pulse raced as if his veins were injected with a shot of magic. He told himself that he was jarred because the execution was part of a past he dragged around in chains, not because he saw his birthmother and clipped her head from her body with his own two hands. Taking a deep, shaky breath, he swallowed hard and rebuilt the barrier stone by stone, like he'd taught himself to do whenever a memory smashed it down.

War was blind. It didn't discriminate. Elders, women, kids were all the same to it. He'd witnessed its destruction in the rubbles of the southeast and heard its deprivation in the laughter of Wardens perching on the rooftops, pointing their crossbows at kids scavenging for food in the ruins, like it was target practice at the Guild and the civilians nothing but a series of bullseyes. He'd seen cold-eyed Rangers shove families inside tents and set the tents on fire. Burning them alive. And he'd walked through camps in the sick after-silence of crackdowns that'd turned into massacres. It wasn't a search for rebels. No, never that. It was the continuation of a cleansing ritual instigated centuries ago when Khansadun became the Strips.

When one nation was ripped apart at the seams.

He didn't need a damn reminder because he carried it all with him every day. Before he became a Cutthroat, he was a Ranger deployed in the southeast. There was no other with his skill, speed, or strength. He led the units, spoke the words of a killer's creed at executions, butchered in the Firawn's name. Kanoni was right. He changed. It started with a slow desensitisation of his mind, his heart, and it turned the cries of the clans into distant noise.

That inner void? It was the darkest place inside him. Like the bottom of a very deep ocean.

And he didn't think he'd resurfaced yet.

Dropping his hands from his face, he looked at the white sheets covering the divans, cabinets, and bed. His mother's things were long gone, but the memories attached to her private quarters, her fading scent, lingered and crumbled his defences, so he stayed on the floor with his back against the doors for another moment. His gaze shifted to the red velvet curtains behind which he used to hide, escaping the cups of milk she'd plead with him to drink, and the lanterns on the ceiling whose shadows he'd watch while she sang him to sleep.

Like the furtive Ghameq, he moved to his feet, quick, quiet, and examined every nook, crook, and piece of furniture. His fingers sought the crevices, opened the drawers. His sight caught the smallest specks of dust in a ravenous hunt. Ripping down the sheet, he yanked open the closet doors. Empty. Still, he explored it to the seams before he slammed the doors and leaned his brow on the wood with tight shoulders.

What exactly was he looking for? Her private quarters were cleared, all traces of evidence erased. But he couldn't leave it alone. His emotions blinded him like they'd done for days now, so he wrestled them down, uncoiled his muscles, head silent, eyes sharp, as they roamed the walls with their Middle Khansāri scripture carved in gold on white stone and stalled on a grille above the bed. His ears caught the echoes of conversation from the lower regions.

The chatter of slaves in the palace kitchens.

"Yaya."

Haya's voice pulled his attention from the grille. He turned to her. "Does your mother know where you are?" he asked. Thumb in her mouth, Haya shook her head and—eyes full of trust—slipped her hand in his. He wouldn't thaw. Crouching down, he brushed a finger under her chin. "You can't keep running off, kid. She worries. You understand?" He saw words in those big eyes, but she didn't know how to speak them. She put a hand to his cheek and he blinked in surprise. Nobody ever touched him like that. Nobody, except his mother, and Mai.

Haya dropped her hand and darted toward the doors.

Malev narrowly evaded her as he walked into the chamber. "Looks like you got a stalker, brother," he said on a chuckle.

Throwing the sheet back over the closet, Leviathan stepped out into the connecting archway and Malev followed him past silk curtains and slaves, through courtyards and up staircases to Leviathan's private quarters.

"Did Junho fill the boys in on the water haul?" he asked his companion.

"They're ready," Malev answered.

"And the food?"

"Delivered."

Last night, they'd hauled rice loads and dried fruits from the city storage. Compared to the things Leviathan had done during his training as a

Cutthroat—like breaking out of detainment without any equipment and surviving assassination attempts by incapacitating the assassins before they got to him—stealing from the storage had been a breeze. The haul wouldn't end starvation, but it'd ease the ache of hunger, and it'd have to do until he found a better solution.

"Did you remind them to hide the haul outside the camp?"

"All taken care of, brother."

"How's Mai?"

"Strong as ever."

She would be. Khiraa's suicide had shaken her, but it hadn't broken her. As for Seth, it'd caused damage, and not the kind that could be seen unless you knew where to look. He was quiet. Too quiet. Leviathan knew that silence. There was a storm inside the kid. Growing. Sooner or later, it'd devour him. He didn't want Seth on that path, so when the kid had asked Leviathan to teach him how to fight, Leviathan had made him a deal. He'd teach him as long as he didn't look for trouble.

"Mai asked for you," Malev said at length. "She wanted to know why you didn't come with the haul yourself."

Leviathan didn't respond. If he'd delivered the food himself, it would've put the clans in a difficult position. They would've been forced to accept it from somebody they hated. Somebody whose hands were stained with their blood. They would've done it out of desperation, but he didn't want them to think they were in his debt or feel they betrayed their own by taking anything from him. This way, they could pretend he had nothing to do with it. They held no dislike for Malev and Junho. Besides, the important part was that they'd managed the haul without any issues and delivered it safely to the camp.

So, he should've been content.

Why wasn't he?

Pushing the discomfort aside, he changed out of his sleeveless undershirt, yanking a black *kurta* over his head, rolling the sleeves up to his elbows. He had to make an appearance in Biranpur tonight. The Firawn's in-laws were in the city. He was expected to honour their presence with his own. Losing face would push the Firawn past reason, snap his patience, and Leviathan knew what happened when reason abandoned the Firawn.

The Firawn's in-laws had powerful connections which made them important in his political game. It meant nothing to him that Leviathan had killed two

Wardens. It didn't affect the Firawn's position. Sustaining the power balance and manipulating people's perception of him? That meant something. As his sole heir, Leviathan was supposed to represent him, remind the people of him. Not all battles should be fought when it came to the Firawn. Hell, most shouldn't. And Leviathan had learned to choose his battles with care.

Leaning a shoulder on the doorframe, Malev crossed his arms. "I did some digging," he ventured. "Children have been vanishing from all over the West Strip for some time and the number increased about a month ago. They're targeting orphans between five and fifteen."

Because nobody would miss them, Leviathan mused, as he slid his knives into place. Being armed no matter where he went was another habit from his training at al-Mawt, but keeping his knives on him was more than a routine. Without them, he felt wrong. Incomplete. Like he was missing a limb.

"Last night, three children went missing in Rania," Malev disclosed. "Two vanished outside Sial around the same time."

"Get in touch with Kai," Leviathan responded.

"Already did, brother."

Passing Malev on his way out, Leviathan slapped a hand on his shoulder. "Take care of the water haul," he said, striding through the archway. "Get Junho and meet me in Biranpur when you're done." He turned a corner and stopped, unhurried. Cecilia stood in his path in all her raging glory, eyes wild, looking like she wanted to skin him alive, so he figured she'd heard about the dead Wardens.

If she knew, the Firawn knew.

Leviathan motioned for Malev to move ahead without him, and his companion walked around the two of them.

"Is this what you returned to Ferozi for?" Cecilia snapped. "To spit on your father by murdering the guardians of our city?"

"So much anger, Mā Saheb," Leviathan said calmly and strolled to the stairs. "Mind that blood pressure."

Cecilia tailed him down the marble steps. "The Wardens are soldiers, Leviathan, protected by our state laws. Do you honestly believe your father will let it slide without consequences?"

"No."

"Foolhardy is what you are. You've no fear right now, but soon you'll regret it."

"I won't be the only one with regrets. It's barely been more than a week and I've already rattled your little reign."

"This is what you learned at the Guild of Guardianship? To behave like an animal?"

"That seems to run in the family."

She pursued him across the hall, barking at his back. "It's true what they say. No matter how hard you train a mongrel to behave like a human, it only spreads filth in your home. That's why it should be throttled at birth. Bitch and babe."

Leviathan stopped and turned. Taking slow, deliberate steps, he closed the distance between them, eyes glittering with something dangerous. "The Firawn raised me, Mā Saheb, and do you know what he taught me?" The hot rage rising in him when she called his birthmother a bitch now cooled to frost. "There's no such thing as a universal morality. There's just your moral code and mine. The most righteous act, in my belief, would be to make you suffer like my mother did."

For the flicker of a second, he saw real fear in her eyes, real panic. It was beautiful. "You keep mistaking my patience for weakness. You forget it's the Firawn who cultivated me for fifteen years." He cocked his head, a prowling purr in his voice. "And if there's anything he taught me that'll prove useful when I decide to hunt, it's how to prey on those who consider themselves predators."

"You can't touch me, Leviathan."

"Want to wager on that?"

Her breath hissed out. "I despise you. Your existence is a stain. Such *filth*. Your birthmother was the same. Badriya seduced him. She became his little whore and birthed a bastard under my roof. Oh, how I celebrated when she bled to death in labour," she crooned. "Did you know? I celebrated when you killed her. How many more have died for you, Leviathan? Don't you wonder? How many more will die?"

Slipping a knife to her throat, he backed her against a pillar. "None," he said, very softly. "None if I end you now."

Her laughter was crude. "Go on, mongrel. Slit my throat." Grabbing his wrist, she pulled the blade closer until it touched skin. Her eyes gleamed with madness. "Do it."

It was tempting. To cut open her throat. To watch her bleed right in front of him. To be released from all the rage and pain she caused.

But he didn't move.

"You can't do it, can you?" she said with a victorious smile. "You fear your father." His jaw clenched at her words, at the gnawing in his gut. "Growl all you want, Leviathan, but deep down you're still a frightened little boy." She clawed a hand over his heart. "And one day, I'll cut out your organs and feast on them. I'll feast on your blood."

"You want my blood? I'll give it to you." Stepping back, he flipped the knife. "This is the only chance you're going to get, Mā Saheb. Better make it count."

She took the knife with her manic stare on his. "I won't be baited, Leviathan. Your father would never forgive me if I damaged a hair on your head. You're his favourite hound."

His teeth flashed. "I'm his only hound," he corrected, reminding her that she was deficient to the Firawn beneath her flawless appearance. He was the Firawn's sole heir—and she was nothing but a pawn in an alliance. Her hold on the knife tightened. "You know, I get it. Must be hard to watch your husband pick other women over you. Take them to his bed. Your bed." Her nostrils flared. He leaned closer. "When was the last time he asked for you?"

"You *bezaat* son of a whore," she hissed.

He clicked his tongue as he backed to the doors. "Careful, now, Mā Saheb," he said, playfully chastising. "Such harsh words might break your delicate bones." Turning his back on her, he reached for the door handle, and the knife sailed past his head, jamming into the wooden frame. He chuckled. "Looks like you missed your shot."

CHAPTER 17

Roma slipped into Biranpur's bustling courtyard with a heart that still pounded a frantic beat. She should tell Jirani about the thieves, but she felt reluctant to reveal what she had witnessed. The thieves had seemed disturbingly accustomed to the task of clearing the containers, moving about Jirani's stall as if it weren't their first time. She had disrupted a routine. Why hadn't they harmed her? Didn't they fear she would report them to the Wardens?

She would never approach a Warden, not even if her life depended on it, but she could report the thieves to the Panchayat. Her belly clenched at the thought. The Panchayat would suspect Jirani for the knives in his containers and persecute him. She wouldn't do that to him whether he was involved with the thieves or not. He was a good man with a wife and daughter who needed him. There had to be a reason he aided those masked men.

If he aided them at all.

Threading through the crowd, Roma found her sisters, joining them in watching the fire breathers conjure firestorms from their throats, the plumes of heat burning the air in hypnotic swirls—and her pulse scrambled at the sight because the amber hues reminded her of the thief in black with his golden eyes who had spoken to her in Middle Khansāri.

'*Your eyes could ruin a man,*' he had said.

"Roma," Hani called with a beckoning wave. When Roma managed to weave a path through the mass to her, she handed her a ceremonial platter. "Bring this to Amma by the temple stairs. *Lavakara*. It's important."

Roma rushed toward the temple stairs with the platter balanced between her hands. People craned their necks and peered over at the temple terrace where the Firawn's in-laws lounged. Bāba Saheb slumped in a chair with large, silver wheels. His wife, Māsa Saheba, and their four daughters—Mā Saheb with her three sisters—sat on velvet settees beside him with their husbands. Jewels and diamonds sparkled on their limbs. The children—six boys and three girls—perched on separate divans. There were other relatives, but none of them were from the Firawn's side. If he had any blood relations apart from his son, it wasn't known to the people.

Noticing a familiar face, Roma's steps faltered. The Firawn's son reclined in one of the farthest chairs. There were no adornments on him but the leather string with the small, curved-sword pendant. His hair shone like black onyx in the torchlight. Girls watched him with an unveiled hunger in their stares and whispered about him. Their words would have brought heat to the cheeks of someone more innocent than Roma. What possessed him to appear tonight? He hadn't cared for the festival before. His eyes wandered over the crowd, cold and dispassionate, and came to rest on Roma. She lowered her stare. She didn't like the sharp focus in his. He always saw her and she never wanted to be seen.

"Roma," Amma said in an impatient tone. "*Yē.*"

Holding the platter with care, Roma ascended the temple stairs behind her. Mā Saheb was swathed in a white pashmina gown with gold threadwork. The bodice was made of gold jewellery that bared her skin in places and covered it in others. Her white velvet veil was pinned on the crown of her head. She beckoned Amma to approach her parents with an elegant hand gesture.

Amma arranged her lips in a smile that held subtle seduction. "Welcome, Bāba Saheb and Māsa Saheba. I've prepared a ritual to bless you. May I perform it?"

Bāba Saheb squinted at Amma through circular, gold-framed glasses that sat on the bridge of his narrow nose. He wore a sapphire blue *sherwani* with a shawl fastened on his right shoulder and drawn around the back to be draped over his forearm. His silver hair and beard was oiled. He couldn't speak or move, so Māsa Saheba leaned toward him and listened to the guttural sounds in his throat.

"You have my husband's permission to proceed," Māsa Saheba said in a voice unsteady with age. She was draped in a similar blue *chanderi* gown with a cropped muslin cape over her shoulders. Triple-moons and a nine-pointed star were painted in gold oil on the back of her creased hands. The sacred symbols were worn by the worshippers of the stars. Her lucid blue eyes so alike her daughter's studied Amma. "You've aged gracefully, Jainaba Begum. The stars must favour you."

"*Meharbani*, Māsa Saheba."

Turning toward Roma, Amma dipped the neem leaves in the blessed water, sprinkling it on Bāba Saheb and Māsa Saheba. She tied beaded bracelets around their wrists before feeding them the honey. Māsa Saheba wiped her husband's lips with a silk napkin. The ritual was repeated for all the Firawn's in-laws—and then Amma stepped toward the Firawn's son. He remained at ease in his seat with his observant eyes on her. Glancing at the skin on his forearms, Roma noticed several raised lines. Scars. Some of them disappeared beneath his rolled sleeves.

"We lost hope that you would ever grace our festival, Saheb," Amma trilled. "Please allow us to perform the ritual."

"Sure," he said in an idle tone and nodded at Roma. "But I want her to do it."

Roma stilled behind Amma.

One of the sons-in-law laughed. "Take a look over here, sister," he commented, smirking at Mā Saheb. "Who would've thought Firawn Sai's son would bend to a slave girl's charms? The apple doesn't fall far from the tree after all." Mā Saheb pinched her lips. Her violent expression made him clear his throat and drink deep from his wine glass to hide his mirth, but his wife laughed out loud with a hint of triumph.

"Women and harems are given to men as dowries, Chiram. She's just a slave," Māsa Saheba said. Raising her hand, she moved it in a dismissive gesture. "Let him enjoy himself. Nothing ill can come of it."

"Nothing but another *bezaat* bastard," Chiram Saheb murmured.

The scheming glimmer in Amma's eyes was unmistakable. "My girl's auction will be held on the Night of Dhātu-Anwat," she said. Roma's cheeks burned. They spoke of her as if she were an object, as if she belonged to the Firawn's son because he insisted she perform the ritual.

"It's a blessed month for auctions," Māsa Saheba stated. "Perhaps you should auction the younger *dēvadasis* as well."

"I would, Māsa Saheba, but one of the young is a babe still, and the other hasn't yet received her blood."

"The lower *zaat* should dedicate more daughters on the next full moon, especially with the current threat of a drought in the lands."

"*Hō*, Māsa Saheba. Several have offered their daughters to the Mother Goddess, but we must wait for the auspicious moon."

"Naturally."

Looking at the Firawn's son, Amma smiled. "May we proceed, Saheb?" There was a moment of silence. He unfolded from his seat and it charmed Amma. None of his family had stood for the ritual. Amma turned toward Roma and jerked her chin. Unclasping her hands, Roma doused the neem leaves in the blessed water, sprinkling the drops on him. His eyes were cold iron punctuated by black, needle-sharp cores. She couldn't grasp why they troubled her so. Why they pushed and pulled at some wilful part in her. She tied one of the beaded bracelets around his wrist with care, so as not to touch his skin, and raised a spoonful of honey toward his lips.

Chiram Saheb chuckled. "Ah, but Leviathan doesn't like sweets," he remarked.

Her hand stalled mid-air. Watching her, the Firawn's son eased forward, accepting the honey. She saw his eyes take in the scars on her face, making her speculate if he had insisted on her performing the ritual just so he could have a closer look at them. It was a notion that perturbed her more than she already was in his proximity.

"It's time for Roma's performance," Amma said. Stepping back behind her, Roma breathed a sigh of relief. "If my Sahebs and Sahebas would excuse us?"

"We always look forward to your girls' performances, Jainaba Begum."

"*Meharbani*, Māsa Saheba."

Sādin Saheb ascended the temple stairs to greet the Firawn's in-laws as Roma hurried down the steps after Amma. She was relieved to escape the draining inspection, and once the musicians initiated the performance, she would draw her strength from the beats. The performance tonight would praise Mother Lamia. Roma hadn't practised for her unaccompanied dance, yet her mind held the collection of their spiritual dances and her shell knew how to stitch them together from beat to beat.

Amma swanned to her seat. "Drums," she shouted over the noise.

The drumbeaters struck three hard beats and all of Biranpur fell into silence. Lifting the veil over her head, Roma concealed her face, turning her back to the temple terrace. Her anklets chinked when she posed.

Then she waited for the sitar's thrum.

It started with a sound like falling drops in a lake—slow and soft—and then it became mysterious like a shadow gliding through a lamplit, smoke-filled chamber. Roma embodied Mother Lamia, the seductress, as she turned on a quick drumbeat and cast the veil back from her face. The strumming of the lutes tugged at her in serpentine movements, depicting the allure of the Mother Goddess, and the songsters sang of a goddess striking men like a thunderbolt and lighting up the earth.

The curling smoke from incense-burning lamps saturated the air around her. Spinning in circles, she matched the bells on her anklets to the harder beats. She was lost amid the swift meld of lutes as she denoted the dark passion of Mother Lamia—a passion which could be a beautiful love or terrible revenge. Catching the two firerods Yoshi tossed toward her, Roma swung them in elegant arches, and they crackled like sweltering wood. The enchanting movements of the sword dancers were engraved into her memory, but she painted them in her own colours, in her own language—the lethal language of Mother Lamia's unforgiving counterpart, Aranyada—as if she knew the dance of battle.

The spectators gasped and sighed, watching her like a serpent would a serpent charmer, following the slender lines of her shell with unblinking stares, enthralled by the low bend of her spine, graceful gestures, and shameless eyes that sliced like a blade, mirroring a fatal trait cajoled to the surface by the quickening beats. Roma slammed the firerods on the ground. The instruments and emotive vocals hushed.

Biranpur was silent for a breathless moment before it erupted into wild cheers.

"*Wah,*" Amma shouted. "Divine."

Roma lifted her head. The Firawn's son had vanished. A *birandasi* took the firerods from her and Sādin Saheb's lips curved in a superior smile as if she had impressed all the Sahebs and Sahebas for him. Hani circled a burning incense stick around Roma's head to shield her against an evil eye because Amma didn't want her fortune spoiled so close to her auction. The unwelcome reminder brought a sourness on Roma's tongue and, all of a sudden, the curious looks from the women and the ogles from the men crawled under her skin.

Searching for her sisters, she found Sunbel, Caliana, Ara, and Yoshi standing around a shared platter mounted with seafood. She started toward them, pausing as laughing children chased each other in a circle around her before plunging back into the horde.

"Where's Chirag?" Roma had told him to stick with their sisters. "Why isn't he with you?"

"Oh, he's around here somewhere," Ara shrugged with a mouth full of seafood. "The prawn is so delicious, I swear."

Sunbel looked at Roma. "Try it, Roma," she said, holding up the pink, shrivelled meat.

"Not right now. I need to find Chirag."

The courtyard was full of newly wedded couples. People tended to marry their sons and daughters in the Sacred Months, such as the Sacred Month of Biran, believing it would bring their children good fortune. A father would wed his son downward in *zaat*, because males provided stature, even if the females were mere washerwomen, but he would never wed his daughter with the lowest in *zaat*.

A boisterous burst of derisive laughter drew Roma's attention to the side terraces where the higher *zaat* lounged. The source of their mirth was a familiar form that moved around in an attempt to imitate her performance. Tripping over his feet, Chirag recoiled when the men and women jeered, throwing shredded flatbread at him. Torrid heat rushed to her head and roared in her ears. Hurrying across the distance to Chirag, she caught his hand and pulled him behind her. He huddled against her back with bewildered eyes as she faced the higher *zaat* laughing at his expense.

"Temple whore," a woman slurred, leaning heavily on a man beside her. He inspected his crystal glass as if nothing else existed around him. Roma recognised him as Amma's patron; the higher *zaat* man who had fathered Chirag. The drunken woman was his wife. She crooked a finger and beckoned Roma to her. "Yes, you. Come here. *Yē*." Her pronunciation of the Khansāri word was awkward. "*Yē, yē*."

Roma nudged Chirag in the direction of their sisters. "Go and eat with the others," she said to him in a low, firm voice. "*Jā*."

Biting his bottom lip, Chirag bolted without complaint. Roma's shoulders dropped the slightest bit in relief the moment he was out of sight. She stepped over to the demanding woman.

"You ruined our fun," the woman admonished. She smelled of sweat, perfume, and wine. "Now, be a good little whore and pour us all another round. We've run out, haven't we?"

There were snorts and laughter.

Picking up a crystal pitcher, Roma poured for her. The woman swept a scornful stare up and down Roma's shell with a cruel twist to her painted lips. "You know," she continued, her voice thick with alcohol. "You temple bitches wreck homes. You strut around acting pure, but I know what you really are." She gulped down half of her refilled wine as Roma poured for her husband. "You're worse than the Flags and the brothel whores. They don't hide behind the gods. They're dirty and they act like it."

"Natasha," her husband murmured. "Dignity, please."

"You robbed me of it." She pinched his cheek. "When you lay with that whore."

"You've had too much to drink."

"I haven't yet had enough to forget."

Pouring for the other higher *zaat* one at a time, Roma closed her ears to their taunts and her eyes to their leers with a growing rigidness in her back. She feared the men might misbehave with her, so she was quick about her task and soon reached the last couple.

A familiar smell raided her senses, assaulting her mouth and scratching in her throat, and she was paralysed when a brutal tide of memories bonded to that smell breached the dam of her will, bursting from the depths of her mind. Damp hands chained her wrists, pressing her into silk sheets that smelled sickeningly sweet, like rotted roses in a humid chamber. A tobacco breath whistled over her skin, the abrasive stroke desecrating her while his weight crushed her lungs.

'*You're the loveliest little pet.*'

Lifting her gaze to the higher *zaat* man in the chair, she looked into small, downturned eyes in a plump face.

It was *him*.

CHAPTER 18

THE CRYSTAL PITCHER slipped from Roma's hand and splintered against the tiles, splashing the cerise liquid on her former patron's trousers. Recoiling from him as he leaped to his feet, she looked down at his steeped velvet slippers in shock. His wife screeched in a fit of rage, shaking her pashmina skirt, her pugnacious outcries snagging the attention of those closest around. Straining their necks, people peered toward the source of the disturbance. They were a blurred backdrop in Roma's world. A world drained of colour and sound.

She couldn't breathe. Her chest refused to relent for air.

She wanted to run and never stop.

Never stop.

She wanted to take a crystal pitcher and smash it into his head.

"By the stars, look at my gown. It's soiled," his wife shrieked. "It was worth more than your lousy life, you imbecile. Do you have any idea what you've done?"

"There, now, Giselle. There's no need to cause a scene," the patron soothed. The searing swell of anger and hatred coursing through Roma distorted to panic. She was enfeebled with each stressed breath as his sordid voice slinked into her head. She couldn't escape its malignant hold. The sharpened edges of suppressed memories threatened to rip her apart. Each scar on her skin itched and burned as if infected.

For so long she had feared his presence. The sound of his voice. None of her sisters understood it because he was just a patron and no different than others who acquired their service. Her sisters never experienced night terrors, never fought invisible hands and awakened on a scream, and so she learned to be ashamed of her fears. She choked them into a silence that was nothing like silence but repressed noise.

"Just look at my gown, Alan. The wine will never wash."

"The *dēvadasi* lost her hold on the pitcher," one of the higher *zaat* men reasoned.

"That may be so," a higher *zaat* woman said, "but she has spilled sacred wine."

"We should confer with Sādin Saheb," someone shouted in the crowd.

"What if she has angered the gods?" another questioned.

"We barely had any rain this season."

"Sādin Saheb!"

Roma licked her lips. She saw her sisters rushing through the gathering. Amma pushed past them to the front and Binti whispered into her ear. Shaking her head, Amma planted her hands on her hips and crinkled her nose, staring at Roma with a rigid expression on her face. She wouldn't interfere. Roma was on her own. She bit the inside of her cheek and tasted blood on her tongue, but it kept her from trembling like a coward.

Floating to the terrace, Sādin Saheb squinted at the spilled wine before his convicting eyes skipped to Roma. "Bow down to the Saheb and the Saheba," he snapped. "Beg forgiveness."

Roma lowered herself to her knees and pressed her forehead to the cool tiles. "Forgive me," she said in a voice which didn't sound like hers. It sounded distant and weak. She burrowed deeper within herself for strength. "Please."

"Stand," the patron ordered. She obeyed. An unpleasant smile cracked his lips. His eyes journeyed over her shell and her skin scuttled to escape his lewd attention. "Accidents happen. You're forgiven on my part." Giselle Saheba squawked in protest, but he raised a hand to silence her and bared a row of narrow teeth that sent a hostile shiver down Roma's damp back. "However, I'm concerned for the people. Water is scarce nowadays. The gods seem awfully discontent. Merely nights ago, the Kāhinah performed a rain ritual and it'd be tragic if it were all for nothing."

People murmured and nodded in consent.

He sauntered in a half-circle around Roma to approach Sādin Saheb where he stood with his hands folded inside the long sleeves of his robe. She looked at the wine on the tiles, her mouth parched, her heart in her ears, and forced down the lump in her throat. From the corner of her eye, she saw Sunbel's sympathetic stare and Chirag's anxious face.

Alan Saheb placed a hand on Sādin Saheb's shoulder. "It's a terrible sin to spill sacred wine, isn't it, Sādin Saheb?" he asked.

"It most certainly is," Sādin Saheb agreed.

"Then repentance would be required?"

"It would."

"And in order to repent, one must be punished."

"Indeed, Alan Saheb."

Alan Saheb strolled toward Roma, but she remained rooted, even as his smell congested her chest. His fingers caressed her arm. She cringed. Her tongue was layered in a sourness so sharp, so profuse, she thought that she might vomit and add insult to injury. Men weren't permitted to touch a *lamiadasi* unless in a patronship with her, yet he touched her in front of all of Biranpur—and none said a word.

None.

"You've grown up quite well, pet. You were just this tall the last time I saw you." Holding up his hand, he indicated her height. She hated that he remembered her. "You were such a lovely little girl. A pity, those scars, such a pity." He didn't mention the scars *he* had given her. He didn't speak of the bite marks on her shell or the ones on her soul.

"It's an auspicious night," Sādin Saheb said. "Let's not summon the Panchayat to settle the matter. I'll leave it to you, Alan Saheb and Giselle Saheba, to decide her punishment."

Giselle Saheba crossed her arms. "Give her a proper punishment, Alan," she demanded in a shrill tone.

Roma lifted her eyes to Alan Saheb's. The malice in his stare prodded her. She shuddered as he sent her spiralling down a bottomless hole, his hands reaching for her in the darkness, his fingernails scraping against her naked skin, but her stare didn't falter, even when she felt the crude lick of fear in the back of her throat.

Where did this sudden sliver of nerve come from? She didn't know, but she gripped it with vigour, and she felt a sense of power. The arrogant curve of his lips and dominant shine in his eyes revealed that he was blind to it. He heard only her silence and tasted only her fear. It fed monsters such as him. The power burned in her blood like a fever as she imagined slamming a cleaver down on his wrists, severing the hands with which he had vandalised her, his screams resonating in the halls of her vivid imagination—resonating while she sliced and hacked at him.

"You understand sins require repentance. Don't you, pet?"

"*Hō*, Saheb," she whispered.

Ambling toward the largest fountain, he spread his arms and looked at the crowd. "Do you all see this wondrous fountain? When Biran wandered lost in his search for Lamia, he wept upon the ground and it sprouted a spring from his tears." His lips stretched wide in a broad smile. "What better way to clean oneself of one's sins than to be awash in the tears of the High Lord? The *lamiadasi* will stand in the fountain below this stream until dawn."

Roma's shoulders lowered on a slow breath. She would take all kinds of excruciating punishments as long as it didn't involve serving the patron.

"If she steps out even for a second—" Alan Saheb's leering eyes crept to her sisters, latching onto Goldie, and Roma's bowels knotted at the keen interest on his face. "—then she'll be replaced by that little gold-haired fairy."

Goldie leaned into Sunbel with a quivering bottom lip.

"Go now, child," Sādin Saheb commanded. "Let's not keep the gods waiting."

Roma ripped her stare from Goldie's frightened face and walked to the ridge of the fountain where she removed her slippers. The polished alabaster was ice beneath her feet. The water was even colder. Threading through it to the spring, she stepped under the harsh stream, gasping as the chill penetrated her flesh and raided the heat from her bones in seconds. It pounded her head, cascading over her shoulders and down her shivering shell. Her garments clung to her skin. Breathing in shallow gulps, she pinned her arms against her belly and cupped her elbows against the painful onslaught.

The crowd lingered for a moment. Then grew bored and scattered.

Digging her fingers into her upper arms, she squeezed her eyes closed, losing sensation and sense of time. When she peeled them open to look at the skies, they showed no hint of an imminent dawn. The punishing weight of the stream persuaded her eyelids to droop in defeat. She couldn't feel herself shivering anymore, but a strange fire blistered in her like an illness trapped inside her veins. Lurching from lightheadedness, she reached out for support, touching the pillar upon which the statues of the divine lovers were erected.

A hand seized her forearm and pulled her out. Drinking in a sudden breath, she almost panicked as unhindered air rushed back into her thumping lungs. Darkness swam across her vision like a hood drawn over her head. Solid arms swept her up and carried her out of the fountain. When she blinked the black blotches from her sight, she discovered the face of the Firawn's son inches from her own. Before she could scramble out of his arms, he lowered her on the ridge and his eyes remained on hers as he straightened. The dark undercurrent surging behind the deceptive calm held her transfixed. She saw temper. Danger.

People amassed to stare and whisper. Alan Saheb exposed his narrow teeth with a livid expression on his face. Tipping back her head, Roma looked up at the Firawn's son while questions ran through her mind. Why had he interrupted her punishment? Why had he risked the outrage of his own *zaat*?

"Lamia *re*," Amma exclaimed, rushing forward. "Saheb—"

The Firawn's son didn't spare her a single glance when he moved past her and sauntered toward Sādin Saheb. His companion, Junho, strolled to the higher *zaat* tables, picked an apple from a platter, and chewed loudly, which earned him disgusted looks from the men and women.

"Leviathan Saheb," Sādin Saheb said in a tone that might have placated a child, but it didn't have an impact on the Firawn's son, who tipped his head to the side as if entertained, only mirth was absent from his cold face. His inspection of Sādin Saheb was similar to the one he had aimed at the Wardens before deciding their fate. Sādin Saheb licked his lips. Roma had never seen him so intimidated. It reminded her of how human he was beneath his arrogance.

"Tell me, priest," the Firawn's son said. "Who made the *dēvadasi* stand in the fountain?"

Clearing his throat, Sādin Saheb bowed low. "Ah, she spilled sacred wine, Saheb, and our customs dictate—"

"I'm not interested in your customs. Answer the question."

Sādin Saheb's jaw slackened and his mouth dropped open, but no sound came from his throat. Standing on her stinging feet, Roma walked to Amma's side, dripping water on the stone. The suggestion of a smile teased Amma's lips as she watched the Firawn's son.

Alan Saheb pushed out his chest. "*I* decided her punishment, Saheb. She didn't just soil my wife's attire as well as mine, but the wine she spilled was sacred."

"It's a sinful act, Leviathan Saheb," Sādin Saheb hastily added, "and a terrible dishonour to the High Lord."

"I don't know much about your gods," Reaching out, the Firawn's son yanked the collar of Sādin Saheb's robe as if to straighten it, causing him to wince in anticipation of pain, "but if you put her in that fountain again, you'll meet your High Lord ahead of time."

Junho whistled, jerking his head toward the skies. "*Samajalē?*" he asked and chuckled.

Sādin Saheb's face turned white.

"Are you challenging the gods, Leviathan?"

The sweetened voice belonged to Mā Saheb. She descended the temple stairs with her eyes on the Firawn's son, and it was as if a battle ensued between them. A battle for power. It wasn't the absence of affection that chilled the air in Biranpur, but the absence of boundaries. They faced each other like adversaries on a field, prepared to murder at any moment. People sensed the perilous atmosphere and the hostility between the Firawn's son and Mā Saheb, shifting on their feet and watching with parted lips.

There was some awful history between them for certain.

Raising her chin, Mā Saheb tipped her head to the side. Her smile was layered with ice. "Will you bring down the wrath of the gods upon us all for a slave?" When she swanned closer to him, Roma saw the muscles in his forearms tighten. The smile on Mā Saheb's lips pulled higher. A strange, mad light was in her translucent eyes. "Someone must repent, or the gods will smite us. Will you take her place, Leviathan? Will you stand in the fountain?"

Laughter erupted among the higher *zaat*. Mā Saheb laughed herself, but it was a soft sound in her throat. She didn't notice the calculative glint in his stare, nor how his muscles uncoiled against the fabric of his damp *kurta*. It struck Roma then that Mā Saheb couldn't read him as well as she thought. She toyed with a fire she didn't understand, seeming as if she controlled it, but she was reckless and had yet to recognise the nature of the element.

That to burn others—the fire had to burn as well.

With the liquid grace of a cheetah, he closed the final inch of distance between them, stepping so close Mā Saheb tipped back her head to meet his eyes. Her fingers trembled at her sides. The longing to wrap her hands around his throat was perceptible in her stare. His eyes travelled down to study the twitch before he stepped around her and snatched the collar of Alan Saheb's *sherwani*.

The patron gasped. "What in the name of—" His voice was detached with a jerk of his collar as he was hauled toward the fountain. Elbowing each other, people clustered closer to watch the spectacle. Alan Saheb stumbled over his own feet to keep pace with the Firawn's son, his resistance trampled in a second, and Roma relished the panic that slackened his face.

"Leviathan," Mā Saheb snapped. "What're you doing?"

"Somebody must repent," the Firawn's son said calmly. He shoved the patron down on his knees by the ridge of the fountain. "Get in."

CHAPTER 19

Alan Saheb stared up at him in disbelief and the Firawn's son kicked him in the side, sending him soaring over the ridge into the fountain, the frigid water splashing high under his weight. Rolling onto all fours with a groan, he staggered to his feet, favouring his right hip. Roma couldn't untangle what he saw in the Firawn's son, but it drained his face of colour and made him hobble to the spring without a protest, and she savoured his shivers as the water saturated him. She wanted him to die a slow death. This agony should feel like a lifetime to him.

Yet it would never be enough. *Nothing* would ever be enough.

He had demolished an irreparable part of her and turned her into a disassociated husk that couldn't love nor be touched with love. He made her feel powerless and ashamed. She heard his rasping voice inside her head when she was weakest at night.

"Alan," Giselle Saheba screeched. Descending on Sādin Saheb like a predatory bird, she shrieked about humiliation, demanding he save her husband. He nodded and murmured in an attempt to pacify her, but Roma saw the hesitation in his furtive looks at the Firawn's son. When she squawked louder, Junho flinched and squeezed his right eye closed, slipping a finger into his ear, as if her screams had shaken loose his eardrum.

Giselle Saheba rushed around Sādin Saheb and approached Mā Saheb next. "This is a crime, Mā Saheb. We're higher *zaat*. I won't stand for this humiliation of my husband. You must—"

Spinning on her heels, Mā Saheb slapped her so hard across the cheek that Giselle Saheba's head snapped to the side on a pained breath, and a collective jolt passed through the crowd. Giselle Saheba lifted a trembling hand to her reddened cheek with tears of mortification in her eyes. Her lips pinched together on a whimper. She didn't dare to unleash another sound.

"You won't command me, wench. I'll have your skin peeled from your flesh," Mā Saheb hissed. Giselle Saheba's shoulders hunched as she retreated. Whipping toward the Firawn's son, Mā Saheb narrowed her eyes and curled her fingers like claws. "You've crossed a line, Leviathan. You'll regret it."

"Promises, promises," he murmured.

She snarled orders at her nervous *bandis* and marched to the palanquin with her fez-wearing slave behind her. Sādin Saheb watched her leave with a dark expression, his withered lips downturned, and a deep line between his eyebrows. The Firawn's son seated himself in a chair in front of the fountain and leaned forward on his elbows. There was a cigarette tucked into a corner of his mouth. He didn't light it even as he toyed with a lighter.

Tossing aside the core of his apple, Junho picked up a platter and dumped rice, meat, and seafood on it. If it were his habit to eat such a wealth of food, it didn't show on his lean frame. He wandered over to Malev, waving the platter under his nose in a teasing manner, and Malev's hand whipped out to smack him behind his head. Ducking out of a second swing with a grin, Junho pulled a higher *zaat* boy out of his chair by the collar and took his seat to devour the mountain on the platter.

"Lamia *re*," Amma murmured, staring at Sādin Saheb while he spoke to Giselle Saheba in hushed tones. She nodded at his promises and wiped her tears. Catching Amma's eye, Sādin Saheb motioned for her to come over and she strutted toward him with a guarded expression. Roma twisted a piece of her veil in her damp hands. What did he want from Amma? What promises had he made Giselle Saheba?

Yoshi moved to her side and leaned toward her ear. "Alan Saheb has been humiliated. They can't punish the Firawn's son," she whispered. "Who do you think they'll punish instead?"

Roma buried her fears for later, so she could survive for now, as Amma sashayed back and pulled her aside. "Giselle Saheba is furious," she said in a lowered voice. "She won't be pacified unless her husband is pardoned, and you're punished for his humiliation."

Any hint of emotion on Amma's face appeared and disappeared before Roma could define it. "Go to Leviathan Saheb. Tell him you choose to repent.

Insist. If he believes you, he'll pardon Alan Saheb, and some of the damage will be repaired. As for the wine, the Kāhinah will perform a public cleansing ritual, so the patrons won't be dissuaded from bidding on you."

"What will happen if he doesn't pardon Alan Saheb?"

"Let's hope we don't have to find out. *Jā*."

Roma swallowed the bitterness in her throat. She was to convince the Firawn's son that she chose to stand in the fountain, to be shamed, or Sādin Saheb would punish Lamiapur. She looked past Amma at Chirag. Even standing among her sisters, he appeared misplaced, as if he were apart from them and felt it without knowing it.

Regardless of how much she wanted to refuse Amma and oppose Sādin Saheb, she wouldn't have Chirag or Goldie punished for her misstep. She should have been more careful. She knew not to give Sādin Saheb and the higher *zaat* an excuse to penalise them.

With a shakiness in her rigid limbs, she drew the soaked veil over her head. The Firawn's son didn't as much as glance in her direction as she approached him, but she knew that he saw her, because there was too much awareness in him, all too much sharpness, to miss a single speck of dust in his presence.

When his intent gaze remained on Alan Saheb, she stepped between them to force him to look at her instead of the shivering patron. "Saheb," she said in a careful voice. She should have bowed first, but she forgot, and now it would seem sardonic. She felt Amma's penetrating stare on her face. The crowd watched her as well. "There's been a misunderstanding. I think I might've given the impression that I was being punished. I wasn't. I chose to repent, Saheb."

After what felt like an eternal silence, his low-pitched voice sounded in her ears.

"What's your name?"

She hesitated.

Giving her name wasn't what she wanted. It was one more feature through which he would know her, and she didn't *want* him to know her, but she couldn't refuse to answer. She had slighted enough people tonight. Insulting someone as powerful as the Firawn's son would bring about consequences that Lamiapur couldn't bear. It was just a name—and he would soon forget it.

"Roma, Saheb."

"Roma," he repeated slowly as if he were rolling it on his tongue and testing its mass. Unfolding from his seat, he pushed to his feet, and she hated that the movement startled her. She wouldn't retreat as he advanced on her but remained rooted with her shoulders straight. She would never cower before a man again, regardless of his power and stature.

There were only a couple of steps between them when the Firawn's son stopped. He might not be able to hear her thrashing heart, but he would notice the scrambling pulse in her throat. She couldn't calm it no matter how much she attempted it.

"Are you lying to me, Roma?"

She stilled. "*Nā*, Saheb," she managed.

"Look at me."

Her fingers tightened on the veil. Slowly, she lifted her eyes. There was iron in his, and she didn't know what it meant. Was he angered? Irritated? Was he even the slightest bit convinced of her lie? It disturbed her that he watched her with such steadiness as if he were picking her apart within his mind and piecing her back together to understand how she functioned. The sense of cold examination made her think of the rumours about the Firawn. People said he looked at one as if exploring one's strengths and weaknesses, seeking what one attempted to hide from him.

The Firawn's son inclined his head. "You want me to pardon him," he said.

"I—it was a misunderstanding—"

"You want me to pardon him."

"*Hō*, Saheb."

"The answer is no."

He turned his back on her and she dropped her veil. "This is my debt to pay, Saheb," she told him. "The gods would want me to repent. It's the way of our people. We must all pay for our sins."

"You believe that?"

"Yes."

"How do you know what the gods want?" he asked her with a note of cynicism under the curious tone in his voice. He gestured toward the skies. "Do they drop a hint? If a glass of wine is so sacred to them, why don't they prevent it from spilling? Do they like watching you suffer for it?"

People shifted and bristled at his words, but none spoke against him.

Amma glared at Roma in an attempt to prompt her into insisting again, but Roma's mind emptied of lies and his questions resounded within her head.

He was right. How could anyone know for certain what the gods wanted? If they were infallible, shouldn't they be merciful toward the fallible humankind? Shouldn't the God of Creation forgive rather than punish when he made them?

Perhaps the spilled wine was only that—a spilled pitcher of wine.

Amma laughed to pierce the tension, but it sounded shrill and false. "We practise caution, Saheb. Repentance is a spiritual practice and a sacred custom. Roma has always been more god-fearing than the rest of us, so she wants to repent to clear her conscience. She has such devotion for our gods, bless her soul." Tipping forward, she offered him a bashful smile touched with seduction. "We're *dēvadasis*, Saheb. Devotion runs in our veins."

The Firawn's son waited for her to finish, and then—

"Is your melodrama over?" he asked.

Amma's aplomb crumbled along with her smirk and Roma's mind was a hive of frantic thoughts. The consequences would be austere for them if Alan Saheb remained in the fountain, but lies weren't how she could convince the Firawn's son and salvage the situation.

Sealing her fear deep within herself where she kept all other fears trapped, Roma stepped between Amma and the Firawn's son. "Who're you punishing Alan Saheb for?" His lips parted to speak, but he was silent. She shook her head. "If this is your justice, Saheb, I don't want it."

For a moment that felt far too long his hardened eyes stared into hers with a determination which matched her own. "Junho," he said without breaking stare. "Let him out."

"*Hō*, Bhau."

Roma wanted to close her eyes in abrupt relief, but she lowered her head instead, even as she felt no respect nor gratitude toward him. Calling her *bandis* to the fountain, Giselle Saheba collected her dripping husband from the fountain—and Roma saw Alan Saheb's pointed glance at Sādin Saheb as he was rushed out of Biranpur.

It wasn't over.

The Firawn's son moved past her, so close his sleeve brushed her arm, so close she recoiled from him, and the people parted to peer after him with both reverence and judgement in their stares.

"Amma," Roma said.

Amma lifted a hand to silence her. "Not a word," she snapped. Leading

Amma back to her seat, Hani handed her a cup of water and kneeled beside her, while their sisters clustered around in concern, but Amma's eyes were locked on Sādin Saheb's in a silent conversation.

Pressing a shaky hand to her belly, Roma curled her fingers in her veil. What had she done? What had she unleashed? Sādin Saheb was infuriated. She saw it in his grim expression that he hadn't pardoned Lamiapur for her mistake. What if Amma dedicated Chirag to Lord Biran? What if she sent him to Biranpur as a *birandasi*?

"Tai?" Chirag wrapped his arms around her waist. She didn't mean to wince and the woundedness on his face pained her. "I'm sorry, Tai."

"It's all right," Roma reassured him, but she failed to conceal the quiver in her voice. Chirag had seen her when she was auctioned to Alan Saheb. When she returned to Lamiapur with bruises on her shell and fractures within her soul—and he remembered.

"Don't be sad, Tai. When you kill him, it'll make your hurt go away."

She looked down at him. "What?" she breathed.

"The stars never lie."

CHAPTER 20

Blue tones from the magic-powered dome washed over the crowd below. Shadows twisted with raw hunger. Watching the Ghameq slither like black serpents, Leviathan thought about the *dēvadasi.* Thought about her bold eyes and scars. Thought about her dance with the firerods cutting through the air like she was born to wield swords. She'd moved with understated grace. If he'd had any less self-control, he would've been as hypnotised as everybody else in that courtyard. She'd met his stare with even force. With a nerve that showed him just what kind of a man she thought he was.

She didn't like him. Not in the least.

Seeing her standing in that fountain had enraged him. She feared retaliation, he assumed, so he'd pardoned the bastard. It irritated him that these priests could spew out the most irrational claims about their gods, and somebody like her didn't question it. She was smart. Too smart to accept a punishment for spilled wine. Maybe his interference had made matters worse for her. Maybe it'd scared off her punishers.

And maybe he should just stop thinking about her.

He wasn't shocked at how the *dēvadasis* were treated. Sacred or not, they were prostitutes. As far as he knew, there were three kinds of prostitution in the Strips. The Women of the Flags were typically mothers or widows. The *dēvadasis* of the temples were young girls dedicated or born into the system. Then there was the most ruthless kind of prostitution—the brothels where women were sold to settle the debts of their families. It placed another debt on the women. They weren't bound to the brothels through sacred customs, but they couldn't leave unless they paid their owner the amount he'd paid for them, plus interest, which meant they had to work, hard, to buy their own freedom.

"They're lower *zaat*," Kai said, pulling Leviathan from his thoughts. Downing half of his beer, Kai wiped his mouth in his sleeve. "They snatch the kids for coin."

"What the hell are you saying?" Junho raked a hand through his messy hair. "Why would villagers do something like that? It makes no sense."

It made perfect sense. The snatchings increased in number about a month ago. Not long after taxes were raised by a full ten percent. The lower *zaat* were already in a tight spot—desperate to feed their families, to make ends meet—and survival was an ambiguous bitch. She pushed you to the brink of endurance, beyond, and incited you to do things you wouldn't have thought yourself capable of. Like delivering orphans to keep your own kids from starving.

When people lived primitive lives, striving to cover their basic needs, humanity was bound to shrink. There was no optimum system to secure them, to ensure they had the surplus of mental and physical resources to lead humane lives. The regime did everything it could to reduce their thinking down to plain subsistence. That way, they were too preoccupied surviving to fight for their rights, much less realise they *had* rights.

The fact was that the West Strip was dying from a perpetual drought like the one ruling the east. The northwest was a hub for human traders and the southwest was a military zone. Border controls prevented anybody from leaving unless they had coin to bribe with. It was a fruitless venture regardless because Dariadun and Suradun were suffering like the Strips. The constant threat of soldiers, human traders, and rebels meant that people chose the known reality of their communities over the costs of the unknown.

The Firawn wanted to keep the people scattered and distracted, but within the regional borders, so his officers could detect trouble and deal with it immediately. He'd placed Prince Jasadan on the seat in the East Strip and two other princes in Dariadun and Suradun with his military to carry out his commands. The princes were pampered with riches, but if they showed ambition or gained too much authority—like two of the last Darian princes—they were executed. The Firawn made sure the Darians understood that his power reached across the sea by sanctioning punitive expeditions and executing the princes publicly.

Leaning back in his seat, Leviathan turned the lighter in his hand. "What else?"

Kai drummed his fingers on the table. "The kids are given to handlers. Not sure how it all works, but they've got some kind of evaluation ritual and a bunch of safe locations. They don't want other traders to sabotage their shipments."

"Shipments?"

"It's not a domestic organ trade. It's overseas."

"They've got foreign clients paying for the organs?" Junho sputtered.

Malev rubbed his jaw with a pensive look on his face. "How often?" he asked, his voice tense. "The shipments."

"Maybe twice a month."

"Who do the handlers work for?" Leviathan inquired.

"Some human trader named Volos. He runs two of the big ones in Makhmoor. Sex and alcohol."

"Describe him to me."

Kai turned the bottle in his hands. "Can't. Few people know what he looks like. They won't talk. All I got is his rep. Rumours say he's a crazy son of a bitch, and he's been doing business with foreign clients for a while. Got people everywhere."

"Makhmoor's his territory?"

"Solid."

Makhmoor was a big chunk of West Durra closest to the coast. It was a thriving place, especially rich on brothels. Volos wasn't a low-end supplier if he owned that place. Traders didn't infringe on each other's zones, but the section of West Durra under Volos' control crawled with drug and weapon trades—two of the trades he didn't run—which meant he made deals with other traders, allowed them to sell on his ground. Alliances like that were rare and lucrative. He was a greedy but smart bastard.

Slipping the lighter in his pocket, Leviathan's eyes focused on Kai. "You've got information on one of the lower *zaat* involved," he said. Kai shifted in the chair and avoided his stare. He cocked his head. "I need a name."

"Can't give you that."

"A name, Kai."

"Bhau—come on. You know how it is."

Moving up behind Kai with a wolfish grin, Junho slapped his hands down on Kai's bony shoulders, making him jolt.

Leviathan leaned forward. "Name," he repeated.

"All right, fine," Kai spluttered, licking his lips. "The one my contact dug up—Jasir—works in the coal mines."

"Where?"

"Kantalaa. Gambles every night at the local tavern. The Black Goddess."

"What does he look like?"

"I don't know, Bhau. You can't just—"

"I can't?" Leviathan interrupted softly.

Kai swallowed hard and rephrased. "What I mean is—if you go after him, he'll know somebody delivered the information to you. It's going to be my ass. I follow—*we* follow a code. You know that. We don't name our sources and we don't name our sources' sources."

"You just did."

His knuckles turned white on the bottle. "This is exactly what I mean with you commissioning me for shit that'll get me in trouble."

"You offered, Kai."

"I'm fucking regretting it, aren't I?" he countered. Leviathan tossed him a leather pouch. It struck his sweaty brow and dropped into his lap. Rubbing the sore spot, he picked up the pouch and weighed it in his hand with a pursed mouth. "Guess I can live with a bit of regret."

"We're done, for now."

"Get out of here." Junho messed up Kai's hair with a rough hand. "Dumbass."

Knocking his hand aside, Kai got to his feet and shoved the pouch into his back pocket. "Wasn't planning on sticking around with you lot anyway."

Leviathan watched him disappear down the stairs with shadow vines at his heels. Seemed like they all had a bit of darkness to tempt the Ghameq. He'd never asked Kai about his family, or his life before this, but he didn't think anything was left of it. Boys like Kai didn't end up in this line of work if they had something to lose apart from their heads.

"This Volos sounds sharp," Malev pointed out, a grim twist to his mouth. He leaned against the rail, the blue dome at his back. "Keeps on the move, doesn't show his face to outsiders. Tracking him down won't be easy."

Nothing ever was. Leviathan wasn't in it for the easy.

Junho straddled Kai's vacated chair. "What now, Bhau?" he asked, impatiently tapping his foot. "How're we getting to Volos if we don't know what the *harami* even looks like?"

"Through his handlers."

Malev frowned. "We'll need to identify them first."

"That's where Jasir comes in."

"*Jhakaas*," Junho grinned. "When do we leave?"

"You're not coming." Before he could protest, Leviathan silenced him with a look. "I want you in Makhmoor. Scout out Volos' area, draw a map. Brothel locations, alleys, alternative exit routes—I want everything. We need to get familiar with his territory."

Mapping was one of Junho's cannier skills. He had the ability to create visuals of lands, structures, and weapons. Something Leviathan had told him, in specific terms, to keep quiet about. If his skills were discovered, he'd be deported to Shadowhold, the underground prison in Intisar, unless he agreed to work for the Wings. They couldn't have people with his talent running free.

Pushing back his chair, Leviathan stood and looked at Malev. "Watch the camp," he told him. "If they need anything, see to it."

Wisps of black smoke swirled around Leviathan's arm, lapping up the dark promise in his corded muscles, the Ghameq savouring his emotions.

'*Blood,*' they whispered. '*Violence.*'

He knew what his mother would've wanted. What she'd have asked of him. He hadn't been able to save her, but he'd save those kids. Whatever it took, he'd find them. Maybe then the weight on his chest would ease some.

Junho spun Kai's empty bottle on the table. "What about you, Bhau?" he asked, deflated, because he couldn't come with him.

Looking down at the shadows, Leviathan closed his hand around them.

"I'm going hunting."

CHAPTER 21

LEVIATHAN PULLED CINDER'S reins northeast of Kantalaa. Letting his eyes wander, he examined the bones of the village, his trained eyes seeing past the shadows that packed the streets. Rundown houses colonised the slopes with their cracked planks for doors and rags for curtains. Nothing like the brightly painted fronts of Sefu, but you'd still find the same dark alleys and flagged roofs, the same chancy nooks and infected hounds here. That much never changed in any part of the Strips. The ringing bells and pounding drums reminded him that people celebrated their gods even in the poorest places. He didn't mind it tonight as it'd make his presence less conspicuous in the tavern.

Leaping from the saddle, he spoke softly in Cinder's ear, bribing her with a persimmon, so she'd leave him at the border. The village was small, and he wanted to slip through unnoticed. Flipping the hood of his cloak over his head, he stepped among the shadows like he was one of them, observing the people parading in costumes, the smell of flowers and piss soaking the air.

And, soon, meat.

The Black Goddess appeared ahead, pressed tightly between two alleys, the idle smoke twisting over a crooked chimney. It looked pathetic from the outside but wasn't as pitiful on the inside. Dark tables, divans, and cushions took up most of the cramped space. Men lounged around platters of meat and flatbread, smoked hookahs, and drank. The rattle of voices and bawdy laughter boomed over the sitar's twang. Women in scant clothes danced between the tables, the brass coins of their headdresses glinting like gold. His gaze roved past the naked, black statue of the southern goddess—Uzzā—above the fire pit and to the walls lined with tinted liquor bottles, the wet dream of any man with a weakness for the false bliss of inebriation.

Settling in a private corner, he combed the horde for Jasir, his eyes cutting to a company of miners at a centre table, dealing a round of As-Nas. From his seat, Leviathan could see three of the old, faded cards in one of the miners' coal-smeared hands—the beastly figures of the ace, *as,* locked in a battle; the *bibi* with a child; and the lowest card, *lakat,* a couple of dancing girls.

"Welcome, Saheb," a woman said. The flirtatious voice came with a pair of tawny eyes. She wore the traditional dress of the lower *zaat* women and it hugged her curves like a second skin. The corners of her mouth pulled up in a perceptive smile. She was used to the attention. "What can I get you?"

"Tea. Black."

"Anything else?"

"No."

"I'll be right back with your tea, Saheb."

Leaning back in his seat, he watched the miners, the grey of his eyes shining below the hood. She returned with a tulip-shaped glass and a pitcher. "We don't see many higher *zaat* in here, Saheb," she ventured, pouring for him, eyes curious. "Are you passing through?"

"Something like that."

Her smile was an invitation. "Let me know if you need anything else." She gave him another long glance before she left his table.

One of the miners slammed his fists down on the wood and sent his cards flying. Five-ten, broad in build, clumsy by the look of how he manoeuvred ineptly between cards and coin. It could've been the result of the empty shot glasses next to him if it wasn't for his neutral complexion, which revealed he was still sober.

"Damned," the furious miner growled. "Damned."

"Not your night, Jasir," his playmate chuckled.

"Is it ever?" another chimed in.

"You up for a third round?"

"Deal me."

Knocking back his tea, Leviathan dropped a few copper coins on the table and stepped out in the alley. It stank of sewage and piss. He gave in to the urge for a cigarette, lit it, and inhaled, the muscles in his shoulders relaxing against the tavern's stone wall. Clamping his teeth on the cigarette, he spun a knife between his fingers.

Waiting.

The darkness in the alley would've bothered him once. Seemed like a lifetime ago. Cecilia hadn't exaggerated when she'd called him sensitive. As a kid, he used to be uncomfortable in crowded places and when exposed to loud noises, lights, even scents. They'd overstimulate him. He was so affected by atmospheres and other people's pain—like when the slaves were punished or somebody suffered in the camp—that it gave him sleepless nights of anxiety.

He was ruled by his fears to the point where he wouldn't let his mother go anywhere without him, making her promise to wake him up every morning before she left him in bed to bathe. His emotions always came in extremes. Fear, anger, love—he'd feel too much, too deeply, so she'd take him to her quarters, dim the lanterns, and tuck him under the blankets until he felt calm, safe.

Less breakable.

When he was sent to Verdite, everything changed. Suddenly, there was no sweet mother to cuddle him anymore. The Firawn had no patience for his sensitivities. He enrolled Leviathan in the military academy before he turned seven. The Guild was created to crush who you were and rebuild you as a soldier. The only way to survive was to become as ruthless as everybody else. You were taught how to read people—their weaknesses, their pain tolerance—and how to break them. The competition to emerge at the top, the pressure to kill and to prove yourself, the expectations from your superiors who recorded your every move, then decided your fate—it would've been more than he could handle if he hadn't toughened up.

Looking back, he didn't recognise the kid who cared too much, the kid who gripped his mother's skirt and shadowed her wherever she went. What would she say if she saw him now? With blood on his hands, cold in his heart, and darkness in his mind. He'd failed her in more ways than one. Now he tried his damnedest to make up for at least some of it while he searched for leads and battled dead ends.

It was selfish that he put his mind to retrieving the kids so he could live with the guilt of her death. No, not just that, but so he could prove he wasn't a villain to the powers that be who hadn't done shit to ease his path. Fate had dealt him this fucked-up hand, yet he'd still be penalised for having survived it however he could.

'*We must all pay for our sins.*'

He'd be paying for a long time then.

Something watched him from the alley's shadows. Tensing, he straightened. He felt the presence, an otherness like when the Ghaib were close, but he couldn't see it. *Ghameq*. It was always harder to distinguish them in the dark.

The door swung open and Jasir staggered out.

Crushing his cigarette under his boot, Leviathan vaulted himself up onto the tavern's roof, eyes fixed on Jasir as he leaped soundlessly from rooftop to rooftop. It wasn't a long journey. Jasir's worn boots tracked dirt to the creaky steps of a deprived house a short distance from the village. It looked deserted. No livestock, no crops. Nothing but the caving walls. Leviathan waited for Jasir to open the door. Then he dropped down, stepped in behind him, and kicked it shut.

Jasir turned, eyes bloodshot. "What the devils?" he shouted, fumbling for his dagger and swinging it at Leviathan.

Leaning away, Leviathan evaded his slash by an inch, measuring his strength, speed, and balance. When he lashed out again in a downward stab, Leviathan blocked his arm, landing a right hook in his face. Jasir grunted. Trapping his hand, Leviathan twisted it in a swift joint lock which bent Jasir over on a hiss and, taking advantage of Jasir's lost balance, brought up his knee in a diagonal strike that rammed into his ribs, breaking bone despite the restrained blow.

The dagger fell from Jasir's hand. It was one hell of a beauty. Black, stainless steel, straight blade. Between six or seven inches in length, Leviathan estimated, while Jasir groaned on the floor. It wasn't a dagger a coal miner should've been able to afford. He kicked it aside as Jasir scrambled for it.

Stumbling back on unsteady feet, Jasir came at him with his left fist. Leviathan shifted away from the line of his sloppy punch, bending his arm in another bone-cracking lock that buckled his knees, and spiralled him into a chokehold. Not giving him any time to struggle, Leviathan tightened his hold, applying pressure to Jasir's neck until the stubborn bull passed out. Dumping the miner in a chair, he removed the thick laces of Jasir's boots, using them to tie his ankles to the wooden legs.

The house consisted of one sparse chamber. A table, two chairs, and a wide sleeping mat occupied most of the tight space. The stench of mildew and waste spoiled the air. Dead flies floated in a bucket of dirty water. The fire pit looked like it'd never been cleaned out, ashes clogging it up, and the fractured door had a broken lock.

Leviathan picked up the bucket and threw the water in Jasir's face. Jerking upright, Jasir gasped for air like a drowning man, blinked, then glared. "Who the hell are you? What the fuck are you doing in my house?" he barked.

"Not much of a house, is it?" Leviathan nodded at the damaged lock. "Got any visitors lately?"

"What's it to you?"

"Good point."

Jasir's eyes narrowed to slits. "I don't know you," he snapped. Leviathan saw the wheels turning in his head, trying to figure out if Leviathan was one of the people to whom he likely owed coin. "You're not one of Faisal's hellions. Who are you? What do you want?"

"Information. I'm looking for a trader. Goes by the name Volos."

He tried to shrug but winced at the pain in his dislocated shoulder. "Don't know any traders. How the hell did you find me anyway? Who do you work for?"

Flipping up Jasir's dagger with the toe of his boot, Leviathan caught it on the fly. When he was done with this guy, he might just keep it. "You've got a busy mouth, Jasir, but you're not telling me anything useful."

"Look, you fuckhead—"

Leviathan rammed his boot on the chair between Jasir's legs with just enough force that the chair skated back, slamming into the wall and rattling Jasir's broken ribs. He roared in pain. He hadn't been stone-cold sober before, but he was now.

Bracing a hand on the back of the chair, Leviathan leaned down and levelled their eyes. "Tell me everything you know about Volos and his organ trade."

"He'd kill me if I talked," Jasir rasped.

"I'll kill you if you don't."

Jasir's lips peeled back. "You've got no fucking idea who you're dealing with. Volos makes those high and mighty Rangers look like little girls. He'll hunt you down, cut you open, and feed your innards to the fucking wolves."

"I'm shaking."

"You should be. Who told you about me?"

"You're a gambler, Jasir," Leviathan cautioned, his gaze unwavering. "Look at the hand you've been dealt. If I were you, I'd fold."

"Up yours."

"Let's try this one more time."

Leviathan yanked the scarf from Jasir's neck, rolled it, and shoved it violently inside his mouth. Jasir growled when Leviathan slammed his injured wrist down on the table, fingers splayed out, and panic invaded his eyes. Raising the dagger over his hand, Leviathan hammered the hilt against his index finger, crushing it with smooth, methodical precision. The miner's eyes crossed. He panted through his nose as Leviathan moved on to his middle finger to the sound of his guttural screams.

"Ready to talk?"

The miner glared.

Leviathan spun the dagger around, about to slice right through his finger. Making aggressive noises in his throat, Jasir tried to get Leviathan's attention before he chopped off his precious flesh. Tugging the gag from Jasir's mouth, Leviathan waited as the miner dragged in a few breaths and swallowed hard, the spittle hanging off his bottom lip.

"Volos wants the children for their organs," he wheezed.

"That much I know. Ever met Volos?"

He clenched his teeth against the pain. "No, I'm just one of the delivery guys. His handlers deal with the trade. We're given a location. We deliver. They take the stock somewhere else. From what I know, Volos likes to oversee the shipments personally."

Leviathan's jaw hardened. *Stock.* Like the kids were objects for sale. He crossed his arms with a tautness in his neck muscles. "Where do you deliver?"

"At random, isolated locations. It varies."

"When's the next trade?"

Moving his damaged hand, Jasir grimaced. "It happened last night. The stock would be relocated by now. You're too late," he snarled.

Dark, cold rage rose in Leviathan. The kids might've been relocated, but that didn't mean they'd crossed the sea yet. It sped up his internal clock. "When's the shipment due?" he inquired.

"Three days from now."

Three days. That bought him some time.

"Where can I find the handlers?"

"Volos' brothel. They oversee the sex trade, too."

"Location?"

"Makhmoor."

"Be more precise."

Jasir spat blood. "Queen's Chamber at Saheba's," he ground out.

"And you know all this how?"

"The handler I sell to offered me coin for delivering girls."

"I want the names of the handlers."

"I only know one. Name's Rado. He approves the trade and moves the stock."

"Describe Rado."

"Dark hair, green eyes. Got some ugly ass sideburns and talks like he's some big shit."

Leviathan leaned back against the table and it creaked under his weight. Every sex trade usually had a premise. Something that made the human trader's business different from his rival's. "How does Volos' sex trade work?"

Jasir coughed on a laugh. "Why? You interested?" Leviathan spun the dagger and his amusement fled. "It's—you show up with a good stock, offer it to the handler. If he approves, he pays you."

"What's a good stock?"

"Volos prefers girls between three and twenty, especially the tribal wenches and dancing whores from the temples. If they're virgin, he pays double. If they're damaged, he doesn't want them."

The mechanics of it started making sense. Prostitution was a legitimised business, normalised as an economic activity. Leviathan knew that. But the grim reality of it still made his jaw stiffen. Volos wasn't just prostituting women. He was prostituting kids. The more Leviathan learned about the sick asshole, the more he wanted to hunt him down and skin him to the bone.

His features hardened, his stare implacable.

Jasir gnashed his teeth. "Look. You don't know shit about how we survive, you self-righteous son of a bitch. Don't you think I see your leather and shine? You're fucking higher *zaat*. Why're you even interested in this? It's got nothing to do with you. Who the hell are you?"

"I appreciate your cooperation, Jasir. It's nothing personal."

Staring up at Leviathan, Jasir shuddered, understanding dawning on his face. "Hold on, I—I told you everything I know. Why don't you just turn around and—"

"That's not an option," Leviathan interrupted, straightening now. "I don't leave loose ends, Jasir. It keeps me up at night."

"Wait a fucking second—"

"Add in the fact that you'll send a message to Rado, tell him all about our little date once I'm out the door—" he continued, "—and you see how I can't let that happen."

"Wait—please—I have—"

Leviathan stabbed him in the throat. Quick and clean. His body jerked, his head lolled to the side, and he went still. The blade gleamed red for the life taken.

Changing his mind about keeping the dagger, Leviathan tossed it on the table, turning toward the door.

And froze.

A kid stood on the threshold, face pale, his hands clutched around a kite, and a dark-haired woman appeared behind him.

"*Jasir*," the woman cried. "Jasir!"

CHAPTER 22

AN UNKIND FEVER seared beneath Roma's skin. She roused at dawn with a burdened heart, an illness in her blood, and Caliana's and Ara's bright laughter resonating out in the courtyard to one of Yoshi's crude anecdotes. Turning onto her side in the sensitive morning glow, she squeezed her eyes closed, barring the world just for a moment longer.

Tomorrow night, she would enter her second patronship.

Her throat twisted into a knot.

A cleansing ritual was performed on her last night. The Kāhinah had chanted in Middle Khansāri, pouring purifying milk over Roma to rinse her fortune to the relief of Amma and the villagers. A few days had passed since the fountain debacle. Sādin Saheb hadn't come to Lamiapur, nor had he summoned Amma to discuss the consequences, and it unnerved Roma. She couldn't have been pardoned without punishment. The insult of the higher *zaat* was as severe as an insult to the gods. She wanted to speak to Amma, but Amma refused to even look at her, and Binti and Hani never opened their mouths about anything.

She was forced to wait and anticipate the worst.

When she was dedicated to Mother Lamia as a child, the villagers had treated her like a goddess. They had decorated her shell, carried her in an ornamented chair, and told her that she was blessed, but it was nothing more than a mother's lie whispered in the dark to soothe a frightened child. Women weren't goddesses. It was apparent in how people consulted the Kāhinah for rituals to ensure the birth of sons; in how they buried their newborn daughters alive in the Lonesome Forest beyond the plains; and in how a father was subjected to contempt and ridicule if he chose not to follow the custom, like Jirani when his wife birthed him a daughter. It was visible in how women were forced to raise the red ribbons for sustenance and were named 'characterless whores' by the same men who darkened their thresholds come nightfall.

The bells on Roma's anklets chinked as she stepped out in Lamiapur's courtyard. Her sisters had prepared platters of adornments blessed for the preauction ceremonies. Caliana poured coconut oil in a small bowl while Ara stirred the henna in another. Their faces were alight with excitement. Rawiya Mai perched beneath the willow with a happily bouncing Aimi in her lap. Glancing at the old woman, Roma faltered, needing her tales, if only to ignore the impending doom. She always experienced an intimate connection to the tales Rawiya Mai spun as if they could have happened in front of her eyes.

Hani approached her with hurried steps. "Are you up at last, Roma Saheba?" she said acerbically. "Come. We're about to start."

Meriel tapped her fingers on a hand drum, spurring their sisters to sing. Chirag and Goldie danced, their laughter mingling with the ballads. Roma lowered herself on a short stool and Sunbel loosened her braid until her thick tresses tumbled down her back to brush the ground. She dreaded this ritual. They would have to touch her. She would have to bear it. Every inch of her skin recoiled at the thought of it.

"Binti," Amma said from where she lounged on a *charpai* with her hookah. Her nostrils expanded to release smoke. "Open the gate."

Women brought in platters of food as a tribute for Roma's ritual. They were familiar faces. Wives and sisters of men who wanted the favours of the gods through her blessings. Pregnant women asked her to touch their bellies for sons, and Roma moved without thought in a painful cycle that continued into the afternoon.

When the gate closed behind the last woman, Roma's kaftan was damp with fever sweat. Caliana massaged coconut oil into her hair to soften it. Binti expertly painted swirling henna patterns on her hands, forearms, and feet. The overly sweet scent nauseated her. She never liked the smell of henna. Binti finished at last, and Roma returned to her chamber. She wanted to lie down, but she squatted in a corner instead and stared at the colourful threadwork on her sleeping mat.

"You look ill," Yoshi remarked from the threshold.

Roma didn't glance up as she stepped over to a pail near the chest, removed the cover, and dipped a cup inside it. She held it out to Roma. Accepting the cup, Roma touched it to her lips. The water doused her parched mouth, but she had to force it down her throat.

Yoshi watched her with folded arms. "There's something you should know. I overheard Binti and Hani talking about your auction last night after you went to sleep. Amma has promised you to Alan Saheb."

Roma's eyes snapped to Yoshi's. "What?" Her fingers tightened around the cup and then started to tremble. "You're wrong. You must've misunderstood—"

"I know what I heard."

"Amma would *never* do that to me."

"If you believe that, you're dafter than I thought."

She shook her head in denial while her mind struggled for reason. Amma might possess an innate aptitude to make harsh decisions, but she couldn't be so cruel as to hand Roma over to that monster again. The undertow of repressed memories dragged her downward. It was as if she stepped outside her own shell to watch a child version of herself scream and sob for Amma while she was tormented in her patron's bed.

Stumbling to her feet, Roma ran past Yoshi and across the courtyard, climbing the temple stairs two at a time to the antechamber where Amma was lighting oil lamps. She stopped to catch her breath. The light of the moon pressed against her back, framing her in a pallid glow, and her nose itched from the sandalwood incense burning on the dais. Sweat speckled her fevered skin and trickled down her neck to dampen her kaftan.

"Your auction is merely hours away," Amma said without turning around. The brass *jadai* pinned along her braid glittered. "You should be resting."

"Would you have told me?" Roma asked in a voice that trembled with anger. "Or would you have had me discover it when I was in his bed?"

Amma was silent a moment. Then she sighed.

"It would've been better that way."

Tears pricked behind Roma's eyes. Betrayal. An utter sense of betrayal consumed her. She tipped her head to the side in a shattered motion. "How could you do this to me? You know what he—*you* know. Why would you send me to him again? Is what he did to me not enough?"

"What did he do? *You* used a knife on your face, *ladoba*. You were the one who scarred yourself. What did he do other than play his part as your patron?"

Speak. Her mind pleaded with her to voice what he had done to her. What he had taken from her. But doubt and shame stirred within her. Hadn't she stood at her own auction? With her lips sealed as she was sold. When was she a victim? Did a victim follow her violator to his bed? Did she lie down and let him touch her? Was it even a violation when she was silent?

Amma arched her eyebrows. "*Kāy*? You don't have an answer, or you're not sure if it's the right answer?" She clicked her tongue. "Does it matter whether it's him or someone else? You'll have to serve all the same *na*."

A fire ignited within Roma at Amma's apathetic words. It wasn't a fever. Yet it seared as one.

"I won't do it."

Amma laughed, long and shrill, and then stopped.

"What did you say?"

"I won't—"

Her hand cracked against Roma's cheek and Roma fell down from the force of it. "You won't do it?" Amma repeated in a soft voice. "Won't?" She slapped her again, and Roma tasted blood, but she didn't whimper. Gripping Roma's cheeks in one hand, Amma turned her face upward. "Three years. Three years I let you to run free because of the Kāhinah's prediction, and you think you have wings now? *Aikā, ladoba.* If you cause me trouble, I'll sever those imaginary wings. You won't as much as levitate, *samajalē*?"

"Then sever them," Roma rasped.

Grabbing the top of her braid, Amma yanked back Roma's head and her scalp screamed for relief. She looked right into Amma's seething eyes. "Don't provoke me, Roma. Don't force me to summon the village men and drag you to your patron's bed. I'll do it if need be."

When Amma released her and started to leave, Roma caught her *lehenga*. "Amma, I'll do anything you ask of me, but the auction—I can't survive it again," she pleaded.

"Then you'll die. But you won't refuse your patron."

"I can endure any other punishment—"

"Even if you shaved your head, Sādin Saheb would have you serve Alan Saheb. It's done, Roma. Embrace the sacred will of the Mother Goddess—"

"It's not *she* who sells me to a monster."

"*Khallas,* Roma." Curling her upper lip, Amma snatched Roma's chin. "You won't ruin what our ancestors have shed blood and tears to protect. You won't endanger Lamiapur. You will, however, stand at the auction tomorrow night like a good girl."

"Endanger Lamiapur?" Roma stared up at her. "What do you mean?"

"You know what I mean. You know whose mercy we live on."

Roma parted her lips and a tremulous breath escaped her. "We're *lamiadasis,*" she said, repeating the mantra she was raised with, even as it singed like a lie on her tongue. "We're—We're the sacred vessels of Mother Lamia and our patrons are the embodiments of Lord Biran." When Amma laughed, Roma heard a bitterness so harsh she wanted to wince and cover her ears. It resembled the claws of the wind in her dreams of the banyan. "What are we, Amma?"

"What does it matter? We are what we are with or without a name." Turning on her heels, Amma looked at the statue of Mother Lamia. "We should be grateful. We could've easily been the Flags or the brothel whores."

'Temple whore,' the higher *zaat* woman had said.

"Prostitutes," Roma whispered. She looked down at her palms, at the symbols of the gods on her skin—and she realised that she had always known it in some suppressed part of her. Nothing ever felt right in Lamiapur, because it never *was* right. Hadn't she wondered more than once why they were exempted from taxes, but had to deliver coin as a tribute to the gods when their service was supposed to be of a sanctified nature? Didn't she see the likeness between Thana's life and her own? The only distinction was that the bidders in the world of *dēvadasis* were called patrons.

Perhaps the truth should have liberated her somehow, but a numbness spread within her instead. She drew in a shallow breath. "The coin from our patronships—it's not a tribute to the gods."

"The villagers pay their taxes to the Firawn. We pay ours to Sādin Saheb. It's the same," Amma insisted in a vexed tone. "This isn't the epoch of Jehangir Khan where prostitution was outlawed and coinless women cared for. Where we could have respectful positions and own properties. *Dēvadasis* might've been revered temple dancers once upon a time, but we haven't been for too long, and never will be again. We must earn our keep in the temples."

Roma rose on her feet with renewed strength. There was hope. It sparked like small embers in the ashes of their past. If they were once temple dancers, not slaves of men, then their fate wasn't written in stone. Kanoni said one had to take a chance to change one's circumstances. It was true. Why should they remain in a prison when there was the possibility of freedom?

Choice meant to write one's own fate.

"We could leave Lamiapur, Amma," Roma said in a breathless voice. "We could live in the desert like the Desert Clans."

"Nonsense."

"Amma—"

"We must stay. It's the fate of our *zaat*."

"Fate has nothing to do with—"

"Don't you dare provoke Sādin Saheb and the villagers with your blasphemy. They're frustrated enough as it is because of this heedless drought." Squinting her eyes, Amma stepped closer to Roma. "You spilled a sacred wine, *ladoba*. *Dēvadasis* have been burned alive for less. You'll stand at the auction and you won't breathe a word of this to anyone."

How could she live on as a *lamiadasi* when she knew it wasn't her fate? And how could she keep the truth from her sisters?

"You want to continue a deception—"

"I want us to survive," Amma snapped. "Your sisters believe everything they do serves a divine purpose. It's their conviction that pulls them through this life; the conviction they've gained the favours of our gods and will be rewarded in the end. Don't shatter that illusion."

This was what Amma meant when she said lies and illusions were how humans survived. Shaking her head, Roma looked at the cobra pendant around Amma's neck. "No matter how painful the truth is, it's still freedom, Amma. Your illusion is a gilded cage," she said with a vehement shine in her eyes.

"This gilded cage has sustained you. Remember that."

"At what cost?"

Amma caught her arms and shook her. "Sādin Saheb made it very clear to me that he won't tolerate any more trouble from Lamiapur. Think about your sisters, Roma. Think about Chirag."

A habituated fear churned within Roma at Chirag's name. It swirled just like in her dreams when she watched the banyan bleed. Amma had conceded that the sacred nature of their service was a lie. It never existed. If they wanted, they could refuse. If they wanted, they could leave. Roma could take Chirag far away from this place. Sunbel didn't have to birth her unborn child in

Lamiapur, and Goldie and Aimi didn't have to become *lamiadasis*. Yet fear of the consequences of a rebellion against Sādin Saheb and their village dimmed the searing flame in Roma until it was all but extinguished.

"Their circumstances won't change, even if you told them the truth," Amma persisted. "They'd still have to serve. They'd have to endure. Your sisters would never choose persecution over the safe walls of Lamiapur. That is if they believed you." She lifted her chin with a self-assured curve to her lips. It struck Roma then that she *wanted* to keep them all in Lamiapur. She wanted the cage. Perhaps because she had lived her entire life inside it and never tasted freedom, or perhaps because she had completed her service and now reigned like a queen in her own queendom.

Anguish throttled Roma's anger and buried it. She peered at the dais where the oil lamps burned, unblinking against their sharp glares, and struggled to unravel her thoughts. What was she to do with the truth? Should she burden her sisters with it? Should she deceive them as well?

Amma patted her sore cheek and Roma jolted at the pain. "You might not be the brightest girl, but you'll choose the path that'll secure your sisters' peace of mind and safety. Go to sleep now. You want to be well-rested for the auction," she said, strutting toward the temple stairs as if nothing had happened, as if she hadn't just shredded the world Roma knew.

"Why have you told me the truth?" Roma asked in a hollow voice without turning around. "Why not let me live with the illusion, too?"

"Because you never believed it, *ladoba*."

Roma swallowed past the throbbing pain in her throat. With all her harshness, her edges, and her schemes, Amma was the only mother she had known. She was the woman who fed and clothed her; the one who raised her. There would always be a cord between them that she couldn't sever, and so Amma's careless words stabbed her heart. Was she only a sacrifice to secure Lamiapur's peace and Amma's position? Was she nothing more to her?

Amma glanced over her shoulder. "It was a matter of time before you uncovered the truth on your own. And I'd rather have you uncover it on my terms."

CHAPTER 23

Leviathan never denied he liked violence. The cracking sound of a punch. That solid friction and dark hum of power. The obscene spill of blood. It was an old dance, raw and real. He used to be too scared to hit a kid twice his size, and then it was the only thing that made sense. It became instinctual. All that mattered was how pounding on somebody obliterated everything else.

Combat came easily to him once the Firawn beat the fear out of him. He was a quick learner; fast, focused, persistent. Ruthless. It was wrestling at six, hand-to-hand at nine, swordsmanship at eleven, before the blades and crossbows were replaced with guns. As a Trainee, he had to learn the mechanics of every weapon available, and he had to learn it under the Firawn's attentive eye. Mistakes meant punishment. The Firawn didn't punish lightly. He understood the crux of life as a kid in the dire hours he spent locked up inside a rice chest until he proved that darkness and hunger didn't touch him, until he purged his fears to the Firawn's satisfaction.

Survival. It always came down to survival.

When he became a Junior Recruit, he was sent to live in a dorm with four Senior Recruits. It was like being chucked into a den of wolves. That he was the Firawn's blood never granted him immunity. It made him a bigger target. He was a rumoured *bezaat,* and tribal blood wasn't welcome. The Senior Recruits wanted to show him his place in the hierarchy of soldiers, so they shoved him around, pissed on his cot, acted like bullies with masked inferiority complexes, but he was patient until they cornered him one night. Things turned bloody. He killed one, incapacitated three, and ended up with several broken bones himself, yet he emerged an alpha, just like the Firawn wanted—and the bastards never howled at him again.

That was survival.

He crossed the line between life and death, between mercy and intolerance. With execution after execution of assumed rebels, he started losing pieces of his soul, and it'd be a lie if he said the fear his name evoked didn't feed some demented part of him.

How did you come back from something like that?

The answer was—you didn't.

Innocent blood never washed. He might've survived the Firawn's brutal upbringing, but it'd cost him. Being an executioner was a habit now, like fighting. He'd forgotten it for a moment until he met the terrorised stare of a kid whose father he'd just tortured and stabbed in the throat.

Not survival. Brutality, that.

As he walked to the camp, he thought about the lives he'd taken. He didn't deserve to be near anybody pure like Mai, yet he still prowled north of the camp. Drawn, denied, and desperate.

Pathetic.

Seth already waited for him. Squatting on the ground, he hacked at the dirt with a branch. He'd been here for a while, Leviathan suspected, eager to start his lessons. He took a moment to study him. Seth was a skinny kid with a mob of hair that needed a cut to ease his vision, but he was tough like his brothers and sisters in the camp. There was a unique strength in the clans, in the way they carried on loss after loss, and Leviathan wanted to keep that strength alive.

It was hope, even if it wasn't enough to save lives.

"Hey, kid," he called. "You ready?"

Jumping to his feet, Seth turned around. "*Hō*, Bhau." His eyes used to be a clear brown. They were dark and broken now.

Leviathan signalled for him to step closer. "Hand-to-hand combat isn't about size. It's about skill. It's about speed, mobility, defensive stances, and offensive strikes. With me so far?"

Seth frowned. "*Hō*, Bhau," he said intently.

Taking a defensive stance, Leviathan pushed his fist against Seth's solar plexus. "First thing you need is proper balance. If I'm putting my weight behind every jab, it means I'm off balance, and my opponent can pull me in.

Try it." Imitating his stance, Seth pushed a fist against Leviathan's abdomen, using his weight, and Leviathan grabbed his wrist, yanking him forward. His feet skipped over each other to regain balance. Catching his elbow, Leviathan blocked his fall. "You don't want to move anything but your punching arm, feet solidly planted on the ground."

He demonstrated again with some restraint, jabbing swiftly, and Seth staggered back, eyes going round with understanding. "I felt that," he rasped, rubbing a hand over the spot. "I felt it all the way in."

"You good?"

"*Hō*, Bhau."

"Second thing you need is proper breathing. It doesn't matter if you're the one punching or getting punched—you want to exhale with every strike."

"Why's that?"

"Controlled breathing keeps you balanced and gives your movements energy. Show me your fist." Seth clenched his hand and Leviathan tapped it. "Don't curl your fingers like that. Make sure your connection point is a flat surface. Flat means less damage to your hand and wrist." Raising his hands, palms out, Leviathan nodded. "Strike."

Seth punched. The sound was shallow.

"Lift your arm. That's it," Leviathan guided. "Relax your shoulder. Relax it." He squeezed Seth's shoulder and gave it a firm shake until Seth loosened up. "Move your arm back from your upper body and swing from your shoulder. Strike on a sharp exhale." Seth punched again on a harsh breath. The sound changed, but it still lacked depth. He had grace and speed. With more muscle on him, he'd generate the right force behind the blows. "Anchor your hips, rotate your upper body. Strike. Speed it up. Contact and retract. Don't think, Seth, feel it."

Seth was working up a good amount of sweat. He practised the technique on Leviathan's palms, his face scrunched up in concentration. He'd forget to breathe in between hits, then remember it, and regulate it quickly.

The *smack* of his strikes changed.

Leviathan's mouth curved. "You hear that?" he asked.

"It sounds different," Seth panted. "Deeper."

"Because you're getting it right. Get one of the other boys to spar with you every day."

"Are we done? I'm not tired yet."

"No, but your muscles are. For core strength, I want you doing sit-ups and planks. For the upper body, push-ups and bear crawls. And for the legs, squats and lunges. Run laps and climb trees. Breathe through your nose when you train, not your mouth, until it's a habit without strain."

"*Hō*, Bhau."

"You did well, kid."

There was embarrassment on Seth's face. He wiped at his sweat with a torn sleeve. "I want to be strong enough to protect Sara Tai and Mai and everybody else in the camp," he said, his voice carefully bland and Leviathan pretended not to hear the shame underlying it. "When the Wardens came for my sister, I couldn't protect her."

Leviathan's gaze skimmed the camp. "There's a difference between being strong and being brave. You can build up muscle, Seth, but building up courage is the hard part. Teaching yourself to be firm in the face of danger, to choose fight over flight, requires another kind of strength. The strength of the heart. You have it."

"How do you know?"

"You punched a Warden. You came up to me at Khiraa's grave and asked me to teach you how to fight."

"I was still scared."

"Fear can drive you, or it can cripple you. You made your choice."

"Are you ever scared?"

"All the time."

"What scares you?"

The darkness residing in him, the absence of humanity.

He clasped Seth's shoulder in a companionable squeeze. "It's almost dawn. Mai will worry. Go on back." As Seth ran back to the camp, Leviathan watched him go. If he could help the kid channel his grief and rage, Seth would be able to hold his own in a fight.

Sensing Malev's and Junho's approach, he checked his emotions out of habit more than need. He hadn't told them about Jasir yet. The ride back to the city a couple of nights ago after the encounter had set his mind straight. If he wanted to find the kids before it was too late, he couldn't afford to dwell on Jasir's family. He'd done what was necessary to achieve his objective. The world wasn't a goddamn wonderland where actions founded on the right moral motives resulted in the optimal result.

So, he'd calculated the most effective courses of action and last night he'd taken Junho's map and left for Makhmoor alone. Scouting out Saheba's in person, he'd assessed Volos' security, familiarised himself with each crack in the brothel's outer structure. The problem was it consisted of more than a hundred chambers divided on several levels—and one of them was the Queen's Chamber. He could penetrate the security, torture the information out of a guard, but it'd be a waste of time. There was a faster way in. It'd require minimal groundwork, a smaller chance of raising suspicion, and cut a clear path to Volos.

"We're running out of time, Bhau," Junho said. "The shipment's tonight. What's the plan?"

"I'm going into Saheba's as a lower *zaat*. To trade."

If he'd gauged Volos right, he was a confident bastard, but he wouldn't risk rival traders finding out about his shipment locations. There was a chance he'd be in the Queen's Chamber during the sex trade. If he was—Leviathan would single him out. A wolf pack always reacted to the alpha's presence. If he wasn't—Leviathan would still have identified the handler. All he'd need to do was follow Rado and his men to the shipment location.

It wouldn't end with Volos. Traders were middlemen like handlers, or removing them would shut down entire trades. No, there were backers involved. Powerful people who profited off a widespread socio-economic system like prostitution.

And he wanted the names of those investors.

"The only thing they trade in that place—" Malev said slowly, "—is women and children."

The words hung in the silence between them. Shrugging off his companion's long stare, Leviathan said nothing. Malev didn't have to like it, but it was the most efficient method to get inside Saheba's without expending time and resources they didn't have. He wasn't about to let moral questions block his path. There was always a risk. He'd considered different scenarios and devised alternative courses of action in case he had to ditch his initial plan, but some things you just had to play by ear.

Either way, he wouldn't fail.

"Who're you using?"

He almost winced at Malev's choice of words. Wiping the emotion from his face, he concealed it behind a mask of indifference, even though masks weren't of much use around Malev who tended to read people's stillness, not their emotions.

"The *dēvadasi.*" Her name was on Leviathan's tongue, still he took his time saying it. "Roma."

"Maybe we should find another way."

"There's no time."

"Using some girl is extreme, even for us, brother."

"She's our way in," Leviathan said, his tone clipped, and Malev's frown deepened. He was quiet, but it was a loaded silence, hanging over Leviathan's head, the weight pressing down on him. He had his reasons for choosing her. She was a *dēvadasi.* It'd draw the interest of Volos' handler and get him close. She was scarred. It'd ensure the handler wouldn't want her once he got a good look at her. And she was strong. She wouldn't break from the experience.

"It's a good plan, Bhau," Junho agreed. "I'll go in with you."

"I need you and Malev on the outside."

"But, Bhau. You shouldn't go in alone. Let me—"

"No."

"But—"

"Do you have to fucking argue about everything?" Leviathan said between his teeth, the temper hot under the ice in his voice. Junho clamped his mouth shut. Glaring at him, Leviathan chewed back the anger. "Focus on your damn part."

Malev stepped closer. "Roma isn't the only one I'm worried about in this," he said, eyes focused on Leviathan.

Leviathan's relaxed tone was laced with cynicism. "If you're worried about my soul, it's already long past retrieval. And as for yours? I don't need you to do the dirty work, Malev. I just need you to watch my back."

"You don't have to ask for that."

"Then what's the problem?"

"What happened in Kantalaa, brother? You've been different ever since your return."

Turning his back to them both, Leviathan let his eyes wander over the steppe. A restless muscle ticked in his jaw as he considered telling Malev the truth. It'd cut too close to his companion's sense of honour, the emotions which ran beneath it, but a self-destructive part of Leviathan wanted to see how far he could push Malev before he decided to walk away from him.

"I killed Jasir," he told him.

"Figured you would. Leaving him alive would cost us the children."

"He had a wife and kid."

As expected, Malev went still, but it was enough. His reaction twisted like a knife in Leviathan's gut, yet he held his gaze, cool, levelled, observing the flicker of anger and disappointment. It took a great deal of self-control for Leviathan not to flinch. Junho glanced between them and rubbed a hand over his head with unease. Malev's past wasn't a secret. He had never been a saint, but he had his principles, and they were simple. You didn't mess around with somebody's family. You didn't rip apart somebody's home.

"Did you know?" Malev asked quietly.

"Does it matter?"

"You didn't know."

Leviathan stared toward the golden line of dawn, irritated, pissed at himself, at Malev. "Don't try to reason it out just to prove I'm not as dark as the deed. You and I both know I would've killed him either way."

"What you did as the Blade is in the past. You're not the same person you were three years ago."

"I'm exactly that person."

"No, you're not."

Leviathan shot him an exasperated look. He wouldn't admit it out loud, but standing in that house, he'd searched for signs of a family, and had been too quick to decide Jasir had none. Seeing that kid, his shocked face, the horror in his eyes—Leviathan had fled like a coward. Maybe one day somebody would corner him like he'd cornered Jasir, pass their judgement, and bleed him out.

The irony of it would be fitting.

"I don't have a problem taking lives, Malev, I don't think twice about it. Whether they have wives and kids doesn't play into the equation for me. Those Wardens I killed? They had families, too."

"They would've raped again."

"And Jasir would've sold kids again."

Malev nodded. "Right," he agreed. "What're we disagreeing about?"

"You thinking Jasir's family would've changed what I did to him."

"It would've."

"That kid was Hashaan's age."

It was a straight hit. Painful. He saw it in Malev's eyes when they blanched. He was sorry about it, too, but his companion needed to be reminded of what kind of person he was because he'd forgotten it.

Locking his jaw, Malev moved toward him and looked him in the eye. "Hashaan is the reason I *know* you wouldn't have done what you did to him," he said in a lowered voice.

Feeling like an asshole, Leviathan said nothing.

"Bhau," Junho said hesitantly. "Zuberi."

Turning around, Leviathan followed his line of sight. The slave kid raced across the steppe toward them. He was a few years older than Seth but shorter and skinnier. "Bhau Saheb," he panted, skidding to a stop and bending over to clasp his knees.

"Take a deep breath, Zuberi."

The kid shook his head, the sweat rolling down his face. "I've got a message for you from Firawn Sai, Bhau Saheb. He wants to see you in Ghada before noon."

It looked like the consequences of Leviathan's actions had caught up.

Finally.

CHAPTER 24

Roma dwelled in a shadowed corner of the practice hall, listening to the laughter of her sisters in the courtyard and watching the gods and *dēvadasis* on the stained screens. For centuries a sham was sustained, the pitch of oblivion cultivated until truths and lies melded as one and cautionary phrases founded on fables shaped their belief. She realised now that the cacophony within her existed without her. It had endured in all the *dēvadasis* before her and it would endure in all the *dēvadasis* after her. She was but a small, insignificant piece of a larger arrangement enforced by countless covetous Sādin Sahebs over time.

Fate was an excuse. It was a manacle that enchained one to passivity. It had a grip on one's mind and spirit, convincing one to remain shackled out of fear. There was no peace in understanding certain incidents in her life hadn't been within her power to change, but within the power of others, because she was still the one to bear the consequences. Would she have chosen a different path had she known what she knew now, or would she have convinced herself of the lie because it was safe?

"Roma?" Sunbel stepped inside the practice hall. "We're waiting. Come out."

Drawing in a deep breath, Roma rose on her feet, following Sunbel outside where her sisters sang ceremonial ballads. Platters of polished adornments, vermillion fabrics, and scented oils sat in a circle on a white sheet. Amma reclined on her *charpai* with a hand curled around the mouthpiece of her hookah. Her expression was proud. Roma didn't know what she hoped to see on Amma's face, but it wasn't pride, and she couldn't ignore how Amma's indifference affected her.

Sunbel, Caliana, and Yoshi circled Roma with a blanket to cover her and Roma slipped out of her kaftan. Nudging Roma down on the short stool, Hani poured rosewater over her head. The cold liquid cascaded over her naked shoulders and her teeth chattered while she was scrubbed raw with a pumice stone. When Hani dipped her fingers in the lavender oil, Roma swallowed a thick lump in her throat. This was the part she dreaded the most. Sunbel sent her a sympathetic smile as Hani massaged the oil into her skin. The unwanted touch made her want to crawl out of her shell, but she clamped her teeth together and detached herself from the moment—or she might begin to scream like a hysterical child.

Spreading out Roma's hair, Hani held an incense burner under the damp tresses, steeping them in the lavender-scented steam. Roma concentrated on Aimi's laughter rather than the swelling illness in her belly as Hani dressed her in a backless *choli* and a *lehenga* with gold *zardosi* threadwork on the skirt. The blanket was dropped. Caliana coiled Roma's hair into an elegant knot and pinned a hair ornament with dipping chains in the centre.

"Bring the other ornaments," Hani ordered. "Be careful with them."

A gold-plated choker embedded with a range of pearls and stones, and a long neckpiece rounding on a pendant were placed around Roma's neck. Caliana fastened chandelier-shaped earpieces on her earlobes and a pearl-studded *nath* in her nose. The double-chained *mathapatti* was settled along her hairline. Hani slipped the bangles onto her wrists and tied a thin beaded chain around her waist. Each ornament felt like another shackle to hold her down.

The afternoon sun began to lower in the horizon.

Leaving the hand drum, Binti came over to draw mythological patterns in gold above Roma's eyebrows and down her temples to the corners of her cheekbones, stopping near the black-inked symbols of her *zaat*. She dusted Roma's brow bone and eyelids in gold, lined her eyes with kohl, and painted sharp wings that made them appear even wider. Her lips were dyed the colour of pomegranate seeds to harmonise with the red shade of the fabric. Roma slid her adorned feet into a pair of slippers embroidered with gold threadwork, and Hani lifted one of the layers of her veil to pin it on the crown of her head.

Goldie clapped her hands. "You look pretty, Tai," she gushed with an excited smile, dashing over and touching the ornaments on Roma with a longing sigh.

"Soft as silk, sharp as steel," Binti praised. "Who'll notice the scars with those eyes?"

"I'll wear what Tai's wearing when I'm auctioned," Goldie said, spinning toward Amma. "Won't I, Amma? Won't I?"

Amma laughed and patted Goldie's cheek. "Of course you will, *ladoba.* We'll decorate you like a princess. Hani, let the villagers know their *lamia-dasi* is prepared for her departure. She'll step out once she has sought her blessings from Mother Lamia." She turned toward Roma. "*Jā*, Roma. We'll wait outside."

Gathering the folds of her *lehenga*, Roma climbed the temple stairs, her adornments chinking and clinking with her movements. She looked at the returned statue of Mother Lamia. The polished bronze gleamed in the billowing light from the oil lamps on the dais among the artificial marigold blossoms tipped with red. She didn't kneel before the Mother Goddess tonight. She wouldn't. Why should she bow down and beseech her? Prayers never aided humans. None prayed more than Ghanima Mai, yet her people suffered the most.

A keening noise disrupted the silence. Roma turned around as Nilo came out of the shadows. She shook her hand in a repetitive motion that could have been excitement or frustration, pacing back and forth in the antechamber, until Roma stepped in her path and forced herself to touch Nilo's shoulders to still her.

"What's wrong, Nilo?"

Nilo wouldn't look her in the eyes, but she made another shrill noise in her throat and then tapped a brass hairpin against Roma's forearm. When Roma took it from her, Nilo walked back into the practice hall, and the noise in her throat faded with her steps. The hairpin was beautiful. The head was carved in the shape of desert sages and a brass sheath with intricate scrollwork concealed the narrow pin. Roma curled her fingers around it, removing the sheath, and stared down at a long blade.

Her heartbeat staggered.

She wondered where Nilo had come into the possession of this. What had made her offer it to Roma? She wanted to follow Nilo and ask her about it, but she remained in the antechamber and traced the desert sages with her henna-saturated fingertips. She thought of the hours she had spent fantasising about what it would feel like to slaughter the demon that haunted her. It was all a lie. Their service, their *zaat.* No divine power bound her. For once she felt a freedom to choose and saw another path stretch out before her. She would take it. She would accept Nilo's present, and she would carve out her own fate with it.

Reaching up, she slid the hairpin into her knot, so only the desert sages were visible, and deserted the temple. A high chorus of singing women surrounded her as she walked in the procession, stepping on blossoms, her pulse calm, her senses numbed, and her mind closed to the colours and sounds. The rigid presence of the blade in her hair soothed her. Perhaps she should have been frightened, but she felt removed from it all, as if it wasn't her heart pounding within her chest, nor her lungs pushing out her breath.

Was this how Khiraa felt when she took her own life?

Sādin Saheb performed the ritual in Biranpur's courtyard, sprinkling blessed water on her as the custom demanded. The *birandasis* heaved over a struggling camel. Roma placed her hand on its head as Sādin Saheb chanted, pointing the blade of his ceremonial dagger toward the skies before cutting open the camel's throat. The roaring animal juddered, collapsing onto the ground. Thick blood flowed from the gaping gash, and the metallic tang of it permeated the air. The *birandasis* sliced open the camel's belly to pull out its organs as offerings for Lord Biran.

Roma entered the Grand Temple alone with Sādin Saheb. It hadn't changed since her last auction. Flickering torches illuminated the elaborate carvings of the children of Lord Biran. Her eyes absorbed the familiar contour of Lord Mawt, God of Death, his stare as black as the titanic feathered wings that sprang from his shoulders. Souls of the dead writhed in his unyielding claws. She let her fingers brush over them and trailed Sādin Saheb into the ceremonial auction chamber.

Twelve statues of Lord Biran's oldest children lined the walls, towering over her like a Panchayat deciding her fate. Gliding to the circle of oil lamps, she stopped in the heart of it, waiting while Sādin Saheb spread a veil outside the circle for the coin the patrons would leave. He would count each bid, scribble it on a piece of paper with the patron's name, and the patron with the highest bid would take her with him tonight—or so it would have been if she wasn't promised to Alan Saheb.

But it would all change tonight. It was only fair the one who ruined her should restore her.

With his lifeblood.

CHAPTER 25

"YOUR WEAPONS, SAHEB," the Warden said, eyes smug. Leviathan drew the knives from his leather bracers, tossing them to him without a warning, and he fumbled to catch them out of the air. Shifting on his feet under Leviathan's stare, he stacked the knives on the rack against the stone wall. "You may proceed, Saheb. The Copper, however—"

"I'd be very careful now," Leviathan interrupted.

The Warden's chin jutted out, but he kept his mouth shut. Wisely so. Malev removed his gun. Surrendering all weapons outside the main part of the palace was protocol, even though Ghada was one of the few locations in the West Strip where foreign weapons like their imported guns were harmless because of remnants of magic still in the earth. Crews after crews were sent into the Sleeping Forest—a wood at the edge of Ghada which showed signs of living magic with its vibrant tones—but those who entered never returned. It spoke volumes of the kind of magic existing there, and it drove the Firawn mad that he couldn't access it.

The Warden stepped aside with some haughtiness. Leviathan quelled the urge to ram an elbow in his self-important face and climbed the steps. He'd arrived two hours before noon and, as he expected, the Firawn made him wait in a precinct of the Palace of Mirrors until it was late into the afternoon. It set him on edge because now he wouldn't make it back to Ferozi before nightfall. The Firawn tended to yammer for hours about things he had zero interest in. It was about the power balance. The Firawn liked to control the conversation. He decided when it was over. He enjoyed that he could make you sit there and listen to him, sweat over when he'd drop the hammer on you, and Leviathan knew he'd be trapped with him for a while.

It was mental torture.

Leviathan walked out on the terrace overlooking the central courtyard. Slaves in brown trimmed the gardens and *bandis* in black moved through the archways of the palace. It stood thirty feet tall in all its ancient glory—a trace of a forgotten past—with innumerable rows of latticework windows. The Firawn preferred this place over others and kept his women in the conjoined harem.

Being back always stirred old memories. When Leviathan was six, he'd been brought here without his mother. He was terrified to be separated from her, to be alone with the Firawn, all because Cecilia told the Firawn about his sensitivities. The Firawn had asked about his interests, his love for animals, and the hoopoe bird with a damaged wing that'd sit on his shoulder, even after it healed. His nerves had started to settle.

Then a slave had arrived with his bird. The Firawn had taken it in his hand, and Leviathan's heart had raced in his throat, imagining him wringing its neck. Instead, he told Leviathan to kill it. Up until that point, he'd submitted to the Firawn out of fear, but he held the hoopoe—the one he cared for, the one that trusted him—and refused to do it with one shake of his head. In the end, the Firawn snapped the bird's neck, and Leviathan was sent to Verdite.

A hellish punishment for a stupid mistake.

He should've killed it.

Cutting across the courtyard with Malev a pace behind him, Leviathan strode through the familiar archways and chambers, ignoring his hundred reflections in the mirrors on the walls and ceilings. The replications would confuse the clearest of minds if you paid too much attention to them. No Wardens guarded the inside of the palace, except the Firawn's private quarters, the outer walls, and the gates, because the Firawn didn't believe anybody could harm him.

He wasn't wrong.

Leviathan signalled for Malev to wait in one of the outer chambers and continued down a corridor to the panelled doors leading into the Firawn's dining hall. With a hand on the doorknob, he paused for a moment, recognising the baritone coming through the gap between the doors. It belonged to the Commander of the Surya Wing who controlled the West Strip division of the Firawn's army.

"—grown in numbers. They're well-trained and well-organised. I've conferred with Commander Reed on conducting a comprehensive assessment of every ambush in the prior ten years. Their leader performs the interceptions with strategic precision, Sai. He's inconsistent with his procedures which makes it problematic to predict when and where he'll launch an attack. The single consistency in his approach is that he chooses to attack from blind spots in challenging terrains, like the Pashmina Pass, where both our overview and movement are limited. Despite setting numerous traps, the rebels have evaded them without trouble. Likely with the aid of trained scouts."

"You sound impressed, Commander."

"Ah, not impressed, Sai. Disturbed. The rebels haven't succeeded in seizing all the caravans, but they've done extensive damage each time. The eastern supply and trade routes are now continuously compromised. However, Wardens have been stationed on the perimeters of the eastern camps. If the rebels come near to distribute the loot, we'll capture them."

"Your mind has weakened, Commander. It shows in your abortive strategies. You have failed to subjugate the rebels, and now they have spread like cockroaches in my state. Do you recall my words to you on the day I handed you this position?"

"Yes, Sai. The rebels are enemy combatants. They must never form an identity among the people. They must be eradicated before they establish themselves as an opposition."

"And have the rebels not accomplished as much?" There was ice in the Firawn's voice, the brittle kind which coated a very dark lake. "Rumours have spread throughout the east. Whispers of warriors. Tell me what they call them, Commander."

The Commander faltered. "Ah—the White Wolves, Sai," he stuttered out.

Now, *this* was interesting.

An organised opposition intercepting guarded caravans on the road, stealing supplies, and getting away with it? These operations required stealth, skill, a sharp leader. Leviathan could appreciate the group pissing on the Firawn, but he doubted it'd be anything more than a transient rebellion, breaking apart on its own or turning into a bloody tug-of-power with the Rangers, which would have the clans paying the heaviest price. Previous rebellions all ended the same way—camps destroyed, people massacred. Rebels didn't care for civilians. No better than the military.

"I cannot stand incompetence, Commander."

"I assure you I'll handle the rebels, Sai. With discretion."

"Discretion? Oh no, Commander. I want noise."

"Noise, Sai?"

Stepping into the dining hall, Leviathan leaned against a wall, observing the Commander. He was five-ten, full-bodied, with an oiled moustache twirled up at the corners. Sweat gleamed on the back of his neck and darkened the collar of his black dominion coat. Refined silver pauldrons sculpted like the head of a hooded cobra glinted on his shoulders. For somebody who ruled the Surya Wing with an iron fist, he was reduced to nothing but nerves in the Firawn's presence.

A feeble moan snapped Leviathan's attention to the mirrored ceiling where an old slave hung upside down from one of the magic-powered fans. He was gagged, eyes bloodshot. His sweat dripped on the tiles as the fan rotated. By the look of his ashen face, he'd been hanging for a while. Leviathan's hands flexed with unease.

"Have you tested the new munitions?" the Firawn inquired.

"I—There wasn't enough magic to properly test all—"

"What *have* you done, Commander, other than waste my time?"

"I've collected reports on the situation in the southeast, Sai," the Commander said with too much desperation in his voice, his fingers twitching behind his back. "The lower *zaat* in Tabassum have been aiding the camp outside their village. Commander Reed reassured me that he would deal with the villagers—"

"By executing them?"

"It would contain the situation, Sai."

"Your short-sightedness is astounding, Commander. This is an opportunity and you want to waste it."

"Sai?"

"Give one of the tested munitions to the Scorpions. Tell them to disguise themselves as the White Wolves and raze Tabassum to the ground. Let the lower *zaat* believe the deception. And take heed, Commander. I want a wound so deep it damages a vital organ. Take down temples and shrines. Nothing maddens these illiterate rats more than an insult to their gods. As for all the eastern villages—announce a one-year tax exemption to anyone who delivers potential rebels."

"Your will, Sai."

The muscles in Leviathan's shoulders tautened. The situation in the East Strip was especially grim because the Great Drought left people with little food and water. They starved while their prince ruled safely from Badru. The Firawn wanted to strike a match near a leak of oil. It sounded like people had finally started uniting in the southeast, but this fire would burn down the delicate alliance, provoking another civil war which would keep them occupied while the Firawn tapped their lands of resources.

The East Strip was the primary host of magic, gold, oil, and steel, but difficult to navigate because magic protected most of the regions. Apart from that, there were costs to consider, like the financial expenses of supplying the Rangers deployed in the east and running a military academy to churn out more soldiers. Regular shipments of guns arrived in the southwest. They didn't come from Dariadun, which exported sulphur, copper, salt, and uranium, or Suradun, which exported coal, phosphate, and mounts. Leviathan suspected the involvement of foreign backers. A trade of arms. Somebody supplied the Firawn with the economic reach to run his militia.

The Firawn signalled for the Commander to step aside and, the moment he did, Leviathan felt the full weight of his attention. Looking at him was always like looking in a goddamn mirror—the same hooded eyes and sharp jaw, the same straight nose and full mouth, and the same tall, muscular build—so Leviathan's eyes cut straight to his predatory stare, focusing instead on that cold, hard blue. It was the only physical feature that set them apart.

Small fucking mercies.

"Ah, and the sun sets upon Ghada." The Firawn opened his arms without standing from his chair at the end of the long dining table. "Leviathan, come. Sit with me."

Moving to the table, Leviathan pulled out a chair, his lungs itching for a smoke. His senses picked up on another presence. Turning his head, he saw the shadowed figure standing in a corner. He should've noticed him before. It unnerved Leviathan that he hadn't, but the Kāhin was an elusive man. With white skin and skeletal features, he looked like somebody on the brink of death. It was his dark eyes that made him look alive. They watched and stored. Tattoos of symbols and numbers from some ancient language covered his face as a self-protective measure against possessions.

This was a man who dabbled with *sihr*. Dark Magic. Kāhins and Kāhinahs were well-known for their amulets and rituals, but these soothsayers played with powers that were forbidden to humankind. *Sihr* was about casting black spells to impact the mind and heart. There were those who worked with trapping the Ghaib to their service for that exact purpose.

Leviathan had looked into it to understand his own ability to see the Ghaib. You could bind them through specific grid systems that included their names and liturgical numbers drafted on paper with a particular type of ink. But it was a complicated process. Their names weren't known to humankind. And summoning them was a dangerous business. The Firawn's soothsayers studied the ancient books, like the Esoteric Testament, in a search for the names. An entire department at the Archeion was devoted to translating them. This Kāhin had been around since before Leviathan was born. Whatever he did for the Firawn, it was something dark, and the reason the Firawn couldn't be harmed like a normal man.

"You remember my son, Commander?"

"Indeed, Sai. He graduated from the Guild at the top of his class."

A whimper sounded from above. The spinning slave's condition slowly eviscerated Leviathan's composure. Focusing on the lighter in his pocket, he forced himself to relax, muscle by muscle, keeping his face neutral, under the Firawn's scrutiny. Otherwise, the Firawn would use his unease to further torment the slave.

"Binay." At the Firawn's call, a slave kid rushed through the doors into the dining hall. He looked no older than ten. His anxious eyes darted to the ceiling. "We shall feast now. Bring in the wine first."

"Ah—Sai—"

"Not now, Commander. I am about to dine with my son. You are dismissed."

Bowing low, the Commander left.

The Firawn took the wine pitcher. "It has been a while since we last dined as a family, Leviathan. Let us drink together."

"I'll pass."

He cocked his head. "Drink with me, son—" he said, his voice merry, "—or watch Binay swallow the shards of your scorned glass."

The slave kid paled.

Grinding his teeth, Leviathan gave a clipped nod. The Firawn poured the wine, then deliberately eased back to watch him in his alien way, while Binay served platters of steaming buffalo meat. The choice of food triggered a memory. Leviathan was five or six and it was one of the times the Firawn had come to al-Abyad Mahal for dinner. He'd dropped a large piece of buffalo ribs on Leviathan's platter and Leviathan's mother had shifted next to him, troubled, because Leviathan didn't have a taste for meat. The spicy chunks had burned down his throat, but at some point, he'd managed to swallow that last unpleasant mouthful. The Firawn had only turned to him, given him a cool, deliberate smile, and dropped another slab on his platter.

Thinking back on it now, Leviathan thought it hadn't hurt him as much as his mother, who'd been forced to watch, her eyes more pained than his stomach, knowing if she spoke in Leviathan's favour, the Firawn would triple his portion.

The Firawn looked at him now with that same deliberate smile.

"Eat."

Leviathan tore a slice of flatbread, dipped it in the buffalo stew, and shoved it into his mouth, too used to the spices and the meat, even though they still made his stomach roil.

Biting into a chunk of meat, the Firawn chewed briskly, the juice trailing down his chin. "How is your Mā Saheb?" he inquired, like he didn't already know.

"Fine."

"She complains about you. She claims you do not attend the festival."

"I'm on leave. Thought I could do whatever I wanted."

The old slave groaned. Binay swallowed hard.

"You disrespected her for a *dēvadasi*."

"She was a pretty *dēvadasi*."

The Firawn threw his head back and laughed. "You certainly are my son." He licked his fingers. "Do not disrespect her again. I will not take it lightly a second time." With that, he went on in a more conversational tone, "I have received demoralising reports from my tool pushers. Magic continues to shrink. What remains of it has retreated too deep into the earth. It senses our intention and refuses to succumb, Leviathan, but I will have it, if I must extract it from the heart of the earth itself."

Apart from a few locations in the west, the east was the only place showing signs of magic existing on a surface level. For one thing, foreign arms like guns were useless there. It might just be a matter of steel. Guns built from Khansan steel might work, but the Firawn hadn't considered experimenting with it yet, his focus on tapping magic and finding ways to tie it to different components, and Leviathan didn't plan on sharing the notion.

Another reason the Firawn believed the east held a large quantity of magic was the Great Drought. It'd emerged in the aftermath of Jehangir Khan's assassination. According to the Firawn's theory, the Great Drought was produced by magic preventing anybody from accessing it—and Leviathan thought the same.

"I delivered a beautiful Darian boon to Prince Jasadan as an appreciation of his soothsayers aiding the drillers in tracking magic. A lesson on alliances, Leviathan. You need not use unnecessary force. Men such as the avaricious prince have been bought ever since our ancestors broke the Khanate. They are useful. When they are not, you replace them. The system remains intact, but the symbol alters its appearance."

Likely why rebellions never had any surviving impact. You had to uproot entire existing systems, replacing them with something better, which required a lot more than the beheading of a figurehead. Leviathan doubted manmade systems would ever be optimal. Flawed beings couldn't create perfection.

The Firawn wiped his mouth in a napkin. "Magic is our greatest resource. Without it, we would be abbreviated to lighting our torches like the common lower *zaat*. Without it, we could not provide our people with impeccable medicine. It is an extraordinary resource which possesses secrets we have not yet uncovered." The zeal in his voice was thick as tar. This was all about power. Not some ethical shit about the welfare of the higher *zaat*. Whoever magic served held supreme power over everything crucial to the establishment of societies and the survival of humankind—like rain, produce, and clean water. "I like challenges, son. They amuse me."

Leviathan's throat muscles worked, tightening along his neck. His ears were sick of the Firawn's grating voice. *Fuck it,* he thought and lit a cigarette. Glancing at the Kāhin, he breathed smoke. The soothsayer hadn't moved an inch from his position.

The Firawn swirled his wine. "I shall force magic to the surface. I shall bend it to my will. Even a whipped hound submits to its master in anticipation of pain. Yes?"

Swallowing a humourless chuckle, Leviathan watched the smoke vaporise. Magic was an essence, a living organism, and the Firawn wanted to control it the way he controlled everything else—using force, intimidation, and punishment. It'd never occur to him to persuade it out of the earth. It'd never cross his mind to question why it served Jehangir Khan in the first place.

The hanging slave had gone quiet. Leviathan resisted the urge to look up and crushed his cigarette. Smoking wasn't helping like it should.

Easing back in his chair, the Firawn studied him again. "I am discontent, son. I have been surrounded by obese, incompetent fools long enough. Thus, I have decided to remove Commander Gilani from his position. Permanently."

'Permanently' carried the jarring sound of a gunshot.

The Firawn's eyes glittered. "I am replacing him with someone much more capable of governing the Surya Wing. I believe the soldiers will thrive under a younger leader, a sharper mind, and a pitiless hand." Leviathan's stomach hardened, heart in his mouth, as the Firawn took his sweet time sipping the wine. "You will supersede Gilani as Commander, son."

Leviathan went still. He wanted to smash the pitcher against the wall, ram his fists into the nearest convenient asshole. He clenched his teeth. Becoming the Commander meant leading the Rangers in massacres, issuing crackdowns and death sentences, and murdering more of his birthmother's people. *His* people.

His mouth turned sour.

Did the Firawn know he'd visited the camp? No, this wasn't about the clans. This was about him. It was another way for the Firawn to chain him down. He wanted Leviathan to be the Blade. To be his weapon. Slaughter in his name, spread fear in his name. Leviathan had proved he could rule the soldiers, even with his *bezaat* blood, because he was without mercy. Those under his command hadn't revered or respected him. They'd feared his madness, seen it in his eyes.

The void.

He wasn't going back to that.

Gripping the leash of his rage, he yanked it back like he would a rabid hound. His voice was quiet when he spoke. "I don't want it."

The Firawn cocked an eyebrow. "Did I give the impression you have a choice in the matter?" If it wasn't for the creases on his brow, you wouldn't know he was older than his own in-laws. That he was, in sinister ways, ageless. At that moment, Leviathan was reminded of how he once watched him pull a knife from his gut with the casual motion of somebody flicking dust from the sleeve.

There was a reason for the rumours of his assumed divinity.

Leviathan swallowed hard. "Why?" he asked.

The Firawn's eyes fixed on Leviathan's, an unnatural stillness in them. "Are you questioning my decisions now?"

"Looks like I am."

Leviathan saw it coming, but he didn't block it. Right now, it was either hitting or getting hit, so he took the blow. There was a time when he would've pissed himself every time the Firawn walked in, looking tall, mighty, and scary as hell, but Leviathan had outgrown him in size since then. He watched the Firawn wipe his blood from the knuckles and let him believe he'd beaten him. Leviathan hadn't forgotten what he'd done to his mother—what he'd done to *him*—and one day he'd pay him back in full, *māshapath*.

The Firawn was oblivious to the hate sealed behind Leviathan's cold stare.

"Why did you shoot the Wardens?"

"They disrespected me."

"An acceptable argument. Yet there is power in restraint, Leviathan." Bullshit. The Firawn didn't work with restraint. He was all about extreme reward and punishment. "Your Mā Saheb has requested a penalty for your actions. You were given three months of leave, but you will now return to Verdite in one and take your place as Commander." Getting to his feet, the Firawn straightened his *sherwani* and Leviathan almost flinched when he put a hand against his cheek. "I have great plans for you, son, and I have equally great expectations. Do not disappoint me."

Then he strolled out.

The Kāhin detached himself from the shadows to follow him. Leviathan ran his tongue over his stinging bottom lip, licking the blood from the corner. He'd stepped right into the Firawn's trap. He'd exposed his weakness by sharing what he *didn't* want when he should've kept his mouth shut. As frustrated as he was about the slip-up, it reminded him that he needed to be careful. He couldn't be seen near the camp. Not if he wanted to keep Mai out of the Firawn's sight.

Guilt gutted him. He'd been selfish.

Tamping down on his emotions, Leviathan moved to his feet, leaving the slave dangling from the rotating fan as he walked out. Cutting him loose would just worsen his punishment. The evening chill did nothing to cool Leviathan's blood when he crossed the courtyard. Malev rose from a bench outside and walked with him. Retrieving their weapons at the gates, they headed to the stables where Cinder snorted and stomped as soon as she sensed Leviathan's approach.

Malev mounted his Khansan mare. "You look ready to murder," he said at length, pulling up next to Leviathan.

"I'll have my chance soon enough. Get in touch with Kai and tell him to investigate a group called the White Wolves. I want everything he can find on them." Brushing a hand over Cinder's soft brow, Leviathan vaulted up into the saddle and turned her down Fateh Road.

"What did the Firawn say to you?"

"He wasn't in his usual chatty mood."

"Looks like his fist was." At Leviathan's silence, Malev frowned. "Whatever he said—"

"Malev, I don't want to talk," Leviathan said through his teeth. "I want to track down Volos and I want to make him pay."

"All right, brother." Malev leaned over to clasp his shoulder. "All right."

CHAPTER 26

Patrons streamed in one at a time and dropped *fals* on *fals* in the veil. Peering down at the glinting copper, Roma saw her worth in the coins with their Middle Khansāri numbers imprinted on the metal. Prostitutes should know the face value of a coin. How else would they measure their own worth? She clasped the cobra pendant around her neck until it bruised her palm as bitterness rose within her. The coins seemed to taunt her with their coppery shine in the torchlight.

She was aware of the scars on her shell, of their shape and depth. The ones Alan Saheb had caused and the ones she had caused. Their rigid existence bred a restiveness in her that she was never able to soothe. It augmented now when she stood in the auction chamber with the gods as her witnesses and transformed into the talons of a beast that craved blood. She wouldn't make it painless. No, she would draw it out until he begged her like she had begged him for relief. The Panchayat would sentence her to death for his murder, but death no longer frightened her.

Sādin Saheb stepped toward her with downturned lips, his robe dragging over the ground. "Well," he said in a thwarted tone, squinting at the *fals*. "The gods aren't happy, child."

A laugh caught in her throat. Knowing the receivers of the coin were the Firawn and Sādin Saheb made her want to comment on his lie—if only to observe the shock on his face when he realised she knew what a fraud he was—but she swallowed her remark. He wouldn't matter to her soon enough, nor would his venomous lies.

Nothing would matter.

The thick, purple veins on the back of his hands twitched as he gathered the veil and summoned a *birandasi* to take it from him. "Your service to Alan Saheb will have to account for your poor worth, I suppose," he continued, turning toward her with an arrogant smile. "Indeed. Alan Saheb has spoken for you. A man with an injured pride is dangerous, child. He won't be kind. Now, it's time—"

"Hold your chants, priest."

The aggressive companion of the Firawn's son—the one called Junho—sauntered into the auction chamber in an orange *kurta* over black trousers. His nosepieces winked as he passed the torches on the wall.

Sādin Saheb glowered at him. "You," he snapped. "How dare you enter the sacred temple of the High Lord, *boy*?"

"Don't choke." Shaking a leather pouch full of coin, Junho tossed it to Sādin Saheb. With a frown on his face, Sādin Saheb untied the pouch. His eyes widened at the silver. "That's your payment from Leviathan Blackburn for the *dēvadasi*. She belongs to him now."

The air snagged in Roma's throat while her mind scrambled to understand. The Firawn's son was *bidding* on her. He bought her. She never thought highly of him, but she considered him above this. Hadn't he defended Khiraa's honour? Hadn't he touched Ghanima Mai's feet in respect and listened to Kanoni's accusations in silence? He had pulled Roma out of the fountain. Why had he done that if he was the same as other men? How could he defend one woman and purchase another?

For a breathless moment, she wanted to believe that he bought her to protect her, as he had seemed to do in Biranpur, but perhaps his intentions were never pure. He insisted on her performing the ritual on him, and then, tonight, he paid *rajat* for her. Men didn't purchase women unless they wanted to use them. Her hands trembled. She clutched one of the bracelets on her wrist. She was a fool. All men were the same. Their exterior was a parade of virtues, but beneath it, one would find perverse intentions.

Sādin Saheb still stared in astonishment. Junho clicked his tongue. "Bhau's paying silver for her. Get it? Need me to repeat in another language?"

"I understand perfectly," Sādin Saheb bit out. "It's an honour to have Leviathan Saheb enter into a patronship with one of Lamiapur's daughters. He shall be mightily blessed by the gods and—"

"Yeah, yeah. Look, Bhau doesn't want any delays. She's going to the palace now."

"As Leviathan Saheb wishes."

"*Jhakaas*. Let's go."

Roma didn't have the surplus of mental strength to consider what this unforeseen alteration might mean for Lamiapur. She was focused on what it meant for her as she followed Junho and Sādin Saheb outside. The blade in her hair was promised blood, but she couldn't assault the Firawn's son, because he wasn't just a prince. He was a soldier whose strength and speed she had witnessed. If she attacked him, she would lose. She didn't want to imagine what he would do to her after an attempt on his life.

Then she had only one choice.

With a pulse that thundered in her ears, she lifted her chin and stepped out on the temple's terrace. The villagers showered the stairs with blossoms. Her sisters were among them. This would be the last time she saw them. She should have told them the truth. It wouldn't have made them rebel or run, but deception was cruel. She despised illusions herself. How could she keep them in the cruellest illusion of all?

Junho walked to a waiting palanquin covered in ornamented silks. Four palace slaves stood in the front and four in the back. He shouted orders before making a path through the crowd. Turning to her sisters, Roma saw Chirag. Food stained his mouth and his hair stuck to all sides because she hadn't combed it for him. She had been too preoccupied with her auction when she should have spent more time with him. Her heart panged. He looked at her with sadness and fear, not knowing what she might return as after tonight. She had promised never to leave him, but she couldn't keep that promise.

"I'm sorry, Chirag," she whispered.

Yoshi stood beside him, and Roma caught her stare.

Amma stepped between them with a ravenous shine in her eyes. "You're fortunate, *ladoba*," she said under her breath, smiling as she draped an arm over Roma's shoulders, steering her toward the palanquin. Amma should have been concerned since the bargain with Alan Saheb had failed, but she appeared pleased. Roma found Goldie beside Meriel, throwing blossoms and beaming in excitement. Amma would auction her. How else would she placate a predator like Alan Saheb? What other reason could there be for her absolute composure?

When Amma cupped Roma's face, Roma looked at her. "Lord Biran has chosen Leviathan Saheb as your patron despite our plans. This is our chance. If you conceive before the patronship ends, you could birth Firawn Sai's grandson. It would elevate our status. We'd have more power than Biranpur, Roma. Perhaps you'd never have to lie with another patron again because of your invaluable service. You could become Leviathan Saheb's mistress."

Roma tasted bile. She wanted to wrench Amma's hands from her face. She wanted to hold them between her own and ask her how she could be so apathetic. Staring into her eyes now, Roma searched for the mother who raised her, hoping she existed somewhere inside her. That she hadn't been another illusion. Yet all she saw in Amma was the hunger, and all she felt was the cold.

"Roma, *samajalē*?"

"*Hō*."

"Good girl. Caliana? Give Roma a hand with her *lehenga*."

"I'll do it," Yoshi volunteered. Lifting the folds, she helped Roma inside the palanquin and fussed over the skirt as she prompted, "What?"

"Amma will sell Goldie to Alan Saheb. You can't let it happen." When Yoshi didn't even glance at her, Roma swallowed her discomfort and grabbed Yoshi's hand. "The gods are an excuse, Yoshi. We're not sacred vessels. We're prostitutes. You have to tell the others and protect Goldie."

"How do you propose I do that?"

Roma noticed the neutral note in her voice and the unworried expression on her face. "You knew," she whispered. "You knew about the taxes and—for how long?"

"For someone who doubts so much," Yoshi said, "you should've seen the truth sooner."

"Yoshi—"

"Be concerned for yourself, Roma. You can only try to change your own fate."

Pulling her hand from Roma's, she slipped out before Roma could speak another word. The silver curtains dropped back into place, blocking Yoshi from her view. Dragging her knees to her chest, she steadied herself as the slaves lifted the palanquin onto their shoulders. Yoshi had seen through all the lies. Roma hadn't. How oblivious she was. How ignorant of the one thing she claimed to understand better than anyone else.

Illusions.

She rubbed a hand over her heart as her breathing turned shallow, thinking of Khiraa's and Sara's laughter, Seth's broodiness, Chirag's slanted smile, and the hours the five of them had spent hunting beehives in the Lonesome Forest.

Those were memories that made life bearable.

"Mā Saheb will be furious," one of the slaves murmured. "She'll punish us once she finds out we brought a *dēvadasi* into the palace."

"If only the Young Saheb would see the Flags like everyone else. Why does he want a *dēvadasi*?"

"Perhaps he believes she's pure."

"The higher *zaat* want finesse even in a prostitute."

"A *vēshya* is a *vēshya*."

Reaching the city gates, the slaves hushed. Roma held her veil over her face, huddling behind the scarce protection the sheer fabric provided. The Wardens ordered the slaves to stop and their shadows moved beyond the silk curtains. Her heart thudded as a Warden drew closer to inspect the palanquin.

Parting the curtains, he peered inside, but he didn't speak, and she didn't look at him. "All right," he drawled, stepping back. "Scurry on, rats."

The gates slammed behind them. Her breath stuttered out. Lifting her veil, she dared to push aside the curtains and glanced out at the city. Blue and ivory bungalows strained skyward behind trimmed courtyards. Fan-tailed birds swarmed the narrow paths which interweaved like the alleys in Sefu, only the drains were clean, the air was fresh, and there were no starved animals in the streets. Pillars and fountains decorated the spaces, the cornices and brackets skilfully crafted, and unpolluted ponds held rainbow-coloured fish sparkling in the clear water. Lemon and fig trees, pomegranate and olive trees stood in the gardens untouched by the aridity.

If she looked toward the northern skyline, she could make out the stone walls enclosing al-Abyad Mahal—the White Palace—where it rose high on the precipice, the gold cupolas and minarets grazing the night skies. Roma wasn't certain how much time had passed when they arrived at the palace gates. The slaves lowered her in a courtyard. Gliding out of the palanquin, Roma looked around at the shallow ponds, fountains, and gold pavilions. Stone paths and steep stairs vanished in and out of view as if devoured by hidden archways in the shadows.

A Darian *bandi* approached her with a torch in her hand. It was the first time Roma came so close to the magical fire. The brilliant blue flame didn't radiate heat. She wondered whether she would be burned if she touched it.

"I'm Hasibah," the *bandi* said. Her silver *nath* indicated she was one of the higher-ranked *bandis*. "What's your name?"

"Roma."

"*Yē*, Roma. Follow me."

Roma trailed after her through the courtyards and gardens, past chiselled statues of battling tigers, and up winding stairs without rails. Bunching up her *lehenga*, she glanced down at the large cages full of birds with green heads, purple throats, and dark tails. No creature should ever be sentenced to life in a beautiful cage. It was the cruellest form of deceit.

A garden in a distinctive precinct of al-Abyad Mahal housed a structure with wide balconies and terraces. Peacocks strutted around the pavilion and lotus blossoms drifted in the ponds. Roma tipped back her head, staring up at the latticework screens and stained-glass windows dyed hues of red, blue, and purple. She felt swallowed in this place. The splendour and dimension of it were so intimidating that her heart beat like the wings of one of the trapped birds.

Terrace doors opened into a hall with floral-patterned tiles in pink and white. Mirrors embedded in the walls reflected the torchlight as Hasibah slipped in between the shivering gossamer curtains in the archways, leading Roma through the individual part of the palace. She paused outside another pair of doors with stained-glass entrenched in a gold frame. The chamber beyond the doors was a similar pink and white. Gold chandeliers dangled from a domed ceiling. Embroidered silk divans and satin cushions shimmered in the dim light from several lanterns situated around the chamber to create an intimate mood.

Hasibah walked to a massive bed with carved motifs on the wooden bed-posts. She patted the silk sheets. "*Basa*," she said. Roma's eyes lingered on the rose petals strewn across the bed and her insides revolted at the sight, but she gathered her skirt and climbed onto the bed. Pulling her knees to her chest, she clasped her arms around them. Hasibah picked up a silver pitcher from a table and poured the water into a bejewelled cup. "You must be tired. Auctions run for hours *na*. Here. Drink this. You needn't fear Leviathan Saheb. He's not as unkind as he might seem."

Sipping once from the cup, Roma returned it to Hasibah. She didn't care for the *bandi's* opinion of him, nor would she place her faith in it, because she wouldn't let him or anyone else touch her ever again. When Hasibah closed the doors behind her, the lock clicked from outside, but it didn't matter. If escape had been a choice at all, she would have done it sooner while restricted only by the walls of Lamiapur. Running could put Chirag in danger. She would never sacrifice him for her own freedom. No, she wouldn't attempt to escape what she had once believed was fate.

She would change it.

Stepping down from the bed, she reached behind her head and pulled out the hairpin, unsheathing the beautiful blade. It twinkled in the lamplight as if it knew her intentions.

The lock's quiet *click* sounded behind her before the doors opened.

"No sound and no tears, Amma," she whispered.

PART II

"When the Nur asked:
'Why create yet another race that will shed blood?'
The answer came:
'We know that which you do not.'"

Shamsuddin Codex, Volume II, ***al-Ghaib***

CHAPTER 27

Roma clutched the hairpin in her hand. The daunting frame of the Firawn's son was shrouded in a black cloak, the curved-sword pendant tucked out of sight, but his hood was drawn back from his head. Shadows haunted the hollows of his face and obscured his emotions to anyone who might search beyond the surface. She met his unwavering stare with a cumulative numbness within her chest and the promise of blood in her eyes. She didn't want to feel such despair, nor did she want darkness to swaddle her mind, but she had accepted that her auction would end with her death.

What did it matter if it were an executioner who took her life or if it were her?

When the Firawn's son took a deliberate step toward her, the blood promise blazed like a fuelled torch, and she touched the tip of the blade to her throat.

"Don't come near me," she warned.

Every sound, smell, and taste overpowered her heightened senses. Her frantic pulse throbbed like drumbeats in her ears. She smelled the scattered rose petals and tasted the subtle vibration in the air at his slightest shift. It somehow reached her, pricking her sensitive nerves and exposing his invisible stealth. She shifted as he did. Her mirrored movement caught his attention, and he looked at her with a different awareness.

"You don't want to do this, Roma."

She despised that he spoke her name as if he knew her. Tipping back her head, she pressed the point of the blade into her skin. A warm line of blood seeped down the side of her bared throat. His facial muscles hardened and his movement stilled.

"I don't want you to touch me."

"If I wanted to touch you," he said, disturbingly calm, "you'd already be on the bed."

Her knees trembled from exhaustion and her skin still burned from the fever. Fear had eroded her for hours, days, years. Now she came full circle. It would all end tonight. "Then why am I here?" she asked in no more than a whisper. He was silent. Because he didn't have an answer that could convince her of his lies. "I'm not educated like you, Saheb, but I'm not stupid."

"No, you're not," he murmured.

"I know what you want. You want power. And it makes you feel powerful when you subdue me." The blade burrowed deeper and the blood trail thickened. A surreptitious shadow of emotion came and went in the nadirs of his eyes. She didn't care to define it. "I won't be broken by your kind again."

"My kind?"

"Your kind, Saheb. Men."

"You're a survivor."

"This is my survival," she whispered.

Drawing back her hand to stab her throat, she saw him close the distance in mere heartbeats. She should have killed herself, but an instinctual part of her—a part far too strong that always sought life over death—overwhelmed her, and she switched to sink the blade into him in the very last second.

It was a mistake.

He caught her wrist with the point barely a breath from puncturing his throat. There was a moment of stunned silence in which they both realised how close she had come, and then he spun her around in one smooth motion that ripped the veil from her head, slamming her against his chest and trapping her arm behind her back.

"Like I said, a survivor," he said. "Next time, don't let me read the move in your eyes."

Panic licked the inside of her throat. Flattening her free hand on his chest, she attempted to create the illusion of a barrier between them, but his breath brushed against her face, and she almost ruptured from the agonising pressure within her. Desperate to escape him, she twisted and yanked her ensnared wrist with such ruthless force that her bangles shattered, the shards burrowing into her skin under his grip. He released her with an abrupt shove. Stumbling back from him, she stepped on the shards that had scattered on the carpet, gulping in air with ravenous heaves of her chest.

Nilo's hairpin was in his possession. He had slipped it from her trapped hand while she panicked. She failed to kill him and now she would pay for it. Refusing to speak the burning plea on her tongue, she held his stare, clenching her damp hands at her sides. Ghanima Mai always stood with her head held high when Wardens raided the camp. She draped herself in dignity and never surrendered to her oppressors.

Neither would Roma.

His gaze lowered to her bleeding wrist. An edginess ruled his stance. This wasn't a hunter in front of her. Hunters could still be human. It was someone darker. She backed until she was pressed against the wall as far from him as possible. With her mind arrested in fear, her eyes darted to the doors. She didn't think of Chirag now, nor the consequences, if she managed to escape.

"You wouldn't make it," he told her.

"You said you wouldn't touch me," she breathed.

"I won't. If you cooperate."

"What do you want from me?"

"Take off your gold."

Bile soured her throat.

"If I—if I refuse?"

The Firawn's son advanced on her. She ran for the doors. He caught her arm before she had taken more than a few steps and pulled her up against the wall. Planting his hand beside her head, he leaned down to stare into her eyes with unreserved calm. Her hands trembled. Her nails chewed at her palms. She pushed back against the wall in a distraught attempt at sinking away from his body so close to her own.

"Don't test me, Roma," he said in a low-pitched voice. "You can take it off yourself, or I can help you. Choose."

It was the quiet threat that unravelled her. Closing her shaking fingers around the cobra pendant, she drew it over her head and it dropped among the wrecked bangles. Tears burned in her eyes as she removed the ornaments, feeling as if she were stripping down to her skin. She wanted to be stronger than her fear, but she couldn't control the shivering in her limbs nor her shuddering breaths, and she depised herself for submitting without a fight.

She hated him.

When she had lost all the adornments, barring her anklets, he allowed enough space between them that her breathing could ease. She looked up at him then, her eyes following him like a serpent primed to strike, but her bite would just provoke him. She jolted as he tossed her a pale blue bundle. Catching it, she stared down at the intricate threadwork on the cotton, recognising it as common *dēvadasi* attire. She licked her lips.

"Must I change while you watch?"

He blinked. "Two minutes," he forewarned.

Before she could draw another breath, the Firawn's son slipped out of the chamber. Standing still, she closed her eyes. Her entire shell started to shiver as if it were ice water in her fever-charred veins. She wouldn't fall apart. Breathing deep through her nose, she released the air through her parted lips and changed into the blue garments with quick movements. Then she looked around for an object she could use as a weapon.

What did the Firawn's son want with her? If he didn't want to lie with her, why did he bid on her? She was certain that he hadn't bought her to keep her here in the palace, untouched, until he chose to end their patronship. He was faster and stronger than her, but she would wait for her chance. It would help if she could find a weapon—

Her cobra pendant.

The cobra's pointed tail wasn't as piercing as a blade, but it was sharp enough to injure if buried in a sensitive place. Pulling the pendant out of the chain, she shoved it behind her waistline, stepping away from the adornments on the carpet just as the Firawn's son came back inside. He had drawn his hood over his head. She couldn't see his eyes in the shadow of it, but she felt their disquieting focus. For an alarming second, she thought he knew about the pendant. He cornered her in three quick strides, and panic's claws closed around her throat again.

"Show me your hands," he ordered.

She lifted her hands between them. Before she had a chance to grasp his motive, he slipped a rope around her wrists and pulled the knot tight.

Panic transformed into terror.

"No," she rasped. Heedless of burns or bruises, she wrenched her wrists to yank free, but the knot tightened the more she struggled. Her voice was shrill. "Release me." She was back on the silk sheets and Alan Saheb's hands clamped around her wrists. "Take it *off.* Let me—"

"Listen."

"Let me go—You have to—You have to let me—"

The Firawn's son pulled her to him. "*Aikā*," he snapped. Her breath hitched in her throat. "If you cooperate, I'll return you to Lamiapur before dawn." She shook her head at his lie and he caught her eyes with forced patience. "Untouched and unharmed. You have my word, Roma."

The resistance drained from her shell. She dropped her shackled hands. "Your word is worthless to me, Saheb," she told him in a hoarse voice.

"Right now, it's all you have."

CHAPTER 28

Roma threaded her fingers through the coarse mane of the scarred mount. Her name was Cinder. She was a nuance of ash that glistened a molten silver in the ethereal light of the moon, a melancholic grey in the shadows, and a silken black in the absolute darkness. She soared like a desert storm across the plains and the hills, her powerful muscles bunching and rippling as if she were born for it, and the thundering vibrations resonated deep within Roma's bones. The mount knew her rider well because the Firawn's son didn't need to direct her with more than the pressure of his knees.

His chest against Roma's back and the unknown destination chilled what heat the fever borrowed her. With a belly that churned and clenched in anxiousness, she huddled inside the thick cloak he had slipped on her shoulders and recalled how he had spun the elaborate knot with the rope. What would she do even if she managed to loosen it by some miracle? How would she fight him? Where would she escape to? Reason had replaced terror and reminded her that if she disappeared, Lamiapur would burn for her desertion.

It could be Chirag.

Leaving behind the hills, they descended into a canyon with unsound paths leading out to a desert. It stretched so far she couldn't see where it bounded. White sand drifted over the hard ground and the sharp air stung in her arid throat. A city rose ahead. The Firawn's son pulled the reins and dismounted. Roma watched him with nervous eyes while he murmured to Cinder as one would to a companion. Turning toward Roma, he reached for her waist, but she dropped down on her own to avoid his touch.

"Where are you taking me, Saheb?" she attempted again, staring at him as he freed the rope from the saddle and sent Cinder back into the canyon. Her question was countered with continuous silence, yet she refused to succumb to the hopelessness within her. "Saheb, please—"

Wrapping the rope around his knuckles, he strode across the desert, hauling her along with him. Fever sweat covered her throat and collarbone, and her heart stumbled over a beat when she was pulled into the city.

It was a bedlam of sandstone houses painted pink, blue, and orange. Torches and lanterns burned, lighting the fronts, and the crowd was so thick that the bodies pressed against her until she felt invaded from the touch of strangers. The chaotic current of dissonant sounds and smells assaulted her senses. No one looked at her twice as the Firawn's son dragged her down the crammed streets. Guards with guns stood around stalls full of weapons and alcohol, observing people with nonchalant expressions on their faces and sharpness in their stares. They didn't intervene when the Firawn's son towed Roma past them. Women in low-cut *cholis* and knee-length *lehengas* dallied on the thresholds of the houses, shouting obscene promises to passing men, and Roma's belly coiled into a knot as a horrible thought crawled into her mind.

Was she here to be sold to a brothel?

She swallowed forcibly. It couldn't be. The Firawn's son promised her he would return her to Lamiapur. Untouched. Why would he bring her to a place of brothels if not to sell her? Why would he even *need* to sell her?

Fear burned a damp path down her back.

They arrived in a courtyard bustling with hijras and women whose loud laughter resonated in the enormous space. The brothel had long rows of latticework windows and painted doors, fragmented stairs and narrow balconies. Prostitutes leaned against the pillars and over the balustrades. Roma had no choice but to follow when the Firawn's son moved toward the stairs.

A woman with a plunging neckline blocked his path. She blew out smoke from between her red-painted lips while her kohl-lined, brown eyes appraised the Firawn's son as if she undressed him in her mind. "What're you looking for, handsome?" she asked with a suggestive smile.

"Queen's Chamber," the Firawn's son said, unvexed. "Where can I find it?"

Feigning sullenness, she pouted. "What's the hurry? Why don't we settle a price first, have a little bit of fun?" She trailed a fingernail down his chest. "Then you can go and do your business."

He caught her hand dangerously low.

"Queen's Chamber."

The woman shrugged. "Fifth level, fourth corridor, red door. If you change your mind, come and find me."

Brushing past her, he ascended the stairs. The prostitutes on the steps turned to watch them. Roma recoiled as they reached out, touching her hair, her face, uttering lewd puns in Khansāri followed by laughter. The unwanted raid by their eyes and hands threatened to unleash a repressed scream caged in her throat. She wanted to crawl into a corner and cover her head until the world ceased to exist, but she shoved at their invasive hands as much as her restricted movement would allow.

The red door appeared somewhere deep within the tangled web of the brothel. They stepped inside a chamber immersed in a golden glow from lanterns and thick with smoke from cigarettes and hookahs. Men lounged on cushioned divans, drinking out of long glasses, and touched the dancing girls in manners that sickened her.

A hijra approached the Firawn's son in a purple *choli* and *lehenga*. Her wavy hair cascaded over one bared shoulder and a pink rose snuggled behind her adorned ear. "What can Rubina do for you?" she asked in a husky voice with a feminine note beneath the baritone. "Oh, let me guess. You're one of Rado's delivery boys."

"*Ay*, Amma," a woman called, strutting over to Rubina. "That bitch Suman is stealing one of my regulars again. If she doesn't stop, I swear I'll scar her in her sleep."

"I'll talk to her."

"Just make her stop—"

"Get back to work, *vēshya*, I'll handle it."

Placing a hand on her hip, Rubina leaned back, her eyes scraping over Roma and dwelling on her anklets. She lifted one of her painted eyebrows. "A *dēvadasi?* You're a rare commodity." She looked at the Firawn's son. "Mother Manāt might bless your fortune tonight if this one catches Rado's fancy. Unless her scars scare him off first. Take a seat. He'll find you."

Roma pulled at the rope before the Firawn's son could venture further into the chamber. Turning halfway toward her, he looked into her eyes. She shook her head with a desperate appeal on her face, but his jaw tightened, and he held her gaze as he moved closer. "If you want to survive here," he said quietly, "keep your bold eyes down and your mouth shut."

Then he hauled her toward a vacant table.

The terror that encased her was still rather than frantic. His promise to return her to Lamiapur was a lie. She knew it. Yet a part of her had hoped against common sense. She should have killed herself. She had wasted that one chance to escape. How would she survive in a brothel? How would she bear the violations from countless men? The awful churning inside her at the sight of the brothel prostitutes returned with a vengeance. She watched with dread as the Firawn's son seated himself and waited for the man named Rado.

It wasn't a long wait.

"Ruby says you've got a *dēvadasi* for me." The nasal voice belonged to a young man dressed in a turmeric-coloured *kurta* and trousers. Brown hair was slicked back from an oval face with sideburns. Perching on a chair opposite the Firawn's son, he draped his arm over the back and shook a narrow, iron bracelet on his wrist, looking Roma over with a probing stare that made her skin crawl. "So, that her?"

"Depends." The Firawn's son tipped his head to the side. "Who's asking?"

"Who do you think? I'm Rado."

"So Volos sends a kid to bargain for him."

Picking an olive from a glass bowl on the table, Rado popped it into his mouth. "Why don't you name your price, Big Guy? I've got other places to be."

"Four thousand *rajat*."

"You've got to be fucking kidding me," Rado laughed. "She's got scars. That's damaged goods. Two thousand."

"I can make a better deal with Bor's handlers."

"Three."

"Four, or I'll take my business elsewhere."

"Three, and you can spend a few hours with one of our girls without charge." When the Firawn's son stood, Roma thought for a second that she was spared. She took a step back with feet that wanted to run toward the door. Rado squinted at the Firawn's son and nodded. "Fine, four, then. Sealed?"

"Thought she was damaged goods."

"What's a few scars in this *dhanda*? As long as she can work, Volos is happy."

Her heart plummeted. She stared at the Firawn's son. He didn't move. It was impossible to tell if he hesitated or calculated, but it mattered not since he accepted the deal with a short nod. She fought against the rope again, pulling with violent force, as Rado tossed a leather pouch to the Firawn's son. He snatched it from the air, inspected the contents, and turned to leave. Her breath stuck in her lungs and the chamber closed in around her.

"Saheb, don't do this," Roma beseeched him, gripping his cloak. He stopped. "Please, don't leave me here. *Please.*" Looking into his eyes, she pleaded with him and saw hesitation on his face for the briefest moment. Before she could press her advance, he clenched his jaw and strode toward the door, his cloak ripping from her hold.

No.

"No, you don't, sweetheart," Rado drawled. She didn't realise she had started after the Firawn's son until Rado's arms banded around her from behind. Thrashing in his grip, she screamed and kicked back, hitting him in the leg. "Fuck! Easy, easy! Noisy bitch."

A fever shivered within her blood, but this one was distinctive. She had sensed it before as a child when Alan Saheb tortured her in his bed. A heat in her veins. A ferocious *apart* presence inside her. She wasn't able to touch it, even as she strained to reach that power, but it was like catching dust out in the steppe. Her fingers closed around it, yet when she opened her hands, they were empty.

Whipping her head to the side, she almost caught Rado's arm between her teeth. "*Ay*—Ruby! A little fucking help here!" he shouted. "Ruby!"

"You better work on your puny muscles," Rubina smirked, strutting toward them. "She's got you sweating."

"Shut up and drug her."

"You poor thing." Rubina pinched Roma's chin. "Hold still."

The piercing point of a needle sank into Roma's throat and the last thing she saw was the red door close behind the Firawn's son. Then darkness dragged her under, swallowing her screams and burying her in silence.

CHAPTER 29

HUNKERING DOWN BEHIND the saw-toothed boulders, Leviathan scanned the lay of the coastal desert. Fissured planes and pastel dunes ruled the western shore. Beyond it, he could see the undulating body of the Bitter Sea. Cold currents had formed Tundra Desert, varnishing it in a vague mist, and his eyes examined each gap and grain, pursuing the hoof marks in the sand to the two hundred feet tall temple structure less than a hundred feet ahead. The entrance was two massive wooden doors. They wouldn't open to anybody at this hour. Scales and vultures carved into the brass frame represented the goddess of fortune and trade—Manāt—especially worshipped by traders.

It was a solid base. Nobody would suspect the temple as the safe location for shipments. He hadn't had time to scout it out, but he wasn't worried, because temples had columns, alcoves, and chambers, and it was enough leeway for somebody trained to move unseen. He rolled his shoulders and checked his knives. His fingertips brushed Roma's hairpin in his leather bracer. Guilt burned low in his gut. Despite her questions and pleas, he hadn't shared the truth with her for three reasons.

One—deception was an effective means to an end. She had to perceive his intentions as something other than what they were. He wanted her to believe he *meant* to sell her because he needed her fear to convince the handler. Two—he couldn't trust her. Three—telling her the truth meant depending on her for his plan to work which was a power imbalance he wouldn't allow. Handing her over to Rado had been a necessary move. If he'd declined after Rado agreed to pay the full price, it would've raised the handler's suspicion. Part of the reason he picked her was because of her scars. He'd been ninety percent certain she wouldn't sell, but that ten percent risk turned the tables on him.

His stomach muscles tightened at his own incompetence.

No matter how hard he tried to get her bold eyes out of his head, he couldn't forget the way they'd implored him. Hell, they'd cleaved right through him like a sharpened blade, and he'd almost turned back for her.

Almost.

Junho watched the brothel in case they shifted her to another. Leviathan had made a promise to her, and he intended to keep it. Once the kids were safe, he'd return for her. The image of her with a blade to her throat was still fresh in his mind. She'd been prepared to take her own life, but her will to survive turned out stronger, so she'd tried to kill him instead, and he had a lot of respect for it. For people who fought to live despite their circumstances.

Something about her was unnatural, though. The focus in her eyes. Her speed. That sinuous way she mirrored his smallest movements. For reasons he couldn't explain, it bothered him.

He couldn't afford to think about her right now.

Shutting down all thoughts of her, Leviathan whistled quietly as a signal to Malev, leaping over the boulder, soaring to the shadow below the rise. Malev already moved in the direction of the temple, closing in from the north. Keeping the hood over his head, Leviathan advanced from the south, stepping without sound, his shape nothing more than an elusive silhouette to the untrained eye. Maybe the rush of exhilaration in his blood should've shamed him. It didn't. It roused the hunter in him.

He levelled himself against the southern wall, listened, catching the skittering of scorpions hiding in the cracks, the echo of chanting from the temple. Stepping back with his crossbow in hand, he set his boot in the stirrup and cocked it. The muscles in his arm tensed as he raised it, sighted, and pulled the trigger. The grappling hook spiralled up and hooked in the window above. Seconds later, he scaled the wall, swinging sideways over the ledge into a dark archway, slipping behind one of the columns.

The square-shaped level had the archway stretching all the way around above an open hall. A red agate cube sat in the centre downstairs—the statue of the western goddess. Four *dēvadasis* circled it. The soft thuds of footfalls reached Leviathan before a door opened up ahead to reveal a priest. Coming up behind the priest, Leviathan locked him in a chokehold, hauling him back into the dim-lit chamber he had exited from. Sandalwood scented the air. A cot occupied the otherwise naked chamber.

Clamping his hand around the priest's throat, Leviathan rammed him up against the wall next to the door. "Where's Volos?" he demanded.

The priest clawed at Leviathan's hold. "I—don't—understand," he wheezed, face red.

Leviathan pressed the tip of a knife under the priest's bulging eye. "Let me help you understand," he offered softly.

"Wait—please—I don't know—where he's gone."

"Where do you keep the kids?"

"Courtyard—a kennel—I only—provide shelter—for them while—he awaits the ship—I swear—on Mother Manāt—"

"A kennel for hounds? That's your definition of a shelter?" Leviathan's teeth flashed. "How many men does Volos have with him?"

"Three—with him," the priest rasped. "Four in—courtyard."

Running the blade's tip to his throat, Leviathan pushed it against his jugular, but the sudden flash of Jasir's pale-faced kid made him hesitate. Clenching his teeth, Leviathan spun the priest around and struck him in the back of the head, dropping his unconscious body on the floor. He wouldn't get up for a while. Moving back out into the archway, Leviathan shut the door, and his muscles coiled when he vaulted over the balustrade, landing on his feet in the hall and startling the praying *dēvadasis.*

"The courtyard?" he asked.

They shivered and pointed.

Two men rushed him on the terrace. His knives arrowed through the air, striking one in the hand as he pulled a gun, and the other dead centre in the head. Leviathan blocked a punch, stepped across, and rammed his elbow into the guard's face. There was a satisfying *crack*. Landing a blow in his side, Leviathan smashed his ribs in and, for good measure, punctured his lung. The guard let out a guttural sound. Forcing him down, Leviathan sent the heel of his boot into his spine, breaking it, and the guard didn't move again.

The violent spill of blood and snap of bone cooled Leviathan's system. Pulling his bloodstained knives from their flesh, he stepped over their bodies, keeping to the shadows as he passed through another archway leading him out into the courtyard. Rado and a second guy sat around a table outside the kennel, drinking beer and shuffling cards. Malev emerged in the archway across from Leviathan and Leviathan met his companion's eyes in a wordless signal before he strode out.

"Got a spot for a third player?" he asked.

The two men cursed and shot to their feet. Coming up behind them, Malev grabbed the other guy and kicked the gun out of Rado's hand to give Leviathan time to reach him. Rado dived for it, but he was too slow. Leviathan closed the distance in three quick strides and slammed his boot down on Rado's hand where it touched the gun on the ground. Rado howled as the bones in his fingers were crushed. Furious, he jumped up and swung at Leviathan with his uninjured fist. Trapping his wrist in a painful joint lock, Leviathan twisted his arm around his back.

"Where's Volos?"

"Fuck you," Rado spat.

"I'll ask you one more time. Where's Volos?"

"Fuck you again."

Leviathan put his mouth at Rado's ear. "You want to play hard? Let's play hard." Flipping a knife, he sank the blade into Rado's spleen and his strangled scream reverberated in the courtyard. Leviathan kept his back to the kennel, not sure if the kids could see. "Talk."

Sweat rolled down Rado's face. "He's not here, asshole," he gasped and coughed.

"Tell me where he is."

When Rado clamped his mouth shut, Leviathan twisted the knife. A primal sound ripped from his throat. "He's—He went—down to the pier," he panted.

Wrenching out the knife, Leviathan slit his throat and dumped his body behind the kennel. Malev joined him as he moved to the cell door. Strange inscriptions were carved into the brass frame around it. He recognised the language as part Ancient Khansāri and part something else. Eleven boys and ten girls huddled inside the kennel, eyes wide, faces pale, but alive, and Leviathan felt his lungs unclench as if they'd been compressed for days. Opening the cell door, he was careful not to make any sudden movements. Their eyes followed him, bodies coiled, ready to flinch. He crouched down, so he didn't tower over them.

"Hey, I'm Levi. This is Malev. You're safe now," he said and held out his hand to one of the girls. "Want to come outside?" She watched him for a minute, eyes full of tears, then she wiped her nose and slipped her hand into his. There was a mark on her arm. A heptagon. The other kids had similar marks. It looked familiar, but he couldn't place it, so he filed it away for now. Picking her up, he passed her to Malev. "Take them to the mounts. I'm going after Volos."

As Malev persuaded the kids to follow him out, Leviathan turned to leave the kennel and stopped the moment his eyes cut to the small figure balled up in the corner. Crossing to the girl, he crouched down beside her. She looked like she was sleeping, but she was too pale, too still, and too cold when he touched her cheek.

His stomach did a slow roll.

This wasn't right. It couldn't be right. Running his hands over his face, he shoved them into his hair and swallowed hard. This wasn't how it was supposed to happen. He'd planned everything down to the smallest detail. He wasted no time and made it here. How could this happen? It had to be some cosmic joke. He was meant to retrieve the kids alive, *all* of them—

"You're playing me, aren't you?" Leviathan whispered to the powers that be. "You're fucking playing me." Bending his head, he pressed his palms against his eyelids. He couldn't make himself look at her again, at her tiny body curled up like she was still in pain. He wanted to beg her to breathe. She'd died alone. Nobody should die alone.

Dropping his hands, he clenched his jaw, staring down at her. It took more than strength to tamper down on the guilt and grief which blocked his throat. It took a part of him, a frozen part, to control it all.

If he didn't move fast, he'd lose more than he could handle tonight.

The darkness in him spread like poison in his veins. His mind turned to Volos and rage filled him to the rim.

He would end the bastard. *Slowly.*

Removing his cloak to cover her, Leviathan leaned down, brushing his lips against her cold brow. "*Inna lillaahi wa innaa ilayhi raaji'oon,*" he said under his breath. "Go with the angels, love."

CHAPTER 30

Leviathan stalled outside the kennel as his senses prickled. Pivoting, he threw a knife. It arrowed straight for a figure cloaked in the kennel's shadow. The stranger swatted the blade aside as if flicking off a fly and eased into the moonlight. Narrowing his eyes, Leviathan sized him up. Six-three, broad in build. Brown leather banded across his large chest over a white *kurta.* His face was hidden behind a shemagh, but his silver eyebrows revealed his age.

"Leviathan Blackburn, son of the Firawn," the stranger said. The words were rounded and drawn out like the Almasian dialect. He was an easterner. "It's an honour to finally make your acquaintance."

"I'd say the same to you, but I'd be lying."

His eyes crinkled. "Not the friendly sort, are you?" he asked, amused.

"Not a friend, are you?"

"Friend or foe. Life's rarely that simple, is it?"

The stranger charged at him. Leviathan dodged his front kick, blocked his right hook punch, and tried to ram his left elbow in the stranger's liver, but the stranger sidestepped his blow lightning fast. Locking Leviathan's punching arm, he slammed an elbow below his ear and Leviathan let out a sharp exhale. The impact to the nerve centre faltered his balance for the better half of a second. He took a knee strike to his ribs and rolled with the stranger's second blow.

Smooth bastard.

His age and weight didn't slow him down. If anything, they were evenly matched. Leviathan had never been evenly matched before. Instinct took control of his muscles. Rotating his body, he swung his leg with blinding speed, smashing his boot in the stranger's face, following it up with quick knife hands to his nose and throat, but the stranger fended off his attempts without breaking a sweat.

Trapping Leviathan's arm in a joint lock, he tried to manipulate him into a chokehold. Leviathan evaded it and, seeing an opening in the stranger's defence, snapped back his shoulder and let his fist rip forward. It connected with the stranger's sternum, but the asshole was barely winded. The jabbing and blocking continued with Leviathan brutally striking the closest points and the stranger effortlessly limiting his freedom of action. He chuckled low in his throat, deflecting Leviathan's blows, his eyes flashing with the heat of the challenge.

Feigning a left hook, Leviathan shifted his weight at the last second, jabbing him in the ribs. The stranger bent over on a huff. Leviathan grabbed the back of his head in a clinch, about to bring up his knee to smash it in the stranger's face, but he was thrown off as the stranger clamped his arms around Leviathan's waist, lifted him up in a wrestling move, and slammed him down on the ground. It should've knocked the air from Leviathan's lungs, but he'd been smacked down harder than this. Flipping up to his feet in a swift motion, he drove the stranger back, gaining some distance, and spat blood.

Then he reassessed him as they circled each other.

"You seem frustrated, my *chhokro*."

"I'm not your boy."

Sweat slid down Leviathan's spine. His muscles flexed, his jaw tensed. The stranger was clearly trained in fighting from positions of disadvantage. Leviathan couldn't read his intentions. A voice in the back of his mind reminded him that Volos was out there. That Roma was in the brothel. He needed to speed this up if he wanted to keep his promises—the one he made to Roma before he abandoned her in hell, and the one he made to the lifeless girl inside the kennel.

The stranger cocked his head. "Would you prefer to be called by the name your father gave you?" he inquired. "Leviathan."

Locking stares, Leviathan beckoned him. "How about you give me yours?" he suggested.

"Names hold power. They should never be shared lightly."

The corner of Leviathan's mouth quirked. "Afraid I'll take away your power?"

The stranger chuckled again. Leviathan attacked with more force, more speed. He dodged one of the stranger's straight jabs, ripped the leather strap from his chest, catching his right hook with it and yanking the strap tight before twisting the stranger's locked arm behind his back. The *crack* and grunt were music to Leviathan's ears. The stranger whacked his cheekbone with his rear elbow, switching their positions, and looped the strap around Leviathan's neck.

"I only fear one thing in this world," he whispered in Leviathan's ear.

Pummelling him in the ribs, Leviathan pulled out of the chokehold. When the stranger lifted his leg in a high kick, Leviathan bent back, hooked his arm around his calf, and dropped, which forced the stranger down with him.

It was a stalemate.

Sliding a knife from his leather bracer, Leviathan released him. As the stranger jumped to his feet, Leviathan smashed his boot against his shin. He fell back on the ground and, in that second, Leviathan was on him, his knee pressing down on the stranger's chest, his knife pushing against his throat.

"Looks to me like you've lost your power."

The stranger laughed. Deep and savage. "You've been trained well." The tone of pride in his voice disturbed Leviathan. Wanting to see his face before he slit his throat, Leviathan reached for the stranger's shemagh. Two masked men leaped from the kennel's roof, flipping through the air, landing on their feet in a tight half-circle around him. Blades touched the sides of Leviathan's throat, making him drop the knife, and he spread his hands, neutralised.

They looked identical in their white clothes and shemaghs, but they were shorter, leaner, younger. The one on his right with narrowed blue eyes stared down at him in obvious contempt; the one on his left with brown eyes held no animosity, nothing. Leviathan recognised their swords. Distinctive wave patterns specked the crucible steel, marking the eastern blades as Durokshan scimitars. The asshole he fought was their leader. He saw it in how the men looked to him for orders, the deference in their body language.

Brushing dust from his sleeves, the leader turned to Leviathan. "You have anger in you, *chhokro*," he observed. "It can be your weakness or strength, but that's a choice you have yet to make."

Leviathan stared him down. "Who are you?" he asked with cold impatience.

"We have many names. Rebels, warriors, thieves."

Easterners trained in combat, dressed in white, and with feudal weapons.

"You're the White Wolves."

"Ah, our reputation precedes us," the leader responded, sounding pleased.

"What do you want?"

"Nothing from you. Not quite yet. We're here for the children."

"What children?"

"The ones you so valiantly retrieved."

"Don't know what you're talking about," Leviathan said. "I came here to pray."

"By yourself?"

"That's me. Broody, loner type."

"Your companions might disagree with you."

Leviathan looked to his left, his stomach hardening as four other men marched Malev and Junho forward at sword point. His eyes ran over their bodies. A few cuts and bruises. Nothing visibly broken. They'd found Junho, brought him here, which meant Roma was alone in Makhmoor. He swallowed hard. She could be hurt, and he could be too late.

The men shoved his companions to their knees. Junho's head dipped in shame, his left eye swollen shut, but Malev looked at Leviathan and gave a faint shake of his head. The leader stepped between them. "What your friend is trying to convey is that the children are no longer in his possession," he said with a merry gleam in his eyes.

The vein in Leviathan's neck throbbed.

"What did you do with them?"

"That's none of your concern, *chhokro*."

"If you touch them, I'll hunt you down," Leviathan ground out. "I'll find you. You don't want to be alive when I do."

"I admire your confidence and passion, Leviathan. The children leave with us." He nodded at his men. That second of a distraction was all Leviathan needed to slip the knives from his boots. Jamming one in the right guy's thigh, he used the other to block the left guy's sweeping blade. The impact of steel against steel caused sparks. Leviathan glided his knife's blade along the scimitar's, diverting the attack, and struck the side of his opponent's head with his elbow.

"Enough," the leader commanded. Leviathan froze. His companions had taken down the men who restrained them, using his diversion to their advantage as he knew they would, but now the leader had a fistful of Junho's hair and bared his throat to a blade. His eyes were cool and amiable. "Step inside the kennel."

"Kill him, Bhau," Junho rasped heatedly, struggling against the hold. "Just kill him."

There was no guarantee he'd let Junho live if Leviathan complied, but Leviathan gritted his teeth, backing into the kennel, and Malev followed. The brown-eyed guy he knocked down earlier slammed the cell door shut, and the blue-eyed one picked up a piece of metal and bent it around the bars to seal them in. The stab wound in his thigh bled. Glaring at Leviathan, he deliberately stuck Leviathan's knife into his leather waistband.

Junho's defiance resulted in a blood trail down his throat. Leviathan gripped the bars of the cell door. "Stop moving, Junho," he snapped, and Junho went still.

"I must thank you for leading us here, *chhokro*," the leader said, annoyingly polite. "We wouldn't have found the children without you. If the Creator wills it, we'll surely meet again."

And he knocked Junho out cold.

CHAPTER 31

With a sharp heave of her chest, Roma blinked open her eyes.

Thirty women clustered together on stained sleeping mats in the enclosed chamber. A rancid smell of sweat, perfume, and bile assaulted the air, and loud sobs resounded against the walls. Roma's head pained as if thousands of needles pinned it all at once. The rope around her wrists had been removed. Turning onto her side, she dry-heaved on the stone. Her belly cramped from the strain, her damp skin glistened in the low lamplight. Drawing several deep breaths, she swallowed the sourness in her throat, crawling toward the door with the chamber spinning around her.

"I wouldn't do that if I were you," one of the women said in a strange accent. "The corridors are guarded. You'll be beaten."

Roma hesitated and crawled back to the corner. She glanced over at the woman. Leaning against the wall with an elbow propped on her knee, she looked as if she were never more comfortable. Thick, auburn hair framed a fair-skinned, angular face with almond-shaped eyes and a small, wide nose with a septum nosepiece. The symbols drawn over her prominent cheekbones and dimpled chin revealed she was from the Mountain Clans.

How had she ended up in a place such as this?

The sobs became a keening wail and the clan woman sighed. "Lisha, *shirina*. Keep sobbing like that and the guards will come." The shrill sound shrunk. Catching Roma's stare, she angled her head. "What's your name, then?"

Roma's voice was hoarse. "Roma," she answered through the pain.

"I'm Thwayya. You're a *dēvadasi*. What's that like?"

"Like being sold for coin."

The clan woman laughed, and it was a rich, beautiful sound. "I like you, Roma," she said. Slipping her fingers into her cleavage, she pulled out a betel leaf swollen with an orange paste. "Do you want? It'll numb your soul before they take your body."

Roma swallowed bile and shook her head. Thwayya shrugged, shoving half of the betel leaf inside her mouth. The paste turned her lips the colour of persimmons. Tipping her head back to rest against the wall, she breathed as if she were at peace at last. Her jaw moved slowly while she chewed on the betel leaf.

"That's where you were the other night?" a woman snapped at Thwayya. "Taking care of Volos' hunger, so he'd give you the Phantom's Breath?" There were no tribal symbols on her dark skin, but her accent sounded distinctive. She wore a tight *choli* and knee-length *lehenga* like Thwayya and the other prostitutes. Her green eyes harboured indescribable experiences that reminded Roma of Kanoni, of how the clan woman carried her sorrow like an aged scar which might tear open and bleed again.

"It was well worth it, Layl," Thwayya hummed, peering up at the festering ceiling as if she saw past it to the constellations in the night skies. Roma looked around at the women. Some of them cried in silence while a few stared down at their feet with a despondent shine in their eyes. Their distinctive garments told her they were new like her because they didn't wear the common attire for prostitutes, but those in similar *cholis* and *lehengas* as Thwayya and Layl chattered among themselves and passed cigarettes to one another.

"Where are we?" Roma asked.

Sliding her tongue over her bottom lip, Thwayya shuddered, speaking words in a rhythmic tongue Roma didn't understand. With a distracted smile, she lolled her head to the side, looked at Roma, and explained her words with a simple, "Far from home."

"Saheba's. Unless you were brought here blindfolded, you should know."

"Don't be a bitch, Layl."

"The *dēvadasi* asks stupid questions."

Lisha wiped her reddened nose in her sleeve. She was younger than the rest of them. Perhaps not much older than Goldie. "What will happen to us?" she squeaked.

"You're in a brothel. What do you think will happen?" When fresh tears overflowed Lisha's eyes, Layl pursed her lips. "Look, Fountain of Tears. Sobbing like a babe won't help you now. You're not getting out, *samajhliyo,*" she added in her eastern dialect.

"How long have you been here?" one of the other women asked.

Layl shrugged. "I was a child when I was sold to Dragan by my father, so he could pay his debt to the coinlender. Dragan told me I owed him two thousand *rajat*. I worked for him, took almost thirty men per night, but then he sold me to another trader for three thousand. It didn't matter I'd paid off some of my debt. I had a new one." She turned her head and scowled at Lisha. "So stop wasting your tears. Work and pay. Because if you don't, Volos will make sure you wish he'd kill you."

"Why don't you run?" Roma asked in a quiet voice.

"Run?"

"What's the point of paying an endless debt?"

"You're really stupid, aren't you?"

"Give it a rest, Layl," Thwayya murmured. She looked at Roma with vacant eyes. "Don't try to run. Volos has men everywhere who'll drag you back, and he'll make an example out of you in front of the other girls."

"Salma pissed blood when he was done with her," Layl remarked. "Wonder where she is now."

"Probably in one of his brothels for sickos."

"I want it, Tai," Lisha blurted. "I want the Phantom's Breath."

Lowering her forehead to her knees, Roma heaved in a breath and counted to ten within her mind. This wouldn't be her life. She owed no debt to anyone. She would escape. Her fingers searched her waistline, but the pendant was gone. They must have found it on her while she was unconscious. The thought of their hands on her shell nauseated her.

"What's your story, *shirina*?" Thwayya asked.

Roma closed her eyes. "I don't have one," she answered.

"Everyone's got a story."

"She's a *dēvadasi*," Layl said in a deprecating tone. "*Dēvadasis* lie with men because they believe they're gods. Isn't that how it is?" When Roma remained unresponsive, she snorted. "It always begins and ends with the gods."

"It begins and ends with humans," Thwayya said airily. "If there were no gods, people would still prostitute their children."

The abrupt resonance of footfalls reached Roma. She clambered to her feet with the other women, but Thwayya, Layl, and the prostitutes remained seated. The door swung open. Five men entered with Rubina close behind, shouting for them to move and pushing them out into the corridor. Roma caught herself against a wall and looked at Lisha when her cries provoked one of the men. Gripping her arm, he hurtled Lisha through the entrance of the chamber.

"Go easy on them, Rust," a prostitute said in a cautious tone. "They're new."

"Shut your mouth and mind your own fucking self."

Roma battled an amplifying feebleness as the men shoved them down narrow corridors and steep stairs. The lurid sounds of chatter, laughter, and string instruments melded together to a cacophonous noise, quieting when they were stashed inside another chamber with obscene murals on the walls and cages dangling from the ceiling. Naked, bruised children peered down at them through the bars. Roma barely processed the abused children before Rubina and the men started stripping the women down to their skins.

Frightened screams filled the chamber. The women who struggled were slapped into submission. Roma covered herself with her arms, humiliated and terrorised, as three of the men picked up large steel buckets from a carved basin in a corner. Water, frostier than the night air, slammed into her, and she choked on her own breath. Rubina tossed them towels to dry themselves and passed out garments. Shivering from shock and cold, Roma slipped into her *choli* and *lehenga*, staring up toward the silent children.

One of the doors into the chamber opened. A man in a green *kurta* strolled inside. Blond hair was scraped back from a narrow face with blue-green eyes so transparent they seemed wraithlike. She had never seen human eyes so bereft of life. Boosting himself up on a table, he lit a cigarette and bared his tobacco-stained teeth in a wide grin.

"Welcome to Saheba's, darlings," he greeted them. "You can call me Kazi. I'm your handler."

Lisha ran.

Kazi watched her sprint to the nearest door as if he were a spider watching an insect squirming in his cobweb, allowing her a single breath to realise the door was sealed before Rust gripped her throat, dragged her back, and threw her at his feet. Lisha's sobs ricocheted within Roma's head. Shuddering at the malevolent shine in Kazi's stare, Roma struggled to remove herself from the scene. She wanted to disappear. She wanted it all to be an illusion that she could shatter with her sheer will.

Kazi tipped his head to the side. "That was rude," he told Lisha in a cutting voice. "You could've at least waited until I finished my introduction."

Rust slammed his boot into her belly.

Lisha screamed and screamed at first, but then her cries became agonised moans. Curling herself into a protective ball, she coughed up blood as Rust's assaults rained down on her, as he kept striking her tormented body for endless minutes. Rubina jerked her head in contempt with a hand on her hip. The women huddled together in terror, but Roma couldn't move from where she stood.

"Rust, my man," Kazi said, tossing his cigarette. "You planning on breaking her bones? Nobody pays for fucked-up whores, for fuck's sake."

Rust stopped.

Rasping for air, Lisha closed her eyes. Kazi turned his attention to the women. "Like I was saying before this little sweetheart interrupted me—I'm your handler. You girls are lucky, you know. It's a jungle out there. You could've ended up with a real monster like Bor, but Volos doesn't mistreat his girls for no reason. He's got a simple system. Follow his rules, and it's all good."

Leaping from his seat, he crouched down beside Lisha, wiping blood from her lips with his thumb. "Think of him as a father figure. We're family here. We take care of each other." He licked her blood from his finger. "You were chosen for Saheba's and that makes you real special. Work hard, pay your debt, and you can leave. Sound fair?" None opposed him. None dared. "Excellent. Line up, darlings. Let's have a look at you."

Roma stared at an immobile Lisha as Kazi circled them one at a time, his eyes raking over their bodies and examining them like raw meat in a butcher's stall. "Send these four to Night Queen's." He gestured to the trembling women on Roma's left. "They'll be good for business there."

Rubina pouted. "I wanted to keep the curvy ones. I've got men complaining about skinny whores. If I don't have what they seek—"

"Don't sulk, Ruby. You'll have plenty more. But we've got to end Night Queen's dry spell. Volos' orders." Roma braced herself when Kazi turned toward her. His smirk evaporated. "And what do we have here? Short, damaged. Was Rado blind when he bought her?" The men snickered. Kazi inclined his head. "Look at those demon eyes, though. You going to eat me, darling?"

His laughter was a slow, soundless rasp that sent an awful shiver down her back. He took her chin between his fingers and she smacked his hand aside. Kazi's men shifted behind him, but he only grinned. "Feisty one, are you?"

Rubina smiled. "She's a *dēvadasi*," she told him.

"*Dēvadasi*," Kazi repeated, stepping back to run his eyes down her shell. "A temple *vēshya*? How did she fall into our hands?"

"Some lower *zaat* snatched her up."

"Did he, now?"

"Rado paid four thousand *rajat* for her. She'll bring in a crowd."

"I've always wanted to see the famed *dēvadasi* dance. Looks like I finally will. Go on. Dance for me, darling. Let's see what all the fuss is about."

Roma stared at him. Panic attempted to touch her, but she was beyond its reach. She didn't know how or where her defiance came from. Whether it was courage or madness. Her frantic pulse thumped and the cold dissipated until all she felt was a searing heat within her veins and a gaping abyss within her mind.

"Are you deaf, bitch?" Rubina snapped. "Dance for him."

Kazi squinted at her. "Eyes down," he ordered. She held his stare for another heartbeat, and then lowered her eyes. When he stepped closer to her, she smelled smoke and sweat on him. "Now, dance."

She didn't move.

The air vibrated a second before he backhanded her. She staggered from the impact. Black spots marred her vision and blood stained her lips, but she wouldn't cower when he advanced on her. "Little bitch." Gripping a fistful of her hair, he hauled her across the chamber while she scratched at his hold. Her eyes watered and her vision blurred. Throwing her into an adjoining chamber, he bolted the door behind them. Roma caught herself on a cluttered table, her hands slipping on the surface, and scrolls and pencils scattered all over the floor.

Charging like an angered bull, Kazi struck her across the face. She fell on the stone, bleeding and rasping as he straddled her. "You give me attitude? You whore."

His weight crushed her chest. The pain from his assault blinded her. She pleaded with her goddess for each smack to be the last. Grabbing a handful of the soil that had spilled from a shattered pot, he shoved it into her mouth and it poured into her throat, congesting her chest and blocking her breathing. She would die here. She would die now. The fire within her escalated, erupting like a volcano, burning through her flesh, and her back arched with such abrupt force that Kazi almost lost his balance.

When he shovelled the dirt into her mouth this time, she sank her teeth deep into his hand. "Fuck!" he screamed, ripping back his arm.

Gasping for air, Roma fumbled for a weapon and clutched a letter opener, thrusting it into his eye. Kazi howled and jerked back. Falling on the ground, he squirmed like a worm, the blade jammed so deep inside his head only the handle was visible. Roma turned onto all fours and vomited soil. Blood and dirt smeared her lips. She scrambled to her feet, catching her breath as she stared at an unmoving Kazi sprawled among the mess on the floor.

"Kazi? Kazi!" Rubina pounded on the door. "Rust, break in."

Stumbling over to a window, Roma unlatched it on her second attempt and stepped onto the ledge, peering down into the alley below. It was a higher drop than Lamiapur's walls, but not as high as the banyan. Her head pounded and whirled. Dragging in a painful breath, she balanced and then leaped just as the door swung open behind her.

CHAPTER 32

Roma ran through the serpentine alleys.

Her hair tangled with blood and sweat, her breath came in gasps, and her right ankle panged from the drop. She weaved around chattering hijras and playing children, pushing her bruised feet forward despite the sharp jolts of pain. Guards shouted and cursed at the people in their path as they pursued her through the slim passages of the city. Desperation wanted her to plead with the hijras to hide her, but she knew none would aid a woman in this place. Staggering from a torrent of vertigo, she leaned against a wall to catch her stuttering breath.

Don't stop.

She threw herself back into the sprint and didn't see the hijra in time, slamming right into her and sending her basket through the air. Blossoms showered down on them. The hijra shouted after her in a burst of temper. Just as it seemed that there was no end to the labyrinth, Roma rounded the corner to an alley which opened out to the marketplace with its hustle and bustle of bartering people between the stalls.

The crowd was thick enough for her to vanish in it.

With a burning throat, she glided past a stall, snatching a shawl while the seller was preoccupied with four loud prostitutes. Spiralling the shawl around herself, she concealed her face as she threaded hastily through the horde, retracing the path that the Firawn's son had dragged her down.

When she spotted the alcohol stalls, she knew she was close to the border.

She turned her head and locked eyes with a guard moving along the outline of the mass. As soon as she discovered him, he dived for her, shoving people aside with mean force. Discarding the shawl, Roma jostled past the men and women, bursting out into the open and surging out of the city. A cold, furious wind lashed her. White dust layered her tongue. The ceaseless quivering in her limbs and the throbbing in her ankle warned her that she couldn't run much farther. She needed to hide before she collapsed, but the desert surrounded her, and the great canyon was still far ahead. Her chest rose and fell with each strenuous breath as she sprinted toward the mouth of the cleft with three guards at her heels.

Her feet struck against the fragmented ground, and the violent pain in her ankle made her stagger. The world tilted around her. She fell. A keening noise trilled in her ears. When she exhaled, the sand drifted over the cracks. It was over. The sharp vibrations in the air revealed the guards were too close for her to escape now. The keening became a low hiss. She lifted her head in a daze and met the eyes of a black-skinned serpent. It must have slithered out of one of the deep cracks in the ground. Rising before her, it watched her with eyes like sweltering rubies. Then it lowered itself and moved toward the guards.

"Watch out for the Black Yuxa," one of them shouted. "It spits venom."

"Shoot it!"

Taking advantage of their diverted attention, Roma clambered back on her feet with a spinning mind, hurtling herself toward the canyon. She reached the cleft to the sound of a blast, but she didn't turn to see if the serpent was dead.

Hide.

Fleeing into the canyon, she spun this way and that for a place to hide. The air vibrated again, too close, but it was a deeper sound. Thundering. She skidded to a stop as three riders appeared from the depths of the canyon, galloping toward her like black-shaped wraiths in the night, and she recognised the front rider's mount at a single glance.

Cinder.

The guards arrived behind her. She was trapped between them and the Firawn's son. Something glinted and whistled past her shoulders. She swivelled around to see two of the guards drop onto the ground with knives impaling their eyes. The last one drew a gun from his waistband, but a knife sliced through his wrist, detaching his gun-wielding hand, and his scream resounded against the canyon's walls before another knife made his body crumble like a puppet whose strings were snipped.

With shallow breaths, Roma watched the Firawn's son dismount. His companions remained at a distance as he advanced on her with a caution that suited a man who had discovered a wounded animal in his path. She was shaken and spent. Too drained to run and too livid to surrender.

"Don't come near me," she rasped.

His steps wavered.

Then he stepped close enough to touch. Emotions darkened his eyes when he took in her battered face. His own was covered in bruises as well.

"Roma—"

Her palm smacked against his cheek. Junho cursed and rushed forward, but the Firawn's son raised his hand without looking away from her hateful stare. His companion stopped in a disinclined silence. Malev hadn't moved at all.

"You sold me."

"Yes."

His quiet acceptance fuelled her rage. Everything within her blistered. If she had possessed claws, she would have raked them across his face. She wanted him to bleed, bleed, *bleed* until he experienced the same agony he caused her. How could Ghanima Mai sing this man's praises? How could she see anything honourable in him? The dispassion with which he had sold her wasn't the trait of a human.

"The worst kind of monsters, Saheb—" Roma said through gritted teeth, "—are those who pretend they're human."

He flinched. It was nothing more than a faint twitch in his expression, but it pleased her that she injured him somehow and that his composure disintegrated to show she *could* injure him.

"I'm taking you home." His voice was impassive. "Get on the mount."

"I'm not coming with you."

"Get on the mount, Roma."

"No. What will you do? Force me? Beat me? *Mār.*" She slammed her palms against his chest and he stepped back from her. It only enraged her more that he relented. She shoved him again. "*Mār.*" Her voice rose until she was shouting it at him. "*Mār!* What's wrong? You can't hit me, but you can sell me? You men are all the same. It doesn't matter if we're a stranger or your sister. You would sell your own mother if it—"

He reached out, cupped the back of her head, and pulled her face to his. So close she felt his breath on her skin and her own dispelled within her lungs. She stared into his eyes, refusing to tremble, even as she loathed his fingers in her hair.

His eyes had hardened. "Don't," was all he whispered.

The emotion behind the word lay him bare. She had made him bleed. But it wasn't enough. She was assaulted and hunted because of him. She was ill so deep within herself that she wanted to crawl out of her shell, yet all she could do was feel the humiliation when she was stripped naked in front of those men in the brothel, and the pain when she was beaten and strangled.

Why should she suffer alone? Why should she spare him?

"Brother," Malev intervened.

The Firawn's son released her as roughly as he had seized her and turned from her. The muscles along his back moved with his breathing. "Get her back to Lamiapur," he said in a low voice. Leaping into the saddle, he turned Cinder around, and Junho glowered at her before he climbed onto his own mount and followed the Firawn's son, the dust rising and settling behind them.

Remaining at a distance, Malev reached inside his cloak, drawing out a canteen. He raised it over his mouth, making a show of drinking from it, and then held it out for her, but she didn't take it. She cared none for his compassion. False, or not.

"I'm sorry, Roma," he said, his eyes open and honest. "I know that doesn't make anything right, but you deserve an apology. You deserve more than that."

Roma closed her eyes and slid down to sit in the dust. Her ankle burned. She couldn't fight him if he attempted to drag her back to the brothel because the residue of her strength had waned, and he was as large as a bear. Malev crouched down and set the canteen near her. "We didn't mean for things to go as far as they did."

"You didn't mean to sell me to a brothel or leave me in a brothel?" she asked bitingly. "Which is it?" The illness within her threatened to unleash the chaos she had repressed since her auction. "Your apologies mean nothing."

"I'm still sorry."

Contrition was evident in his voice because he didn't guard his emotions like the Firawn's son, but she ignored his penitence.

"You claim you're sorry, yet you follow him."

"He wasn't always like this." Malev rubbed the copper bracelet on his wrist. "A part of him still isn't. I know it's hard to believe. Sometimes you stick around people you care about because you don't want them to lose themselves completely. I'm not trying to excuse him—I'm trying to explain. You were the means to an end. We wanted to save some kids from an organ trade and needed a face on the handlers involved. So, we used you to enter their brothel. That's fucked up. We all know it. He knows it."

Children. She hated that he told her this because it made it worse. She thought of the children in the cages back at the brothel with a twinge in her belly. The Firawn's son put her through a nightmare. His reasons didn't change that she was abused because of him. How could he sell her to save children? What sort of twisted heroism was that? Wasn't she human to him?

Malev seemed to read her thoughts. "In Levi's head, it's all about things that work and things that don't. That's how he's been wired. It doesn't mean he considers you less than those children. It means he thought this path served his aim the best and he acted out of habit. Roma?" His voice was gentle and kind. He waited for her to look at him. "Will you please let me take you home?"

"I don't trust you."

"I know, but the problem is we're in the desert. If I leave you here, you'll end up back in the brothel because once those guards over there don't return to their posts, they'll send others after you."

What choice did she have? Wandering in the desert until she perished from the cold and thirst, or until she was caught and hauled back? Reaching for the canteen, she raised it to her lips, suppressing a need to pour the water over herself. It burned through her tender throat, but she tipped it higher and gulped it down.

"Can I take you home?" he asked again. "Please."

"Don't touch me."

"I won't. You have my word."

A man's word was a void.

CHAPTER 33

Something demonic pounded through Leviathan's system, rippled in his muscles, clinched around his heart. Thick, hot, and raw. He had a need for violence, but he knew it'd alleviate nothing—silence nothing. Not this time. He didn't know how to stop feeling anymore. Years of honing that damn skill and it was useless to him now.

As he paced his chamber, he pulled out his knives, tossed them on the dresser. Then he removed his leather bracers and chucked them, too. The Wolves had *stolen* the kids from him. By the time he'd broken out of the kennel and reached the pier, the foreign workers were dead, gutted on the shore, and Volos was long gone.

"Bhau, it's not your fault," Junho said with caution. "The *dēvadasi* only said all that shit because the *haramis* assaulted her. You tried, Bhau—"

"Ride back to Tundra," Leviathan interrupted coldly, stripping out of his filthy *kurta*. "Track the Wolves as far as you can. I want to know where their trail ends, *samajalē*?"

"But we already—"

"Do it again."

"*Hō*, Bhau."

"Any news from Kai?"

"Nothing yet," Malev responded.

"Put some pressure on him."

"I'll see to it."

Junho rubbed a hand over his hair. "Bhau, I know we didn't get the kids, but you had a plan. You even had a backup plan. The Wolves screwed everything up."

"Drop it."

"You didn't know those assholes would waltz in out of nowhere and—"

"I said, leave it alone."

"But you're beating yourself up like—"

"Goddamn it, Junho." Leviathan shoved the knives off the dresser with a ferocious sweep of his hand. The dresser followed next and smashed against the tiles. He moved toward Junho in a flash, standing in his face, eyes dark and dangerous, and a muscle pulsing in his jaw. "No matter how many times I repeat myself—" He tapped Junho's temple, hard. "—it never gets through your thick skull, does it?"

Junho winced but didn't back down. "What're you going to do, Bhau? Punch me? Go ahead. I'll lay down my life for you if it'll make you feel better."

Leviathan cuffed the back of his head. *"Dokyala taap devu nakō.* Get the hell out of my sight."

"That *dēvadasi* called you a monster after you saved her life—"

"Junho," Malev warned.

"If anyone ever trashes you like that again," Junho said with heat, backing toward the doors. "I'll break their ass in half, *māshapath*."

"*Junho*."

"*Jāto, jāto.* I'm leaving."

Leviathan glared after him. Running a hand over his face, he rubbed his mouth, breathing through the smothering emotion in his throat. *Monster*. Yeah, he was a monster. He'd killed without a second thought. He'd sold Roma like she wasn't human—made that decision in cold blood. The dead kid he found in the kennel? Maybe it was a punishment for assuming the end justified the means, or maybe for enjoying the hunt a little too much. It made him feel powerful to reach the kids, to know even for a second that he could save them. He felt it now. The self-disgust. Things were easier for him when he didn't have to control his demons, so he let them run savage, and as a consequence people around him got hurt.

Leaning a shoulder on the doorframe, Malev crossed his arms. "He's right about the Wolves. You couldn't have predicted they'd show up," he ventured, his voice bland, but Leviathan heard the things he didn't say.

That what he did to Roma wasn't right.

Leviathan squeezed his eyes shut. "How is she?"

"Hurt."

He inclined his head. "I thought like the Firawn. I picked my objective and acted without any regard for her life." He could've found another way if he'd put his mind to it, but he hadn't wanted to waste time or resources. He'd made it personal—seeking relief, thinking if he saved the kids, he'd find some kind of peace. He walked toward the bathing chamber. "This is on me. All of it."

"Brother—"

Slamming the door on Malev, he crossed to the mirror, bracing his hands on the basin, staring at his own reflection after a long time. Roma had looked at him with ravaged eyes. Like he violated her. When she'd hit him, he'd welcomed it. It made him feel better that she lashed out at him because he didn't know how else to deal with the look in her eyes.

'*The worst kind of monsters are those who pretend they're human.*'

God, he slipped.

Hard.

How the hell did he end up here? So much like *him*, exactly like him. How didn't he see it before? The aching in his throat intensified. He stared at his own face, the Firawn's face, and smashed his fist against the mirror, shattering it, the cracks running like cobwebs and obscuring his features. Not his reddened eyes. No, they looked back, suddenly burned-out, dead.

He rinsed the blood from his knuckles and stepped back into the chamber. Malev had left. He was grateful for that. Pressing the heels of his palms against his brow, he dissected the night in his head, thought of all the ways he could've spared Roma, and tormented himself with alternatives. Maybe it would've changed the outcome if he hadn't used an innocent, if he hadn't been so obsessed with getting to Volos, but focused on taking care of the kids first. The Wolves had known about the organ trade. They'd known he was on to it, and they'd tracked him without his knowledge.

How?

If they'd had somebody follow him, he would've known. His senses would've picked up on a scent, sound, or movement. Something. He might've suspected Kai sold him out, but the kid was too scared to double-cross him, and he didn't think the Wolves worked like that. They wouldn't need him to do the tracking for them if they could've gone through Kai and Jasir on their own. Their leader had skill, but he didn't want to be seen. Instead, he operated in the dark like he wasn't yet confident enough to come out in the open.

Dragging a hand through his hair, Leviathan worked to swallow. It was barely dawn when he left the city and strode to the steppe, chased out by shadows of pricking memories and a noose tightening around his throat like a chokehold.

The camp still slept as the skies turned blood red. Before he knew it, his feet carried him to Mai's tarp, and his hands parted the opening. She was asleep on a mat next to Seth. The dullness in his chest was regret. What was he doing? He shouldn't be here, risking their lives.

Stepping back out, he walked north of the camp where he'd trained Seth. Something was wrong. His hands were ice, his heart raced. He couldn't breathe right. The last time he felt like this was when he was fourteen, standing with a loaded gun pointed at a clan woman, his commanding officer telling him to shoot her.

He swallowed hard, again and again.

"Levi?"

He froze.

Sucking in a breath, he steadied and turned. His eyes were blank as they met hers. Mai was smiling softly, but one look at his face killed it. "Levi," she gasped, coming to him, brushing her fingers over his bruises. "*Kāy jhāle*? How did this happen? Are you all right?" He stared down at her, undone. She'd suffer. Still, she'd ask him if he was all right. "Why won't you answer me? What happened?"

"I sold somebody tonight."

Her hands dropped from his face. "What?"

"I sold a girl to a brothel," he said, holding her shocked stare, "and I didn't look back."

"Levi—"

"I killed a man and his kid saw me do it."

"Stop."

"You know how many men I've cut down? I've lost count. Their faces blur together sometimes, but I remember them all. Your people."

"Why're you telling me this?"

"Because this is who I am, Mai. I'm his blood. His voice is inside my head even when I don't think I hear it." His tone was raw; helpless, desperate. "I'm following him. I can't—he's in my head."

"You need to stop, Levi," she said in a trembling voice.

He spread his arms. "What's the point? I don't care, Mai. I don't care about any of you. I pretend I do, so I can manipulate you into loving me like he does. That's what monsters do. They play you."

She shook her head, denying his words. "You do care," she insisted with tears in her eyes.

"I don't."

"Stop this nonsense, Levi. What's happening with you?" Her hands reached up to frame his face and brushed along his shoulders. "You want me to despise you? Is that what this is? You want me to despise you so you can use it as an excuse to fall deeper into that inner void of yours?"

"Why don't you hate me?" His voice faltered. "Why do you always look at me like that?"

"Because I know you can be better. I need you to be better than this—"

"I'm not your hope. I'm nobody's hope. Don't make me—don't expect that from me, Mai. People like me don't—you don't know what I've done."

"Levi." She reached for him again. "Please."

"You don't believe me?" he asked softly, stepping back from her. "You want to ask the girl I sold tonight? You want to ask her how I tied her hands, dragged her into the brothel, and handed her over for silver?"

Mai slapped him. A sob escaped her throat, and it ripped him apart. When she lurched on her feet, he picked her up in his arms. Cradling her to his chest, he moved to a boulder and set her down on it. He took her hands in his own with a pained breath and pressed them to his eyelids, but she pulled free like his touch was poison.

"Mai."

"*Nakō*. You don't care, remember?"

"You're shaking."

"Leave me be."

"I can't."

"Women are mothers, sisters, daughters, and companions, Levi. Not cattle. What you've done to that poor girl—you've sullied Badriya and shamed Gabrielle." She looked away from him and it cut him deep. "Badriya was fire. She was compassion. Even when that demon violated her, she carried you in her womb and loved you. Children born into our world are known by their father's name, but Gabrielle named you Leviathan bin Badriya. Your birthmother didn't die in labour so you could dishonour her when she battled the likes of Cecilia Blackburn to bring you into this world."

Her words punched him in the stomach. He took three steps back. Afraid to touch her, afraid to stain her. Mai looked up at him and saw too much. "When your sins push you to your knees, you crawl toward redemption, Levi. You don't surrender. I prayed for you. I wanted you to see what you were, where you are, and who you must become."

"It's dark where I am. It's always been dark."

"Light a candle."

His eyes glittered. "I can't sleep, Mai. All I see is smoke and dust. All I smell is blood and death. I'm more like the Firawn than you know."

"You're not like him. You were a sensitive child, Levi. You always felt deeply for others, humans and animals alike. Why would he take you away to a place of darkness if not because of the light in you? Thieves don't enter an empty home and demons don't raid an empty heart. There's still time to make amends."

"You don't understand. He's in my head."

"Cast him out."

He slammed his eyes shut and lowered his head. Something clawed at him from the inside, clawed to be voiced, heard, and he clenched his jaw from the pain of it. *He broke my mind*, he wanted to say. *And no matter how hard I try, I can never fix it.*

"Please," she begged him. "Make amends, Levi."

"I don't know how."

Her features hardened. "Then you better figure it out, and you better not return until you do. Show me who you can be, Levi, or don't return at all. Do you understand me?"

"Yes," he whispered. "I understand."

CHAPTER 34

LAMIAPUR WAS SILENT. Roma slipped into the bathing chamber and drew the curtain closed. Leaning against the wall, her bleak eyes moved over the bar of soap, the extinguished oil lamps, and the bucket of water. Her bruised arms pinned against her belly as if the maelstrom within her might tumble out should she lower them. Her mind was dark. It wasn't the sweet darkness of oblivion, but the painful inferno of awareness that consumed her. The pressure within her wouldn't ease. She saw the brothel. She tasted the blood and the soil, heard the laughter of men, and felt the weight of the handler on her hips.

Her skin itched without cease.

She was tainted.

Without removing her garments, she took the small bowl in the bucket and filled it with the water, clumsy in her haste, and poured it over her shoulders to erase the stains. Their imprints on her. Within her. But her soul continued to thrash. How could she put an end to it all? She poured again and again, and then she tossed the bowl with a clatter. Lifting the entire bucket over her head, she emptied it on her shivering shell in a distraught attempt at purging herself, scrubbing her forearms, shoulders, and face with pitiless force, heedless of her protesting injuries.

Gasping from the pain and the cold, she slid down and sat in the blood-stained puddle, pulling her knees to her chest to hold herself in one piece, pressing her lips into the saturated fabric. She wouldn't sob. She wouldn't shatter. Never again. There was a shadow within her. An existence without a name or a face. It pushed her toward a widening chasm, coaxing and pleading, and she wondered what she might discover beyond it. Grasping at the threads of that shadow, she thought it tasted like a promise of power, but she couldn't touch it even as she strained toward it. Forbidden, a voice hissed. Perilous. Never had she been so close to it as in this moment when the walls of her mind crumbled.

A bitter hardness encased her as she deserted the bathing chamber. It silenced the whispers of the storm. She slipped into the unoccupied shed. Her sisters would expect her return because few patrons wanted their *lamiadasis* to remain with them past dawn. She changed into a simple *choli* and *lehenga*, leaving her hair unbraided to relieve her raw scalp and tossing the sheer veil over her shoulders before she stepped back outside.

Gathering all the sleeping mats from the sheds, she hung them up on the washing lines, knowing she should be in the antechamber for dawn prayers with her sisters, but not caring in the least for the gods. Her bones and muscles complained when she picked up the rug beater. Her hollow belly ached. The pain distracted her from darker sensations.

The sun rose higher into the skies as she swung the rug beater, slamming it in a repetitive motion against the sleeping mats, her long tresses sweeping around her. Motes of dust swirled in the air. She recalled the gnawing chill in the desert, the suffocating feeling of soil in her throat, and swung harder until light sweat shimmered on her collarbone. If anyone looked at her now, they would see a vengeful goddess. Her eyes slashed anything they touched and her hair whipped like a panther's tail. Spinning gracefully, she swung the rug beater again, but a hand caught hold of it mid-air.

She stopped.

The Firawn's son stood before her. No men but Sādin Saheb and his *birandasis* were allowed to enter Lamiapur, but it didn't surprise her that the Firawn's son considered himself above such laws. She wondered what would happen if she called for Amma. Would she reproach him for breaching a rule, or shower him with blossoms because he was the Firawn's son? Roma knew the answer, so she didn't call for her. The sleeping mats might hide them both from plain sight, but prayers should have ended, and her sisters would come down any moment to discover her battered condition. They would believe it was his hands that caused her injuries.

It might as well have been.

"Is it safe to let go, or are you going swing at me next?" The mirth behind his words didn't soften her, nor did it make her smile. "Guess I'll have to take my chances." He released the rug beater, and she lowered it, even as she wanted to strike him with it. His eyes observed her bruises. Glancing away from her, he cleared his throat. "So, this is home."

"What do you want, Saheb?"

"Nothing. I'm here to release you from our patronship."

"That's kind of you." Her voice sounded so hollow that she wondered if her soul had found a path out of her shell at last. "It's one less vow on your conscience." Amma would find another patron for her soon enough. She wasn't released from anything but his vices.

"It's not the only reason I came." He moved his hands to his hips in an uncertain movement and, as one settled, the other lifted to rub his forehead. "I wanted—I came to—I'm not doing this right." He drew a deep breath. "Everything you said last night is true. I sold you. It wasn't what I wanted to do, but I did it anyway." His eyebrows pulled together. "I'm sorry."

"Your sorry doesn't change what happened."

An emotion came into his eyes, but she didn't care to read it. "You're right," he said softly. "You have to pay for your sins, right?" He watched her for what felt like an eternity. "But you think—you think you could ever forgive me?"

She shook her head with decisive deliberation.

He nodded as if he hadn't expected a different answer and, drawing a vial from his pocket, moved closer to her. She retreated from him. It wasn't fear, but resentment. She couldn't stand his presence. It reminded her of everything she wanted to erase. If her withdrawal bothered him, he didn't show it. He held out the vial to her.

"It'll heal you. Take it, please."

Magic wouldn't heal her soul. She didn't think he would leave unless she accepted the medicine, so she took it from him and slid it behind her waistline without a word. "I've got a question," he went on while his eyes searched hers. Gritting her teeth, she shifted on her feet. She was irritated now and she didn't hide it, yet he still asked. "How did you escape from the brothel?"

Her hands squeezed the rug beater as she recalled being hauled into a chamber, straddled, beaten, strangled, and she wanted to slam the rug beater into his head. "I don't care to tell you," she told him. His lips twitched. It frustrated her that she humoured him somehow when she wanted to hurt him.

Raising the rug beater between them, Roma swung it with unnecessary force, missing him by an inch. Dust sprawled in the air. He evaded another swing and tipped his head to the side. "Roma?" She glared at him in answer. "If you ever need anything, you can send for me." He took a step toward her as if to seal the sentiment behind his statement. "Whatever it is, I won't refuse. I know my word is worthless to you, but you have it."

"I don't want anything from you, Saheb."

"It's Levi."

Names were for people who considered each other equals, and she and the Firawn's son would never be equal.

He backed from her and turned to leave.

"Did you save them?" she asked in a voice which betrayed no emotion. "The children."

When he looked at her this time, she saw what she wanted to see. Pain. But it didn't fill her with the satisfaction she had hoped for.

"No," he answered quietly. "But I will."

She turned her back to him in dejection. Relief poured through her when she sensed the subtle shift of the air and heard the almost inaudible *click* of the gate. If he meant what he said about their patronship, perhaps she would never have to see him again.

"Roma?" Sunbel walked toward her with eyes widened in shock. "Lamia. What did he do to you?" Her voice dropped to a whisper. "Are you all right? You should be resting. *Jā*, lie down. I'll you bring you balm for the—"

"I don't need it."

"You should—"

"No."

"Roma—"

"Stop." Roma threw the rug beater. Her head screamed. "Just *stop*."

Sunbel pressed her lips together. "There's something I must tell you." Tears trailed down her pale cheeks and dripped from her delicate jaw. "It's important."

"What is it?"

"Yoshi is gone."

Roma's thoughts scattered like shards of shattered glass against stone. Staring at Sunbel, she drew a breath as she parted her lips, struggling to form a sentence. "Gone, how?" she asked in an unsteady voice. Sunbel wrung her hands and Roma took a step toward her. "Gone, *how*, Sun?"

"Last night, she abandoned her service while we were all in Biranpur after your auction," Sunbel answered, wiping her tears with the back of her hand. "And she wasn't alone. She ran with the son of a higher *zaat* family. His parents are furious and out for blood."

A horrible realisation made Roma's heart tremble in her chest.

"Where's Chirag?"

"You have to understand, Roma—"

"Where *is* he, Sunbel?"

Sunbel closed her eyes and released a quiet breath. "Sādin Saheb summoned the Panchayat in the square. They're all there," she whispered.

CHAPTER 35

Breathless, Roma darted toward the crowd assembled around the shrine of Dathan, God of Justice, and pushed past people until she saw Chirag. His hands were bound to a pillar, his widened eyes held blatant fear and tears, and she smelled the urine on his trousers even from the distance. She rushed toward him, but a hand clamped down on her wrist and hauled her back from him. Spinning around, she looked at Binti whose face was arranged in a pitiless expression. Hani hovered behind her, primed to step in, if necessary.

The Panchayat sat in the shade of a willow. All the landowners were dressed in *kurtas* and *dhotis*. Brass adornments of their finer *zaat* decorated their ears and necks. The Sarpanch, an old man with a red shawl draped over his shoulders as an indication of the highest status in the Panchayat, observed in silence while the other elders debated, and Amma stood beside Sādin Saheb with calm on her face and calculation in her stare.

"A line was crossed last night," Farasat Babu declared in his lisping manner. "It was crossed when a *lamiadasi* deserted her service to the gods. Not only that. She seduced a Saheb's son. We have strict laws against such crimes."

"Farasat Babu is right," Pawar Babu consented, rolling the corner of his moustache in a repetitive motion. "News of a *lamiadasi* eloping with a higher *zaat* man will soon spread across Durra. It might even reach the southern temples. We can't have one shameless *dēvadasi* disgrace our sacred customs and encourage other *dēvadasis* to do the same."

"And what of the wrath of the gods?" Thabit Babu demanded with a frown. "The monsoon season has come and gone, and we've barely seen any rain. The lands are parched and taxes have increased. We don't need another misfortune."

The Sarpanch raised his hand and the Panchayat fell silent at once. His voice rasped slowly, as if he were unable to pull enough air for sound, or as if he were intoxicated and the air dragged itself out of his chest. "Sādin Saheb," he said, his words drawn out. "What do you suggest? How should we handle this delicate situation?"

"We should follow the laws dictated to us," Sādin Saheb replied. "The *lamiadasi* is gone, and so the punishment befalls her relative. This boy who's her brother in blood."

"No," Roma breathed.

"It won't be enough to remind the *dēvadasis* what happens if you defy our sacred customs," Pawar Babu argued with a taut expression. "A much harsher punishment is required, Sarpanch Saheb."

The Sarpanch moved his hand in a downward motion. "One matter at a time. First, we must ensure the higher *zaat* family is placated, or the situation could worsen for all of us."

"This boy should be castrated and dedicated to Lord Biran," Sādin Saheb pressed.

"Stop," Roma shouted. Twisting her sore wrist in a forceful motion, she wrenched out of Binti's hold. The elders stared at her in surprise and contempt. She ignored their outrageous murmurs as she folded Chirag into her arms. His entire form trembled against hers. "It's all right, Chirag. I'm here."

"I want to go home, Tai," Chirag sobbed.

"We will."

Amma snatched her wrist when she reached for his ties. "Roma," she snarled, her eyes darting to the Panchayat. "Have you lost your mind? This is a trial—"

Roma yanked free of her. "He's not an animal. Don't tie him up like one," she bit out. "And this isn't a trial but persecution."

"Sādin Saheb," the Sarpanch wheezed. "Is Lamiapur not under your authority? Is this rebellious demeanour what we can now expect from the slaves of our gods?"

Sādin Saheb glided toward Amma. "Restrain her," he warned quietly, "before I demand a steeper price than your son."

"Leave, Roma," Amma snapped.

"Not without Chirag." Roma pulled him behind her and held Sādin Saheb's stare. "You can settle a price with Amma, but it won't be Chirag." If they wanted to take him, they would have to kill her. Whipping toward the Panchayat, she looked at the Sarpanch. "I knew Yoshi planned to desert. She admitted it to me when I saw her with the Saheb." Amma cursed at her and Chirag's trembling fingers curled even tighter in her veil. She lifted her chin with resolution in her gaze. "If you want to punish someone, it should be me."

"The *chhokri* makes a valid point," Farasat Babu said.

"Perhaps," Sādin Saheb intervened with impatience. "But she's in a patronship with Firawn Sai's son. She can't be punished until she's released from it."

"Then her trial will happen when she's released."

"I have been released," Roma snapped. "You can ask him."

"Does she jest?" Thabit Babu laughed. "She was auctioned only last night."

"Perhaps she was a disappointment," Pawar Babu remarked.

"Enough. This *lamiadasi* shall be tried when we hear from Leviathan Saheb on the matter of her patronship with him." The Sarpanch hauled himself to his feet. "The boy shall be dedicated to Lord Biran on the Dawn of Tanuf. Adjourned."

"You can't have him!" Roma opposed, stepping in front of Chirag to protect him as the village men moved toward them. She shoved their reaching hands aside. "Don't touch him!" Binti and Hani captured her forearms, pulling her from Chirag. She battled their grip, yanking and twisting, but her attempts were futile. "Let go of me! Let *go*!"

"Tai," Chirag whimpered.

"Nothing will happen to you, Chirag. I'll protect you like I always—"

When Binti gripped her hair, Roma gasped at her aggrieved scalp. Chirag's desperate call sounded in her ears as Binti dragged her through the streets. People stopped to stare and murmur. Binti's strong hold forced her head back until her neck burned and the pain brought tears to her eyes. Towing her into Lamiapur's courtyard, Binti tossed her down on the ground. Her sisters left their chores to gather around the spectacle in confusion and anxiousness.

Amma picked up the deserted rug beater with a contorted expression on her face. "Stupid wench!" she shouted, slamming it against Roma's back. Her bruises wept under each unrestrained *whack*, but she didn't allow a sound past her pinched lips. Anger sweltered in Amma's voice. "You've ruined us all! Conniving bitch!"

"Amma," Caliana said in a weak tone. "Please, stop."

"What sin have I committed in my past life to earn this humiliation?"

"Amma."

"She opened her filthy mouth in front of the Panchayat—"

"You'll hurt yourself—"

"—in front of Sādin Saheb. I won't spare her!"

Sweat trickled down Roma's skin as she thought of Chirag through the intense pain. They would throw him in the hole in the square until his dedication, until his castration during the initiation ritual. It was his punishment for being Yoshi's brother. He would become a *birandasi*. Her fingernails bit into her palms. She had been so careful to shield him ever since his birth, but she failed him, and now he would live the life of a prostitute and the patrons would eat him alive.

She lowered her head and squeezed her eyes closed.

Amma continued to pound the rug beater on her shell. "You knew about Yoshi's little plan? You let her run, wench! This is all *your* fault!" Throwing the rug beater aside, Amma collapsed, sitting on the ground and smacking her palm against her forehead. "Lamia *re* Lamia, we're ruined."

Her keening wail had its desired effect. Gathering close around her, Binti, Hani, Caliana, and Ara comforted her with soft murmurs and softer caresses. Goldie curled into Sunbel's side. Meriel rocked a screeching Aimi on her hip with her concerned eyes on Amma.

Straightening in a slow, painful movement, Roma wiped a trickle of blood from her lips with the back of her hand. "You can't let him be dedicated," she said in an estranged voice. "You can't do that to him, Amma."

"Shut up, Roma! You don't see the disgrace Yoshi has caused. We were once revered. Now we're defaced! This defilement is your fault as much as it is hers." Roma gritted her teeth as Amma's voice shrilled in her ears. "You should've told me about her nasty little plan. I would've beaten some sense into that bitch or killed her with my own hands. If it wasn't for the two of you, we wouldn't have had to stand before the Panchayat like shameful criminals. Chirag's dedication is a mercy—"

"Stop!" Roma screamed. She looked at Amma's astounded face with a violent inferno in her eyes. "Stop blaming us. Stop *lying*. You didn't have to sacrifice Chirag. You protected him all this time only because you considered him a valuable trade within our whorehouse." Her sisters bristled at the crude term. She didn't care for their sensibilities. "You knew Sādin Saheb wanted him and you used him as you've used all of us."

"*Khallas*, Roma," Binti snapped.

Ara glanced between them. "What's this about?" she asked in bewilderment.

"It's about our patronships," Roma answered in a ruthless tone. "They're not a service to the gods. They never were. We have to earn the coin to pay our taxes to Sādin Saheb and the Firawn."

Her sisters stared in a moment of staggered silence.

Hani narrowed her eyes. "How dare you? How dare you soil the gods with your blasphemy?" she spat, clenching her hands at her sides.

"It's not true," Caliana interjected, thrusting out her chin. "Mother Lamia chose us. We're sacred."

Ara shook her head at Roma. "Why're you saying this?" she asked with pursed lips.

"To spread lies and cause havoc. What else?" Amma lamented. "Why she harbours hatred toward her Amma is beyond me. She was an infant when her birthmother left her on my doorstep. I breastfed her. I raised her as my own daughter." She beat her palms against her chest. "Today she accuses me. Today she stabs me in the heart."

"Amma—"

"*Nakō*, Roma. You've said and done enough," Hani interrupted, raising a hand. The harsh derision in her voice and on her face struck Roma like one of Amma's stinging slaps. "I didn't know you were so bitter, and toward Amma?"

The resentfulness of Roma's sisters permeated the air. She saw their refusal to believe her in their reproachful stares and closed expressions. It was like Amma had said. The illusion was safer than the truth. Before she was auctioned to the Firawn's son, before she was sold to a brothel, a moment such as this would have silenced her, but the horrors of last night had emancipated a part of her that she repressed for far too long.

Silence wasn't within her might because silence was suffocation.

"You should be ashamed of yourself," Caliana chided.

"I am ashamed," Roma said in a voice pulsating with all of the anger and pain she ever felt. "I'm ashamed I obeyed you, Amma. I'm ashamed I never questioned it when you sold me as a child. I told you what he did to me and you said 'such things happen', so I choked my own voice like a dutiful daughter." Stifled tears prickled her eyes. "A mother is supposed to teach her child to scream when it's harmed. You taught me silence. I thought you cared for me. Until now. Until I saw how you delivered Chirag to those vultures. If your own blood is so disposable, then what am I to you? What are any of us to you?"

"Roma," Binti snarled. "Apologise!"

"I won't apologise for speaking the truth." Binti opened and closed her mouth without a sound. The anger and pain undulated, becoming darkness, as Roma rose on her feet despite the protest of her abused limbs. "And I won't let Sādin Saheb turn Chirag into one of his prostitutes. If anyone touches him, I'll burn down this village," she said softly. "By the gods, I'll destroy everything."

Amma arched her eyebrows. "Will you, now? You have a bold tongue, Roma, and that's all you have because, in the end, you cower just like the raunchy men sneaking out to visit the Flags at night. You're afraid, *ladoba*. As you should be, as all of us should be. A single offence to the gods and even Lamiapur's walls can't protect us from their wrath."

Caliana and Ara sent each other distressed glances and Sunbel clutched Goldie closer against her. Terror invaded and shone in their eyes. Roma realised her sisters had been frightened for so long that fear was more familiar to them than resilience, but it mattered not, because for the first time in her life Roma felt that she had a choice, even if it pitched her against Lamiapur, the Panchayat, and her village; even if it pitched her against the entire world.

Tonight, she would leave while her sisters slept. She would free Chirag. If she opposed Amma now, if she fought with her, she would risk Amma confining her to the temple, so she had to submit to her one last time to secure Chirag's safety and their freedom.

When Roma didn't speak against her, Amma lifted her chin. "Nothing more to say? Good. Now, we'll all forget Yoshi. Don't speak of her ever again." She looked around at them with eyes narrowed to slits. "We're *lamiadasis*. It's our blessed fate to serve the gods. Get on with your chores. We've wasted enough of the morning."

Caliana and Ara rushed to the cooking chamber and Sunbel sent a sobbing Goldie inside Rawiya Mai's shed. Roma felt far removed from herself. She had chosen Chirag over them all. She had chosen him over innocent Aimi and Goldie, old Rawiya Mai and lonesome Nilo, and over gentle Sunbel who cared deeper for Roma than anyone else in Lamiapur. It was cold to abandon them to the vices of the Panchayat and Sādin Saheb, and selfish, but she uncurled her fingers and started toward the sleeping mats.

Amma stepped into her path. "Where are you going, *ladoba*?" she questioned in a sarcastic tone. "Do you think your punishment is over?"

Binti and Hani trapped Roma's arms. "Let go of me," Roma snapped, twisting to loosen their grip on her. "Let go—*Amma*."

"Lock her up. She's under temple arrest until I say otherwise."

"No! Amma, I'll stay in Lamiapur. I'll do what you want!"

Dragging her up the stairs and into the temple, they tossed her on the floor in one of the ceremonial chambers. Roma whirled around and hurled herself at the door, but Binti slammed it shut and sealed it from the outside.

"Tai, let me out! Tai!" Roma beat her hands against the wood until her palms became numb. "Tai, please!" Breathing laboured, she ran over to the dresser, pulling out drawer after drawer, rummaging through the scrolls in a desperate search for an object she could use to force open the door.

Nothing.

She shoved the last useless drawer closed. Slipping down to her knees, she dropped her head into her hands with one thought on her mind.

Chirag.

CHAPTER 36

Sitting in his mother's moonlit chamber, Leviathan brooded in silence. Nebulous shapes moved in the shadows around him, drawn to his dark emotions, famished for a taste. Blood and sand haunted him. Severed heads and pejorative stares. The Ghameq were on him like hyenas on an antelope. Their intimate whispers drilled past his weakened defences. They touched his mind and found his murkiest thoughts. They couldn't do much but lick to savour, but even darkness without hands could injure, if it knew your secrets and, as he watched, the Ghameq warped into the faces of his victims. It was hard to stay connected to what was real when reality turned on you.

A delicate hand trailed over his shoulders. "Look in their eyes, Leviathan, and see what you are," his birthmother whispered in Ancient Khansāri. "You have orphaned their children. They had mothers and wives, yet you executed them."

He swallowed hard. "I can change. I can be better," he said roughly.

"Can you? Do you even want to?" Stepping in front of him, she brushed her fingers along his cheekbone and he saw himself reflected in her eyes. "Your *fitra* is that of a demolisher. Brutality is in your nature, Leviathan. You kill with such artistic skill, such cruel abandon. You have taken lives from the moment you were born." She leaned down with a smile and levelled their faces. "I was your first."

He cradled his head. "Don't say that," he whispered.

She morphed into the dead girl from the kennel. "Poor, little Leviathan. Forever wallowing in the arms of self-pity. Does the truth hurt? Redemption is for the ones who deserve it. Why should you be forgiven?" She cocked her head and her dark eyes glittered. "You are nothing. Even the higher power of your people does not care for you. Eternal agony awaits you in the lowest depths of hell. Why do you fight it?"

"Stop."

"You are not brave enough to change. You are not strong enough. Be honest. Does your corrupted heart not crave the taste of fear at the mention of your name?"

"No."

"Liar."

"Get out of my head."

The girl sighed, transformed.

Leviathan's breath backed up in his throat. Her face appeared like extracted from his memory and brought before him in living form, and it took him a few swallows to speak. "Amma?" He'd wanted to see her again. So desperately that if this mirage had carried her scent, he would've believed it was her.

"My lovely boy," she said with tenderness. "I know what haunts you. I know everything. I feared you would become your father. It is why I always hid you away behind my skirt. To protect the world from you."

He shoved to his feet, turning his back on her, on what had taken her shape. "*Khallas*," he ground out, shutting his eyes.

"I saw the darkness within you," she murmured against his shoulder. "I saw the *monster*."

"I said, *enough*," he shouted, taking the chair, smashing it against the wall. The Ghameq spiralled around him, relishing his torment, and fled his rage without a trace. Breathing hard, he ran his hands over his face and into his hair. He needed to get out of here. He needed distance from the palace, this city, all of it, or he'd drown in his own goddamn head.

Something had shifted inside of him since he found the dead kid. Since Roma. Something he had no control over. His temper was unpredictable; his emotions were volatile. Truth be told, it scared the hell out of him. He'd dropped his guard long enough for the Ghameq to ride his doubts. He felt like a coward. Too afraid to confront his demons. Too afraid, period. Hadn't he already paid a heavy price to eradicate his fears?

"Bhau?"

He looked up. For a beat, there was no recognition in his eyes. Just an emptiness. Eyebrows pulled low, Malev moved around Junho to stand in

Leviathan's line of sight, the splinters of wood crunching under his boots like glass shards. It was loud in the quiet chamber and cleared the stupor that clouded Leviathan's mind. A shadow flickered over his features half a second before he checked it.

"You all right?" Malev asked, eyes wary. "You look lost, brother."

"I'm fine." Striding out, Leviathan headed through the archway, needing the movement more than the distance now. His companions fell into step behind him. If they'd heard what would've sounded like a senseless one-sided conversation with the shadows, they didn't mention it. "What do you have on the Wolves?"

"What we already know. They're a resistance on the rise. People have seen them operating in the east, seizing caravans and stealing supplies. Seems to be their prime objective. But it begs the question of why they strayed as far as West Durra for a bunch of orphans."

"Maybe they're recruiting?" Junho suggested.

It wouldn't have been the first time a resistance brainwashed the youth to build an army of rebels conditioned to destroy without independent thought, but it didn't fit Leviathan's limited profile of the Wolves. If they wanted to brainwash kids for radical purposes, they could've easily plucked them right off the streets. Why target kids in an organ trade? Why bother with a time-consuming operation when the alleys of every village were packed with orphans?

He also couldn't shake the feeling that the leader wanted a confrontation. He could've had his subordinates take Leviathan down sooner, but he'd taken his time and been amused. Knowing the bastard toyed with him pushed Leviathan's temper. The leader knew who he was from the start. He could've held him ransom, seized the opportunity to negotiate with the Firawn, but he hadn't done that. If he didn't want to use Leviathan to force the Firawn's hand—then what was his motive? Why had he wasted his time fighting Leviathan when his men had already taken the kids?

"Did Kai have any information on the heptagon?"

"None of his contacts have seen it before," Malev answered.

"What about Volos?"

"Never returned to Makhmoor. Nobody knows where he is."

Leviathan stepped out into one of the courtyards. Slaves bowed and scattered, eyes anxious, faces pale like he'd snap their necks for breathing in his space. "The foreign clients' interest in the organs? There's more to it," he stated, crossing the courtyard, climbing the stairs to the panelled doors of the conjoined palace structure.

"How do you figure, brother?"

"The kids were marked like it was a ritual."

"What, like for some kind of sacrifice?" Junho asked.

"More like a branding. Decoding the heptagon might tell us who the backers are."

"But Volos is gone, Bhau, so how do we find out?"

"Human trade is a business. Every business has competitors," Leviathan responded and, inclining his head, glanced back at Junho. "I want to know if other human traders are involved in similar trades. If they are, I want names. Volos kept his shipment locations a secret for a reason. He didn't want his rivals to screw up his deal with the foreign clients. As for the heptagon—" he looked at Malev, "—pull on your contact at the Archeion. Remind her to be discrete about the research. We can't lose our sole link to the documented sources. If they catch her prying, they'll deliver her to Shadowhold with a life sentence. Higher *zaat* or not."

Junho hesitated. "Bhau," he ventured.

"What?"

"You wanted me to look into how the *dēvadasi* escaped."

The muscles in Leviathan's stomach went taut.

Roma.

He'd apologised to her with less skill than an idiot. From her distrustful stare, there was no doubt he'd messed it up. She'd jammed herself inside his head all right—with her bruised and broken eyes.

Those eyes.

When he was a kid, the Firawn had locked him inside a rice chest in the Guild's courtyard for three nights. A lesson that had fortified his fear of the Firawn. He'd spent hours screaming for his mother, but he wasn't let out until he learned to be silent in the face of pain. Looking into Roma's eyes sent him back inside that chest. The confinement, the suffocation. He recognised something in her that yanked at something in him.

They were both survivors. They never quit. No matter how badly they were beaten, or how much they bled. She reminded him of a version of himself that he'd buried. The scars on her face resembled the scars on his mind.

He wanted to ask her about them. Maybe he'd build up the courage to do it the next time he saw her. Something he wasn't sure would happen. She made it clear she didn't want to see him again, and he owed it to her to keep his distance.

"What did you find?" Leviathan asked.

"Her handler was a *harami* named Kazi, but the guy's dead. Got himself killed last night."

"How?"

"Don't know, Bhau. Nobody's sharing the details."

"Was he killed before or after her escape?"

Junho shifted on his feet. "I don't know, Bhau," he repeated sheepishly.

Eyes hardened like a frosted lake, Leviathan looked at him. "Let me get this straight. You couldn't find the Wolves' trail and you couldn't get the information I asked for. What have you been doing all this time?"

"Bhau, I tried—"

"Try harder."

"Nobody's talking—"

"Then make them talk," he said through his teeth. "If you can't get it done, tell me now."

Shame and hurt flashed in Junho's eyes. "I can do it, Bhau," he said with passion. "I'll do it." He shot Malev a quick, burned look before walking away.

"You're coming down hard on him," Malev told him after a tense moment, following Leviathan to his quarters. "He's trying. We're all trying."

Leviathan set his jaw at Malev's reprimanding tone. "We're getting nowhere," he said, an edge to his voice.

"That's not Junho's fault. What's really eating you, brother?"

Everything.

"Nothing."

"You asked if the handler got killed before or after Roma's escape," Malev said, letting the subject go for now. "You think she had something to do with his death?"

"Just keeping an open mind."

He thought about his visit to Lamiapur, about how the bruises on her had paled in just a few hours, too fast for a human, not obvious enough to draw attention unless you had an eye for detail. It was a remedial process he would've expected if she'd used magic, except the lower *zaat* didn't have access to curative magic.

So, how did she heal like that?

"A small size like hers against one of Volos' men? Doesn't seem likely, brother."

"Maybe."

Maybe he was losing his mind.

Leviathan unlocked the cabinet and scanned his knife collection. He would head back to Tundra Desert and see if he could pick up a trail—any trace of the Wolves at all—even though their tracks would be long gone by now. Malev was right. It wasn't Junho's fault. It was his. He should've sent his companions to retrieve Roma and pursued the Wolves on his own, but his rationale was compromised ever since his mother's death and, on top of that, he wasted hours in her quarters hoping for an epiphany. Some revelation that'd give him what he needed to bury Cecilia once and for all. It was time to pull his shit together because in a month he'd be in Commander Gilani's seat—ordering crackdowns and executions, using his skills to sow fear, making the lives of the clans more miserable.

He'd become the Blade again.

What he feared was himself. What he feared was the hope in Mai's eyes. That ache in her voice when she told him not to come back unless he was better.

But he couldn't stand against the Firawn.

Not alone.

There was still time before his promotion, and he'd use every minute to track down the Wolves and retrieve those kids.

Settling on the divan, Malev leaned forward on his elbows and watched Leviathan slide his knives into place. "Did you see Mai?"

"I saw her."

"What did she say?"

'Make amends.'

Leviathan didn't know where to start or how to confront his demons. He was hell-bound now. He'd be hell-bound even if the Firawn didn't make him the Commander.

'Why should you be forgiven?'

"Nothing that matters," Leviathan answered. "I'm going to Tundra. Watch the camp."

As Leviathan shut the cabinet door, Malev left, and for a second, one split of a second, Leviathan leaned his brow against the solid wood. Just to breathe. A knot in his throat pulsed. His heart slowed, ached. The motive behind his actions up until this point was about his mother, about him, but from the moment he entered that kennel, the visual of the little girl—her body thin, her skin cold—haunted him in his waking hours. She reminded him of the other dead kids lying in their own blood in the southeastern camps after a crackdown.

He clenched his teeth.

Shut it down.

But the emotions were in his system like an infection.

Guilt, shame, remorse.

Pain.

He licked his lips.

Something prickled his senses. A movement, a sound. Turning his head, he listened, recognising the distinct call of a hoopoe. It came in through the open balcony doors, soaring in his direction with surprising speed, and he caught it out of the air. The bird was a beauty, all black-striped fan-tail, long, curved neck, and orange feather crown. It didn't struggle in his grip but looked at him with strange, glassy eyes as he untied a tiny scroll from its feet. Releasing the hoopoe, he unfolded the scroll while the bird fluttered to his shoulder. He found a message written in the calligraphic swirls-and-twirls of Middle Khansāri.

'Seek the Path which unshackles the Dawn and leads to the Vale turned upside down.'

Below the message was the stamp of a tribal wolf head.

So the Wolves summoned him with a riddle. His muscles pulled tight in anticipation. His resolve hardened. He'd thought he'd have to search long and hard to find them, but they sent him an invitation instead. There was a considerable chance that this was a trap. He expected as much from a faction of masked men who worked in the dark. Yet, their leader was too clever to underestimate an opponent.

It grated Leviathan that their reunion would be on the bastard's premises, but he'd play his game, play by his rules, because it was the only way to reach the kids.

'Seek the Path which unshackles the Dawn.'

"East," he murmured.

The hoopoe *oop*'ed and took flight.

CHAPTER 37

Roma licked her parched lips. Droplets of sweat dribbled down her skin from the humid heat. She couldn't tell the time in this windowless chamber, but it would have been hours since she was locked inside it. The turbulence within her chest caused her heart to thump harder than it should. She feared Amma might keep her confined past the Dawn of Tanuf to ensure she failed to disrupt Chirag's dedication.

Her agitation disturbed the scarlet serpent nestling in a coiled band around her left ankle. It raised a bulbous head and peered back at her. Lowering her forehead on her knees, she released a breath, attempting to hold on to the calm as her mind whirled with terrible thoughts of the present and future.

When Amma unsealed the door, Roma would apologise and submit to her. Then she would escape with Chirag. It was selfish to desert like Yoshi, yet self-preservation depended on selfishness. It might be right or wrong. There would always be people that convicted and people that understood. Ghanima Mai said one had to choose what one believed was right for oneself. What one could stand for. What one could live with.

"Freedom is what I can live with," Roma whispered.

The serpent hissed.

She had lived with the shackles for so long that she mistook them for anklets because they made a melodious sound, but underneath the sacred *dēvadasi* costume she was a prostitute, a slave of men, and she recognised herself in women like Thana and the brothel prostitutes. Those women were pieces of her. Chirag was her final piece, the one that mattered, and she wouldn't lose him to the same cruel structure. She hadn't thought of what would happen to him if she had taken her own life on her auction night. Who would have protected him from Amma? A hand squeezed her heart. Who would protect him now if she couldn't reach him in time?

No, she would retrieve him from the hole and run with him. All she needed was a chance to leave this chamber.

A soft rustling sound came just beyond the door.

The serpent uncurled itself from her ankle's warmth, slithering over to one of the sandstone pillars of their voluptuous goddess inclined against the wall, and disappeared behind the column. She would have risen to inspect the hide closer, but the *click* of the latch jolted her and drew her attention. Sunbel stepped inside with a platter in her hands. She wore her sleeping attire which meant the celebrations had ended for tonight.

Crossing over to Roma, Sunbel placed the platter on the floor near her feet. It held half a flatbread, salt, and a cup of water. The harsh diet was a part of Roma's punishment.

"Chirag is all right," Sunbel reassured. Roma forced a calm she didn't feel out of trepidation that the slightest sign of desperation would prolong her punishment. With the Dawn of Tanuf arriving in hours, she needed to be let out of the temple. If she acted as if she succumbed, Sunbel might speak to Amma in her favour. "Biranpur is the house of Lord Biran, Roma. Chirag belongs there with the other *birandasis*. You know he should've been dedicated sooner."

When Roma continued to stare at the platter in silence, Sunbel offered one of her soft smiles and drew a tin container from her veil. The balm inside it smelled like Hani's dried herbs. Sunbel rubbed her fingertips in the paste. "Amma's beating hasn't softened over the years, has it?" The mirth in her voice was meant to lighten the mood. Roma didn't smile. Her sister reached over to smear the balm on her bruises, but Roma turned her head, and Sunbel dropped her hand. "I forget you don't like to be touched. I know it's difficult for you, Roma. Khiraa's death, the auction, and now Chirag. You're his mother and sister. No one cares for him like you do. We're all aware of the bond you share."

"If you are—why do you take him from me?"

"Amma doesn't command the Panchayat, nor the gods. It's Chirag's fate."

"Where is it written? Show it to me."

"The gods—"

"—are forever passive. Our fate is what we choose. We don't have to be prostitutes, Sunbel. We don't have to be trapped here in Lamiapur and fear Sādin Saheb or the Panchayat."

"We're *not* prostitutes. Someone has filled your head with—"

"It's Amma who told me the truth."

Sunbel looked at her with pity. "Anger is a useless emotion. It'll demand all you have and leave bitterness behind." She sounded so much like her principled birthmother that Roma wanted to laugh, but the pressure in her throat would have turned it into a scream. The impending coldness within her encompassed her heart and thickened to unbreakable ice. Sunbel didn't want to believe her. She didn't want to see. It mattered not. Roma had delivered the truth to her sisters. It wasn't her obligation to liberate them. Weren't they sacrificing Chirag for Lamiapur's peace? What did she owe them when they cared none for him?

"We're blessed, Roma, don't you see? We weren't made to receive, but to give, and our sacrifices will ensure we're rewarded. Mother Lamia's love for us is so vast. Embrace it, please, for your own sake. Men are the essence of the world for a reason. It's through our service to them that we earn our salvation. Don't you want to be rewarded?"

"Yes," Roma lied.

Sunbel relaxed. "I know you're upset with Amma, but please try to understand. She lost both her children in one night. It's hard on her. Won't you be kinder to her?"

"I will."

"I'll talk to her. She might let you attend Chirag's dedication. You should be there."

"All right."

"Will you take the balm?"

"Yes."

"Then I'll hope to see you in the morning for prayers."

The door locked behind Sunbel. Roma waited for the sound of her anklets to wane before standing and moving to the column where the serpent had vanished. The narrow space between the pillar and the wall made it impossible to see what was behind the column. Pressing her lips together, she wedged her hands in the space and pulled to draw the statue forward. It inched across the floor. She squeezed through the gap to discover a low, shoulder-wide opening in the wall. Ducking inside it with caution, she swallowed stale air and coughed against her hand, peering into the dark passage ahead. Bones of rats crunched beneath her slippers.

The serpent lingered as if waiting for her. Her breathing echoed loudly in the restricted space. She didn't need lamplight to see through the impervious darkness, because she sensed the warm vibrations of the serpent's movement as a guiding light, and she knew it would lead her out of Lamiapur if she heeded its call. This was her chance to escape while Sefu was in a drunken slumber after tonight's celebrations. Her palms dampened and her pulse quickened. The consequences of her desertion would befall Lamiapur. She had once condemned Yoshi for the same crime she was about to commit.

As the serpent glided down the passage, Roma drew a deep breath and followed it. The air tasted like the sewers in the alleys. Her feet slipped on the slick surface and the walls pressed in close. She descended a crumbling staircase deeper into the blackness. Her fumbling hands felt along the curious serrations in the sandstone to her right. Rats squeaked and roaches hissed. She stumbled over the last step into a rancid canal brimming with knee-high water so cold it numbed her to the bone and snatched the air from her stressed lungs.

The serpent was gone.

Pressing a hand against the dripping wall, she bit her bottom lip, tasting the acridness to the pit of her belly. She had to be somewhere in the sewers beneath the village. With the wall as a support, she splashed through the foul water and reached a stone rise connecting to a rusted ladder at the end of which she saw the soft light of the moon. Clutching the rungs with slippery hands, she climbed the ladder to the opening above and dragged herself out of the sewer into an alley chalked with Khansāri slurs. The rough sound of male laughter shepherded her into an alcove until the drunken men became a distant echo.

With a heart that seemed to have catapulted into her throat, Roma drew the veil over her head and hurried onward, passing sleeping hounds and orphans so famished their bones showed through their skin. Slipping through the gracious gloom, it occurred to her that she would never dance again. When she and Chirag were far from Sefu, she couldn't show her face without a shawl to conceal the inked symbols of her *zaat*. Perhaps she could work for a milkman for coin. She helped Jirani wash his cows and deliver milk when his wife was ill or Lamiapur needed coin. It would be all right. She would unearth a path, a solution, to provide for Chirag, but first, she needed to secure his safety.

The heated glow of four torches illuminated the square and the chairs of the Panchayat still stood in a row under the willow. There were no men to watch the hole. Perhaps because Chirag was a child. The hole was mined so deep he couldn't climb out of it without aid. At times, if someone was confined inside it, the village boys would pee into it just to torment the prisoner.

Roma peered toward the hole with an agitated heartbeat. Once she walked straight into the square, she would become visible to anyone who happened across it. The late hour didn't make it less likely, because the tavern milled with men, and the Flags were sought out until dawn, but she couldn't stand in the shadow of the alley and wait for Amma to discover her absence.

Dashing into the square, she closed her hand around one of the torches, pulling it from the ground before spinning toward the hole. A wooden crosshatch covered it. She lifted it up, shoved it back, and dropped on her knees. Chirag huddled in a corner at the bottom. When she whispered his name, he tipped back his head to stare up at her, and his lips parted for a sound that didn't leave his throat. She stuck the torch in the soil, hurrying to the rope ladder tied to the shrine and unravelling it with clawing fingers. Her shoulders jolted at the ringing of voices from the closest street. She tossed the ladder into the hole without wasting a second.

"Chirag, climb," she pressed him. "Fast, now."

Chirag crawled to the ladder in his dirt-stained trousers and started the climb with weak whimpers. Roma stretched down her arms, helping him out of the hole, and he collapsed against her. His ragged breathing sounded too loud in the quiet square. She pushed at his shoulders in an attempt to straighten him. "We have to move now. We can't—" She stopped as his whimpers turned to pained moans. "Chirag?" His face was pale and his skin was feverish. The overpowering smell of urine and vomit prickled in her nose, but it was the blood on his trousers that paralysed her.

He'd been castrated.

No.

There were hours yet to his initiation rites. There were rules. How could Sādin Saheb have broken the rules? Despair without sound, taste, or scent consumed her. She couldn't think. Cupping Chirag's damp cheeks in her hands, she murmured soft reassurances, like when he was a babe and she rocked him to sleep in her arms.

"It'll be all right, Chirag." It wouldn't. "I'll protect you." She hadn't.

Helping Chirag stand on his feet, she slipped an arm around his waist and snatched the torch from the soil, supporting him toward the nearest alley where she dunked the torch in a discarded bucket of sullied water to smother the flame. She would bring it with her just because it made her feel better to have a weapon on her, but she couldn't let it burn and have someone notice the light.

Chirag's moans resonated in the enclosed space and she took out the vial of medicine from behind the waistline of her *lehenga*. The Firawn's son had provided Ghanima Mai with a similar vial which had healed Khiraa's injuries. She had to trust it would heal Chirag's as well.

Unplugging the vial, she coaxed him to drink from it. It might not regrow the severed part of him, but it would ease his pain. The evidence was on his face when his half-strangled anguish thawed and his form slouched with relief. She took his hand and led him through alleys, down disintegrated stairs, and into the benign shadows of Sefu with the Lonesome Forest as a destination in her mind. It rested just beyond the plains and used to be the strongest wood in the north when magic still nourished the soil. Evergreen oaks, pines, and wild plants had provided medicine. Now the barks burst with rot; the leaves were a dull brown, the roots freckled with mildew. It would hide them while she decided on what to do next.

The deep note of the Horn of the Gods sounded in the night.

Roma stopped. Behind her, Chirag jolted. The Horn rumbled once, twice, and then the third time. Three long notes were the alerting signal that called for the host of thirteen village men paid for their service to the Panchayat.

Chirag's disappearance had been discovered.

Gripping Chirag's hand, Roma looked out into the street as oil lamps shivered to life behind the curtained windows. They needed to cross to the opposite alley and make it out onto the plains before the village crowded with hunting men. She knew Ghanima Mai would shelter them if she went to the camp, but the clans would be punished if exposed, and she couldn't do that to them. For but an instant, she thought of the promise the Firawn's son had made her and considered it despite her distrust in him. Even if he meant it, she couldn't reach him now.

Chirag shuddered. "I'm scared, Tai," he whimpered.

"We're almost safe," she promised, pulling them toward the alley, but torchlights appeared around the corner of the street. She tugged Chirag into a niche below the stairs in the middle of the path just as the men emerged with their torches. Her heart pounded against her ribs.

"—gone, too."

"These *lamiadasis* must be taught a lesson. They're out of Sādin Saheb's control."

Roma's fingers tightened around the extinguished torch.

"Sādin Saheb is an old, senile man. It's time to replace him, I say."

"Agreed, but he's got Sarpanch Saheb on…"

Their vehement voices faded, but Roma waited another moment, and then hauled Chirag with her to the alley. The entangling passages led them to Sefu's border. Soon, the sharp smell of the polluted Kobe Lake tainted her mouth and the last alley opened up into the street. She could see the plains, the dark shape of the banyan, and the shadow of the Lonesome Forest contoured beyond it. The knot in her belly slackened. They were so close to their freedom. They could reach the wood in minutes if they crossed the plains at a sprint.

Pausing against the alley's wall, she looked at Chirag. "Don't look back no matter what," she told him. "Just run, all right?"

Chirag shook his head. "They'll catch us."

"They won't."

She needed him to believe it, but his eyes were wide with panic. They didn't see her. They stared toward the banyan as if it were a demon in the darkness. The unnerving remains of her dream returned to her in fragmented pieces; the blackened banyan, the abandoned husks of the serpents, and Chirag's quiet words.

'We were all burning, except you.'

"This is how it ends," he whispered. "This is how."

"Listen to me, Chirag—"

"Blood and fire and no stars."

Shouts resounded in the street.

Squeezing his hand, she said, "Run *now*."

Dust rose in the air around them as she towed him down the remainder of the street, her *lehenga* billowing around her legs, her bones moaning from the strain, but Chirag stumbled, out of breath, and she swivelled on her heels to pull him back on his feet. They were so close to the plains that she tasted the parched air. She came to a slipping halt as Sādin Saheb stepped around the street corner into their path with three other men. Whipping in the opposite direction, Roma drew a sharp breath, seeing the torches advancing on them and obstructing the only other escape route.

"Stand down, child. You're surrounded," Sādin Saheb said. His apathetic eyes carried a punishing shine that promised torment in return for her rebellion. "Come, now. Surrender."

Chirag pressed against her. She cradled his head on her shoulder and raised the torch like a sword. The men observed her with contorted faces. The harsh torchlight danced in their eyes, resembling wrathful fires within bottomless pits. She felt their anger and frustration from Yoshi's escape and saw the hunger for blood in their stares. It was the kind of hunger that turned humans into beasts.

She had doomed Chirag. She had doomed them both.

"Sādin Saheb," one of the men barked. "Your slackened leash has encouraged the *lamiadasis* to run rampant. It's time for us to make an example out of them, so no *dēvadasi* in any of our temples ever disgraces our gods again."

Roars of consent sounded all around.

The man lunged for her. Swinging the torch, she cracked it so hard against his head that the wood came apart. He staggered with blood pouring down the side of his face, then dropped on his knees, his eyes rolling back in his head, and collapsed on the ground. Shock rippled through the horde and—amidst their perplexity—she took the unconscious man's torch from his limp hand.

"If you come near us, I'll set you on fire," she warned.

"Beware, the *lamiadasi* has a weapon," Sādin Saheb scorned with a cruel smile. "How many can you harm before you're subdued, child? Surrender now and perhaps you'll live."

Roma's hand trembled around the torch. She wouldn't *want* to live once the men were done with her. Their lust for punishment was a delicate string pulled too tight, prepared to snap at any moment now.

"This is the outcome of allowing one wench to dishonour our sacred laws," a man snarled at Sādin Saheb with his yellowed teeth bared. "Other wenches follow in her path. Tonight, we put an end to it once and for all."

The men bellowed before he finished.

"They must pay!"

"They've sullied our gods!"

"Burn them!"

"Hang them!"

Terror shattered her resolve as the ferocious men pounced. Swinging the torch again, she slammed it into someone's shoulder, but in the next second, it was jerked out of her hand. She was backhanded with brute force and her vision blurred at the edges. Destructive hands wrenched a screaming Chirag apart from her, hurtling him straight into the bowels of the beast.

"No!" Throwing herself at the mob, she clawed at the bulks of men. They tore into him like savage hounds, shredding his garments and pounding on him, their maddened howls drowning out his cries. She was on the threshold of madness herself. Fingers gripped her hair. She scratched and thrashed as Chirag was kicked down where she could no longer see him. "Stop! Stop, please, it's my fault! I made him run!" When her pleas fell upon deaf ears, she screamed in desperation. "Amma! Amma, help us!"

Her bloodcurdling cries resonated over the village, but neither Amma nor the other villagers came to their rescue. The men tossed her down like a sack of waste and beat her to the sound of Chirag's agonised screams. Passing around a rope, they looped it into a noose, their tongues cussing, shouting still, and Chirag's cries became strangled moans.

A fire ignited within Roma's pulsing veins, rippling through her blood, burning through her skin, and the air vibrated with her charring heat. The same sensation as when the handler assaulted her. An ancient presence roused inside her, mounting to the surface, too distant for her to recognise, to touch, but her senses reached across the dust like the tendrils of her heat—seeking out the plains, the hill, the banyan—and then she heard them. Loud, growling hisses that snapped the men's attention to the sixteen-foot-long cobras springing from the shadows.

Dropping forward onto her palms, Roma struggled to breathe through the heat, sensing rather than seeing the six cobras. Alarmed shouts turned to screams. She smelled it. The venom on those who convulsed. The screeching continued like an echo in the outer edges of her awareness. She felt as if thorns embedded themselves in her heart, and her shell crumbled inward. Whispers sounded within her head. Memories. Her hands cupped to hold them, but they slipped through her fingers.

She tasted pride, fear, and shame.

Betrayal.

"Demoness!" a villager howled as he ran from her. "Demoness!"

Then, silence.

With the scorching heat still in her bloodstream, she crawled over the bodies of the poisoned men, the cobras hissing and circling her, guarding her against further threats.

"Chirag?" she breathed as she found his lifeless form. His hair and skin were darkened with blood. "I'm here, Chirag, look." Everything inside her bled. Chirag wouldn't bleed. He was safe now. She loosened the noose around his neck and drew it over his head. "Hush. Sleep now."

The whispers returned like phantoms roaming the halls of her mind.

What had she done?

The air clawed in and out of her chest. "You're all right, Chirag. I'll make it all better," she panted, brushing back his hair.

She felt new vibrations on her tongue and glimpsed blue and silver in the night.

"What in the fucking hells?" The Warden stared down at the bodies of the twelve men strewn all around her on the ground. "Get her tied up."

"The villager called her a demoness," another Warden said.

"Don't be a fucking idiot. Come on. Watch those serpents."

Rising high, the cobras opened their maws and hissed. The Wardens pulled their weapons, aiming for them just as they attacked.

"Son of a bitch!"

Blasts rang out in rapid succession.

CHAPTER 38

Leviathan crouched down to examine the track on the ground. A claw mark. The shape and dents suggested it belonged to a cheetah or leopard. He ran a hand through his damp hair. With the afternoon sun roasting the air, the heat was thick in his mouth. Sweat gleamed on his skin and covered Cinder's coat. So far he'd avoided the main road and taken to a less conspicuous route, crossing the overlapping hills between the western plains and the eastern desert with caution, searching the terrain and the rises for signs of scouts. The Wolves already had an advantage with him meeting them on their turf. There was no need to announce his arrival from a distance. He didn't know the north like he knew the south, and it bothered him because it made him vulnerable.

Grabbing his *kurta's* collar, he yanked it over his head, stripping down to his sleeveless undershirt. He swigged from the canteen as his eyes skimmed the desert. He wasn't alone. Malev and Junho were a mile behind him, shadowing him, but they knew he wanted solitude and stayed out of his way. He would've told them to return to the city, except they'd never leave him without backup, and he had no mind to snap at Junho out here in the open where even a half-skilled archer had a clear shot.

The canteen was almost drained, but he wasn't worried. During his training for the Black Guard, he'd survived without water by tapping the blood from his mount. The lesson, brutal as it were, served him well. He leaped back into the saddle. With a soft murmur, he urged Cinder onward. She powered across the hard desert, her speed calming his mind, and he pushed her until the sun lowered in the skies behind him.

It was unusually quiet. No reptiles, no birds, no predators. Nothing.

Tightening the reins, he stopped on the summit of a narrow escarpment and assessed the shadowed land below it. The riddle mentioned a vale turned upside down. He'd heard about it in the folk ballads sung by the lower *zaat* and clan elders. A fable. *Flesh and bone*, he recalled, *turned to stone*. Something about a forgotten city on cursed land and the people buried alive by a shower of brimstone.

This had to be it. He smelled the sulphur in the air, saw the destruction frozen in time. It expanded to the chain of mountains grazing the skyline ahead. An impressive sight, and purposely chosen. The stationary rock formations posed as obstacles, forcing you to move on foot to reach the dark woodland at the base of the mountains, making you vulnerable to attacks. He wagered the Wolves' hideout was past the trees, if not among them, but it couldn't be their headquarters. They'd never lead him straight to the nerve centre.

Dropping to his feet, he loosened Cinder's reins, sending her back to Malev and Junho. The night became his sole companion as he made his way down to the vale, stepping lightly in the shadows, his roving eyes observing the darkness. He strained his senses—inhaled, listened, scrutinised, and found no indication of movements in the rubble.

Yet he knew he was being watched.

Stalked.

The presence was predacious. Furtive and primal. The muscles in his body went taut. He caught a movement in his right periphery, another in his left, and stopped. *Wolves*. Real white wolves, except they weren't. They were the Adharit tribe from the Ghaib clan, Banu Thib, known to reside in isolated areas, to take the form of birds and wolves. Unusually large and glassy-eyed, they were harmless unless provoked.

It looked like he'd trespassed. Did that count as provocation?

They shot out of the night in tandem.

The first wolf pounced on him. A full-on frontal attack, teeth bared for a bite. He flipped over its arched back, his body spinning in the air above it, his knife slicing at its neck before he landed in a crouch where the creature had been seconds ago. The second wolf came at him from the right, leaping on a growl. Drawing another knife, he raced to meet it, dropping on his knees a beat before collision, his spine bending back as he skated over the ground under it and jammed the blade into its heart. The creature evaporated in a cloud of smoke, like it never existed, then reappeared at his left, while a third charged him from behind.

He kept killing them and they kept coming. As wraithlike as they seemed, their teeth were real as hell when they snapped at him. He never ran from a fight in his life, but this wasn't a battle he could win. Jabbing another wolf, he sensed a human approach and inclined his head, hearing a high whistle that yanked the Adharit's invisible chains, and all seven of them settled in a perfect formation around Leviathan like obedient hounds.

"Sorry about the rude welcome party," a merry voice said.

Two men walked toward him, one taller than the other and dressed in black, unlike his companion in white who had an arrow pointed at Leviathan's heart. The archer was five-ten, broad, his brown eyes shrewd like a fox's and his face hidden behind a shemagh. He returned Leviathan's scrutiny with coolness. It was the tallest in black that spoke. At six-four, he was sinewy in build, and Leviathan recognised the unnatural light in his amber eyes. He wasn't human. Not all of him, at least. He had Ghaib blood in his veins, so he was a Shunned, just like the Assassins of al-Mawt.

Leviathan didn't show his surprise when the guy removed his shemagh, uncovering long hair and a lean, clean-shaven face.

"You see," he continued in that same laughing tone, "they weren't supposed to bite. Swear it on my mother." Showing teeth, he pinched his throat for emphasis on his oath. "But Ferran here knows how badly I wanted to see the Blade in action. Don't you, Ferran?" He smacked his companion's back and the archer growled. "Don't worry. He does that a lot. When he gets really angry, he's almost unintelligible."

"Shut up, Ashar," Ferran snapped. "Get on with the plan."

Laughing again, Ashar stepped forward, cocky as hell. He didn't pull his sword, didn't even touch the hilt as he paused three feet from Leviathan and rubbed his chin. "You're not as tall as I imagined. The rumours made you sound like a giant. Ten-foot giant, eyes of a demon, kills you on sight. Guess rumours are rumours for a reason." His grin came and went in a flash.

Leviathan watched him with dispassion. The asshole had a mouth on him all right. Taking a slow step forward, Leviathan invaded his space. "Don't need to be a giant to snap your neck like a twig."

"Please don't hurt me. I have so many dreams," Ashar deadpanned. "I want to ride unicorns and braid crowns out of daisies."

With blurring speed, Leviathan touched his knife to Ashar's throat, and in that same rapid beat, he heard the rasp of a blade clear its scabbard and felt the tip of a dagger press between his ribs. The Adharit snarled. Ashar flashed his teeth in another grin, eyes hardened to a glint. "Try it, and we both bleed to death, champion," he said, his tone casual. "Would be kind of counterproductive, don't you think? You travelled so far to meet us."

"Where's your alpha?"

"Expecting you."

"Take me to him."

"You don't rule here, son of the Firawn, so play nice. If you will, we will."

He could've slit Ashar's throat before he had a chance to draw a breath, much less push the blade into his chest, but he wasn't interested in bloodshed.

Not yet.

Behind him, Leviathan heard Junho spilling profanities, brawling all the way down to their tight circle. He clenched his jaw and lowered his knife. His companions had been captured by four Wolves in signature white. He recognised two of them from their eyes—curious brown and hostile blue. The latter was the one he'd stabbed outside the kennel. He'd either healed, or he had a high pain tolerance. Not even a limp to his gait. Malev could've taken those two down blindfolded. The other two, though, topped him in strength. They were the same Wolves who subdued him last time.

Junho's face sported fresh bruises. One of the Wolves shoved him and Junho turned on him with a swinging fist. Malev grabbed a fistful of Junho's *kurta,* hauling him back from the armed Wolf, but his mouth kept on going full speed. "Touch me again, *harami,* and I'll kick your ass. You think you're tough? You look like a gorilla in a fucking skirt—"

"*Ay,*" the blue-eyed Wolf snapped. "Shut your mouth, or I'll do it for you."

"How about I smash your goddamn kidney and make you piss blood for weeks?"

"That's it—"

"Hold on, hold on," Ashar chuckled, stepping between them, dropping his hands on Blue-Eyed's shoulders. "*Chodiyo,* Zufar." If his accent wasn't enough indication, his dialect confirmed he was an easterner and Joharian from the sound of it. Westerners didn't add *iyo* to the verbs. "He's a kid, man, come on."

"Hey—not a kid," Junho said heatedly. "I'm eighteen."

Ashar cocked his eyebrows. "Really? You're not just an unusually tall twelve-year-old?" he asked.

"Up yours."

"Stop talking before I cut out your tongue," Zufar warned.

"Bite me, assface."

A muscle ticked in Leviathan's jaw. Enough of this spectacle. He didn't come all this way for them to compare balls.

Turning around, he locked eyes with Ashar. "I've no more patience for games, so why don't you take me to your leader?"

"Your wish is my command," Ashar smirked and shook out a scarf. "If you accept?"

They wanted to blindfold him. Like that'd keep him from mapping every trail when they led him to their hideout.

Beating back his pride, he kneeled, holding Ashar's stare.

"Bhau," Junho objected.

Following Leviathan's lead, Malev pulled Junho to his knees with him. Weapons removed, eyes covered, and hands tied, the Wolves ordered them back on their feet. With one of his senses limited, Leviathan focused on the others. For a trial at al-Mawt, he'd been temporarily blinded with a potion and set free in a wood surrounding a ruin. His orders had been to reach the ruin, unarmed, unharmed, and retrieve an object, while Suran assassins were assigned to incapacitate him. He hadn't evaded them as the assassins anticipated. Instead, he'd hunted them down one at a time and immobilised them before he recovered the object. It came back to him now in pieces. The rapid racing of his pulse, the rush of blood, and the dark thrill of the hunted becoming the hunter.

Leviathan and his companions were marched down trails with a texture too smooth to be part of the cursed land. No hurdles. A steady incline. The thinning air was fresh—crisp, clean—infused with minerals with a sweet base tone. The temperature cooled. They were in the mountains. Their footfalls helped him interpret the sound waves replicated by the entities in his environment. As he moved, he listened to the echoes and figured they'd passed from a larger to a smaller space, a passage from how the sounds bounced between the walls. He picked up on movements, other footfalls, and voices that didn't belong to their company.

Sentries. They'd stationed sentries to guard the passage.

Wood creaked, chains rattled.

He thought about moving forward, quick as a viper, and twisting the rope in his hands around one of their necks, but he wanted to attack the heart, not a limb, so he needed to get to their leader. Still. It was a constant battle between his mind and his instincts. It was fighting a part of himself trained to eliminate a threat on the spot rather than letting it hold the power balance.

A gate slammed shut behind him. He was missing the sound of two pairs of footfalls. Two Wolves had stayed behind. They walked about a mile north-east of the passage, sloshed through water with a pungent smell—algae—and were loaded on a *shikara*; a flat-bottomed Khansan boat.

Junho was shoved down beside him. "Bhau," he whispered. "What's the plan?"

"Shut up and don't move."

"That's the plan?"

Boots clomped on the wood, and the blindfolds were yanked off.

"Welcome to Safa," Ashar said.

CHAPTER 39

Well, he'd be damned.

The vale was made of waterbodies. Lakes and wetlands. Cedarwood houseboats were moored in place with balconies connecting to stairs and docks. Boards served as walkways, intersecting between the handcrafted structures like a village on the water. The painted fronts had calligraphy engraved in the wood and flowers decked every arched, stencil-carved doorframe and ceiled terrace. There were at least a hundred houseboats, if not more, and several *shikaras* operated like carriages between those that weren't connected with boards.

Standing on the terraces, the people watched their *shikara* approach. They would've sought refuge here from the Strips and established this haven over the decades—barred by cursed land, secured by snowcapped mountains—and it would've required faultless craftsmanship, not to mention resources, to develop these houseboats.

Just how had a fraction of refugees accomplished such a feat?

Unless this place existed before the invasion. The calligraphy and design of the houseboats were similar to the architecture of the Khansan palaces. He sensed magic, too. It was on the surface of the mountains and in the depths of the water. He couldn't see it like the cobalt torchlights in the cities, or the dome at Nox, but he felt its consistent buzz, like an itch under his skin. Safa couldn't have existed without it.

The *shikara* docked. Their hands were untied. It could've been a gesture of trust or arrogance. He wouldn't wager on the former yet. If he'd deliberated violence before, he changed his mind now as his eyes locked on a little girl hiding behind her mother's skirt, staring back at him. Boys no older than Haya played on the walkways, their innocent laughter tightening his throat.

This wasn't what he expected. He'd imagined caves and tunnels—the characteristic hideout for any resistance—not a vale inhabited by families. How was he supposed to deal with that? With the women and kids? It shouldn't have surprised him. Rebels used the civilians as a shield. The moment their hideout was exposed, they'd slip out and leave the people to burn.

Ashar watched him. "After you, Blade," he invited.

Keeping his composure, all traces of emotion banked, Leviathan climbed the high rise to the terrace, his wary companions trailing him. He sensed Junho's trapped temper, the painful amount of self-control it took for him to keep his mouth shut, and Malev's guarded movements. Taking the lead, Ashar and Ferran headed down the walkway. The other two Wolves lagged behind, hands on the hilts of their swords, eyes fixed on their captives.

Reaching a red-painted houseboat, Ashar hammered a fist on the door. "Māsa? We're coming in."

They entered a cedar-panelled space crammed with eastern-styled furniture. Landscape paintings drawn by a skilled hand on animal skins covered the walls and the spicy scent of split red lentils hung in the air.

Scanning the chamber, Leviathan's eyes came to rest on a scimitar on the wall. Durokshan steel. A beautiful blade. Long and curved. The silver pommel was shaped like the head of a wolf, red rubies for eyes, and teeth clenched in a snarl. He wanted to touch it, feel the weight of it in his hand, know the blade's nature. Fire or ice? Dark temper or icy calm?

Leviathan's attention snapped to an elder woman in a black kaftan who shot through an opening, swinging a rug beater and catching Ashar in the head with it. The impact made him stagger. She swore in Khansāri, each cuss punctuated by a swipe, fierce green eyes flashing. The Wolves behind Leviathan coughed to disguise their laughter.

"Stupid, useless boy," the woman raged. "You never learn, do you?"

"Māsa—*thāmb re*." Ashar dodged a blow. "*Aikā re*—what did I do?"

"What did you do? Esha's boys came home with their pockets full of glass shards—" she seethed, "—because *you* told them they were diamonds."

"It was a harmless tale. *Ow*," Ashar chuckled. "I was entertaining them."

"How many times have I told you not to spread mischief?"

Grinning wide, Ashar caught the rug beater and picked her up in a disarming move. "Swear it on my mother, Māsa. That anger takes thirty years off you," he said. Zufar made a gagging sound. Ignoring it, Ashar juggled her lightly in his arms. "Say, did you gain weight? Looks great on you."

The woman twisted his ear. "Don't try to charm me," she snapped, fighting a smile. "And set me down."

"I like you where you are."

"I'll beat you black and blue, *chhokro*. Set me down."

Ashar complied.

She walked over to stand in front of Leviathan and tilted her head back to meet his eyes. Assessing him, he thought with a quick flash of appreciation, like he assessed her. The right side of her face was scarred like on victims of acid attacks. "I'm Kalyani. You're Leviathan. Yes?" When he didn't respond, she smiled. "Vivaan?" One of the Wolves with the same green eyes as hers came to her side. "Move the divans for our guests. Come and sit. I've made dinner—"

"We're not here to dine," Leviathan interrupted. "And we're not your guests."

"Hey," Zufar snapped.

"*Ay*," Junho fired.

The Wolves closed in on them, and Leviathan's muscles tensed. He was holding back, yet every second pushed him further past his patience. He wanted to see their leader. He wanted to know what he'd done with the kids and, if necessary, *cut* the answers out of him. It was Kalyani's presence that made him lock down the beast. He'd done a lot of shit in his life, but he wouldn't kill in a woman's home again.

Zufar narrowed his eyes. "*You* just keep that trap shut," he warned Junho through his teeth.

"Make me, Shorty."

"Don't tempt me, Stick."

Ashar watched the tension between the boys with amusement. Ferran shoved his shoulder. "Step in any time and stop this pissing contest," he prompted.

"Now, why would I do that?" Ashar grinned. "This is the most excitement Zufar's ever going to get in his life."

Zufar's lips peeled back. "This kid's just begging to be punched in his ugly face," he snarled.

"*Not* a kid, you—"

"Enough," Leviathan said quietly, eyes on Ashar. "Where's your leader?"

"Eager to meet me, are you, *chhokro*?"

Leviathan should've sensed his approach before he heard him. It irked him that he hadn't. Turning his head, he locked stares with the Wolf leader. No shemagh masked his face this time. It was a sharp-featured face with a full, silver-streaked beard and shoulder-length hair. Dressed in a white *kurta* and *dhoti*, he could've passed for somebody's grandfather, except for his build. He had a bull's shoulders and a wrestler's chest; a warrior's height and a militant's observant eyes.

With a presence short of kingship, he had the Wolves responding to him by backing like one host, their hands dropping from their swords, eyes staying on Leviathan, Malev, and Junho. He walked to one of the divans—casual, calm—and sat down.

"Forgive me," he continued mildly. "I was in prayer, or I would've greeted you myself. After all, it's not every day you invite the son of the Firawn into your home."

Leviathan didn't blink, didn't give any indication of emotion, but his blood boiled. "You've risked your own safety by bringing me here."

Propping an elbow on his knee, the leader brushed a hand over his beard. "I'm not concerned for me and mine. If I were, I wouldn't have opened my home to you. You won't kill without a reason."

"I've reason enough to leave with your head. Where are the kids?"

"Safe and sound."

"You want me to take your word for it?"

The leader smiled. "Never. You're not one to trust a man's word. I'd show you the children, but they're asleep. They've been through a difficult time as you very well know." Stretching out his hand, he beckoned Leviathan to the divan opposite him. "Please, sit down. My wife has prepared a warm meal. You wouldn't break a woman's heart, would you?"

Leviathan moved, and Zufar, Vivaan, and Ferran charged at his companions as they shifted to cover his back. Drawing his sword, Ashar lunged, swinging it in a downward arc that would've split Leviathan's head open, but his attack was deliberately restrained. His hands shooting up, Leviathan caught the blade between his palms, jerking it hard in a backward motion, the hilt knocking against Ashar's face, and the sword fell from his grip. Catching it in his right hand, Leviathan locked Ashar's left hook in his fist, ducking under his arm, and stepping across to land an elbow strike in his liver. Ashar doubled over on a hiss. That second was all Leviathan needed to turn to their leader and press the blade to his throat.

The fight halted behind him.

The leader didn't move a muscle, even though Leviathan knew he had the skill to match him strike for strike. There was no fear in his eyes and no threat—just an annoying patience.

"Tell your boys to toss their weapons," Leviathan told him.

"If I don't, will you stab me as you did Jasir?"

Something in Leviathan flinched.

"Want to find out?"

Kalyani marched over and planted herself between them. "You don't threaten my husband in my home. Lower your weapon. You as well, boys, right now." When Leviathan didn't comply—holding the leader's unperturbed stare—Kalyani stepped dangerously close to the blade and he let her push it aside so she didn't cut herself. She was pale under the anger. "You seek answers, Leviathan." She narrowed her eyes at her husband. "*You* will deliver them to him. It's time, Alam. Tell him who you are."

The leader took her hand, tugging her down beside him. "Vivaan. Bring your Amma some water." He brushed his lips over her knuckles. "Calm down, *jaan*."

"Tell him."

"I will." Without releasing her hand, he signalled to Zufar and Ferran. They stepped out. Malev and Junho moved to flank Leviathan. Leaning on a wall, Ashar exchanged a loaded look with Vivaan as he returned with the water for his mother. He stationed himself behind her, eyes fixed on Leviathan. Alamguir gestured to the divan again. "Shed your hostility for a moment and have a seat, *chhokro*."

Leviathan didn't. "Talk," was all he said.

"Very well. I'm Alamguir bin Talaab."

"Is that name supposed to mean something to me?"

"I'm a descendant of Sultan bin Taib of Banu Yardan." Watching Leviathan, he nodded at him. "You're a descendant of Jehangir Khan. We're sort of related."

"Cut the bullshit," Leviathan said.

"It's the truth."

Grabbing his collar, Leviathan hauled the leader to his feet. Kalyani stood with heat in her eyes, but Alamguir raised a hand to stop her without breaking stare. There was no lie in his eyes. No matter how hard Leviathan looked—there was no lie. Leviathan shoved away from him, his teeth clenching, the vein in his neck throbbing, and tightened his grip on the sword.

Jehangir Khan. The Last Khan.

It wasn't the answer he covered all those miles for. He came to save the kids. He came to confront the man who stole them—and maybe he looked to fight somebody who had the skill to knock him flat on his ass. But this? This revelation that burned bitter down his throat like the Firawn's wine—this unpredicted, sharp-edged clarity inside his head? It was too much of everything he didn't want. So, he chucked the sword and started for the door.

"Running from the truth won't make it a lie. We're of the same clan, *chhokro*, yet you're more. You know it deep down," Alamguir called after him, and as Leviathan reached the door, he raised his voice. "You can see the Ghaib."

That statement stopped Leviathan dead in his tracks.

He swallowed hard.

Junho stared at him. "Bhau?" he said in disbelief.

Malev said nothing.

Not looking at either one of them, Leviathan kept his back turned, breathing to control his temper, sensing Malev's silent questions and Junho's confusion. He didn't know how Alamguir had unearthed something he was so careful to keep buried, to keep a secret, but the bastard had no fucking business sharing it.

Alamguir's voice chafed his ears. "There's only ever been two humans with the ability to see the Ghaib. The first was Jehangir Khan, and the second is you."

Shutting his eyes, Leviathan ground his teeth. There it was. The answer to the question he'd asked himself since the first moment he saw the Ghaib. He knew it couldn't be a coincidence. There was a reason. And this was it? His ability to see the Ghaib, to perceive magic, was because his ancestor was the Last Khan?

He almost laughed at that, but his throat wouldn't cooperate.

Banu Yardan. The ancient clan that branched out from Yardan's sons—

Qabil and Habil—whose bloodlines were exterminated. Dramatised stories. Folk ballads passed down to clan kids at bedtime. What was left of the Qabilids and Habilids was ashes, and nobody could descend from death.

Leviathan turned and looked at Alamguir. "Banu Yardan is nothing but a myth," he said, ignoring his frowning companions.

"All myths still lead to a truth," Alamguir argued.

"This one's been dead for centuries."

"You may think you know your history, Leviathan, but the Guild taught you only the things they wanted you to believe. You're aware of their indoctrination. A mind such as yours would've detected the truth from the lie in a heartbeat."

"Your point?"

"Denial doesn't suit you. You have a willingness to see reality for what it is, regardless of what it looks like, so don't insult your own intelligence."

Leviathan's jaw tightened.

"The truth is you wouldn't have followed my riddle if you believed it to be a trick, and one you couldn't override with your intelligence," Alamguir continued calmly. "You came because you had questions. Who am I? How do I know you? You calculated the risk before you stepped on the path. Since you've braved that path, brave the truth as well. Tell me. Who gave you the pendant you wear?"

All of a sudden, Leviathan was too aware of the scimitar hanging from the leather string around his neck, the Ancient Khansāri inscription on the blade that read Sword of Justice and Truth, and the memory of his mother slipping it over his head before he was sent to Ghada as a kid. She'd told him it belonged to his birthmother. It was one of the only proofs she ever existed.

At Leviathan's continuous silence, Alamguir strode to the wall and retrieved the scimitar. With his stomach in hard knots, Leviathan watched him approach. His heart sped up and his throat went dry, but he wouldn't baulk.

Resting the flat side of the blade in his palm, Alamguir held it out between them. "This blade was forged for Jehangir Khan and fed drops of his blood. It became a part of him. You want to hold it. Go on, then."

"Brother," Malev cautioned.

"Relax. It's not going to blow up in his face," Ashar said.

That wasn't why Leviathan hesitated. The sword called to him, and it troubled him that he wanted to answer the call. He didn't like being controlled, being herded like sheep. Grinding his teeth, he closed his fist around the hilt, and the sword came alive at his touch. The rubies glowed a bright red. He felt the essence of it deep in his veins.

Dark, stark, and powerful.

Durokshan steel was known in the Strips for its unique quality, but this was something else. He'd heard the swords from the Last Khan's time were sometimes bonded with magic. Blood Magic. The secret of binding steel with blood was long since lost like so many secrets of the world. The Firawn had tested Durokshan steel's connection with blood, but without a sword of the past, his blacksmiths couldn't study the correlation.

Raising the scimitar, Leviathan turned it over in the lamplight, noticing the shifting patterns, as if the steel pulsed with life, breathing, savouring their connection. It was weightless in balance. Strong. The spine was as sharp and lethal as the edge itself. Such an ancient blade with such a deadly spirit. Leviathan knew its name before he read the inscription engraved on the hilt, just like the one engraved on his pendant.

"Saifulhaq," he murmured.

"The Sword of Justice and Truth," Alamguir said with a smile.

Tossing the sword back to him, Leviathan slipped his hands in his pockets. The rich power didn't leave his system, but whatever connection he felt, he had no taste for it. "Is this why you brought me here? To introduce me to my dead heritage? To tell me I'm linked to some Khan with a birthright to the throne?"

"Not at all."

"Good. Because I believe in neither birthright nor throne. Magic, blood, heirlooms—these things don't matter to me."

"Then do you believe in a better world?" Alamguir didn't wait for an answer. "Make no mistake. I know what you think of our resistance, *chhokro*. You compare us to other resistances over time that caused destruction. You think we're nothing but rebels."

"Aren't you?"

"We're an opposition. We have our own creed and our own system. We don't use civilians as our shield. *We* are the shield."

"Isn't that what all resistances believe?"

"Not all resistances follow a clear code of honour. Not all resistances are based on the welfare of the people above anything else."

"So, what? You're different?" Leviathan shook his head. "Every opposition starts out the same. Good intentions, for the people. Then it turns into a power struggle, within and without, and it's the people who get trampled."

"We're not every resistance," Ashar responded. "We're the White Wolves."

"That's not much of an argument," Alamguir laughed.

"Neither is his, *yani*." Ashar's eccentric eyes shifted to Leviathan. "Every resistance doesn't turn out the same. The Red Widows have existed for longer than our opposition. They've never been taken with power. It's about the people that make up the resistance, the core principles of it, and their ability to stick to those principles no matter what comes."

"All right. What's your objective? Justice, equality, freedom?"

Replacing the scimitar on the wall, Alamguir returned to the divan. "Those are philosophies, and philosophies never changed the world. They can't unless one applies them. Our opposition wants to implement the system the Khanate was founded upon. Khansadun prospered under Jehangir Khan's rule. There were no human trades, no castes, no civil wars. That's the world we want."

"Let me ask you straight," Leviathan cut in, stepping toward him. "Did you take the kids to raise them as weapons in your war?"

"The children are the Khanate's future. The Firawn knows this. What other reason does he have for targeting them? Why does he oppress the people? He wants to demolish our intellectual wealth, so the coming generations are robbed of reason."

"Vivaan," Kalyani said. "Serve the dinner."

Alamguir rolled up his sleeves and washed his hands in a bowl on the table. "There are two things that make for a perfect slave—absolute ignorance and intellectual poverty. I brought the children to Safa to provide them with a safe environment and education. I have people here who can teach them to read and write, to always think for themselves. They're the future, and they must be protected from the Firawn's annihilation."

"You want me to believe brainwashing isn't on your agenda?"

"What do you know of the Wolves? What do you know of their stories? They all chose their own paths," Alamguir said, his voice steady. "Most of them come from ruin. Their homes were destroyed; their families were slaughtered."

Coming in with the steaming platters, Vivaan set them down on the table. Alamguir poured rice and lentils on a brass plate and served Kalyani first. "They've been pushed mentally, physically, and emotionally to the extent that if they were approached by the wrong people, like the Scorpions, who speak lovely words and commit atrocious crimes, they would've strapped on explosives thinking suicide is martyrdom." He passed Kalyani a cup of water. "They're children of a robbed nation. They need to channel their frustration, rage, and powerlessness in a productive way, and so I train them to save lives rather than obliterate them. Anger without direction only breeds destruction. I think you know of its decay, *chhokro*."

Leviathan didn't react to his last statement.

"What is it you want from me?"

"I want you to join our opposition."

He was silent. Not shocked, but thoughtful. The pieces fell into place for him somewhere around the time Alamguir invited him to dine.

"Why?" he asked.

"Because you'd be an exceptional asset. You have what we need to become a strong threat to the Firawn and an impenetrable armour to our people."

"You see me as a potential weapon."

Alamguir shrugged. "You *are* a weapon. You're the son of the Firawn. Raised as a remorseless soldier, but with the blood of a merciful Khan in your veins. You're light and dark, a question and an answer. You're a choice, *chhokro*. That being said, it's not the only reason I want you," he admitted. "My men are strong, fit and skilled, but they don't possess the refined competence of a soldier trained by the Guild. They're not ready to stand against an army of Rangers. They never will be unless they're taught by someone who knows the mechanics of war. Someone like the Blade."

Bitterness rose in Leviathan at the mention of his second name. He didn't show it because he wouldn't display weakness, but it burned in his throat all the same. "You want me to train your people. To betray the Firawn. Why not just ask me to assassinate him?"

Alamguir watched him. "Can he be killed?" he asked softly.

There were two sides to his question.

It was a known fact that the Firawn had survived assassination attempts in the past without a hitch in his throat, but what Alamguir wanted to know was whether Leviathan could kill the man who fathered him. He'd fantasised about it more than once through the years whenever he suffered at the Firawn's hand, yet he wasn't able to answer. He didn't want to explore the emotions rising in him, so he shut them down, ignoring the sudden flicker of panic. From the corner of his eye, he saw Malev read his silence.

Alamguir cocked his head. "It's not enough to remove a ruler because another will take his place," he went on, like he hadn't noticed Leviathan's hesitation, but they both knew he had. "You know the Firawn better than anyone else. You're closest to him. With any other ruler, we'd lose that advantage. We wouldn't be able to know his mind, his strengths and his weaknesses. We'd have no direct path to him."

"What makes you think you can trust me?"

"Because I've watched you for a long time. Because you won't refer to the Firawn as your father." Alamguir lowered his voice. "Haven't you wandered long enough, *chhokro*?"

The words hit too close to home. His throat closed up. In his head, he heard Mai's voice, pleading him to make amends. In his heart, he held a fear that he'd lose himself once he returned to Verdite. He didn't know much about the Wolves, but he had a chance to beat his own path. Turning away from what could be an alternative to a life as the Firawn's slave and an answer to helping the clans—it wasn't a mistake he wanted to make.

"All I ask is that you stay and observe us. Think it over before you make a decision. If you decide to leave, Ashar will lead you back to the Forgotten City. I won't stop you." Alamguir pushed to his feet and put a hand on Leviathan's shoulder. "You care for the clans. So do we. Trust might be impossible right now, but together we can achieve what we can't accomplish alone, *chhokro*. What do you say?"

"I'll stay," Leviathan answered at length. "For now."

"For now, then."

CHAPTER 40

Darkness surrounded Roma. A void swallowed all emotion before she could stretch out her hands to touch it. The cold weight of the shackles on her bruised wrists and ankles held her down where she lay on the grime-smeared stone. Blood and urine soiled her *lehenga*. Her unwashed hair clung to her skin. The cell door opened only for the Wardens. They drugged her at times, but she didn't mind it, because the substance numbed her and helped her survive the assaults. When they lashed her with a rubber whip. When they violated her.

"You don't exist," they whispered.

Time ceased to be. She didn't know how long it had been since she was arrested. She remembered the blasts and the Wardens. One of them had touched her. His scream still resounded within her head, but it was drowned out by the cries ricocheting in the corridors beyond her cell. Tormented prisoners whose screams would have startled the vultures from their nests.

Demons breathed in the shadows. Demons with soulless eyes that didn't allow anyone to sleep. They came and went behind the cell door and, if she closed her eyes, they poured salt on her wounds. Her enflamed gashes never healed before new ones formed. She didn't attempt to push past the thick haze clouding her mind. Remaining on her side, she curled into a ball, holding herself together.

As if she wanted to live, as if she deserved it.

When she allowed the chasm to consume her, she always saw Chirag. He materialised beside her. She fought to speak his name, but he shushed her, the noose looped around his purpled neck, and she discovered an emotion beyond the borders of saneness. Wrath. It watched her with eyes like fire—a colossal, winged beast that beckoned her closer.

"Don't drown," Chirag whispered.

The clanking sound of a latch pulled her from the vacuum. Chirag dispersed. Fear stirred within her and she wanted to scream, but her throat was parched. She could only stare as the Wardens stepped inside, their faces illuminated in the bright blue torchlight that sliced into her eyes.

"Give her another dose," one of them said.

"You afraid she'll bite?" the other drawled. "She can't even raise her head."

"Hares is bloody thorough."

"Hares is a psycho."

Laughter.

"Why do they want her shifted to Shadowhold?"

"She killed a Warden."

"Markov was bitten by a cobra like the village idiots."

"Not how Coen's story goes."

"You believe Coen? You believe she *made* the cobras attack?"

"There were witnesses."

"Those village half-brains see demons everywhere. They worship rocks and bury their kids alive, for fuck's sake. They're crazy."

The Wardens hauled her up on her swollen feet. She couldn't stand, so they carried her out of the cell. Her sore toes dragged over the stone as she was ferried down corridors with doors behind which prisoners moaned, and outside into a vast courtyard where a caravan awaited. Frigid air pierced her skin. No moon glowed in the night skies. She felt faint from the rough movements, slumped between the Wardens.

"We have your prisoner, Captain Saheb."

A soldier opened the barred door in the backside of the caravan. "Get her inside," he ordered. "Be gentle with her. Firawn Sai wants her treated with utmost care."

"Too late for that, Captain Saheb. She's broken."

They lowered her on a hard cot and chained her shackles to hooks on the wall. She wanted to lick her chapped lips, but her tongue stuck to the roof of her mouth.

The Captain climbed into the caravan and sat down on the bench opposite her. “Send for the two Wardens who oversaw her detention.” His southern intonation was clearer in the small space. “Firawn Sai’s orders.”

The door clicked into place and the caravan set into motion.

“Lower *zaat* bastard,” one of the Wardens murmured. “Does he think that running the Firawn’s personal errands makes him better than us? Suran vermin. They wear our suits and take our fucking positions…”

His voice faded.

Roma coasted in and out of consciousness while the caravan sped down uneven paths, rumbling as it went, the hooves of the mounts like thunder in the night. There were moments when she struggled to open her eyes, the cold touch of panic in her throat, but she couldn’t push through the awful weight of exhaustion.

It could have been hours or days when a hollow pain roused her. Rolling onto her side, she retched. The Captain leaned over with a canteen, spilling drops of water on her bleeding lips. He was careful. She still coughed and gasped for air as her throat struggled to remember how to swallow. The blanket he drew over her shivering shell provided limited warmth. She wanted the drug they injected her with in the dungeon, but she couldn’t locate her voice to ask for it, so she trembled and floated in muted anguish.

The caravan rumbled to a stop.

Sunlight burned in her eyes as the Captain opened the door. He unlocked her shackles. When she inhaled, the sweet aroma of blossoms overwhelmed her frayed senses. It seemed a lifetime since she smelled anything other than vomit and waste. He carried her through gardens and archways. Doors. Beautiful, carved doors. Mirrors. So many mirrors. Her mind spiralled like a tempest, her head lolled on the Captain’s shoulder.

She needed a dose. Just one dose to soothe the illness.

The Captain stepped inside a chamber. The high walls were the deep green of betel leaves, framed by white scrollwork. Gold lanterns suspending from an ornate ceiling were embedded with shards of mirrors that showed thousands of replicas of her and the Captain. Lowering her on an embroidered futon lined with cushions, he stepped back outside.

She was alone.

Her eyes slid over arched, latticework windows, brocade chairs, and burnished tables on sculpted feet. Elaborate paintings decorated a wall. Canvases of lavishly dressed rulers lounging on thick, lush cushions conversing with foreigners in golden halls of palaces; bejewelled women laughing in harems and waited on by *bandis*; tall demons slaughtering men on a battlefield. Fire licked the demon bodies. Fire without smoke. At the front of the demonic army, covered in black armour, stood a taller demon, his black hair braided close to his scalp and tied together on the crown of his head with a gold clasp. The sight of the demon unnerved her.

A portrait of a Khansan ruler with a golden turban on his head hung on a separate wall. His black beard was thick on a handsome face and his skin was almost as dark as his shoulder-length hair. Lucid brown eyes peered out at her—soft and hard, compassionate and assertive. A chain around his neck disappeared beneath his *kurta's* collar. She recognised him in other paintings; one where armed men severed his head in front of a sobbing woman and another where parts of his dismembered body were displayed on spears around a city.

Planting her palms against the futon, she grappled with a surge of nausea, pushing herself up into a sitting position to stare at the portrait again.

"Jehangir bin Aurangzeb," a velvet voice said. "The Last Khan."

Roma shivered.

The door had opened without a sound. She hadn't felt the vibrations of his footfalls. For a moment, she thought it was the Firawn's son in the burgundy *sherwani*, but then his hooded eyes, as blue as magic in its purest form, sealed upon her face, and an ancient fear—sinister and familiar—awakened inside her.

CHAPTER 41

Roma couldn't tear her eyes from the Firawn's. He was a man more handsome than his son with the captivating hollows and planes of his face carved to hold secrets, but whereas his son was mortal in his appearance, the Firawn was preternatural, and she found an alarmingly ancient and concurrently youthful suggestion to the sharp slant of his jaw, the ruling lines of his high cheekbones, and the cool astuteness in his stare.

A stare that seemed to devour her.

"Roma, is it?"

He spoke her name like a prayer, like the sudden prospect of hope on a battlefield, and she dragged her knees to her chest. His smile was unnatural as if he had practised how to curve his lips in front of a mirror.

The elegant yet primal tip of his head reminded her of his son. "Would you like some water?" he asked in a sociable tone that sounded equally rehearsed. "You seem dehydrated. Water is so essential for your health as it cleanses your vital organs of poisons." He walked to a low, circular table holding a bejewelled pitcher and crystal glasses. "It is particularly advantageous in war. Destruction of water supplies results in agonisingly slow deaths. People cannot survive without clean water. Such a waste, is it not? War."

Crossing to the futon, the Firawn held out the crystal glass for her, but then withdrew with another simulated smile. "Ah, but you are shackled." He crouched down to her level and raised it to her lips. She couldn't refuse it. When the liquid touched her tongue, she gulped it with hunger. "You know, in some cultures," he continued as he watched her drink in fascination, "it is said that if a man feeds a woman a single drop of water, then he becomes her god."

She whipped her head to the side, coughing and gasping, and pressed a hand to her throat. Tossing back his head, the Firawn laughed. "Such willpower. Do you know what it is about you that charms me so? Your regal poise. Even as you are shackled, there is that imperial lift to your chin. You are a queen in disguise who wears her scars like a crown. Enthralling."

Winding her fingers around the chains of her manacles, she clenched them until the iron burrowed into her flesh. He leaned toward her. "I have searched for an eternity," he murmured, "and I must know for certain."

Before she could comprehend his intention, he brushed his fingertips lightly over her cheekbone, the mere whisper of a touch, and a dark fever erupted within her. It hissed and singed and ruled with a savage fervour. Crimson fire engulfed the blue of the Firawn's eyes, appearing and disappearing so precipitously she questioned if it existed at all, even as the muscles of his face twitched and his eyelids lowered in pain or ecstasy, or both. She clamped her teeth together to suppress the scream in her lungs as her blood blistered with the fever.

The Firawn rolled his head and looked at her. She had heard the rumours of how he was touched by the gods, but she hadn't believed them until now.

"Have I frightened you?" he whispered.

It terrified her how easily he read her.

Rising on his feet in one graceful movement, he mercifully increased the distance between them, returning to the table and replacing the crystal glass with care. "Do you know of me, Roma? Do you know who I am?"

"The Firawn," she rasped.

"The Firawn," he repeated with a grin. "So formal. You can call me Silvius, for now. I would like for us to become friends. Perhaps even close friends."

"Do you keep all your friends in chains, Sai?"

He laughed again. "Wits as well. You become more beautiful by the second." His eyes glittered. "I should warn you. Beauty is a terrible weakness of mine."

"Where am I?"

"The Palace of Mirrors."

She was in Ghada. But how far was it from Sefu?

The Firawn watched her with an imploring intensity. Her lungs convulsed within her chest. She arched forward, coughing blood until it filled her cupped hand, and the Firawn approached her in his deliberate manner, crouching down, but so close this time his breath brushed her cheek. She realised he possessed no scent.

Sliding a silk handkerchief from his pocket, he dabbed the blood from her hand without touching her skin. "Your life as a *dēvadasi* must have been hard. Dedicated as a child, raised to please patrons. An existence devoted to obliging gods and men," he said in a strange tone. She discovered a penchant for deceit in his measured voice, yet his words still festered within her mind. "You must have loved your brother dearly to have bargained your life for him. I wonder how many sacrifices you made for your *zaat*."

He leaned closer to her and she pressed back from him. "How petrified you must have been when the villagers cornered you. I heard of how callously they murdered your brother. Stripped him naked, beat him like an animal, and strangled him to death." Her throat burned. He sighed. "You only wanted to protect him from a horrible injustice, and your village slaughtered him."

She lowered her eyes as a tear trickled down her cheek.

His voice softened to silk. "You must have called for aid. Did anyone come for you?" When she lifted her eyes to his, he nodded, as if he saw more than the answer to his question; as if he saw her entire past. "Such is human nature, little queen. It is truly a monstrous world. Humans are atrocious creatures."

Her breath hitched in her throat as his fingers reached to caress her hair. Twisting away from him, she turned into the wall with a suffocating pressure within her chest. He barely drew a breath between sentences. "Your brother did not deserve such a fate. Nor did you. You are in so much pain, but I can help you discover relief. We are in distress because we allow emotions such as guilt and remorse into our hearts. Do you not want it to stop?"

Yes.

There was a possessiveness in how he crowded her space. "We are alike, you and I." Tenderness seeped into his voice. It was like a lover's whisper in her ear. "I see it in you as I see it in myself. We have mastered a caricature of human demeanour to exist in this society. The feature that sets us apart from each other is you wear your disguise to hide while I wear mine to conquer."

"What do you want, Sai?"

"What I want is to give you something invaluable. My friendship. I want to become your closest ally. A guardian angel. Someone whom you can trust and lean on; someone who will never mistreat nor abandon you. All I ask is that you accept. Open your mind, your heart to me. I am a well-wisher."

Her instincts snapped and hissed at the familiar resonance of those words.

"Why?"

"Because you are a treasure."

Nothing of what he said made sense. Was this about the poisoned villagers and the Warden? Did the Firawn believe she killed them? Was she brought here so he could lure her to confess? A shudder passed through her shell. She couldn't understand how she had ended up here, how to escape, and the utter sense of entrapment—of being caught in a cobweb—submerged her in a wave of sightless terror. She needed an escape.

"I want my dose," she whispered. "Please."

"Do you not want to punish the monsters who murdered your brother? You do. You want it deep down, past your sorrow and pain, where your anger resides, because you cannot forgive, little queen. You cannot *forget*." Unbearable heat poured through her veins at his proclamation. She trembled with it. He tipped his head to the side. "You want to see the ones who violated you bleed."

The chamber faded and turned into a stone cell. Screams of torture resonated in her ears. Phantom laughter as she soiled herself. Her insides cramping as their violence injured, her skin splitting under the lashes of the rubber whip. She pleaded and screamed when they desecrated her, when they reached inside for her soul and ripped it from her shell.

Blood and pain and terror.

All that her mind had repressed. All that she had pushed down, down, *down* where it couldn't be touched. It now reawakened. She retched. She clawed at her skin, dragging her nails through her hair, across her scarred face until the drug filled her veins, numbed her, silenced all of it, and the darkness cradled her in the crook of a shadow arm.

The stone beneath her evaporated. She returned to the present on a frantic gasp.

The Firawn's fingers hovered a breath from her cheek. "That violation is the result of sacrifice," he said in a bitter tone. "You toil and ransom for a higher power, a so-called greater good, but all you receive in return is more pain and humiliation. Degradation. What value then do your sacrifices have?

What value do you have? We are what they make us until we break them and make ourselves. We can choose not to give another the power to make us feel less than we are. Let me ensure you never have to feel powerless again. Let me offer you that gift."

"Why would you do that for me?" she breathed. "You don't know me."

"I know so much more than you think. Say yes, little queen. Say you want it."

She wanted liberation from life itself.

"Yes."

His fingers unravelled her shackles. "Then I shall give it to you." His lips cracked in a devilishly promising smile. Straightening his *sherwani,* he called, "Khuram," in an imperious voice.

The Captain reappeared through the doors. "Sai," he answered with a respectful bow of his head.

"Bring them in."

"Your will, Sai."

Roma sensed their hideous presence before they entered the chamber. Even in her shattered state, she had somehow memorised the vibrations of their footfalls, the approaching steps of a nightmare, and bile climbed the back of her throat. Their faces summoned the gaping maw of the darkness that held her through the excruciating torture. If she unleashed it, she would fall apart and never be pieced together again.

The Captain shoved the bound and gagged Wardens to their knees. She wouldn't look at them. If she didn't see them, if they were only shadows, they couldn't haunt her. They would remain demonic shapes, crude laughs, and brutal hands.

Faceless and nameless.

Not real.

The Firawn's coaxing voice wrapped around her like velvet. "Look at your violators as I sacrifice them in your name. They will taste the torture they practised on you."

Their strangled voices warmed her chilled bones.

She opened her eyes.

Kneeling bare-chested, the two Wardens stared at the Firawn in terror. The Captain stood behind them with a machete in his hand. The Firawn unsheathed a gold-hilted dagger from a jewelled sheath and sank the blade into the first Warden's belly. He screamed, struggling like the camel sacrificed on her auction night, and the Captain kept him still as the Firawn sliced him open from his navel to his throat. Roma swallowed and swallowed, staring in morbid absorption, while his blood and intestines spilled onto the tiles.

The Firawn sidestepped the mess without pause, his attention moving to the second Warden, who now fought against the Captain's hold, but the Firawn didn't drive the blade into him. Turning toward Roma, he approached her and placed the bloodstained dagger in her palm, his eyes alight with a desire matching the brutality of the monster in his smile.

Her trembling fingers curled around the hilt.

"Show me what you want to do to him," the Firawn said softly, signalling without breaking stare, and the Captain hauled the squirming Warden toward her. "Take your power, little queen."

What she wanted was to sever the hands with which she was assaulted, carve out the tongue with which she was called a whore, and amputate the manhood with which she was raided. The memories smothered her and the emotions mounted until she ruptured. Screaming in rage, she rose on her knees, sinking the dagger into the Warden's chest. Wrenching it out, she stabbed him again and again before dropping down, the dagger clattering on the tiles and her wrath bleeding into silence.

"Finish him," the Firawn ordered.

The Captain bowed his head and set to work.

When the Warden's screams had quieted, his eyes and body still, Roma dry-heaved until she was hollowed out. Her bloodied hands quivered even when she clenched them. The bodies were removed and a pale slave cleaned the tiles. She wanted to lie down and sink far beyond retrieval, but her eyes followed the slave as he scrubbed and scrubbed with a squeaking sponge.

"Do you feel powerful now?" The Firawn smiled with satisfaction. "I can find all of your patrons, every one of them, and deliver them to you. Would you like that, little queen?"

"Firawn Sai," the Captain said in a quiet voice. "Khamisi is here."

"Let him enter."

A short man with brown curls and a narrow face stepped inside the chamber. A white scar strained from his cuff-adorned ear to the corner of his harelip. His soot-stained hands mangled a maroon scarf. "Sai, I bring news from Sefu," he said with a bow, and Roma stirred at the mention of her village. He cleared his throat. "There's unrest among the people, Sai. With the murder of Biranpur's Sādin Saheb and the village men, the *lamiadasis* are accused of *sihr*."

Dark Magic.

Roma's pulse leaped and climbed to a crescendo in her ears at the realisation that her sisters were being blamed for what had happened. Her mind conjured agonising visuals of them dragged, beaten, and throttled as Chirag had been. What had she started? Aimi was in Lamiapur. She was just a babe. What would happen to her? What would happen to all of them? If she hadn't run, Chirag would have been alive. Her sisters would have been safe.

"Your information is valuable, Khamisi. You shall be rewarded for it."

"*Meharbani*, Sai. You're the most generous, most merciful."

Khamisi bowed out of the chamber, and the Firawn turned toward her with a smooth, unreadable expression on his face. "The *lamiadasis* are in peril." His statement fuelled her panic. "You can save them, or you can leave them to their fate. The choice is yours. But remember. They did not come to your aid. They abandoned you."

Roma tipped back her head to peer at him with beseeching eyes. "How do I save them?" she asked in a little more than a whisper. "How, Sai?"

"If it is what you want, I will take care of it."

"It is. Please."

"Then do not be troubled. You are not alone anymore."

She couldn't trust him. His son was unpredictable, but the Firawn was worse. She could discern his ambiguous nature as if she knew it, as if she recognised the pattern of deception, calculation, and a darkness so inherent it made her heart tremble, but she didn't have a choice other than to accept his aid and hope he was true to his word.

With a patient smile, he said, "Khuram, send word to Sefu. The *lamiadasis* are not to be harmed. They have been granted immunity." There was no double intention in his tone, nor a trap in his words, but she knew there would be a price. He wanted something from her. She saw it in how he looked at her and how he coaxed her with his promises.

"Your will, Sai," the Captain bowed.

"And have a dose of the Phantom's Breath delivered for our dear new friend." Leaning close, the Firawn lowered his voice just for her. "We have so much to learn from one another."

CHAPTER 42

STEPPING INTO THE houseboat used for conferences, Leviathan contemplated the regional maps on the walls, skimming the colour-coded pins marking trade routes, camp locations, and military bases. Alamguir had scouted out most of the regions in the East Strip, but a large section of the West Strip lay bare. He either didn't have the manpower to send into the west, or it wasn't a priority. A couple of eastern locations were circled in black. Duroksha for the steel and Nirut for the gold. Those areas crawled with the Firawn's soldiers.

There was one map older than the others. It showed how much Khansadun and the neighbouring lands had changed since the invasion. The largest regions in the three countries used to be provinces, but when the Khanate was colonised, the foreign powers drew new borders, and the administrative divisions created as a method to supervise the Khanate became a matter of ethnic distinction, dialects, and customs. The map was a tragic reminder that conquerors could rip an empire apart, break it into pieces, and convert the places into civil war zones.

Brother against brother, blood against blood.

Pensive, Leviathan studied the Khanate's tribal falcon sigil on a white banner as his mind turned to the kids from the organ trade. Alamguir hadn't lied. They were here in Safa. They stayed close to the women, scared, uncertain, with a starved look in their eyes. It made him think about Seth and the clan kids who lived with that same fear, and it made him think about the dead bodies of infants in the southeastern camps. Every night he walked through those burning camps in his sleep. The cries of the clans got louder and louder inside his head, but instead of *listening*, he'd been shutting them out, drowning himself in his own anger and grief, while people around him continued to suffer.

He couldn't do it anymore.

Malev walked through the door to the conference chamber. "You've been quiet for days, brother," he ventured at length. "What's on your mind?"

What was on his mind? It'd been a week in Safa. That was seven days less until his promotion. If he didn't choose a different path now, he'd become the Firawn's Blade again, and he'd lose what was left of his humanity.

With it, he'd lose Mai.

Pacing to the table, Leviathan leaned on it. "I want to work with the Wolves," he responded, arms crossed. Malev didn't look surprised. He must've figured it out before Leviathan had. Sometimes his companion seemed to know him better than he knew himself. "Bringing food and water to the camp isn't enough. It won't change their situation. Alamguir's got the manpower and resources I don't, and I've got access to information he doesn't." He looked at Malev. "You and Junho need to decide what you want to do."

"It's already settled, brother."

"Don't follow me without reason."

"We never needed a reason to follow."

"Malev—"

"I've made my choice. You want to argue with Junho on this? Good luck with that."

Restless, Leviathan moved back on his feet. "I'm surprised you're not shutting me out like he is." Junho hadn't said a word since he found out Leviathan kept his ability to see the Ghaib a secret from them. Not talking was difficult for Junho, so Leviathan knew his hurt went deep. He hadn't as much as protested when Leviathan told him to leave for the camp without him.

"Junho doesn't get why you didn't tell us about the Ghaib."

"It wasn't because I didn't trust you."

"I know that."

Leviathan was silent for a beat. "Amma knew," he said, throat tight. "I was a kid when I first saw one. She made me promise not to speak of it to anybody. I guess she thought the Firawn might use it somehow if he knew." Because everything with his mother was always about protecting him from the Firawn.

"This whole Jehangir Khan thing is a pretty big deal," Malev said.

"It's just a name," Leviathan dismissed.

"It's your legacy, *chhokro.*"

Leviathan looked over his shoulder at Alamguir and Ashar as the two walked in. "Legacies don't do us any good," he responded, pushing away from the table.

"They're still a part of us."

"Tell me something. How did Jehangir Khan's line survive?"

"I'm overjoyed that you inquire about your lineage," Alamguir smiled. "Why don't I show you?" At his signal, Ashar brought a brass urn from a cabinet to the table. Tilting it, he poured red sand into his hand and threw it in the air. It rotated like a typhoon, then calmed and suspended. Glittering. Leviathan moved closer, eyes on the mass, as Alamguir watched him. "It's sand from the heart of the—"

"—Raging Desert," Leviathan concluded. He'd heard about it. Magic sand with a life of its own, and dangerous to handle for humans, but Ashar wasn't all human.

Malev joined them at the table. "Incredible," he murmured. "I've never seen anything like it. Back in ancient times, the Ghaib used the sand from the Raging Desert to record history."

Ashar grinned. "Still do, brother," he corrected.

"It can do a lot more than record history," Alamguir divulged. "It can take any shape or form. During Jehangir Khan's battle against the Nar, it turned into a battalion of soldiers. Imagine warriors made of sand, faster than the wind, and invulnerable to mortal weapons."

Malev scratched his jaw. "How do you keep it contained in the urn?" he asked curiously.

"The brass traps it," Ashar explained, tapping the urn. "Like it can trap the Ghaib."

Alamguir turned to Leviathan. "You asked me how Jehangir Khan's line survived. His sister was married to Hashim bin Merdas. Do you know of him?"

"Hashim the Blood Traitor," Leviathan said with a clipped nod. "Who doesn't?"

Ashar said Hashim's name. The sand started moving like it was reactivated. It showed a square-shaped prayer house with a minaret and a man and a woman in conversation. Alamguir pointed to them. "Jehangir Khan and his wife, Khairaat Khanum," he clarified. Men with swords rushed into the prayer house, surrounded the couple, and one of them sliced Jehangir Khan's head from his body. "Hashim assassinated his brother-in-law, then placed his sister-in-law and his wife, Jawariya, under house arrest. Eventually, he executed Jehangir Khan's sister to eliminate the bloodline of Qabil."

So, he killed his own wife out of paranoia.

Leviathan watched the sand take the shape of men and women. Hashim sat on a throne, pointing at the people, and his soldiers cut them down. "Hashim sanctioned the executions of every Habilid to demolish Banu Yardan once and for all," Alamguir continued. "Yet in his crusade against the Qabilids and Habilids, he forgot about Jehangir Khan's wife."

Khairaat Khanum reappeared, pregnant now.

"While Hashim was preoccupied severing heads and parading them in Almasi, Khairaat Khanum escaped with aid from a palace servant." The palace turned to mountains. "She found refuge with one of the Mountain Clans known as Banu Bomani."

"Banu Bomani," Malev echoed. "The warrior clan?"

"Indeed."

Leviathan cocked his eyebrows. "And she sought this clan out, on her own, in her pregnant state?" he asked.

"Women have a strength that men don't," Ashar said with a shrug.

There was no arguing with that.

Alamguir motioned for Ashar to rein in the sand. "There's also the fact that she belonged to Banu Bomani because her father was the head of the Bahram tribe."

As Ashar called the sand back into the urn, Leviathan considered the revelation. His ancestors weren't just related to Banu Yardan, but the largest of the Mountain Clans, and if Jehangir had married a woman of a warrior clan that resided in the mountains, it could only be to secure an alliance between them. A move meant to ensure their fealty to the Khan.

Settling in a chair, Alamguir stroked his beard. "I have a book on Jehangir Khan's time as a ruler. An ancestor of mine wrote it. You should read it sometime, *chhokro*. You'll learn much about a past they didn't teach you at the Guild," he said, pride in his voice. "Jehangir Khan was the first ruler to establish militaristic stations at strategic locations in the Khanate, and designate emissaries to provide him with detailed reports of the people's circumstances. Think of a world with public storages of food and medicine. Guided by his faith, he adhered to moral laws above all."

"Maybe that's why magic submitted to him," Malev suggested.

Alamguir's eyes gleamed with appreciation of Malev's deduction. "I agree. There are descriptions of Khansadun before the Great Drought. Trees in full bloom, rich agriculture, rivers as clear as crystal." He shook his head. "All of it destroyed in one sweep of Hashim's blade. Now his descendant rules the east. Jasadan has inherited Hashim's greed."

"Your objective is to reinstate the Khanate," Leviathan said, redirecting the conversation.

"Yes."

"That includes Dariadun and Suradun."

"Of course."

"How do you plan on doing that?"

"We build an army that can overthrow the Firawn's."

"How many Wolves do you have?"

"A few hundred."

"Not much of an army."

"No, but they're men who can be trusted," Alamguir reasoned with calm. "I can't risk infiltration. I started this opposition alone and it hasn't been easy to train the men. You must understand they're not soldiers, but farmers and dyers."

Sympathisers, Leviathan knew. From the villages.

"The lower *zaat* recruits at the Guild were farmers, potters, dyers. Some were promised exemption from taxes for their commitment to the Wings, and others were forced to sign on as conscripts because their families were arrested and tortured," Leviathan argued. "Soldiers aren't born. They're made."

"Point taken."

"I'm not questioning your stance. But if you want to become a real threat to the Firawn, you need more men. It doesn't matter whether they're soldiers bred for battle. They'll be made ready when the time comes."

Alamguir shifted in the chair and spread his hands. "We've been concerned with other critical issues. The camps need food and medicine. Those who know of the Wolves plead to be taken to a safer place." His eyebrows pulled low. "Safa is large, but not enough to house thousands of people, nor is it possible to bring them all here without drawing attention and risking their lives. Improving their condition in the camps is our top priority. We have limited resources which we must utilise well."

"You can still make numbers a priority," Leviathan persisted, moving to the map of the Strips and gesturing to the red pins. "Recruit from the camps. They want to fight. They want a chance to defend their families."

"It would take time to earn their trust. Too many rebels have claimed to fight for their cause only to cause destruction."

"Then talk to them directly," Malev proposed, backing Leviathan up. "Tell them who you are and what you want. What you can do for them. If you go to them, they'll come to you."

"You're focused on your Wolves. That's fine," Leviathan nodded. "But you're not seeing the men and women here in Safa. They have a strength of their own. Organise a few factions to visit the camps and talk to the clans. All they need is a match, and they'll light up like beacons. They have the will to rise, but you have to guide them."

Ashar rubbed his chin. "It's not a bad idea, Babu Saheb," he admitted. Leviathan looked at him from across the table, appreciating his support with a short nod. He'd seen enough of Ashar over the past week to conclude that he was a strong choice as Alamguir's second-in-command. Level-headed, strategic, and superior in combat. Despite his laid-back nature—and annoying charm—he was serious when it counted.

Glancing between the three of them, Alamguir considered the proposal. "If I sanction the factions to visit the camps, and they're caught," he said slowly, "it'll mean death for all of them."

Leviathan held his stare. "There can't be results without some amount of risk," he said. Alamguir took a deep breath and Leviathan moved back to the table. "As long as they steer clear of the roads and villages, they'll be fine."

"You make it sound simple, but it's not."

Sliding his hands in his pockets, Leviathan lifted a shoulder in a half-shrug. "You wanted me for my mind. This is what I advise. If you want to be a strong opposition, you need to become invulnerable. You need manpower, resources, equipment, and space. Those have to be your priorities."

Alamguir sighed and nodded. "All right. We'll try it your way. Does this mean you're one of us now?" he asked, eyes calm and not too gentle.

"It means I'll help you if you help me."

"Fair enough. I pray your advice proves prosperous. The more horrors the clans endure, the more desperate they become."

"Prayers don't save lives."

"Prayers are for ourselves, *chhokro*. They offer patience to bear hardships." Watching Leviathan, the leader smiled. "Discussing faith makes you angry."

"I'm not angry. And I'd appreciate it if you'd use my name."

"You have a viciously throbbing vein in your neck. Don't be so furious at life that you rob yourself of the rare moments of happiness. We need it to live. No matter who or where we are."

"I know how to survive."

"I said live, Leviathan, not survive."

Leviathan ignored his comment. "I'm heading back to the city tonight." He had to make an appearance in Ferozi, or his overdue return would be reported to the Firawn. His freedom was a limited privilege; a privilege Cecilia would love for him to lose sooner rather than later.

"The Firawn watches you."

"Not yet."

"Ashar can lead you out before he leaves with his charge tonight. Ashar?"

"Sure. No problem."

Alamguir interlaced his fingers. "There's one more thing. I need information on particular steel caravans arriving in the Pashmina Pass from the East Strip. An exact time, location, and the number of soldiers assigned to escort the caravans would be helpful."

"I can get the information. Is that all?"

Keeping his eyes on Leviathan, Alamguir leaned back in his seat. "I'd like a private moment with you." Malev looked at Leviathan and Leviathan inclined his head. As the door shut behind Malev and Ashar, the leader cocked his head. "You never answered my question."

"What question?"

"When the time comes—can you kill the Firawn?"

This time, Leviathan didn't hesitate. "I'll do what I have to."

"That's not an answer. We love and fear our creators, Leviathan. It's not something to be ashamed of. It's human."

"I don't love him," Leviathan said through clenched teeth. "And I don't fear him."

"You have unresolved emotions for the Firawn."

Something tried to push past his defence. Something he didn't want to touch. Memories, feelings. The confusion in him as a kid whenever he saw his mother's affection for the Firawn despite how he treated them.

He swallowed hard. “We’re done now.” He turned to walk to the door.

“If you want to destroy the identity the Firawn gave you and reclaim your own, leaving him won’t be enough,” Alamguir said to his back. “You’ll have to break out of his mental prison as well.”

He would. Whatever it took, he would.

CHAPTER 43

Alamguir's houseboat was loud as hell at nightfall.

Four men sat in a circle around a platter of seafood and flatbread, engaged in brotherly banters and scattershot conversations veering between war and women. Companionable shoves and back claps were passed around like the pitcher of water, roaring laughter ringing in the cramped space, and Leviathan's head pounded with a menace. Alamguir and Kalyani lounged on a divan with their eight-year-old daughter, Ghaliya, talking in low voices, smiling at each other with a tenderness too intimate for an audience. It was a rare kind of love that Leviathan had never seen before.

"—heard Naira's been sick," Ashar was saying. "I thought I'd bring her desert sages. Women like flowers, you know? So I bring her a whole goddamn bunch—"

"Ashar," Kalyani cautioned. "Watch your language around Ghaliya."

"Ashar Bhau cursed," Ghaliya giggled.

"Indeed, he did," Alamguir laughed.

"And you know what she does?" Ashar continued. "She throws the flowers in my face. Broke my heart, *yani*."

"Your heart doesn't break," Ferran said without looking up from his food. "It bends like an acrobat. Poets should write ballads about your endless crushes."

"All of which have been unrequited," Zufar added. "Face it, Ashar. Women don't care about your pretty-boy looks. They want heart and soul, *samajhliyo*."

"What do you know about women? You fucking piss yourself every time one walks by."

Luay choked on his water.

"Ashar," Kalyani snapped. "*Language*."

Zufar's cheeks flushed. "I'm ten seconds from punching you where it hurts," he ground out.

"Big talk."

"Five."

"Despite his tragic lack of experience," Ferran intervened and spat out fish bones. "Zufar's right. Women want heart and soul."

"You're married. You only know about *your* woman. Women in plural are different… like sweets."

Zufar rolled his eyes. "Oh, here it comes," he murmured.

Ashar spread his arms with a grin. "There are all kinds of sweets, aren't there? Syrupy *jalebi* and *rasgullah*, dark *gulab jaman* and soft-as-velvet *burfi*, cool *faloodeh*—" He was cut off when Ferran stuffed a large slice of flatbread into his mouth to shut him up.

"You know what I think?" Zufar asked smugly.

"You can think?"

"Shut it, Pretty Boy. You're going to meet a girl who'll rein you in—hook, line, and sinker—and you'll spend the rest of your sorry life courting her like a lovesick poet, *dekhliyo*."

"If she has eyes I can drown in? I'll crawl over burning coal for her."

"*Wah*, a poet, truly," Ferran mocked, slapping Ashar's shoulder. "Leave the heart and soul thing to Luay, brother. You just stick with the grease."

"I'm offended."

Zufar smirked. "Eyes you can drown in, huh?" he echoed.

"Is this about the girl from the village?" Luay glanced between the three of them. "The one who saw Ashar in Jirani Bhau's stall?"

"He wasted five precious minutes staring at her like an idiot."

"Minutes well spent," Ashar said with a slow smile. "Wish I'd had an eternity to look into those eyes."

"Really, brother, enough with the nauseating poesy."

"*Your two eyes—why do they fire such arrows*?" Luay recited. Ashar and Zufar cheered him on, and he shot them a grin. "*They strike bullseye in my soul, though the bow is drawn at someone else.*"

"*Wah*," they acclaimed.

"I'll be sick in a moment," Ferran murmured.

"*Agile tricksters, your eyes, they aim over there yet strike right here,*" Luay finished, clasping his hands over his heart, making Ashar and Zufar howl and hail in response.

"Fucking love it when he recites Khusrau."

"*Khallas,*" Kalyani hissed, stomping over to the men. Everybody sobered up, except Ashar, who had his back to her. Snatching his ear, she twisted it and he yelped. "I told you not to swear in front of the children. Do you listen with your rear end, boy?"

"*Ow*—I'm sorry, I'll listen," Ashar chuckled. When she released him, he caught her hand, leaning back to wiggle his eyebrows at her. "Have I ever told you how incredible you look in the lamplight? Like a goddess, Māsa."

She shoved his head. "Finish your dinner in silence," she ordered.

It didn't quiet down.

Setting his teeth, Leviathan stared at his untouched food, tension coiling in his muscles, his mind tuning out the male noise to a distant echo. Something hounded him. A question, a suspicion. Did Mai know he was a descendant of the Last Khan? Was it the reason she placed her faith in him? Was it why she cared so much? His lineage meant nothing to him, but what if it meant everything to her? Did she see him as a weapon, too?

If that was all he was to her—

'*You are nothing.*'

Glancing up from their shared platter, Malev frowned at him. "Brother," he said quietly. "You all right?"

"I need some air."

What he needed was a cigarette, but he was out, so the air would have to do. Shoving to his feet, he ignored the curious looks at his back and stepped out on the balcony. The sweet fragrance of the mountain flowers hung heavy in the air. Safa was beautiful at night when lanterns lit up the balconies, terraces, and walkways. The chill in the mountains was oddly calming. Not like the hot, dry air of the steppes.

Leaning his arms on the rail, Leviathan savoured the cool breeze passing through, his chest finally easing with each inhale. As a kid, he used to be afraid of the water. It was this deep, dark entity. He imagined beasts under the surface with the Firawn's eyes and alien smile. When his mother bathed him, she'd cup a hand over his brow to keep the water from pouring into his eyes so he wouldn't panic. He overcame that fear and many others, but he never forgot the things she did for him.

There was love in her smallest gestures. Unquestionable, unconditional love.

It pained him that he questioned Mai's.

Turning over his left hand, he brushed a thumb over his mother's name tattooed on the inside of his wrist in Middle Khansāri, right where his pulse thumped. He wanted desperately to find the truth, to avenge her, but he couldn't do it if he wanted to be better. If he wanted to focus on helping the clans. He clenched his hand into a fist. Maybe he couldn't act on his thirst for vengeance now, but when this was all over, he'd extract the price of her murder, because he had both the patience and inclination to destroy Cecilia.

When the time was right, he'd end her the way she ended his mother.

Without mercy.

"If you want for solitude, I'm afraid I can't oblige you," Alamguir said, approaching him, and he dropped his hand. His muscles tensed up again. He'd avoided the leader since their last talk in the conference chamber. It went too far. "Kalyani holds my tea hostage. She insists I spend some quality time with you before you leave. She can be quite frightening. You've seen her temper. She's iron, that woman. The moment I saw her in the slave market, I was in love."

Tilting his head, Leviathan looked at Alamguir. "She was a slave?"

"A *vani*. The family she served didn't want her anymore because of her age. They sent her to the slave market to be sold. Vivaan was just a child, but I remember how he stood by her side, his head held high, and his eyes daring anyone to touch his mother."

Vani. The term was used in the northeast to refer to girls forcefully married to settle blood feuds between families. It was a punishment for crimes committed by their fathers and brothers. These girls were treated as less than slaves by their supposed in-laws.

"You bought her free."

"And she gave me a home."

Silence.

"I know you have questions, Leviathan," Alamguir ventured, looking toward the mountains. "Ask if you'd like."

"How did you tail me to Tundra?"

"Friends of Ashar's have watched you for some time."

"Friends?"

Alamguir rested his hands on the rail. "You received an invitation from one of them and the rest you met in the Forgotten City," he elaborated. *The glassy-eyed hoopoe bird and the wolves. Adharit.* "Ashar gave me a detailed description of your encounter with the Adharit. It'd be quite something to see those creatures for myself. I've heard they're magnificent."

"Ashar's got some interesting friends."

"You may have noticed he's related to the Nar. It lends him certain advantages, such as his natural ability to communicate with the Ghaib or the few tribes that still reside among humankind. The Nar, of course, were banished to a far-off island. Have you heard how Jehangir Khan—"

"You killed the workmen from the ship," Leviathan cut in. He wasn't interested in hearing about Jehangir Khan's endless virtues and feats.

"You don't sound pleased about it."

"They had information on the backers of the organ trade."

"Information on the heptagon symbol, I assume."

"Why'd you kill them?"

"They wouldn't surrender. We had no choice. Volos told us that he received his payment through the workmen hired by foreign handlers to deliver the children across the sea."

Straightening now, Leviathan frowned.

"The backers?"

"He called them the Benefactors. They harvest Khansan children's organs for experimentation. To see if magic can be extracted from them."

Experimentation. Leviathan's stomach turned. Of course it was about magic. It was always about magic. Something didn't add up, though. "If that's their sole objective, why not acquire bottled magic instead? Why bother with abductions and experiments?"

"Because magic loses its preternatural qualities once it leaves Khansan soil. It's tied to this land."

Looking out at the water, Leviathan ran his tongue over his teeth. He never would've figured that magic could lose its qualities. "Thought it was indestructible," he murmured.

"Nothing in this world is indestructible," Alamguir responded.

Except the Firawn.

"What about Volos?"

"We have him."

"Where?"

"I know what you're thinking, Leviathan, but we don't torture our prisoners."

"He might know something important," Leviathan said in a tight voice. "Something that could lead straight to the backers."

"This isn't Shadowhold. We *don't* torture. If we stoop to that inhumane level, we're no different than the Firawn."

Leviathan shook his head and clenched his teeth. Alamguir's goddamn principles were a problem. Volos was a link to the backers. If nothing else, he could give a name or the location of where the ship took the kids, and Alamguir was too bloody righteous to force it out of him.

Sabotaging the organ trade had at least put a dent in the business. Whoever was involved would lay low for a while. News of Volos' disappearance, his safe location being compromised, and the fact that the ship never returned with its stock to the foreign handlers, would eventually reach the backers if it hadn't already. They'd regroup. Somebody else would take Volos' place. It didn't matter because he'd find a way around Alamguir to Volos. An opportunity would arise—and he'd seize it. He wasn't surrendering the one lead he had to unmasking the backers.

"Your prisoner, your rules," Leviathan said with a change of tone. "You're making a mistake."

Alamguir cocked his head. "You're welcome to criticise my methods, Leviathan. Are you open to the same?"

"Criticism of my methods?"

"Criticism altogether."

"Knock yourself out."

Turning around, he leaned back against the rail. "You don't sit with the Wolves. You don't dine, or speak with them. It seems out of character for someone who makes it a habit to know his environment before trusting it."

"Never said I trusted this place."

"It's difficult to form trust if you don't engage with anyone." At Leviathan's silence, he continued, "Kalyani and I didn't raise the boys to be men. The definition of manhood is flawed. If you ask a boy to be a man, he thinks he's meant to rule. We raise custodians. The Wolves are taught to protect and defend the people. They understand they're the ones to serve, not the other way around. It's a notion that keeps a man humble. Knowing he serves as a custodian of those weaker than him."

Tucking his tongue in his cheek, Leviathan considered his words. "Why're you telling me this?"

"Because you watch the Wolves with judgement."

"That's not it."

"You don't assess them?"

"I do, but—it's not judgement."

"Then what is it?"

The breeze picked up around them. He let his gaze roam the trees beyond the water and chose his words with care. "I'm not good with people," he answered. "And add to it that I'm the Firawn's son—I doubt they'll want to trust me."

"If you don't spend time with them, how will you earn their trust?"

"Look, I'm not one of your lost boys, all right? I wasn't found on the streets or bought at the slave market. I wasn't brought up with your values and virtues. The kind of morals I've been raised with? They lead to the gates of perdition. I can't pretend I'm one of your adopted sons any more than they can pretend they want me here."

"Do you think we base our brotherhood on blood? If that was the case, would you have an orphan such as Junho as your friend? You care more for your companions than you let them see, but you would kill for them. They're your brothers. Not in blood, but in heart, mind, and spirit. What you fear, Leviathan, is rejection, and so you've already rejected us."

Leviathan locked stares with him. "You're wrong."

"Am I? You keep everyone at a distance, even Malev and Junho. Did they know of your ability to see the Ghaib?"

"You're way out of line. Again."

"You can't battle the forces of darkness alone, Leviathan. We need to become one host if we hope to stand a chance against our enemy. Without unity, we're doomed."

"I know the psychology of war."

"I don't doubt it. You know what's required of you." Alamguir nodded, eyes hard. "You may not be one of my boys, but you're a part of this now. I didn't invite you only for your mind. Your heart must be in it as well."

"Fair."

"Then we understand each other."

"Perfectly."

A shadow leaped from one of the *shikaras* to the dock. Narrowing his eyes, Leviathan recognised Vivaan's quick, nimble movement before he hit the walkway, the old wood groaning under his boots.

"Babu Saheb," Vivaan called urgently, and Alamguir moved to meet him. Hearing the call, the other Wolves stepped out of the flaking houseboat, faces sober, joining them on the walkway. Sweat dampened Vivaan's *kurta*. His breathing was shallow from the race. "There's been an explosion in the southeast, Babu Saheb."

"Conference," Alamguir ordered, leading the way through the scattered houseboats. Malev fell in step with Leviathan a few paces behind. Entering the conference chamber, the Wolves gathered around the worn table while Luay lit the lanterns. Shadow and light flickered off the wooden walls. The Wolf leader looked at Vivaan. "Report."

"A massive explosion in the southeast has wrecked Tabassum. There's nothing left. Hundreds are dead. Men, women, and children, all lower *zaat*. The area's covered in a poisonous white mist. Some acidic weapon that burns. Coyan says people are boiling from the inside out."

"White phosphorous," Leviathan stated, and they all looked at him. "It's incendiary. This contact of yours—did he say anything about charged air? Blue sparks?"

Vivaan nodded sharply.

"What does it mean?" Ashar asked, eyebrows pulling low.

"It means the white phosphorous was fused with magic to create a temporary dome over the area. The Firawn doesn't want the chemical to spread outside Tabassum. It's contained annihilation."

"Send a message to Coyan," Alamguir told Ferran. "Tell him to gather as many Wolves as he can and ride for Tabassum."

"There's no point," Leviathan said.

"What do you mean there's no point?" Zufar demanded, slamming his hands down on the table. It shook from the impact. "We have to help."

"The dome can't be breached until the air's detoxified."

"What do you suggest we do?"

"Wait it out. Then search for survivors."

Ferran stared at him. "We're not leaving those people to die," he countered.

"They're either dying or already dead. It's done."

"We have to try."

"If by some miracle you do breach the containment—you'll die with them."

"We're not afraid of death," Zufar snapped.

"Babu Saheb," Ashar intervened without heat. "What do you want us to do?"

Pressing his fingertips against the table, Alamguir stared down at a map, noticeably warring with himself. The animal skin curled at the edges around the visual of the Strips. A moment passed in anxious silence as they all watched Alamguir intently. It wasn't an easy call to make, and it didn't surprise Leviathan when Alamguir's visceral need to do the righteous thing overpowered his rationale.

"Tell Coyan to ride for Tabassum," he repeated to Ferran. "Take some of the men with you in case he needs more hands." Ferran signalled for Luay to follow him and Alamguir looked at Leviathan. "I appreciate your counsel and I agree with you on a rational plane, but we don't abandon hope in our opposition. We must act. If we ask the people to place their faith in us, we must show them that we're with them in life and in death. That they're never alone."

"That's very noble," Leviathan said with calm, "and a waste of resources."

"It's the right thing to do." Alamguir dropped a hand on Vivaan's shoulder. "What of the camps?"

"They were far enough from the village to avoid destruction. There's one more thing, Babu Saheb. Rumours are spreading that rebels were behind the attack. They're saying it was the White Wolves."

"What? They're saying *we're* behind this?" Zufar growled. "Where would we have attained the damned white phosphorous and pounds of magic?"

"You can't expect people to reason in the face of tragedies, Zufar," Alamguir reminded him before turning to Leviathan. "What are your thoughts? Why was Tabassum of all places targeted?"

"That doesn't matter." Leviathan's words made them all tense up. "Look, this is a False Flag operation. The Firawn's focused on you, the lower *zaat*, and the clans. He doesn't want you to unite, so he's making sure you take care of his problem by ripping each other apart. The blame for the attack will fall on your opposition, and since you're directly linked to the clans—"

"The lower *zaat* will punish them in their rage," Ashar finished. "Another civil war breaks out."

Zufar swore.

Pushing away from the wall, Leviathan stepped into the light. "The Firawn is using his guerrilla group to smear your name while destroying any potential alliances between the lower *zaat* and the clans. You need to do damage control. You need to show the people the truth, so they don't believe the lie."

Alamguir shook his head. "If we come out in the open, we won't be provoking the Firawn. We'll be outright challenging him. We have far more to lose than gain from such a dangerous invitation."

"I'm not talking about coming out in the open. The opposite, in fact. Deception. Make it look like the explosion in Tabassum intimidated you and use it to appear as if you've withdrawn. If you're not considered a pressing threat, you'll be temporarily off his mind, which will buy you time to appeal to the clans, recruit, and reach out to the lower *zaat*, too."

"Would the Firawn fall for this deception?"

"It's one course of action you'd have more to gain from."

It wasn't an answer to his question, but Alamguir didn't pursue it. Leviathan saw it on his face that he understood there was no certainty when the Firawn was concerned.

"I suppose it's not that different from what we've done so far. Perhaps we were too rash with our recent interceptions," Alamguir mused with regret. "It has drawn the Firawn's complete attention."

"But the camps need the supplies," Zufar protested.

"What about a distraction?" Malev suggested, catching Leviathan's eye. "Taxation day is coming up."

"An opportunity," Leviathan murmured.

"Um, we're not all mind readers here," Ashar said, raising his hand. "Elaborate, please."

"Taxation day is tense for the lower *zaat*. Emotions run high. People are frustrated, angry, scared. Most can't pay the demanded rate," Malev explained. "It'd be easy to trigger a riot, which might unite the people, and remind them the Firawn is a tyrant, a common enemy, not a god. Remind them what he takes from them and what they've got a right to keep."

Alamguir frowned. "It'd become violent with the Wardens present."

Leviathan glanced around the chamber. Everything from the ragged drapes to the peeling paint on the walls spoke of their lack of resources. "Leave that part to me," he said. He hadn't told Alamguir about his Commander position yet, but now seemed like a good time as any to drop the news. "I'm being promoted as Commander of the Surya Wing."

There was a moment of stunned silence.

Ashar cleared his throat. "Well, doesn't get fancier than that," he remarked.

"Commander?" Zufar spat out. "Of the Firawn's army?"

Alamguir focused on Leviathan. "What does it mean for us?"

"It means you'll have somebody on the inside for a while." Until the Firawn discovered his game. Leviathan left that part out.

"And for the people?"

"I'm not going to order a massacre." He kept the bitterness out of his voice. "If that's what you're concerned about."

"How the hell do we know for sure?" Zufar squinted at him, eyes cynical. "How do we know you won't become your father's little pet again?"

A muscle ticked in Leviathan's jaw, but his irritation was quelled by a tightness in his throat. He grew up in Verdite, a place where humanity didn't exist, and he wore a soldier's skin most of his life. Acting human was different from being human. If he returned to the military city, it'd be a matter of time before he fell into old habits, like an opium addict back in the opium den, because, at the Guild, he wouldn't even have to *act* human.

Zufar pointed at Leviathan. "The second he becomes Commander, he's going to continue killing our people," he snarled. Malev clenched his hands on Leviathan's left. "We never should've brought him here. We should've locked him up with that *harami* Volos. That's where he belongs. I knew this was a bad idea from the start, but nobody ever listens to me."

Ashar shot him a look. "Does it hurt?" he asked.

"Does what hurt?"

"The huge stick up your ass."

Zufar glared at Ashar, opening his mouth to bite back, but Alamguir held up a hand, and whatever the Wolf was about to spit out was swallowed. The mood in the chamber was dark and agitated. One of the lanterns guttered in the breeze that whistled through a wide crack in the wall. Malev seethed in silence and Leviathan held Alamguir's even stare. He didn't fully trust the Wolves, and the Wolves didn't trust him, especially not now with his upcoming promotion. It'd put him in a too powerful position.

"How much time do you need?" Alamguir asked at length.

The leader might have his plans, but Leviathan had his own. There were some things he wanted to accomplish before he left that life behind.

"Give me a few weeks."

A few weeks, and he'd be out of there. For good, this time.

Alamguir straightened with steel in his eyes. "Let's discuss taxation day before you leave for the city," was all he said.

CHAPTER 44

It was late in the night when Leviathan and Malev camped on a hill near the strategically situated fortress of Liyana; a four-thousand-feet tall prehistoric structure overlooking a massive vale, so old a structure it should've crumbled centuries ago, but the calcareous bones stood strong. Minarets slashed the skyline, cupolas cast shadows, and windows invited travellers into the dark. Built before the Ghaib and humankind existed, Liyana was from the time of a different race of creatures. Like the Forgotten City, it was considered cursed and left alone.

There were forces even the Firawn wouldn't touch.

Too restless to sleep, Leviathan took the first watch. Smoke rippled over the woodpile. Moonlight filtered through the awkward branches of the willow behind him. Desert creatures scuttled in the dark. Their restlessness was like his own. Maybe it was the proximity of the fortress that disturbed him, the strange verve emanating from those high, dusty walls, but it didn't bother his companion. Malev slept a short distance from the fire, his cloak rolled up as a makeshift pillow. Their mounts didn't stir either. He'd been riding Cinder hard, piloting her down the shortcuts Ashar showed them, hoping to reach Ferozi before the next dawn, but the mounts had needed rest, even a Suran breed like Cinder.

Watching the flames hiss and cavort, Leviathan went over the argument in the conference chamber. He was starting to understand the mechanics of Alamguir's mind. In the leader's head, the means didn't justify the end and the end didn't justify the means. Both had to be ethical. Leviathan was raised with the conviction that morality played no part in leadership and war. Were humans just numbers to him? He wanted to help Tabassum, but his mind worked like a cost-benefit scale. It was so easy for him—so easy to trade people's lives for his objectives.

'How do we know you won't become your father's little pet again?'

Alamguir was right about one thing. Names held power. Leviathan was called the Blade, and each time it made him feel a little less human inside.

His senses prickled, agitated. It wasn't the fortress. It was something else. Looking up, his eyes locked on a figure standing on the rampart in a white kaftan, the layers billowing with her long white hair. But there was no wind, not even a breeze. Moving to his feet, he made for the wall. She cloaked herself in the invulnerable darkness and vanished before he could get a closer look at her.

Malev came up behind him. "What is it?" he asked, fully awake.

"I don't know."

Rubble crunched under Leviathan's boots as he walked up the steps to the gates. They were carved with encryptions, resembling the ones he'd seen on the kennel. Strange lines intersected with symbols shaped like geometrical patterns overlapping with Ancient Khansāri letters between the ornamental rule lines. The iron hummed with aged magic; a pulsating power that got under his skin.

"This language," Malev pondered out loud, studying the encryptions. "It's from the Esoteric Era when the Arcanes walked the earth. Those markings? They're scriptures from the Esoteric Testament. The language is Arafataic. Middle Khansāri and other languages are all later variations of it."

Nobody knew much about the Esoteric Era, the Arcanes, or their mysterious language, except that they'd been one of the sources to Khansadun's magic. Absorbed in the encryptions, Malev went on, "That particular symbol there appears in countless Ancient Khansāri texts. It's a name. Shamsuddin. He's said to have been the first ruler of the earth and parallel dimensions. He wrote six volumes in at least a dozen variants of Arafataic on the creation of all beings, including his own race and the Ghaib. This encryption is either an instruction or admonition. Could be both."

"How can you tell?"

"There are theological texts at the Archeion about encryptions on ancient structures, claiming the Arcanes might've used a liturgical variation of Arafataic to create magic seals, making it difficult for anyone to enter their domains unless able to read the words. The symbols and Ancient Khansāri letters have one thing in common. Both are difficult to translate. A mispronunciation or change in the swirl of a letter can alter the entire meaning of the word itself. Like that symbol." He pointed to one of the curlicue lines. "It looks just like the Middle Khansāri word for *burn*, but depending on the shape and pronunciation, it can mean the opposite: *extinguish* or *quench*. If the meaning is *burn*, I'm guessing it's a warning."

Leviathan rolled his shoulders. "Watch the mounts," he said, approaching the gates alone.

"Be careful, brother."

Touching the cold, oxidised iron handle, he shoved it sideways, expecting it to jam and deny him access. The magic was so strong it jolted through him, making him clench his teeth at the sharp buzz, but the handle slid through the hooks without resistance. Shoving the gates open, he stepped inside, and a chorus of disembodied whispers in Ancient Khansāri—some in a tongue that didn't even sound human—ambushed him at once.

'Wanderer. Tread with restraint.'

'You walk upon consecrated land.'

'A blood trail you leave.'

'Sword of the Cursed One.'

He turned in a slow circle, his intent eyes searching the shadows, trying to track the owners of the voices. He'd never heard anything like it. The Ghameq were always tangible, their voices textured like velvet sliding over skin, but these whispers felt like air, like the phantom pressure of the wind on his body after it'd passed. He knew it was real, but he had no proof of it.

This place was haunted.

Taking caution, he stepped without a sound on the primordial stone, moving through cobwebbed archways, up broken stairs, and past hollow-eyed structures. Serpent sloughs cluttered the courtyards. The rational part of his mind told him to leave. What was he doing here? But another part of him wanted—needed—to find the white-haired woman. He was drawn to her like he was drawn to Jehangir Khan's scimitar on the wall. With a bone-deep knowing.

'Such implacable darkness.'

'A lost, lost soul.'

Laughter sounded all around him, from the ground and walls, and bounced back at him. He saw her then. She stood in a courtyard, barefoot. The ground beneath her was carved with narrow channels leading to a deep indentation in the centre. She wasn't old. She was ancient. With skin so creased that the furrows held shadows of their own, and bones so worn that her fingers curled like claws. A silver ring with a black stone sat on her middle finger. She'd seemed taller on the rampart, but she was a head shorter than Mai. She had no eyes. Yet, she stalked him as he circled her.

"Come closer, child," she said to him in Ancient Khansāri.

"What are you?"

"A keeper of secrets."

"I've been solving a lot of riddles lately. Not in the mood for another."

She spread her arms. Sand levitated in the air around her, spinning like a whirlwind, swallowing her up, then rushing at him. It wasn't a show of power but an answer to his question. He felt her timelessness. The sandstorm rotated in front of him, settling to reveal the sightless woman, and white hair swelled around her like moonlight underwater. She wasn't old anymore. Her skin was smooth, unscarred, but even in this form she was blind.

"You stand on consecrated land. Barefoot you must be." She waved a hand and his boots vanished from his feet. "This is the birthplace of Shamsuddin; the Horned King and Binder of Demons. It is a sacred place, Blade of the Firawn, a place that bares your soul. You are naked here."

He swallowed hard. "Do you have a name?" he asked.

"I have many."

"Give me one."

"Rawiya."

"Rawiya. You called to me. Why?"

"I have been tasked with forewarning the descendants of the Last Khan and so I come to you with a warning," she answered. "You must find the one of dual nature. The *nāgin*. She is in peril."

Nāgin.

An old word that referred to—

A female serpent.

Something inside him froze, making the connection, recognising it, like he'd known all this time, but hadn't been able to understand it until now.

He still asked.

"Who is she?"

"You know her as Roma."

From the moment he saw her in the procession, he'd sensed it. The quick and sharp element about her; how she mirrored his movements; how she almost accomplished stabbing his throat when she'd pointed the blade at her own just a beat ago; the otherness of her eyes, their focus. She healed faster than a human. Hell, it seemed impossible—and yet, he'd seen things far more impossible than this.

So, she wasn't human, after all.

Rawiya circled him. "For so long she was hidden. Now she has been discovered. If her memories are unsealed, darkness will follow. Such darkness that the world has never seen."

"What're you talking about?"

Before he could evade her, she touched her fingers to his brow. A searing, hot pain shot straight through his skull. His hand clamped around her wrist, but a bone-jarring force threw him back across the courtyard, ramming his back against a pillar. He dropped forward on his knees, the stone cracking and crumbling behind him, and his sight blurred. The world reshaped around him. It happened in high speed at first—a street, torches, shouts. Men and cobras. Dead bodies, dead cobras. Roma in shackles. Screams.

Then everything slowed to a crawl.

A familiar chamber. Paintings and lanterns. The Palace of Mirrors. A voice sounded in his head. Cold, dark, known.

'Open your mind, your heart to me.'

'I am a well-wisher.'

'Searched for an eternity.'

'Treasure.'

Jaw clenched, the muscles in his face and throat twitched as he swallowed. The rushing visuals subsided, leaving him shaken, and he coughed and spat blood. Sand and dust from the collapsed pillar scratched in his lungs.

Lifting his head, he narrowed his eyes, looking at Rawiya as she advanced. "You see it now," she whispered. "You understand."

He'd seen far more than he wanted. "What does the Firawn want from her?" he asked, his voice hoarse.

"What she knows. What she keeps."

"Which is *what*?"

"The treasure she protects is not meant to be known. If it comes into his possession, it will mean the destruction of humankind. Find her, hide her. Ensure her memories remain sealed."

"Wait—"

"She can never remember who she is, nor what she keeps."

And the woman was gone.

Shit.

Gaining his feet, he snatched up his boots, moving quickly. He didn't understand everything she'd told him, but at this point all that mattered was reaching Roma. The Firawn wouldn't have taken her if she wasn't somehow important in his obsessive hunt for magic. When it came to power, the Firawn was unscrupulous. He had her escorted to the Palace of Mirrors and took the time to manipulate her. It confirmed as much that Roma had something he wanted.

Malev met him outside. "I was about to come in after you, brother," he said with a frown. "What happened in there?"

"I'll explain later. Right now, I need you to track down Ashar," Leviathan said, striding to Cinder. The glimpses he saw of what was done to Roma made him sick to his stomach, but he forced the visuals from his mind. *Get her out now. Deal with the damage later.* "There's a woman in his faction. A former prostitute named Naira."

"I remember her."

"Bring her with you to Kantalaa, the northern border, and I'll meet you there on the fourth dawn. I'm heading to Ghada." Because he knew Malev cared about her and would want to know, he added, "Roma's in trouble."

His companion tensed. "How bad is it?"

"Bad."

Roma had spent time in a detainment cell in Ferozi's dungeon where she was tortured and raped. She wouldn't be in a condition to want him—or any man—anywhere near her. She needed a woman. Naira was the best choice. He'd seen her engage with other victims in Safa.

Tightening the back cinch, Leviathan checked the saddle in a quick, rough inspection and reached into the saddlebag for his shemagh. His thoughts kept circling back to Rawiya's warning. "Does the word *nāgin* mean anything to you?" he asked.

Malev's eyebrows pulled low. "It derives from the root word *nāga* mentioned in Khansan fables as a sacred race. Worshippers of the Serpent Goddess,

Lamia, sometimes call her a *nāgin* because of her association with a triple-headed cobra, but those fables have been passed down by word of mouth for generations, brother, embellished and altered, and they differ from region to region. Is this about Roma?"

"We'll talk later." Leviathan swung into the saddle. "Find Ashar."

"Be safe, brother."

CHAPTER 45

Roma wandered in a nightmare bounded by blood-smeared stone. The stark smell of human waste burned in her nose. Brutal hands touched her. Brushed and clawed and snatched. She wanted to sleep, but sleep meant pain. Time was an immeasurable existence inside the Palace of Mirrors. She couldn't determine if it were days or months since she arrived. When she asked for her dose, the *bandi* assigned to her refused because she wouldn't eat, nor would she swallow more than a few sips of water.

"You can't have it, Saheba," the *bandi* said. She was younger than Roma. Her brass *nath* revealed her low rank among the *bandis*. "You haven't eaten. You must at least try—"

"Just one more," Roma beseeched.

"You must eat and rest as well."

"I can't sleep without it."

The *bandi* chewed on her bottom lip. "All right," she whispered, looking past her shoulder at the closed doors beyond which Wardens guarded the corridor. Roma had been confined to these quarters ever since the Firawn murmured promises in her ear. He allowed only the *bandi* and himself to enter and leave.

"I'll bring you a dose if you promise to eat a bit. You mustn't fall ill again, Saheba."

"What was your name?"

"Aura."

"Will you say mine?"

"Your name is Roma, Saheba."

"No, I have—it's not my name."

Her physical injuries healed. The doses were merciful enough to steal her emotions. She became a shell without a soul. She bathed in rosewater in the sumptuous tub and dressed in the silks that the Firawn sent to her quarters. Embroidered, backless *cholis* in indigo and scarlet, emerald and marigold. *Lehengas* with *zardosi* threadwork and brocade borders. Gold neckpieces, nosepieces, and bracelets delivered with personal notes written on scented paper from the Firawn.

She was decorated like a queen, but she was an ornament.

Her quarters consisted of columns straining toward a ceiling of mirrors. Sunlight sieved in through ornate windows, casting outlines of floral patterns on painted tiles and lush carpets. Gold sconces and large paintings adorned the walls. Divans were mounted with embellished satin and velvet cushions, silk curtains stirred in the openings between chambers, and a colossal bed with dark wooden bedposts carved with elephants and camels was raised on a platform. It was a prison of mortal beauty, but she only craved her doses.

She sprawled on the carpet with a fever one afternoon while Aura had vanished to the kitchens to fetch towels and cold water. The last dose layered her lips in a bitter paste—the inside of her mouth so parched she couldn't move her tongue. Her blistering skin shimmered with fever sweat; her heart pounded a tremulous beat as if it might stop in a moment.

Aura returned from the kitchens and kneeled beside Roma. Dousing a towel in the water, she twisted it between her hands to drive out the moisture, pressing it against Roma's forehead to cool her skin. She sighed in relief from the welcome chill. Her damp eyelashes fluttered when she fought the weight of exhaustion to open her eyes the slightest bit.

The doors opened.

Aura rushed to her feet and bowed low as the Firawn stepped inside. He came to Roma's side, his gold-plated slippers soundless on the carpet. Crouching down, he inclined his head, his hair glistening like burnished black opal, and his gaze travelled over her shell in a disquieting caress. Roma looked back at him through heavy-lidded eyes.

"How is she?"

Aura licked her lips. "She has another fever, Sai," she said in a quivering voice.

"How many doses has she had today?"

"Two, Sai."

"I have someone I would like for you to meet, little queen," the Firawn said softly. "A close friend of mine. Aura—why are you still here?"

Aura jolted. "Forgive me, Sai." She hurried toward the doors. The second she closed them behind her, a tall man emerged from the shadowed corner. His thin form was shrouded in a black kaftan. His skin was deathly white with symbols inked on it. A turban clasped his head from under which black curls spilled to his shoulders. The protruding bones of his face made it seem as if his skin was dragged over his skull and stretched beyond its means.

The Kāhin kneeled on her other side with an eerie grace. Drawing a dagger from his long sleeve, he sliced open his palm, moving his pale lips in a silent chant. With a cold fingertip, he painted a line of blood between Roma's eyebrows and tipped back his head, staring up at the ceiling in utter stillness before a shudder journeyed through his body, his head dipping to peer at her again.

The Firawn looked at him. "Well?" he demanded.

"The seal on her memories remains strong. The ancient magic is too powerful for the usual rituals I perform, Sai. It might take years to weaken it."

"I want the seal removed *now*."

"I could attempt a different ritual."

"Do it."

"I need rare ingredients that would take time to acquire."

"Acquire them."

Bowing his head, the Kāhin hesitated. "Her mind is frail, Sai. A forceful removal of the seal could shatter it, and no magic will heal her once it is done," he emphasised.

"Prepare for the ritual."

"Your will, Sai."

The Kāhin glided out of the chamber.

"Khuram."

Stepping inside, the Captain bowed. "Sai," he answered.

"Is my mount ready?"

"It is, Sai."

"Perfect. Make certain she is well guarded while I am gone. No one but you and Aura is to enter or leave this chamber. If anything happens to her, I will make you watch as I cut open your wife and children. Rest now, little queen."

And she was alone again.

Raising a trembling hand, Roma trailed a fingertip over a line of sweat on her forearm where the bruises had healed. Without a sense of time, she drifted in and out of shallow waters. When she forced open her eyes, she discovered that stars dusted the night skies through the intricate framework of the large windows. The sound of grunts brushed her consciousness. She heard the *click* of a lock and felt the vibration of footfalls.

Fingers brushed her hair back from her face. Fear roused her. Wardens. They came to violate her. Lashing out against her perpetrators, she drew a sharp breath when a hand caught her wrist. Her eyes met those of the Firawn's son. A black shemagh covered his face beneath his hood, like on the sword dancers.

"Saheb?" she whispered.

This wasn't real. It was a fever dream.

He sprinkled the water from a pitcher on her face, the cool drops jarring her senses, and she gasped and blinked in bewilderment. He held the rim to her chapped lips. She gulped the water down, pushing it higher for more, even as it threatened to spill, but he took control of the pitcher.

"Easy," he murmured.

The drowsiness started to subside.

Taking her forearms, he helped her stand on unstable feet. The movement caused a mean spinning in her head, her limbs burning as if her joints were ablaze. She would have fallen against the window, but his arm banded around her waist, pulling her to him and holding her until she regained her balance. If she hadn't been so detached from her own emotions, she would have recoiled from him.

A loud clatter sounded just beyond the doors.

Aura screamed.

Grabbing Roma's hand, he pulled her past the terrified *bandi.* The corridor was strewn with bodies of Wardens, the ones that had guarded Roma's quarters, and soldiers leaped up the stairs and swarmed their path. The Firawn's son raised a sword in his left hand with a measured calm, his right still sealed around hers, and stepped in front of her with the magical torchlights on the walls glinting on his blade.

"The girl musn't be harmed," a Warden snapped. "Kill the son of a bitch."

The Firawn's son walked toward them, drawing her with him behind his back, and she staggered after him. Flourishing his sword, he began slicing a path to the stairs. A blond-haired Warden swung at his head. The Firawn's son ducked, slamming his elbow into the Warden's temple, and turned his blade to slash another's throat. As the Warden fell to his knees, the Firawn's son kicked him aside. A third Warden rushed at him. Sidestepping him, he flipped his sword, running it through the Warden's chest from behind.

Blood spattered Roma's face. The Firawn's son released her hand and continued in a swift tempo. Strike, slit, stab. Strike, slit, stab. The corridor vibrated with the clanging of steel, the guttural groans of Wardens, and the Firawn's son slaughtered as if it weren't life and death but a task of leisure. The enclosed air was ripe with a metallic tang.

Roma pressed herself against the wall. The Firawn's son switched the sword to his right hand an instant before two Wardens attacked him. They were all so trained, so skilled, but it was in a savage manner and clashed with his clean lines. The Firawn's son was a blur of movement, spinning on his heels, cutting down one Warden, snapping the neck of a second, and throwing a knife in a third's eye.

It happened in heartbeats, and Roma was ill. So ill. Breathing laboured, she forced herself to stand straight, shivering from the fever and what she beheld in the corridor.

The Firawn's son turned toward her. His stare was cold and untouched. Blood seeped from a gash in his side. He didn't as much as wince when he leaned down to yank his knife from a Warden's head, and then held out a bloodstained hand for her to take. She stared at it as it struck her that he had killed his father's men to help her escape.

"Why?" she rasped.

"There's no time," he said.

A horn sounded over the Palace of Mirrors.

Roma slid her hand into his. Tightening his hold, he led her down stairs, around corners, through archways and chambers, until she lost all sense of direction. Struggling against a need to drop against him, she anchored herself. The voice in her head reminded her that she shouldn't lean on the Firawn's son. He was her escape from the palace, but he couldn't be trusted. He had used her before, and he would use her again.

"Block all exits," a Warden shouted outside the palace. "Search all levels."

The Firawn's son pulled her around the corner of another corridor with mirror walls, ushering her through a door into an outdoor archway that led into an immense courtyard. The scent of jasmine and lemons saturated the night air. Trees were speckled with pomegranates. Sapphire blue and white tiles formed slender paths between carved ponds with pink-tipped lotuses, stretching to a gold pavilion in the heart of the courtyard. Silver tables, embellished futons, and silk cushions were scattered around. A gold cage held white tigers with translucent eyes that stalked them to the pavilion.

This was a part of the harem.

Slumping against a pillar, Roma caught her breath while the Firawn's son pressed down a portion of the circular shrine in the centre of the pavilion, revealing an opening in the ground that held nothing but darkness.

"There's a water canal below," he told her. "Jump."

When she perched on the brink and slid her legs inside, he grabbed her upper arms and lowered her with unexpected care. She dropped into the absolute darkness, landing in the ice water, the chill enveloping her heart and clogging her chest, and the Firawn's son leaped down behind her. The shrine shifted back into position above them. He didn't pause to consider but navigated through the darkness without hesitation. Touching the slick wall for support, she waded after him through the underground tunnels.

After what felt like hours, the Firawn's son climbed an iron ladder to the surface. Licking her lips, she gripped the rungs, hauling herself up. He reached down and lifted her out. Black blotches speckled her sight and heat seeped from her shell, even though she felt cold to the bone. She thought she might faint or vomit.

Brisk male voices sounded in the street.

The Firawn's son caught her forearms and backed her into the shadows. A curved alcove in a wall behind a mountain of garbage concealed them just as four Wardens marched past the alley, their silver buckles and buttons glinting and their boots clomping with an ominous echo.

"—can't get away. Don't harm the girl. She's important to the Firawn, so make sure she doesn't have a scratch on her, or he'll have us all decapitated."

"What about the intruder?"

"Arrest the bastard for interrogation. The Firawn will decide his fate when he returns."

Their footfalls faded.

The Firawn's son stepped out of the alcove.

"Let's move."

CHAPTER 46

Drumbeats resonated through the streets and alleys from festival celebrations in the distance. The chanting of a choir revealed that it was the last auspicious night before the Sacred Month of Yaghuth, God of Strength and War, ensued with a new moon. Roma felt the cavernous percussions through her battered feet as the Firawn's son pulled her into an alley, his back pressing against the sandstone wall behind them, his hand closing around the hilt of his sword, and she heard the voices a heartbeat later.

"Anything?"

"Negative, Captain Saheb."

"Keep searching. *Find* them."

"Yes, Captain Saheb."

"Have you stationed Wardens at the perimeters of the village?"

"No, Captain Saheb. We thought—"

"Do it *now*."

The Firawn's son tensed as the Wardens hurried up the street, inspecting the houses and passages on both sides. Turning his head, he slid his sword halfway from the sheath, estimating the vicinity of the soldiers. He slipped out a knife with his other hand and passed it on to her. She clenched the hilt in her hand. The knife had a narrow, stained blade. She recalled the last time she wielded a weapon; of how the Warden's face drained from fear; of how he struggled to escape his fate within her grasp.

She couldn't forget the taste of power.

A large procession of dancing and singing villagers turned the corner, forcing the Wardens to pull back or be trampled beneath the horde. Men, women, and children hurled coloured powder in the air, chimed the bells to the drumbeats, and their cheers drowned out the impatient curses of the Wardens.

The Firawn's son took her hand. "Stay close," he shouted over the noise and they slipped into the procession as it passed their alley.

Smothered by the press of damp bodies, Roma pushed through the mass. The drums matched her frantic heartbeat and the bells shrilled in her ears. Grinning paper masks of grotesque demonic faces surrounded her, bouncing up and down, chanting Lord Biran's second name.

"*U'lu Hubal, u'lu Hubal!*"

The procession reached an immense stretch. A market embraced a deep stepwell, selling incense, blossoms, tassels, and brass lockets for prayers. She looked toward the great shrine of Ba'alat-Sahra, Goddess of the Underworld, in the heart of the stepwell with *shikaras* rowing people to the sandstone platform. Separating from the procession, the Firawn's son led them through the marketplace. Shouts rang out not so far behind. Glancing behind them, she saw the Wardens violently shove a path through the thick crowd with crossbows in hand. Sellers protected their carts, children huddled against their mothers in fright, and people rushed aside to avoid a collision.

The Firawn's son hauled her past startled men and women, shedding the horde and hurtling down a steep hill with a colossal ruin looming ahead. Beyond it stood the silhouette of a wood with luminous trees. Running toward the ruin, they weaved in between the fractured pillars and crumbled stonework. He tugged her down behind a cracked wall. Their abrupt appearance frightened a serpent among the pebbles. It squirmed with dramatic exertion before stilling to act dead with the maw open.

The Firawn's son glanced at her tight grip on the knife. "You good?" he whispered.

Her throat felt swollen with cotton. "Yes," she rasped. Her gaze fell on his bleeding wound. She should have asked him the same question.

"Run when I whistle." His eyes searched hers. "Can you do it?"

She nodded.

He left her behind the wall.

She pressed a hand to the parched stone and waited with her breath locked within her chest.

He whistled.

She bolted out of the ruin, sprinting across the steppe, toward the wood.

The stars watched from the night skies, sparkling like sequins stitched into black fabric, and she felt disoriented beneath them. It was too far to the wood on foot. The Wardens would capture her before she reached it. The strained muscles in her limbs convulsed, the ground blasted sharp jolts of pain through her feet, and the world around her spun out of control. She sensed a violent vibration in the air seconds before a high-pitched scream shrilled in her ears and a mount skidded to a halt in front of her.

Cinder.

The whistling was a signal to Cinder.

Rearing with a whickering sound, Cinder slammed down her hooves, lowering herself in an urgent invitation. Roma climbed into the saddle, curling her fingers in Cinder's coarse mane for balance as the mount leaped back up. She thought they were headed for the wood, but instead, Cinder galloped in a wide arc, charging back toward the ruin, and Roma felt the mount's fierce determination when she thundered ahead both beautiful and lethal in her devotion.

The Firawn's son emerged from the ruin with his sword dripping blood. Bracing a hand on a low, collapsed wall, he vaulted over it, a spiralling arrow nicking his shoulder. As Cinder passed in a curve, he snatched the reins, leaping into the saddle behind Roma. Her back recoiled and revived from the heat of his chest through his damp *kurta.*

"Told you not to come back for me," he said to Cinder. He didn't steer her. She careered across the stretch with astonishing new speed, the bruising potency of her powerful limbs all but splintering the injured ground.

The wood was close, so close.

Arrows swished through the air, so near she felt them brush past her calves. Cinder made a terrible sound, her hooves skidding and staggering, and the Firawn's son sealed his arms around Roma a mere second before they were pitched from Cinder's back. He switched their positions in the air, his spine striking the unforgiving surface and shielding her from the worst impact. She pushed onto her hands and knees, her skin scratched and bloodied, but the ground tipped beneath her. Dipping her head, she dragged in deep breaths and looked up to see the Firawn's son crouching beside Cinder. Torment was in his eyes as he soothed her in Khansāri. Anguished sounds ripped from her throat. The arrows were lodged into her side and blood turned her silver coat a dark red.

The pounding of hooves in the close distance reminded Roma they were still out in the open with the Wardens on their heels. The soldiers would be upon them soon, but the Firawn's son remained in his crouched position, his eyes never leaving Cinder's, even as the whites of hers showed. He lowered his forehead to press it against hers.

Arrows struck the ground near him. If he didn't move, they would strike him next.

With a hardened face, he stood. Raising his sword, he brought it down on Cinder. Blood spattered his *kurta*. The wounded mount stilled in merciful relief, but her killer's eyes darkened with a nameless emotion. When they met Roma's, she recognised it.

Wrath.

"Run," the Firawn's son said in a cold, cold voice before shifting toward the threat. With the swift slant of his body, he shirked an arrow. Roma couldn't move. She watched him through a haze as he diverted several more arrows with quick, sharp evades, and the flicks of his blade. One arrow struck him in the front, but it didn't stop him. Breaking the end of the shaft, he tossed it aside and moved to meet the four Wardens jumping from their mounts with torches in one hand and swords in the other. Swinging his sword in close, smooth arches, the Firawn's son felled the Wardens, catching one of the torches and using it as a second weapon.

The last soldier slumped under his pitiless assault. Turning back, he lowered the torch to Cinder's coat and the blue flames devoured her. She didn't burn, but bleached. A dozen more torches emerged near the ruin.

Whizzing past Roma, the Firawn's son seized her hand. She saw the ridge too late, but he caught her around the waist without stopping, leaping down with her against his side. For a moment, she was airborne, and then his boots struck the ground. Dropping her back on her feet, he pulled her the short distance to the wood.

The Wardens hesitated on the ridge.

"Go," the Captain shouted.

"But it's the Sleeping—"

"*Now.*"

The wood closed around her. Ice and darkness and soil. She soared over shrubs and brushwood, scampering around trees and rocks while a strange mist trundled over the ground. The frigid air stung in her throat, sticks and stems pinched her feet. The wind moaned, lashing her spine and forcing her onward, even as her fevered mind spiralled. The cold hues of the Wardens' torches were behind them, but it seemed the trees shifted out of their paths to obstruct their hunters. She thought she heard them murmur a persistent war chant.

Blood.

Fire.

Bone.

Ash.

A rumble upset the wood and the trees quivered. The mist began to ascend, heeding a soundless call and dampening the enclosed air. Ripping her calves on a cluster of thorns, Roma tripped, gasping as she steadied herself before she landed in the underbrush.

When she thought that she might collapse, she burst from the chanting wood onto a high precipice. The Firawn's son stood on the verge, peering down, his muscles rippling in his shoulders as his chest rose and fell with each breath. Breathing shallow, she ran to his side and looked down at the source of the roaring thunder. Her belly clenched at the sight. She had climbed trees and walls ever since she was a child, but this was far beyond her experience.

Four enormous columns of waterfalls crested over a semicircle of shale precipices, cascading into a rushing stream over a hundred feet below them. The plunging water was emerald under the frothing surface. How could so much water exist when all the lakes and rivers of the West Strip receded?

Shouts erupted in the wood behind them.

The Wardens were at their back and the free fall at their front.

They were trapped.

The Firawn's son unravelled the shemagh from his head, tethering it around his wrist and hers in the durable knot she had witnessed him tie on her before. Realising his intention, she swallowed the sore lump in her throat. He drew her close and leaned toward her ear. "Hold your breath," he shouted over the raging of the falls.

Closing her eyes against the foaming bottom, she jumped with him, plummeting through the air for an excruciating moment, breathless and weightless, before slamming through the surface into ice water.

CHAPTER 47

Roma huddled on the riverbank with her shoulders hunched from the chill, dripping and shivering, as the Firawn's son dragged his *kurta* over his head and pulled up the hem of his undershirt to clean his injuries. He had drawn out the rest of the snapped arrow where it went right through him. Now he plucked plants and breathed in their scents, crushing them into a paste that he smeared on his wounds. Ripping his *kurta's* sleeves, he pressed one over the paste-streaked injuries. He used the second sleeve as a makeshift bandage around his torso beneath his undershirt.

"Why did you come for me?"

He stilled at her question and inclined his head. "You weren't safe," he answered as he tied a knot on the bandage.

"You never cared before." At his silence, she looked up at him. "What does the Firawn want from me?"

"He likes women."

The Firawn hadn't touched her. Not even once in the time she was with him.

Seal.

He had spoken of a seal, but she couldn't remember.

What had he meant? *What?*

With a shuddering breath, she peered at the pallid trees. Each one towered over her, stretching so high she failed to see where the interwoven boughs ended, nor could she perceive the skies for the impenetrable awning. Tipping back her head, she glanced at the twisted, overhanging branches which carried heart-shaped leaves the luminous colour of the river. Bulbous blossoms in cerise and orange and bell-shaped blossoms in indigo and lilac appeared as if they were dipped in iridescent dye. Strange plants covered the knotted roots of the trees.

The humid air was saturated with the potent smell of enriched soil merging with the headier smell of sweet-scented fruits. Even stranger was the silence. The river didn't babble; the birds didn't chirp. All sound seemed swallowed by an invisible vacuum. No, there was a sound. Whispers. Like a breeze rustling the branches. Roma looked at the river, the trees, and the ground—green, red, purple, blue, a gold so lustrous—and it struck her that she recognised this wood. She heard tales of it as a child from Rawiya Mai.

This was the Sleeping Forest.

It was the sole wood in the Strips that remained intact, unscathed by the fatal touch of the drought. Rawiya Mai had mentioned waterfalls that sprang from an unseen source, becoming ribbons of rivers circling and pouring into an immense well in the heart of the wood. Colours so sharp and radiant one became mesmerised. She had said it was home to the Ghaib tribes who dwelled in waters and woods. A treacherous place one might enter but never leave without their permission.

The Firawn's son turned toward Roma with shuttered eyes. "We need to move," he told her in a tone that held no emotion.

A serpent with emerald scales slithered out between the plants and held her attention. Thorns protruded from its crown. Coiling beneath the roof of a transparent blossom, it watched her with keen interest. Serpents aided her whenever she was trapped. Serpents were drawn to her and she was drawn to them. She could call on them with her emotions. Did the Firawn know? Was it the reason he wanted her?

Who am I?

"Roma."

Who am I?

The disquiet in her chest began to smother her, the scorching heat from the escape subsiding from her bones and baring a tomb of emotions she was too afraid to unseal, so she watched it from afar as one might a foreign creature with a panicked tremor within her heart. There were more than emotions in that tomb. There were the memories she locked inside it to survive.

When the Firawn's son touched her shoulder, she jerked back and stared at him with accusations in her eyes. *Don't touch me, don't touch me, don't touch—*

His expression hardened. “Get up.” A rawness existed beneath his practical tone. The rawness of loss.

She should tell him she was sorry for the death of his mount, for what he was forced to do, because it was the proper human reaction. She should empathise with him, but the lie smouldered in her throat. What did she care for his loss? What would her apologies matter? Sorry didn’t erase what had happened. Sorry meant it was too late. She envisioned herself opening her mouth and screaming from the desolate bottom of her belly right into his face—

And she bit her tongue hard.

She struggled to stand. Her nerves were tattered as if she were stripped bare. She needed heat. A dose. She remembered how the fire of the drug spread through her veins, how it abolished all emotion, all thought, and towed her underneath the darker tide of oblivion she so craved.

How would she survive now?

Panic swelled in her throat. Clutching her elbows, she followed the Firawn’s son, her convulsing fingers burrowing into her skin. The trails were overrun with shrubs. She heard the constant whispers. It sounded like a language as melodious as Ancient Khansāri. He heard them as well. She could tell from how he inclined his head to listen. He moved through the wood with care, disturbing as little of it as possible out of respect for what resided in the trees, and she stepped where he stepped.

Fingers of sunlight reached down through the awning above. They walked for hours, pausing now and then to drink from the emerald river. The Firawn’s son plucked plum berries from the wild bushes, murmuring a word of gratitude in Khansāri, but she refused the berries when he offered them to her and he didn’t push her to eat. She didn’t know where he led her, nor could she care, because a greater fear preoccupied her mind. The longer she went without a dose, the harder it became for her to remain on her feet. Her shell ached for the sensation of the drug, her veins cramped at the memory of it in her blood, and her skin was cold beneath the fever sweat. The emotions that the doses would steal resurfaced in shocking waves.

The Firawn’s son stopped with the excuse to rest, but she knew it was because she couldn’t walk at his pace. Whenever she closed her eyes, the tomb cracked open, and memories with talons reached for her. She was back in Biranpur, hiding from Alan Saheb, but he still found her. He told her that he had a present for her. For his special, little pet. Grabbing her hand, he slid rainbow-coloured bangles onto her wrist. She didn't want him to touch her. She wanted Amma to make him leave her alone, but Amma would reprimand her for it, and she didn't want to disappoint her.

Sunbel caressed her hair. 'Be brave, Roma. Be obedient, be silent, be brave.' If she didn't struggle against him, it would hurt less and be over sooner, but her pain excited him. She cried. She begged. She became silent. He liked to bite. He liked to suffocate her until she scratched at his hands for air. His face transformed into one of the other demons. She saw them all. She felt them inside her, tainting her with their bruising touch, their staining words, and she screamed at herself to fight back and not just lie there like a corpse.

Her staggering feet pulled her from the unwanted memories. She didn't remember rising to follow the Firawn's son. Touching a hand to a tree, she licked her lips. There was a torrid burn in her throat. She arched and retched. The Firawn's son moved toward her, but she shook her head. "I want my dose," she said in a hoarse voice. "The dose—I need it."

"I don't have it."

"You can find it."

"Maybe," he said softly. "But I won't."

"Then I'll find it on my own."

"Roma—"

"My name is *not* Roma." Her heart pounded too fast and too hard. "Leave me alone."

"I can't do that."

"You can."

He took a slow, careful step toward her.

"I know—"

"You don't know *anything*."

"Just let me—"

"Stop! Stop talking!" she shouted at him, pressing her hands against her ears. "I hate your voice!"

He didn't speak again.

The evocative darkness of the Sleeping Forest raised more demons. Without her doses as a shield, she remembered with clarity. It wasn't disjointed memories anymore, but absolute ones, so detailed she relived the torment. She was in the cell. The whip sliced through her skin. The Wardens wanted to hear her scream, so she chewed her tongue, chewed until it bled. Never would she allow them the satisfaction of a sound from her. She lost even that battle. Insects bothered her wounds for hours. She heard the Wardens violate other prisoners like her, and she curled together in an attempt to disappear.

I'm the wind. I can't be touched.

Trailing sightlessly behind the Firawn's son, she was swaddled in a tumultuous storm of emotion. She stared at the back of his head. Would he touch her? Would he violate her as well? Was he waiting for her to collapse from exhaustion, so he could assault her while she was at her weakest? She should kill him. She should carve him open like the Firawn had the Wardens. If she hadn't lost his knife, she could have stabbed him from behind. He deserved death. They all deserved death. She deserved death.

"I'm cold," she said that night.

His eyes touched her. She hated that they touched her.

"We can't light a fire," he said in that same soft voice.

"I need heat."

He started to move closer.

"Don't," she snapped.

"What do you want me to do?"

Why did he speak to her as if she were a breakable child?

She wasn't breakable. She wasn't.

"Light. A. Fire."

"It'll disclose our location to the Wardens."

"I don't care."

"We'll be out of the wood soon."

"Give me my dose."

"I don't have it."

She stood in a rush.

"Don't follow me."

Knowing he would if she strayed too far, she walked down to the river, climbed on the large rock over the stream, and sat with her legs clutched to her chest. The whispers were a consistent drone in her ears like the hushed chanting of *lamiadasis* at prayers. She picked the scars on her face until her skin bled. She peered into the river. To be conscious while the memories raided her was torture. The demons had stolen everything from her. Why would they still not leave her alone?

"Powerless. Stupid, worthless, *powerless*." Dragging her fingers into her tangled hair, she cradled her throbbing head. "Stupid, stupid, *stupid* bitch." Her breathing came in erratic gasps over the furious sounds in her throat; the sounds of self-disgust, anger, and hatred.

Stop, stop, stop—

Lowering her hands to the rock, she dipped one foot into the river, then the other, and slid down. The rushing water reached her collarbone. It was cold. So cold that her skin numbed, her bones ached. So cold that when she sank even lower, the air hitched in her chest. The stream pushed against her as if it wanted her, as if it beckoned her. Silence and oblivion waited on the other side, it promised, the absolute extinction of thought and emotion.

It could stop. It could all stop now. She squeezed her eyes closed and dropped under the surface. Submerged in the freezing pressure, she opened up to the darkness. Fear and panic stirred somewhere in the fringes of her consciousness, but not powerful enough to trouble her. It was the river that raided her this time. She called to it.

Please.

Whispers sounded in the water. Whispers like the ones in the trees.

"It is not yet your time, *nāgin*."

Strong arms banded around her waist.

No.

Dragging her from the deep, the Firawn's son broke through the surface with her. She gasped as he carried her to the riverbank. Thrashing in his arms, she clawed and scratched, but he pinned her against his chest. "Breathe, Roma," he said into her ear. "Breathe."

"No! Let me go!" She wrenched herself around in his hold. "Let me *go*!" He pulled her right back, trapping her again, even as she struggled like a hunted animal.

"It'll pass. I promise it'll pass."

"No, it *won't*."

She slammed her clenched hands against his chest, pounding and shoving, but he wouldn't relent. The river called to her. The whispers had betrayed her. She was furious. She struck out from the rage. "Let me go!" she shrieked until her vocal cords burned. "Let me—just let me—"

He was too strong.

She felt a crack within her. And something split wide open.

A keening sound tore loose from deep inside her. It wasn't a human sound. She screamed, at last, screamed like she would never stop again. He buried his fingers in her hair, cupping the back of her head and keeping it locked on his shoulder, and she crumbled against him, driving him down into a crouch. Caging her fists between them, he held her as if afraid she might break free and run for the river.

Tears spilled down her cheeks.

The ones she subdued for years; the ones that didn't bewail Chirag; the ones she didn't relinquish even when she was tortured and violated. Her teeth ground in anger and agony, her cries were pained and vicious.

She wept until she was emptied, until she was hollowed out.

The delicate light of the moon slipped through the crevices in the canopy above them as the clouds drifted on with time. Her throat felt raw, her mind felt numb. Wrath still burned within her, but it was now a cool flame, and the chill of it spread through her bloodstream.

She saw Chirag's shattered form on the ground.

Saheb lowered his hand from her head to her back. "I know what it's like to be invaded, Roma," he said in a quiet voice. "I know what it's like to have somebody leave their imprints on you. To lose who you are and hate what you've become."

She heard herself scream for aid and the silence of the village.

"But everything doesn't have to be a reminder of what you've lost. Some things can be a powerful symbol of what you've survived."

She felt retribution burn bright with the frigid flame.

The emerald serpent weaved through the underbrush at a languid pace and slithered over the sword that Saheb had abandoned in the grass. Tasting the air with a forked tongue, it caught and held her stare. She forced her shell to shed the tension, surrendering to Saheb's hold, and felt the muscles in his arms tighten in surprise. He pulled back from her. She looked up at him. Raising a hand toward her face, he almost touched her cheek but withdrew with a jerk.

His throat moved to swallow. He released her at last and turned his back to her. "We need to go," he told her in a hoarse voice.

While he drew a deep breath, she reached for his forgotten sword. "Saheb," she said in a whisper-soft voice, rising behind him. When he turned toward her, she slammed the hilt into his injury with such force that he pitched forward in shocked pain. She bashed it in his head next. Dropping on his knees, he coughed and lurched.

It required a third strike before he collapsed.

"You didn't read my eyes this time, Saheb," she whispered to his unconscious form. Blood leaked from a gash on his head. "You're right. There's power in survival."

And now she would wield her own.

EPILOGUE

THERE WAS BLOOD on the moon.

Beneath its sanguine shade stood the hill, and upon the hill stood the banyan. Sensing Roma's presence before she reached the plains, it called to her. A mother in mourning reuniting with her lost child. The song of sorrow tasted like saline tears on Roma's tongue and the supplication of the banyan whispered through her mind.

'*Come, child. Come and see what the humans have done,*' it moaned. '*Witness the dark deeds of the creatures we protect.*'

Scavenging vultures circled over the banyan. Among the twisted boughs, she found her sleeping sisters, their naked bodies dangling from nooses, their cadavers swarming with insects. The rot invaded her throat and congested her lungs. Falling to her knees, she dropped forward on her palms. Her fingers curled in the soil. A rapacious scream ripped from her chest, tearing through her throat and colliding with the night skies.

The vultures scattered like flies waved from an infected wound. Such was the rupture in her that it shook the entire hill. So violent was her rage that the banyan quivered. It fevered like an erupting volcano, the spines and roots coming aglow, crackling until the ancient barks burst with fire. Engulfed in smokeless flames, the banyan burned. With it, the carcasses of her sisters.

The Conch of Aranyada fell out of the blazing branches.

White, unscathed.

At the bottom of the hill, a horde of villagers assembled, their wide-eyed stares full of terror.

"It's the Dark Goddess! She has descended for vengeance!"

"Biran, protect us!"

Taking the Conch, Roma rose to her feet. Her shadow on the ground stretched in the shape of a hooded cobra, her hair whipped around her head, and her eyes shone like black pearls in an impassive face.

The men and women all shivered as one.

"For what you've done," she said in a whisper that carried down to them, "I sentence you to death. You will bleed as we have. You will scream as we have." She raised the Conch to her lips. "I won't forgive, I won't forget."

And she blew the horn.

GLOSSARY

***Abba*:** The informal title for *father.*

***Aikā*:** *Listen.*

***Amma*:** The informal title for *mother.*

***Ay*:** *Hey*. It is used as a negative/disrespectful exclamation to interrupt and/or to warn.

***Babu*:** The informal title for a male elder outside of a blood relation.

***Babu Saheb*:** The formal title for a male elder outside of a blood relation.

***Basa*:** *Sit down.*

***Bāba Saheb*:** The formal title for *grandfather* inside/outside of a blood relation.

***Bezaat*:** *Casteless.*

***Bhau*:** The informal title for *brother* inside/outside of a blood relation.

***Bhau Saheb*:** The formal title for *brother* inside/outside of a blood relation.

***Birandasi*:** Slave of Biran.

***Bitiya*:** *Daughter.*

***Chodiyo*:** *Let it go.* Pronounced *cho-ree-o.* The dialect is common for easterners.

***Chhokri*:** *Girl.*

***Chhokro*:** *Boy.*

***Choli*:** A backless, short-sleeved blouse that reaches just below the bust with strings to tie at the nape of the neck and the middle of the back. Tassels and bells often dangle from the strings as decoration.

***Dahab*:** *Gold.*

***Dekhliyo*:** *You will see.* Pronounced *dayk-lee-o.* The dialect is common for easterners.

***Dēvadasi*:** Slave of God. It is used to refer to slaves of deities in Biranpur, Lamiapur, Manātpur, and Uzzāpur.

***Dhanda*:** *Business.*

***Dhoti*:** A long piece of fabric wrapped around the legs, folded, and knotted around the waist. It is lower *zaat* menswear.

Dokyala taap devu nakō: *Don't give me a fever* (i.e. headache).

***Fals*:** *Copper.*

***Firawn*:** A special title reserved for the ruler.

Fitra: *Nature* as in human nature.

***Ghaib*:** That which is *hidden.* Creatures created before humankind.

***Hō*:** *Yes.*

***Harami*:** *Bastard.*

***Hijra*:** A transgender.

***Jā*:** *Go* or *leave.*

***Jaan*:** *(My) life.* Term of endearment.

***Jadai*:** A hair ornament pinned along the braid.

***Jāto*:** *I'm leaving.*

Jhakaas: *Awesome.*

***Jhoomar*:** A multiple-chained hair ornament with beads and gems worn on the side of the head. Northern higher *zaat* womenswear.

***Kāhin*:** A male talismanic soothsayer considered an intermediate between gods and men.

***Kāhinah*:** Female equivalent of a *Kāhin.*

***Kamarbandh*:** A waist ornament with beads or gems attached to it. Lower *zaat* womenswear. The clan women also wear *kamarbandhs.* Theirs are made from iron or brass with whorlwork.

***Kāy*:** *What?*

***Kāy jhāle*:** *What's wrong?* The *j* is pronounced as a *z* sound.

***Khan*:** *King.*

***Khanum*:** *Queen.*

***Khansāri*:** Language spoken by the native people of Khansadun.

***Kurta*:** A long-sleeved tunic that reaches around mid-thigh with slits in the sides. It can be simple or embroidered around the collar and cuffs. Lower *zaat* menswear.

***Ladoba*:** *Darling.* Term of endearment.

***Lamiadasi*:** Slave of Lamia.

***Lavakara*:** *Hurry*. Pronounced *low-karr.*

***Lehenga*:** An ankle-length skirt with multiple layers. It can be simple or adorned with threadwork. Lower *zaat* womenswear.

***Mār*:** *Hit (me).*

***Mā Saheb*:** The formal title reserved for the Firawn's First Wife.

***Maangtikka*:** A head ornament shaped like a beaded chain with a gem attached to the end. It is pinned along the centre hairline. Northern and southern higher *zaat* womenswear.

***Mai*:** The formal/informal title for a female elder outside of a blood relation.

***Manātdasi*:** Slave of Manāt.

***Māsa*:** The informal title for *grandmother* inside/outside of a blood relation.

***Māsa Saheba*:** The formal title for *grandmother* inside/outside of a blood relation.

***Māshapath*:** *Swear on my mother*. Pronounced *maa-shup-patt.*

***Mathapatti*:** A single or multiple-chained hairline ornament with pendants and beads. Lower *zaat* womenswear. Clan women also wear *mathapattis* made from iron or brass.

***Meharbani*:** *Thank you.*

***Na*:** A sound used much like *yes/no* at the end of a sentence.

***Nā*:** *No.*

***Nāgin*:** A female serpent.

***Nakō*:** *Don't.*

***Nath*:** Nosepins and hoops. Some have chains that dangle along the cheekbone with a hook pinned in the hair. Others are chainless. Higher/lower *zaat* as well as clan womenswear.

***Panchayat*:** A council of the wealthiest elders.

***Rabb*:** *God.* It is used by the clans to refer to the Creator.

***Rubab*:** A string instrument with a distinctive sound.

***Rabbrakha*:** *God protect you.* It is used to say hello and goodbye.

***Rajat*:** *Silver.*

***Saale*:** *Bugger* and/or *dude.* A slang among friendly men, but can also be used as an abusive term depending on the context.

***Sādin Saheb*:** The formal title for a High Priest.

***Saheb*:** The formal title for a male of a higher stature. It can also be added to reinforce the power of someone such as the Firawn's First Wife.

***Saheba*:** Female equivalent of *Saheb.*

***Sai*:** A royal title reserved for the Firawn. The word means *lord.* It can also be used to refer to the Creator.

***Samajalē*:** *Understand/understood?* The *j* is pronounced as a *z* sound.

***Samajhliyo*:** *Understand it.* Pronounced *sa-maj-lee-o.* The dialect is common for easterners.

***Sarpanch*:** Judge in a Panchayat.

***Satyanāsh*:** *Ruin(ed).* An expression used when something has gone wrong.

***Sherwani*:** A royal version of a *kurta* made from luxurious fabrics. Northern and southern higher *zaat* menswear.

***Tai*:** The informal title for *sister* inside/outside of a blood relation.

***Thāmb*:** *Stop* and/or *calm down.*

***Uzzādasi*:** Slave of Uzzā.

***Vēdī*:** *Crazy.*

***Vēshya*:** *Whore.*

***Wallahi*:** *I swear on God.*

***Ya*:** *Oh.*

***Yani*:** *I mean* or *meaning.* It is mostly used by easterners.

***Yē*:** *Come.*

Yēto: *I'm coming.* It can also mean that the person will return.

***Zaat*:** Caste.

ACKNOWLEDGEMENTS

THIS BOOK COULDN’T have been completed without the support of some incredible people in my life. First and foremost, I’m thankful to God and my family: Baba *jaan* and Mama *jaan*, Babar *bhai*, Maha, Nayyab, Muna, and Inaya. A special thanks to Anila *baji*, Sabahat *baji*, and Baseerat for always motivating me, Shakila *baji* for being an inspiration and a pillar of strength throughout the conception, development, and conclusion of this painful but rewarding journey, and to my soul sister and best friend, Anne, who never ever gives up on me. You have all chased my doubts and fears with pitchforks to ensure I didn’t quit this book, even when I tossed it in the trash multiple times.

A heartfelt thanks to Jenny, Jojo, Caleb, and Gercy for suffering through different editions of the blurb to make it the best that it could be. To my closest friends, Diane and Kris, for their constant love and support. To Debra L. Hartmann and Fiona McLaren who provided invaluable critique that elevated the content to a point where it might be worth people’s hard-earned money.

Last but never least, I want to thank every reader who takes the time to read this book and, perhaps, appreciate it. What I wanted was to spread awareness about the sacred prostitution, caste system, and half-creature perception and abuse of transgenders in South Asia; the ethnic cleansing of the Rohingya People; the exploitation of once-resourceful places like the Middle East and Afghanistan; the occupation of and war crimes against Palestine; and the human trafficking of adults and children across the globe.

I’m not an exceptional writer (and this book is far from perfect), but I hope that it depicts the fall of humanity, the absence of it in our world, and raises important questions about morality, identity, and the power of choice.

With love and hope,
Ana

Ana Lal Din is a Danish-Pakistani author currently based in England. When she doesn't have her nose in a book or her fingers on a keyboard, you might find her in the nearest Caffè Nero. *The Descent of the Drowned* is her debut novel. Follow her on Instagram and Twitter @laldinana.

CPSIA information can be obtained
at www.ICGtesting.com
Printed in the USA
LVHW010803190122
708825LV00019B/1194/J